UNDER HEAVEN'S SHINING STARS

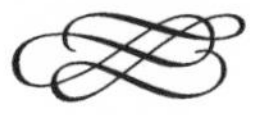

JEAN GRAINGER

JEAN GRAINGER

UNDER HEAVEN'S *Shining* STARS

Under Heaven's Shining Stars

Copyright © 2016 by Jean Grainger

All rights reserved. No part of this book may be used or reproduced in any manner whatsoever including Internet usage, without written permission of the author.

This is a work of fiction. The names, characters, places, or events used in this book are the product of the author's imagination or used fictitiously. Any resemblance to actual people, alive or deceased, events or locales is completely coincidental.

Print ISBN: 978-1517115258

❀ Created with Vellum

OTHER BOOKS BY THE AUTHOR

THE TOUR

Shadow of a Century

Safe at the Edge of the World

The Story of Grenville King

The Homecoming of Bubbles O'Leary

Finding Billie Romano

What Once Was True

Return to Robinswood

Trails and Tribulations

Letters of Freedom

The Future's Not Ours To See

What Will Be

The Star and the Shamrock

Catriona's War

So Much Owed

Dedicated to my inspirational friend, Pauline

Close friends are truly life's treasures. Sometimes they know us better than we know ourselves. With gentle honesty, they are there to guide and support us, to share our laughter and our tears. Their presence reminds us that we are never really alone.

—Vincent Van Gogh

CHAPTER 1

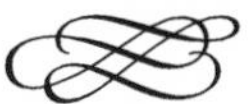

Cork City, Ireland, 1963

The clanging bells broke through his dream, just as an angel was explaining in great detail how to score a point from a side-line cut at the fifty-yard line. The noise was deafening since the house was only seven doors down from the entrance to the hallowed church of St Teresa on the north side of Cork city. Mammy always said how lucky they were to live so close to God's house, some people had miles to go to get to Mass on a Sunday or during Lent but the Tobin family was blessed; they only needed to run up the street anytime to be in God's house.

'Pop in and say a prayer on your way home, Liam,' she would always say as she brushed his brown curly hair neatly and sent him off to school to the brothers armed with a bottle of milk and a doorstep of bread and jam for his lunch. He was luckier than most of the lads in his class he knew, to have a lunch every day and good shoes and an overcoat in the winter.

Liam dragged himself out of bed, the edges of the mattress cold to his skin as he blearily looked for his clothes. He sighed as he spotted his trousers, shirt and pullover on the floor as usual, despite his folding of them last night. Con always threw his clothes off the chair when he came in. Liam was sure he did it as a matter of course just to annoy his younger brother. It was hard being the youngest. The girls more or less ignored him or laughed at his seven-year-old thoughts on things and Con liked winding him up. He was four years older than Liam and much bigger and stronger, but to be fair he wasn't the worst big brother, some other fellas had desperate things to put up with altogether from their older siblings—Con was all right. He always played hurling with Liam even though he was way better. He taught him some great tricks of the national game, and Liam always made the school team because of Con's help. Sometimes, he even gave Liam a sweet if he got a shilling for doing a job for one of the neighbours. He'd hate anyone to know that he had a nice side though; Con liked his hard man image.

Liam opened the grey, shabby net curtains to see what kind of a day it was. Mammy washed them every week, but there was no money for new ones so they were grey with age, the smoke from the neighbours' fires, and the mist off the River Lee didn't help either. He heard her sighing as she hung them back up week after week, and Liam vowed that when he grew up he'd go into Murray's on the Grand Parade and buy her the whitest net curtains they had. Everything looked a bit grey this morning though and as he dressed quickly, he could see his breath in the cold bedroom. At least, the range would be lit downstairs, Daddy banked it down before he went to bed and stoked it up in the morning when he was going out to work so that the kitchen was nice and warm for his family, even if the bedrooms were freezing.

Liam looked out into the street as he put his foot on the windowsill to tie his shoes. Even the famous golden fish weathervane, which adorned the top of the church, seemed less luminescent in the gloom of the morning. Everyone round there called it 'de Goldie Fish' and it was put on top of the church for the whole city to see. Stories varied as to why it was there and what it represented. Some people said it was there as a symbol of Cork being a port city but Mammy said it was because the Lord Jesus was a fisher of men. Whatever it meant, the generations who lived and died under the Goldie Fish considered themselves the luckiest people on earth. There was even a prayer that they learned in school, asking Our Lord and the Virgin Mary and St Finbarr to bless Cork as it lay beneath Heaven's shining stars. A fella in his class asked Brother Aquinas why was Cork so special and wasn't the whole world under Heaven's shining stars, not just Cork, but the priest replied, 'No wonder you don't understand, and your father from Kerry,' and gave him a clout across the head for impertinence.

To an outsider, the north side of Cork city and Chapel Street in particular might look poor and unkempt, and there wasn't much going spare in 1963 that was true, but Cork people had always pitied those other unfortunate inhabitants of the earth without the geographic good fortune to live their lives on the banks of the River Lee. And those who lived on the north side pitied those on the south side of the river, even though that's where all the posh suburbs were. The demarcation was important, and while all Corkonians loved their home there was a respectful distance kept by both sides of the river. Life on the north side was poor and plenty of families had lost people to emigration—to the car factory at Dagenham in England mostly—but there was a pride and a passion for their home that belied its dilapidated appearance. Liam thought it was the best place in the whole wide world.

Liam peered down the hill from his bedroom window. The fog lay heavily on the river as the dawn tried valiantly to break through the thick grey clouds. The distinctive aroma of hops hung in the air, sandwiched as they were between Beamish's brewery on the south side and Murphy's on the north side. Liam loved the malty bitterness that greeted your nostrils each morning. Unless of course the tide was out, then the lovely hops aroma was replaced with the stink of a river at low tide. Rats would scurry around the riverbed among the silt-covered old bicycles and bits of timber. They made Mammy shudder to look at them but Liam thought they were fascinating and Daddy was always telling him what a resourceful little fella the rat was, always managing to survive despite people doing their best to kill him off for centuries.

The city lay at the top of Cork Harbour, the most southerly city on the island of Ireland and the safest natural harbour in the whole world, another thing Liam's Daddy had told him proudly, more than once. The river rose way out in the country and wandered gently through the green valleys and small villages and towns to find its way to the sea, almost at Liam's front door.

The sound of deliveries, bringing milk, bread, and newspapers to the shops around Chapel Street, a few voices, hooves of dray horses on cobbles, and a fog horn further down the harbour were the only sounds in the early March morning. You could set your clock by the arrival of the big horse with the furry feet pulling the milk cart to a stop at their door.

'Ow!' Liam yelped as a flying hob-nailed boot hit him in the back of the head.

'Close the curtain, ya big eejit.' Con pulled the blanket and coat over himself, trying to go back to sleep.

'We have to get up now anyway, Con. Mammy will be up here in a minute. If she doesn't hear us, she'll murder you,' Liam pleaded with his older brother. He hated it when there was anger in the house in the mornings. Daddy and Liam's older sister, Kate, would be gone to work already, but Mammy had to get the rest of them out to school and she took no nonsense, especially from lazy eleven-year-old Con.

'You're serving today, Con, and Father Mac warned you about being late for Mass again. You had your soutane on backwards yesterday, lucky Mammy couldn't find her glasses or she'd kill you.' Liam begged his brother to cooperate. He was so lucky too, not everyone was picked to serve at Mass. Liam longed to be an altar boy like his brother, but he hadn't yet made his First Holy Communion so he wasn't allowed. He always vowed that if he was picked to serve Father Mac he'd never, ever, be late for Mass and his vestments would be immaculate.

''Liam, I swear I'll bate the head off ya if you don't close them bloody curtains!' Con groaned, his voice muffled under the feather pillow. Reluctantly, Liam closed them, knowing only too well that Con meant every word of the threat. He checked himself in the mirror on the wardrobe door. His short trousers had seen better days, having first being owned by Con, and now him. Mammy patched the backside of them so many times they looked a bit mad, but he didn't mind. It wasn't like he was the only boy in the class with patched trousers. Compared to most, Daddy always said, they were lucky. Food on the table, shoes on their feet and a warm bed. And they got to stay in school till they were twelve years of age. Loads of the kids on the street either never went to school at all, or left after a few years, when they could read and write a bit. It was the law that every child was supposed to go, but the authorities didn't bother too much with the kids who lived on Chapel Street. Most of the parents weren't able to read or write very well either, but Mammy and Daddy were very good at it, and Daddy read them the best cowboy stories at night. He could do the voices and everything and you'd swear Buffalo Bill or Billy the Kid was talking when Daddy read to them. Even the girls loved the stories, but they pretended they wanted him to read stupid old romances.

The bells rang again. Mass was at seven and then it was home for a bowl of porridge before being packed off to school at the top of the hill.

'Con Tobin, you better be out of bed and dressed, I'm warning you. If I have to come up to you, so help me God I'll brain you! D'ya hear me?' Mammy shouted from downstairs. Liam went out onto the landing.

'Ah, Liam pet, you're the best boy ever, do you know that?' she rubbed his hair as he passed her on the stairs. 'Is that big lump of a clown out of bed yet?'

Mammy had her second best dress on. Not the one she wore on Sundays but the blue one with the little flowers on it. She made it herself and it was Liam's favourite. He loved how soft the fabric felt against his face when Mammy hugged him. She always made a funny sound like she was being strangled when he gave her extra squeezy hugs and it made him giggle. There was no time for hugs this morning though, they had to get to Mass. Mammy was fixing her long dark hair with pins in the small mirror over the Holy Water font in the hall before putting on her lace mantilla to cover her hair in the church. Daddy always said how lovely Mammy was, and how she was the most beautiful woman in Ireland. She usually just swatted him with the tea-towel and told him not to be trying to soft soap her with his old plamásing, but Liam knew she loved it when he said it. Her cheeks went all red and she smiled a kind of special smile at Daddy.

She looked at herself and was sure she looked respectable.

'Con!' she shouted again. 'Was he up, Liam, when you were coming down?'

Liam hated being a tell-tale on Con, he mostly liked his big brother and anyway, he'd only give him a clatter for telling on him if he did, so he muttered something about getting his coat and ran out the back door.

He pushed the heavy oak door of St Teresa's church—he wasn't tall enough to reach the shiny brass handle—and immediately inhaled. He loved the scent of the incense mixed with beeswax polish, the muted notes of the organ played by Mrs Hegarty who Daddy said was an old lady when he was a child, and the sense of anticipation among the congregation, waiting for the bell to announce the start of Mass. Most of the pews were almost full and he hoped that nobody would sit beside him because there would be no room for Mammy and the twins. Daddy would get Mass on his way back from the dockyard in St Peter and Paul's church in town, and Kate took the patients to Mass in the hospital every day anyway, so in the mornings it was just Con, himself, Mammy and the twins.

He knelt and said his prayers, asking God to make him good, good enough to be able to make his First Holy Communion in two weeks time. Father Aquinas said only very good fellas were going to be allowed to make it, and he told them that the week before the Communion he'd be sending a list to the bishop of the good fellas and the bad fellas and any bad fellas won't be making the Communion, and what's more, they won't get a shiny penny, and won't be able to go to the breakfast in the monastery where rumour had it, sticky buns and lemonade were available to all the good fellas. He tried to suppress a smile at the memory of Jackie Byrne asking Father Aquinas if the bishop was like Santie so, with a good and bold list. The entire class watched the priest's reaction with bated breath, Father Aquinas was very scary. The priest had puffed up like a bullfrog and roared at Jackie not to be so cheeky, thumping him on the shoulder as he did so. Father Aquinas was huge and used to be a brilliant boxer so when he hit you a clatter, you knew all about it.

He felt someone touch his shoulder and he started. He looked up, relieved to see Molly and Annie, the nine-year-old twins, nudging him to push in, their mother behind. He moved along as far as he could, making space for the rest of the family as the piercing ding of the bell indicated the start of Mass. Seamus Daly was on the altar with Con this week, and he walked reverentially across the altar, bowing low before the Blessed Sacrament, then kneeling on the left hand side of the pulpit. Next, came Father Mac, his bald head shining under the lights as he bent to kiss the Bible. Liam scanned the altar for Con, praying he had his soutane straight and on the right way. His stomach lurched as he realised nobody was on the other side. He glanced sideways at his mother, who was rapidly taking in the situation as the colour drained from her face. Where was Con? To shame the family like that, by not turning up for mass in front of everyone was going to be unforgivable. Mammy was going to be mortified and Daddy would go mad. Suddenly, the door behind the altar that led to the sacristy opened with much clamouring and creaking, and a mortified Con, with hair standing on end and one boot missing, crept across the altar. Molly started to giggle and that set Annie off, both girls shaking with mirth as their mother threw them dagger looks. Liam focused on the sanctuary lamp, where the sacred heart of Jesus was covered with a purple cloth for the forty days of Lent. He prayed hard that Father Mac didn't notice Con arriving late, or that he only had one boot. He knew that Con had forgotten he had thrown the other one at Liam for opening the curtains so it was probably under the bed or something.

The Mass went on uneventfully and Liam watched in awe as Father Mac held up the body and then the blood of Christ, but Liam could feel Mammy seething beside him. Poor old Con, she was going to go mad when they got home. The Glen and the Rockies were playing in the hurling County final down in the Park on Sunday and Daddy was taking both of them, but it was looking bad for Con now. There is no way Mammy would let him go after this, and Daddy always bought them chips afterwards and everything. Con would be heartbroken to miss it, but Daddy wouldn't overrule Mammy.

Liam pulled his attention back to the Mass. In school, Father Aquinas was teaching them about transubstantiation, the way that a real miracle happened in front of your very eyes when ordinary old bread, made by the nuns in the Good Shepherd's convent in Sunday's Well got turned into the real body of Jesus Christ.. And then how wine got turned into his blood. Liam was transfixed when Father Aquinas talked all about it, trying to make sense of how a miracle happened every day just across the road from his house, and all over the world as well.

The wonders of Catholicism fascinated Liam. He loved to hear the stories about the missions and how brave priests were leaving the comfort of home and their families to go out and convert the black babies in darkest Africa so that they could be saved and go to heaven when they died. At night in bed, Liam worried that there weren't enough priests to go around, what about all the babies with their big brown eyes and curly hair that never got to meet an Irish priest? Was hell full of black babies just because they weren't lucky enough to be in the same village as a priest?

He'd asked Mammy about it one night and she said that they were probably not in hell, but they might be in Limbo. That place wasn't as bad as Hell, no fires burning for all eternity or the devil and all that horrible scary stuff, but that they would never get to see the face of God because they hadn't been baptised.

'But Mammy, who minds all the babies up in Limbo so?' Liam had asked, getting more and more upset. 'If all the Mammies and Daddies did get baptised, there's nobody there to mind the babies.'

'Oh, Holy God and the Blessed Virgin Mary send very special angels to look after the babies so they're fine, all playing together and lots of nice things to eat and everything,' Mammy reassured him as she peeled the spuds for the dinner. 'They have a great time there, buns and lollipops and everything.'

'Well, I suppose it doesn't sound that bad so,' Liam wasn't convinced, 'but it would be better, wouldn't it, Mammy, if they got baptised into the Holy Catholic Church and then when they died they could go up to heaven with all the other good people?' He watched and waited as his mother peeled the wafer-thin layer of skin from the potato, they had enough, but just about. There was no waste in the Tobin household.

'It would, of course, pet, and sure aren't there priests and nuns going out to the missions every week, doing their best to get to as many of those poor people as they can?' She ruffled his brown curly hair with her wet hand. Mammy always had time for him, even when his brothers and sisters told him to get lost with his endless questions, she would chat away to him as she did the jobs around the house. He got home the earliest since he was the youngest and it was his favourite time of the day, helping her to wash the sheets or get the dinner, and talking away all the time. Mammy had great devotion to St Bernadette, the Little Flower, and St Anthony. She often told him that he looked like St Anthony with his lovely brown eyes, but her favourite angel by far was St Michael the Archangel.

'St Michael the Archangel, Liam, he's the one you want if you are ever in trouble or worried or scared. Sure, didn't he take on the devil himself and won? He's not scared of anything or anyone so he's a great one to have in your corner. And the Little Flower, oh she's lovely. They say that when people who had devotion to her die, the room smells of the sweetest roses.' Mammy would stare off into the distance then and sigh with contentment at the thought of such a lovely death.

'But we'd be lost entirely without St Anthony, wouldn't we, Mammy?' Liam grinned.

'We would indeed, pet, because he's the only saint who can find lost things and we're forever losing things in this house, aren't we?'

Liam nodded enthusiastically. 'Like, remember last week when Daddy couldn't find the key for his bicycle lock and I ran over to the church to the statue of St Anthony and said a prayer and then Con found it in Daddy's old donkey jacket?'

'That's right. Aren't you the smart lad to think of that?'

Liam didn't say that Daddy had given Con a bulls eye for finding the key, but it was Liam's prayers that did it. Con had to put the lovely black and white sweet away till after Lent since nobody ate sweets in Lent. Sure, Con would probably let Liam have it anyway once Easter came. Con pretended to be grumpy and mean to Liam in front of people but he was nice under it all.

'Lost entirely without St Anthony is right,' Mammy laughed, and when she did, it sounded to him like little bells ringing. Mammy was always laughing at funny things Liam and his siblings said or did, but especially she laughed at Daddy. He loved to lie in bed at night, hearing them chatting quietly downstairs, having a cup of tea before bed, or if things were good, and Daddy got overtime, cocoa. One time, he crept downstairs because he'd had a scary dream and he saw Mammy sitting on Daddy's lap. They were just looking into the fire together, lost in thought. Daddy had his big arms around her and was rubbing her hair. Liam watched for a minute but went back upstairs rather than disturb them. Every night she waited up for Daddy, even if it was really late when he finished work, and Liam was relieved when he heard the door open—everything was fine, Daddy was home. And every so often, lying in bed, he'd hear Mammy laugh and Daddy shushing her so as not to wake the children. He knew some of the boys in school had Mammies and Daddies that used to fight, and even sometimes the Daddies would drink too much porter and get very scary and be shouting. Just across the road, Patrick Lynch's Daddy was forever roaring around the street. When he'd wake the whole place up singing and shouting in the middle of the night on his way back from The Glue Pot, Mammy used to say to them, 'Just say a little prayer for Mrs Lynch that he'll fall asleep.'

Last weekend, there was really bad shouting, and Liam got a fright when it woke him up, and Daddy had to go out to try to make Mr Lynch quiet and Mrs Lynch had to go to the hospital because she fell down the stairs. Liam was really glad he had his Daddy who never shouted or drank too much porter or made people fall.

The next morning was Sunday, and Daddy was at home so Liam asked him, 'Why was Mr Lynch making so much noise last night?'

Liam saw his parents exchange a look and then Daddy said, 'Mr Lynch drinks too much porter and then it makes him do stupid things.'

'But why does he?' Liam was confused.

Daddy pulled Liam onto his lap then, 'Ah Liam, Joe Lynch has had a hard life, you know? His Mammy died when he was small, and there wasn't anyone to mind him so was raised in an industrial school up the country and maybe they weren't as kind to him as they could have been. And then he got married to Mrs Lynch and she's a lovely woman, and he was working below in the butter exchange, but they had to let people go when they got the new churning machines so he lost his job. I know he can be a bit scary and all of that, but he's not had it easy either. I'll tell you what, when we were younger you'd dread it if Joe Lynch was marking you in a hurling match. He was the quickest centre forward I ever saw, and he could score from anywhere. One time, I remember he doubled the sliotar over his shoulder and scored a point from about sixty yards out. Even the mighty Christy Ring was beaten by Joe a few times. Sure, I see it now with young Patrick, he's what? A year older than you? And I'll tell you he'll be one to watch. Patrick Lynch is nearly as good a hurler as his father was, and in time, he might even be better. I've watched him when I go to see Con playing, he thinks three moves ahead. Did you ever notice that? Other fellas are tackling in the box but young Lynch is nowhere near, then one of his teammates makes a bit of space and there's Patrick, in exactly the right spot to score. He has it all, speed, skill, accuracy, and most importantly, intelligence. He got that from Joe.'

Liam's eyes were wide as saucers, amazed to be party to such detail of an adult's life. It was true, Patrick Lynch was the best player in the school, and he seemed nice too, though he was ahead of Liam so they just said hello mostly. Liam was anxious to get back to the racket of last night though.

'Did you have to hit him to quieten him last night, Daddy?' Liam liked the idea that his Daddy was the hero of the story.

'Indeed, then I did not, Liam Tobin, what kind of a question is that? I don't go round hitting people and neither does anyone in my family, do you hear me? Joe just had a bit too much to drink and I helped him to get to bed, that's all.'

'Did he push Mrs Lynch down the stairs by accident, is that what happened? Is that why she is in the hospital?'

Liam caught the warning glance his mother threw his father.

'Ah no, I think she just tripped on a loose bit of carpet or something.' Daddy said quickly.

'But the Lynches don't have carpet on the stairs...' Liam began.

'Now then,' Mammy interrupted, 'who wants a sausage?'

The family yelled with delight at the weekly breakfast treat and the Lynches and their stairs were forgotten.

CHAPTER 2

He was panicking. It wouldn't go down. It was only the practice host, the real ones were the body of Christ, but these were just the ones the nuns made before the priest consecrated them. They were using them for practice but though Liam tried as hard as he could to swallow, the wafer disc felt like it was actually blowing up like a balloon inside in his mouth. He struggled again to swallow, aware now how red his face must be as beads of sweat prickled his neck. Father Aquinas was explaining how you must never touch the host with your hands, only a priest was allowed to do that. You had to open your mouth wide when the time came to go up to receive the body of Christ and stick out your tongue to make it easier for the priest.

Liam tried to focus on the priest's boomy voice.

'Under no circumstances must you touch the body of Christ with your teeth. Would you bite the Lord Jesus Christ if he walked up to you here in this holy place? Would you?' His bright blue eyes, almost covered by long hairy eyebrows bore down on Timmy O'Shea whose jaw was moving.

Timmy shook his head quickly, 'No, Father, I would not,' he mumbled.

'Indeed, you wouldn't if you knew what was good for you. Then why would you think, Mr O'Shea, that chewing the body of the Lord your God, with your big yellow teeth like a donkey, the Lord that died on the cross for you, gave up everything for you, would be acceptable?' He roared the last bit, poor Timmy shivered.

Timmy swallowed with an audible gulp and squeaked, 'It isn't ac...ac. . .acceptable, Father.'

With a heavy sigh and a cuff across the back of the head for Timmy, the priest turned his attention to the next part of the Holy Communion Mass.

The monastery chapel was cold and smelled of beeswax polish. The dappled coloured sunlight through the high, narrow stained glass windows played and danced on the ornate brass altar rails. There were only about ten pews either side of the aisle, enough for the brothers, since no members of the public ever attended Mass here. It was much smaller than St Teresa's but it was just as lovely.

One or two of the really good fellas got to put beeswax on old socks and polish the floors of the chapel on a Friday afternoon while everyone else sat listening to the readings and the Gospel for the following Sunday in the draughty high-ceiling classrooms, but they would never tell what it was like. Those lads would probably turn out to be priests themselves.

The class were so excited, being brought into the private chapel as a group was the most talked about event of the school year. Holy Communion practice went on for months in the classroom but to get inside the priests' private house was thrilling. It was hard to imagine them sleeping or eating or doing normal things, they seemed so far removed from ordinary people. Normally, everything behind the big oak door that linked the school and the monastery was off limits and the boys never dared to take a peek at the place where the brothers slept and ate, but in the week before the sacrament, the first Communion class were allowed in and it gave them legend status with the smaller fellas. Even the older lads were kind of envious because it was years ago they were allowed into the private area of the monastery and they were always asking what changes had happened.

Liam tried to take in as much as possible as the priest opened the big door and the whole class trooped through. The smell was the first thing that hit you, not like anyone's house or even like school, it smelled warm and sweet and just like what Liam imagined rich people's houses to smell like. Their feet squeaked on the polished parquet floor as they waited in the hall. There were statues of saints on little tables in every corner and loads of holy pictures on the walls. The silence felt heavy. As they followed the priest past a room that had lots of fancy looking furniture and bookshelves from floor to ceiling, Liam spotted the most amazing thing he'd ever seen. A big brown television stood in one corner of the room, between the huge marble fireplace and the window. There was a television in the window of Fitzgerald's Electrical Shop on the Grand Parade, which the people of Cork marvelled at. There was a cartoon called *Dathaí Lacha* about a duck every Saturday morning and sometimes Con would take Liam into town to watch it through the shop window. No one they knew had one, they were much too dear for anyone living on Chapel Street and yet there was a really big one, bigger even than the one in Fitzy's right there in the monastery.

Mammy and Daddy had laughed when he told the family about his day and the sounds and smells of the monastery over dinner.

'How can someplace smell rich, you clown?' Con laughed, but Daddy gave him a disapproving look.

'I know exactly what you mean, Liam, don't mind him. I did some work in there a few years back, they needed some pipes replaced and it did smell rich, and there was a great smell of cooking too, I remember. They weren't supposed to, I think, but the nuns that ran the kitchen used to bring me a cup of tea and currant cake with butter and jam. 'Twas lovely altogether.'

'Oh I see, Seán Tobin, you prefer the nuns' sweet cake to the stuff your wife makes for you with her own bare hands. Is that the way of it? Maybe you should have been a priest yourself and you'd have a clatter of nuns traipsing after you day in day out feeding you cake!' Mammy sounded cross but when Liam looked at her properly he could see she was only joking with Daddy.

'Ah, but I'd have no lovely wife to be cuddling and kissing then, would I? And sure that would be a fright to God now, wouldn't it?' He winked at the children, who giggled. They loved hearing this story though they'd heard it a thousand times. 'Oh no, I could never have taken Holy Orders because I fell in love with Mary Clancy and even the Lord himself couldn't stop it. He must have said to himself, and he sitting around on a big fluffy cloud one day, with a small little angel beside him playing tunes on the harp, "Sure I don't need that many priests and poor old Seán Tobin down there in Cork is stone mad about Mary Clancy and if they got married they'd have a fine brood of lovely children so I'll leave him off."'

'Seán! Will you stop with all that auld talk, and our Liam about to make his First Holy Communion, isn't that nice chat for him to be listening to over the dinner table. What if Father Aquinas heard that, did you ever think of that?'

Mammy was blushing and trying not to smile, but Daddy was still smirking.

'Sure, maybe he's above kissing the nuns,' Con quipped.

Liam started with the fright he got as his mother's quick temper emerged.

'Con Tobin,' Mammy was not joking cross now, this was real cross. 'How dare you say such a thing about a man of the cloth, a holy, saintly priest like Father Aquinas! And I might add, a priest who was willing to let you serve on the altar even though you can't turn up in time or ever wear two shoes, and you making a show of the whole family in front of the entire parish? 'Tis lucky for you that Father Mac is half blind, God love him, or he'd be onto the school above demanding a new altar boy!'

Mammy was glaring at Con and then at Daddy urging him to get involved. Con wasn't going to be allowed to forget the one-shoed altar boy fiasco in a hurry.

'Your mother is right, Con. Father Aquinas is an ordained priest, and you shouldn't be making a mockery of him.'

Mammy seemed satisfied and it was only when her back was turned, Liam noticed Daddy kicking Con under the table to get his attention and giving him an almost imperceptible wink. Con smiled, and Liam felt himself relax.

He wanted to restore the good humour of earlier so decided to share his latest discovery.

'The brothers have a television, too, in the sitting room.'

Annie and Molly suddenly sat up and took notice of what was going on. A girl in their class had come from England to live in Cork with her granny and she was full of what television they had over there and how much she missed it. The twins thought she was the most glamorous thing they ever clapped eyes on.

'Have they really, Liam?' Annie's eyes were round in amazement. 'What do they want a television for?'

'Ah, go way outta that, Liam! You're joking! Sure there are only old news programmes and fellas going on about farming on it, anyway,' Kate laughed, looking up from the newspaper. She was always looking for a new job; she hated working in the hospital. 'Sure, what business would the brothers have with a television?'

'They do have one, I saw it. It's even bigger than the one in Fitzy's window.' Liam wanted them to believe him, but the twins trusted Kate and if she said it wasn't true, then they believed her. They went back to testing each other on their spellings; they were very swotty at school and always won medals and things for being the best in the class. Liam was fine at school; he didn't get the strap that often for getting things wrong in his lessons, but that was only because Daddy checked it for him and told him if he made a mistake. Con launched into a story, telling Daddy how he scored the winning point in the game against St Michael's. Kate was busy circling things with a pen in the paper. He'd lost everyone's attention except his mother's.

'They really do have one, Mammy,' he said.

'I bet they do, pet, maybe they'll need to know what people are looking at in case it's not suitable,' she replied as she cleared the table. Daddy turned from Con's graphic description of a tackle and gently put his hand on her arm, stopping her from continuing.

'Now, Mary, my love, let you sit there by the stove. Myself and these fine sons and daughters of ours, who you go to such trouble to feed and clothe and educate, are going to wash up and get the place straight, and you are going to have a cup of tea. Now, ladies,' he announced, grabbing the paper from Kate and putting it up on the high shelf, 'tea towels at the ready. Con, scrape the plates for the hens and get coal. Annie and Molly, ye sweep the floor and bring in the washing from the yard and fold it, then ye can hang out the next lot. Liam, you put away, Kate will dry, and I'll wash.'

Groaning only a little bit, everyone went about their jobs. Daddy was not to be argued with, when he told you to do a job, you just did it. Not because he'd slap you or anything, he never slapped them, and he got all quiet whenever he heard any of his children got hit at school. One time, when the nun had really beat Kate for daydreaming, he went down to the convent. Mammy begged him not to, but he said that he wasn't going to have anyone attacking his children. Nobody knew exactly what happened that night, but everyone saw him march up to the front door of the convent and ring the bell, and none of the Tobin girls ever got a slap again. Con was forever getting the strap from the brothers in school, but then Con was forever doing bold things so he never told Daddy about it. The night he went down to the nuns, Liam was only two so he didn't remember it, but Con told him that everyone looked at Daddy a bit different after.

He was a gentle giant really, but people usually did what he said, and he didn't care one bit what people thought of him. Liam knew that none of the other fellas in school would believe that his daddy did the wash up every night, while Mammy had a cup of tea. None of the other fathers would do anything like that, but big, handsome Seán Tobin wasn't like others, Liam knew that. He was taller than most of the men, and he had loads of hurling medals from when he was younger. He always wore a collar and tie and changed into his overalls when he got down to the dockyard. He never walked home covered in dirt like the other men, he always washed up after work, even though he told them that the water was icy cold. For as long as Liam could remember, he would watch him every morning, standing in his white vest, braces hanging from his trousers as he shaved with a cut-throat razor at the kitchen sink, and sometimes in the evening too if they were going out somewhere. One time, when Con was about three, he got the razor and nearly cut his head off trying to copy Daddy, so now the razor was kept on the very high shelf. Mammy and Daddy always insisted that the family were well turned-out. He pushed the pram when they were small, he even cooked dinners and made brown cake when Mammy had to go and stay with Granny that time last year. Though it wasn't as nice as when Mammy made it, they all ate it without complaining. He didn't really drink, which made him a bit unusual too, and after Mass on Sundays he would always take them to the little huckster shop up Murray's Lane and buy them an ice cream or a few sweets. Liam knew he was lucky and other fellas watched with envy as they walked home after Mass licking ice creams and he holding his daddy's hand.

Daddy stood at the sink washing the dishes as Kate dried and put away. She was singing an Elvis song, she was mad about him, forever going on about him, and she told them that she was saving up for a record player.

'Kate Tobin, I don't think that all those songs are suitable for young ladies. Mrs O'Shea was only saying the other day when we were doing the altar flowers how a lot of that music isn't one bit nice and that Elvis Presley is not allowed to do concerts in lots of places because parents, even in America, don't like the kind of influence he is having on their children. And all his songs, well, they only encourage company keeping and all that sort of thing, and I just don't think it's suitable for nice girls to be listening to,' Mammy said in a voice that brooked no argument.

'Ah, Mam, sure he's lovely looking and his songs are great, don't mind Mrs O'Shea, she wouldn't know Elvis from the Bishop!' Kate jumped to her hero's defence.

'Well, the Bishop might have something to say about him and all his...gyrating. If he ever comes to Cork, you for one won't be going to see him anyway. Can't you listen to that lovely traditional music or a choir, or Seán O'Riada, sure his music would bring tears to your eyes. 'Twas on the wireless yesterday, beautiful it was,' Mary suggested.

Kate snorted in disdain. 'Ah Mam, did you ever see the state of him, and them fellas with the fiddles and accordions? They'd bring tears to my eyes all right. They're all about a hundred and that's the music for the old folks, but you've nothing to worry about anyway, I don't think someone as marvellous as Elvis would ever bother his barney to come to Cork. Why would he? He'd want his head checked to even come to Dublin let alone Cork.'

The twins giggled as they swept the floor, they thought Kate was the picture of sophistication.

Seán flicked sudsy water at his daughters, 'And what's wrong with Cork all of a sudden? Sure isn't it the real capital of Ireland, the jewel in the Irish crown, the place where all the best people come from? Michael Collins, Christy Ring, Jack Lynch. Sure wouldn't Elvis be only too thrilled to meet the people of such a fine city?'

Kate responded, 'Ah sure, Daddy, Cork is grand for hurling and fellas dying for Ireland and all that stuff, but it's not cool. Not like London or New York or places like that.'

'Cool? Well, I can tell you 'twas cool enough trying to unload a container of coal this morning below at the quay wall. 'Twas fine and cool, 'twas freezing in fact. Not that you would know anything about that, inside with the nuns and the place like a bake house. I don't know if having the hospital so hot is good for people, sure they'd catch their death then when they came out into the real weather.'

'Well, Sister Gerard insists on having the private rooms roasting altogether, nothing is too much trouble for the *quality*, don't you know?' she giggled, mimicking the staff sister's voice. 'It isn't the same for the poor people in the public wards, the food, the heat, everything is different. Sure, nuns have no interest in poor people.'

Daddy gave her a warning glance, Liam knew he kind of agreed with Kate when they went on about how snobby the nuns were but Mammy wouldn't like any of that talk about nuns or priests.

CHAPTER 3

1968 – Five Years Later

Liam came in from the yard with a bucket of coal.

'Mrs Kinsella said, can you go in and check something in the attic, a creak or a squeak or something?'

His father was scanning the jobs section in the evening paper after dinner. Seán had finally been laid off from the dockyard and spent most days scouring the paper or walking the streets of the city looking for work. The dock was only limping along for years, and it was a miracle it stayed going as long as it did. The problem was most of the men in the city were in a similar position. Too many men and not enough work. He picked up a bit of casual labour now and again but even that was scarce. Liam knew he was one of the few boys in school whose father was still around; most were gone to England working. Liam would never forget the day Daddy came home with his last pay packet six months earlier. Mammy sent them all upstairs doing jobs but he watched them standing together in the kitchen from the top of the stairs. Tears glistened in his mother's eyes. Not saying a word, they held onto each other, Daddy's chin resting on the top of Mammy's head, lost in thought. Liam remembered feeling fear for the first time, like this was something his parents couldn't fix. Things were very tight before but now there was no money at all coming in. They hardly ever had meat, and treats were extremely rare. Gone were the bags of chips after the match or the ice creams after mass. Every penny was accounted for.

The house next door had been occupied by old Mrs Moriarty until her death three months earlier. She had a son in England but he hadn't come home for years so it was the Tobins who looked after her and organised the funeral when she died. She was a nice old lady and she used to give a penny to whichever Tobin child brought her messages from the shop every Thursday.

Her son, Jerome, came back for the funeral, thanked the Tobins for their help with his mother and left, never to be seen again. A few weeks later, a woman moved in with her young daughter.

'But you were in there yesterday, honestly...' Mammy began before Daddy shot her a warning glance.

'Yerra 'tis only a loose window frame or something I suppose,' Daddy said, putting down the paper. 'I'll have a look in the morning. Now, you lot, one decade of the rosary and off to bed.'

The family knelt in the small room, each one facing a chair. It was Kate's turn to give it out, and the family responded to the prayers reverently. Mammy would not tolerate any blackguarding during the nightly prayers. No matter what went on or how tired they were, the Tobins prayed together every night, 'The family that prays together, stays together,' was one of Mammy's favourite sayings. Once the formal prayers were done, it was time for the trimmings, which often took longer than the prayers themselves. Anyone who was sick got a mention, anyone with a worry, a hope, a wish, or bereavement; all were prayed for after the rosary. Regular features were a prayer that Daddy would get a new job, that Mrs Moriarty's soul would rest in peace, that Uncle Jimmy would recover from the bad chest, that Christy Ring's ankle would be better by Sunday in time for the final against the Barrs—the rival hurling team—no cause was left out of the entreaties to a variety of saints. Then there were the saints who required special mention. Mammy knew whose feast day it was every day of the year, so the family found themselves invoking the intercession of St Nicholas Peregrinus or St Cornelius of Armagh on any given day. It was with relief they would say the final prayer of 'Our Lord, Our Lady, and Saint Finbarr, bless Cork under Heaven's shining stars.'

You daren't complain about numb knees unless you wanted a lecture on how lucky you were to have such a charmed life.

When the prayers were over, and guardian angels called upon to protect through the night, Liam, Annie and Molly reluctantly kissed their parents and went upstairs. Kate went out sometimes, over to a friend's house or even to the pictures, and Con was allowed to stay up till nine because he was older and had finished school and started an apprenticeship with Uncle Willy as a carpenter. Liam tormented himself imagining all the great things Con got to do in that extra hour. He was always telling Liam how he met all sorts of interesting people out on the street, or how Daddy told him a great story but it was unsuitable for him because he was too young. It drove Liam mad with frustration, which only made his brother laugh at him.

Con had finished school when he was twelve, every day at the primary school was a persecution for poor old Con and the general wisdom at the time was the sooner he got out from under the brothers' feet the better. Daddy could probably have got Con a job in the dockyard at the time, it was still open then, but Liam knew their parents wanted something better for him. Daddy said the docks were on the brink of closure for years anyway so there was no future in it for a young lad like Con.

There had been talk for a while about him staying on at school, for a few more years anyway, but Brother Malachi had told Mammy that he was a waste of space and she'd only be throwing her money away paying fees for a big lump of an ignoramus like Con. Mammy was upset when she told Daddy , Liam remembered hearing them through the floor discussing it, but Daddy was reassuring. Con was a good lad and a great hurler and Daddy went to all his matches and, anyway, he didn't care one bit about school so he eventually convinced her that it was probably just as well that he finishes after sixth class. He'd get a great start with Willy, and it would all work out fine. Liam knew that if Con had shown any interest in the books, Daddy would have found a way for him to stay on, but Con just wasn't a scholar and that was that. Mammy met Father Aquinas a few days later and he told her what a grand lad Con was and how he'd be a great worker and she felt a bit better about the whole thing.

Liam wished they chatted like that still. Since Daddy lost his job, they were not getting on as well as they used to. Liam lay awake listening to them worrying about money, hankering after the nights of years ago when they would laugh and whisper together when they thought the whole family was asleep.

Liam lay in bed, wide awake. Con was pucking the sliotar off the gable end wall, practicing his accuracy. The rhythmic sound of the little leather ball hitting the bricks was reassuring. Kate was at her friend's house; they were making a dress from a pattern, though Mammy whispered to him earlier with a wink how she couldn't imagine Kate and Kitty Hourihan managing to make anything a person could actually wear. Kate wasn't great with a needle.

Daddy's voice, though hushed, could be heard through the floorboards.

'Mary, I really think I should go, only for a few months, till things get better here...' Seán's voice was pleading.

'No Seán, we've been over this and over it, I don't want you to go to England. I know all the arguments, and sure, the whole of Cork is over there in that car factory but I need you here, the children need you here, something will turn up, you just have to be patient. I'm doing the nine days prayer, never known to fail.' Liam knew that despite his mother's positive words she was ragged from trying to make ends meet.

'Mrs Kinsella wants me to paint her yard at the weekend; I suppose that will be something...' Seán said.

'There's nothing wrong with her yard, honestly, Seán, she's making a fool of you, I know she throws you a few shillings but honestly she...' Liam strained to hear. His mother's voice had dropped to a whisper. Liam wasn't sure why, but his mother didn't warm to the new neighbour much, which wasn't like her at all.

He tried to block out the sounds of them arguing so he pulled his school book out from the satchel he kept under the bed. He wasn't a natural scholar, but he really wanted to stay at school, go onto the secondary, so he needed to show the brothers that he would be worth a scholarship. Liam, like most of the class was twelve now so they would be looking for work, though with no experience or skills, their chances were non-existent. Some were talking of going over to fathers or older brothers in England. Liam desperately wanted to stay on, get his exams, but the chances of it happening seemed fainter by the day. There was no way Mammy and Daddy could pay the fees now, so the only way to keep up his education was to win a scholarship. Even then, it would be tight but without the financial assistance the bursary offered, it would be simply impossible. Liam never even mentioned it at home. He knew Daddy hated not being able to provide for them all, he dreaded the look that came over his father's face when he noted the holes in their shoes or their jumpers threadbare from overuse. If Daddy knew how badly he wanted to go to the secondary, it would only make him feel worse about being out of work so Liam kept his dreams secret.

After school the next day, he was learning his Latin verbs at the kitchen table. Mammy was over at the Lynch's house to borrow a baking tin, Con and Kate were at work, and Daddy had gone down to a man in Glanmire where he heard there might be a bit of labouring going. He didn't know where the twins were, whispering somewhere probably. He was sick of them always saying he was a baby and Mammy's pet. They were only jealous because Daddy was taking him and Con to the Munster final in Thurles tomorrow and it was a no-girls-allowed excursion. One of the men from the dockyard had a car and was going anyway so they had a spin, and Daddy got the tickets because he repainted all the lines of the pitch for the club with the white paint roller. Mammy would make them sandwiches so it was a free day out. Liam and Con were so excited they talked of nothing else for weeks. Liam knew the twins were going mad to be excluded though they let on that they couldn't care less. They thought because they were fourteen, they were so sophisticated. As if there was a world of difference in maturity between a twelve-year-old and them. Sometimes, he really hated being the youngest, but he knew he kind of was Mammy's pet at the same time. She had more time for him, he supposed, since he was the last and there wasn't a baby or a toddler coming up behind him that needed her more. She talked to him about things, and they went to Mass together every day. Con was busy at work, so much to the relief of both Con and the clergy that he had been relieved of his altar boy position. Father Mac had asked Father Aquinas for a suitable recruit, and apparently was dubious when he heard him suggest another of the Tobin boys, but Father Aquinas assured him that Liam was a much more devout boy than his brother. Father Mac gave Liam this information, along with dire warnings that if he turned up late, or his vestments weren't in perfect order, he would be most affronted. Liam didn't really know what that meant, but guessed it wasn't a good thing, Father Mac liked to use big words. He trained Liam for the altar and as soon as was decent, Con's services were dispensed with. Liam loved serving at Mass; he loved the sense of importance he got as he rang the bell at the Consecration or carried the thurible during Benediction. Father Mac didn't trust everyone with it, so Liam felt great he was chosen to be the most responsible of all the altar boys, especially considering how far he'd had to come, living with the legacy of being Con's brother.

Some of the other boys who served said they were only doing it for the money, people gave you a shilling usually for a funeral and sometimes a half crown for a wedding, but Liam did it because he loved it. He'd never admit it to the others, they'd think he was a right dope for saying it out loud, but he loved the sense of peace he got when he went into the church. He prayed every morning and every night at home, and he enjoyed the whole family saying the rosary at night before bed. Everyone did it, he knew that and he wasn't any holier than any of his friends, but he'd get an awful slagging if he said he liked it.

He dragged his mind back to the Latin declensions when there was a knock at the door. The door was always on the latch so most people just tapped and walked in. He expected to see someone pop their head into the kitchen any second but nobody appeared. Sighing, he got up to go and see who was there.

Standing at the door was Mrs Kinsella from next door. Liam's heart sank when he recognised her silhouette through the glass of the front door. She was always asking for Daddy to go round there and do jobs, and she seemed to have a lot of things wrong with her house.

'Is your Daddy at home, Liam?' she asked in her strange accent. Mammy said she was from Dublin or somewhere, and she certainly didn't sound like anyone from around here. She didn't look like anyone either, she was always wearing flowery dresses that went out like an umbrella and her hair was really yellowy-white, and she wore red lipstick. Kate was always asking her about clothes and make-up and boring things like that. She had no husband. Liam thought he must be dead because she never mentioned him, and she had a daughter who was ten. He might have played with her a few years ago but now big lads like him just played with boys and the girls played their own things with dolls.

'No, Mrs Kinsella, he's out,' Liam answered her politely. Mammy would want him to be polite even though he knew from the conversations at night between his parents that Mammy really didn't approve of her. She never came in for a cup of tea and a chat like the other neighbours and Liam knew Mammy didn't like her asking Daddy to do all the jobs in the house. Maybe Mammy wanted him doing jobs at home instead.

'Oh yes, I forgot, he said he would be going somewhere today. Not to worry, I'll call later. There's a mouse in my kitchen and I'm terrified of mice.' She gave a giggly laugh, more like a girl than a grown-up woman.

'Oh right,' Liam answered, not sure what to say next. 'I'll tell him when he comes home.'

As he was about to close the door, he saw his mother coming down the street with a baking tin in her hand.

'Ah, Mrs Kinsella,' she said. 'Is everything all right? Run in and finish your lessons, Liam,' she instructed him. Turning her attention back to her neighbour, she asked, 'Can I help you with something?'

There was something about the way Mammy spoke to her that made Liam linger inside the front door. Mammy was smiling and seemed like she was being friendly, but there was something in her tone that made him interested in what would happen next.

'Oh no, Mrs Tobin, it was Seán I was looking for actually. I have a mouse in the kitchen and I'm too nervous to open the cupboard.' Liam couldn't see her face, but he could imagine it, with her big innocent smile.

'Oh dear, and you from the heart of Dublin city afraid of a little mouse, doesn't that beat all? Well, Mrs Kinsella, I'm afraid my husband is busy today and when he comes home, we are going to visit family so he won't be available to catch your mouse for you then either. I'll tell you what though; I have a fine trap inside. I'll get Liam to set it for you and when you hear the snap sure pop back, he'll empty it out for you. The thing is you need to be very clean in your housekeeping to keep them out. They'll get in anywhere so the trick is not to leave anything for them to eat.'

Liam was confused. Daddy would set a trap in one second, and she never said anything about them going out tonight. Daddy wouldn't mind a bit, he was always helping people; he was great at fixing things. He even found an old bike in the river a few months ago, the wheels buckled and everything, but he fixed it up and painted it dark blue and Liam and Con used it all the time. Daddy told Mammy when she was grumbling about him going in next door again that even though Jerome Moriarty was the landlord, he lived in England somewhere so he couldn't do anything, so she was a woman on her own and needed someone like Daddy next door, who was able to do things.

He ran down the hall just in time to avoid being caught eavesdropping. His mother opened the door and called him.

'Liam, would you get the mousetrap from the pantry and a small bit of fat off the bacon in the larder please. I want you to set the trap for poor Mrs Kinsella here. She is terrorised by a furry friend in her kitchen press.' Mammy was smiling but not her normal smile; it was extra bright and smiley.

The women waited in silence until Liam appeared. 'Oh well, if you're sure, but I'm happy to wait for Seán if it's more convenient,' Mrs Kinsella said as Liam appeared with the trap and the bacon rind.

'No, no, it's no problem. Liam here is well able to do it, and my husband is a very busy man.' Liam was confused, his mother didn't usually use that kind of voice and she usually called Daddy Seán when she was talking about him. Not all this 'my husband' stuff.

Next door was the same size as theirs but only had two people living there so it seemed much less cluttered. He followed her into the kitchen and noticed she was wearing perfume, she smelled nice, like flowers. She quickly moved a bottle of stout off the kitchen table and put it in a press and the pint glass that was beside it. It was weird that she was going to drink a bottle of stout, only men did that. Women didn't really drink at all, Liam thought, Mammy was a pioneer of total abstinence and went to meetings about it and everything. But maybe Mrs Kinsella was thirsty.

'Which press has the mouse in it?' he asked.

'Er, that one,' she replied, pointing to the one she had just opened to put the stout in.

'But you just opened that one.' Liam didn't understand how come she opened it if she was scared of the mouse.

'Em, well, em, I forgot, can you just put the trap in that one please, Liam?' She seemed a bit flustered, she must be really scared, he thought, to be so upset. He felt quite brave and manly setting the trap and placing it in the press.

'Do you want me to wait in case it snaps straight away?' He had spotted a bottle of lemonade in the larder so she might offer him a drink if he stayed.

'No, no thanks, Liam. Maybe it will take ages, so maybe your daddy could look in when he comes home.' She stopped and smiled at him. 'You look like him. I suppose everyone tells you that. I bet he looked just like you when he was small, with your brown curls and big brown eyes.' She smiled and rubbed his hair.

Liam could feel his cheeks reddening at her touch, 'Er, yeah, Mammy says I've his big feet, too,' he blurted, suddenly anxious to get away.

He let himself in to the kitchen as Mammy was getting out the ingredients for a cake.

'Well, did you set it?' she asked.

Liam was going to tell her about the stout and what she said about him looking like Daddy but something stopped him and decided he better not.

'I did. She said it might take ages so not to wait. She said maybe Daddy could look in when he comes home.' Liam went back to his lessons at the other end of the table but was sure he heard Mammy utter under her breath, 'Over my dead body, he will.'

CHAPTER 4

Con was on the ground with John-Joe Murphy underneath him, and Con was battering him, even though John-Joe was bigger. Liam stood by, unsure of what to do. If Mammy found out they were fighting in the street and everyone was watching them, she'd murder them but John-Joe was teasing Con and Liam about Daddy going away to England, saying that he was gone over to Mrs Kinsella. They were walking across the road at the monastery gates and John-Joe asked how the new Mammy was. Con gave Liam the bread he was carrying back from the shop and squared up to John-Joe, sure everyone knew he was as thick as a ditch and dared him to say it again.

John-Joe smirked back at the shower of eejits he hung around with and said, 'Say what? That your auld fella and Mrs Kinsella were at it and now he's gone running off to England after her?'

Another fella jumped in and now there were two of them on Con. Liam had no choice, he had to join in—he couldn't let his brother try to fight them on his own. Liam jumped on the back of Tommy O'Leary and stuck his fingers in his eyes as hard as he could. Suddenly, all of John-Joe's gang were in the fight and legs, arms, and punches were flying. Over the din of boys yelling, he heard a voice he recognised.

'Stop that fighting this instant!' The loud, booming voice of Father Aquinas. He picked up John-Joe by the scruff of the neck and gave him a thump in the back, sending him flying. There was a general scatter of the others until eventually the only ones left were himself and Con. All the boys knew Father Aquinas was the boxing champion in the seminary when he was young and more than a match for John-Joe and his gang. None of them wanted the priest at their door complaining to their parents about their sons brawling in the street so they made themselves scarce quickly.

'Well, isn't this a nice state of affairs and your mother doing her best to cope, I'm sure Seán Tobin wouldn't be one bit pleased to hear his boys were fighting out in the street like common hooligans.' He sighed and pulled a bleeding Con to his feet. 'Ye better come in to the monastery, clean yourselves up and not go home to your mother in that condition,' he said wearily but not unkindly. Con went to protest that he was fine but one look from Liam told him he better not go home looking like that.

Father Aquinas always taught in the junior school, but he was an ever present force around the neighbourhood, if he gave you an instruction, you didn't question it. He always looked the same, Liam saw him around the school all the time even though he was in sixth class now and Father Aquinas still taught first class. His eyebrows were just as bushy as when Liam made his communion but the bit of hair he had left was now totally white. He was tall and muscular, built like a rugby player, he ran the school boxing club though hurling was his passion. He was still as terrifying as he was when they were seven however, so it was with a heavy heart Liam followed his brother behind the priest and into the monastery.

It smelled exactly as it had when he was last in there, five years earlier, preparing for his communion. Their shoes squeaked on the highly polished floor and the priest led them down a warren of corridors without a word towards what must be the kitchen. The large room had a huge black stove at one end and a long often-scrubbed wooden table running its length with a bench on either side. The shelves that lined the walls bore the weight of stacks of white table ware on top and pots and pans beneath. The whole room smelled of baking and heat and plenty.

It was deserted, so the priest indicated they should sit and he went to a sink and filled a basin with water. Looking under the enormous sink, he produced a clean white cloth and a bottle of Dettol and deposited them on the table beside them.

'Now then, you're the worst, Con, so let's have a look at you first,' the priest began.

'Honestly, Father, I'm grand, I'll just clean myself up there and...' Con was anxious to get away.

Father Aquinas held Con by the chin as he protested, turning his head to examine the cut over his eye.

'Your poor mother has enough on her plate at the moment without you coming home looking like you've done ten rounds with Sugar Ray Robinson. Now hold still, this is going to sting.' He dapped the cut with the wet cloth dipped in Dettol and Con winced as the disinfectant entered the wound. The priest did the same for his burst lip and told him to hold the cloth up to it to stop the bleeding. He then turned his attention to Con's hand where the fingers were swelling quickly. Con's eyes were blackening already, and his nose was swelling up, all that Liam could think was that Mammy was going to have a fit when she saw the state of them.

'How'd that happen?' the priest asked.

'Tommy O'Leary stood on it, Father,' Con managed to say, despite the cloth at his mouth. Liam could tell he hated the priest fussing over him like this. Con was sixteen and out working, he resented being spoken to like a schoolboy. Ignoring his protests, Father Aquinas lifted his hand and tried to bend the fingers. Con let out a shriek of pain.

'Broken,' the priest said matter-of-factly. 'You'll have to go down and get it seen in the hospital.'

He took some powders out of a jar and mixed them with water and handed it to Con. 'That will take the edge off the pain till you get to the hospital or if Sister Julia comes back. She's a dab hand with strapping the broken fingers—we'd be lost without her on the sidelines at the underage hurling matches, I can tell you.'

'Now, Mr Tobin Junior, let's see what you've managed to do to yourself, shall we?' he said, turning his attention to Liam. His knees were cut and bleeding and his arm had a big bite mark where one of John-Joe's gang had bitten him and drawn blood. Again the priest cleaned the cuts with the disinfectant and Liam tried not to react but it really hurt.

Once they were cleaned up, the priest brought the basin back to the sink, rinsed it, and replaced the Dettol. He then went about getting two big cups of tea and took an apple tart out of a larder. He cut two huge slices and placed them in front of the boys along with the tea.

They were taken aback, unsure what to do.

'Well, do ye want it or don't ye?' Father Aquinas asked. 'You'll be ages below waiting to get that plastered up so you better eat something or you'll keel over. Maybe Sister Julia will be back, she was visiting her family today and if so there'll be no need of the hospital, but if she doesn't, I'll ask Father Joseph to bring you down in the car. I'll phone the convent there and see, and I'll send someone down with a message to your mother in case she's worried.'

'Seriously, Father, there's no need. Thanks for everything...'Con went to stand up but his legs seemed to go from under him.

'Con Tobin, you could never be told, could you? You're concussed, so just sit down and eat the cake and drink the tea and stop making this more difficult, will you?'

Con sat back down and gingerly took a bite of the tart. Father Aquinas went out to make the phone call and the brothers were alone. The tart was delicious, and they wolfed it down followed by the hot, sweet milky tea. Mammy didn't bake anymore, not since everything happened, so they hadn't had anything nice in ages.

Once they had finished, they sat quietly, afraid to talk in case someone came in. Eventually, Liam asked, 'Is your hand fierce sore, Con?'

Before Con had a chance to reply, Father Aquinas came back, 'Good news, Sister Julia will be up in a few minutes. She'll get you right in no time.' He noted the thunderous look on Con's face, a mixture of pain and fury.

'You'll have to learn not to react, Con, you know that, don't you? You're too big now for that kind of stupid schoolboy scrapping. You have to be the man of the house until your father comes home, and you aren't helping your mother by carrying on like that in the street. And drawing young Liam into it as well, he could have got a right battering, sure that big gom John-Joe Murphy would make two of him, he's only twelve. Your mother has enough to contend with without having her youngest in the hospital and you hauled off by the guards for brawling.'

Liam willed Con just to nod and say nothing but he knew his brother of old.

'He said something about my father, and I couldn't let it go,' Con muttered.

Father Aquinas sighed and walked over to the big window that overlooked the gardens of the monastery. He put his hands in the pockets of his soutane and thought for a moment.

'Do you know what people are saying, Liam?' the priest asked with his back to them.

Liam was embarrassed. Of course he knew, he'd overheard enough the night it all happened to know, and even if he didn't, he heard it every day in school. The Tobins were the talk of the place.

'Yes, Father, I do,' he replied.

The priest turned back to them and sat opposite the brothers at the big table.

'Listen to me now,' he began. 'I know what people are saying, that Mrs Kinsella that lived next door had something to do with your father, something improper.'

Liam was trying so hard not to cry. Everyone was talking about them; even the priests had heard it in the monastery.

'And they're putting two and two together and making ten because she is gone and your father had to go to England looking for work. People are saying they ran off together.'

Con and Liam sat wordlessly. 'Isn't that what ye are hearing?' the priest asked.

Liam nodded, Con glowered.

'Now, you know I can't tell you anything I have heard in confidence in my role as a priest, don't you?' Again they nodded, unsure where he was going.

'But I will tell you this. I *know*, not guess or hope, but *know* for a sure and certain fact, that your father has nothing to do with Mrs Kinsella, now or at any time in the past, beyond being a good neighbour. I've known Seán Tobin a long time, since he was a small boy up here like ye were once, and I know he's as honest as the day is long. He is devoted to your mother and to all of ye and he would never do anything to hurt ye.

'Now, ye need to speak to your mother about this, tell her what's been happening and she'll tell you the same thing. That it is all rumours and gossip and that Seán never looked at that woman in that way. It's not going to stop the gossips, they have nothing better to do with their time, but I want you two to know that when your father told you that it wasn't true, he was being honest with you all, and with your mother, no matter what anyone else says. The fact that the dockyard closed and so many men were out of work meant that your father couldn't get a job here. Plenty of men would just go on the dole, and raise their family on a pittance, but Seán Tobin wants better for his children, so he's gone to get work over in England and he'll be back to you all as soon as he can. Mrs Kinsella is somewhere else entirely and that is the truth. Now, in the meantime, he'd want his boys to be good. So no more of this scrapping, do ye hear me? Just ignore them, you know the truth and that's all that matters.'

Liam looked into the eyes of the big priest for the first time in his life. All of a sudden, he didn't seem so scary; he seemed nice, and kind. There was no way he could raise the issue with Mammy, she hardly spoke to them these days and spent all her time cleaning the house and going over to the church. She never mentioned Daddy or Mrs

Kinsella or the situation at all. Liam had a lot of questions and no one to ask. Kate was just like Mammy, and she was cross with it, so she just told Liam to buzz off any time he asked them anything, and Con was as much in the dark as he was. He deliberated; maybe he should ask the priest about the terrible night.

As he considered it, a nun entered the kitchen.

'Ah, Sister Julia, the very person. We've a young man here with a suspected broken finger, maybe two of them, would you take a look at it and see if we can just strap it or does he need to go to the hospital?'

The youngish nun with tanned skin smiled at them, 'Well, you two have been in the wars and no mistake! Now, let's have a look, don't worry, I'm a nurse,' she reassured Con.

'Sister Julia is home from the missions in Ghana where the nearest hospital to them is about two hundred miles away, so she's able to do nearly everything,' Father Aquinas said.

'I'm visiting the convent below, but my brother is Father Matthew, do ye remember him? He used to play the organ at Mass before the arthritis got too bad.'

Liam had no idea who she was on about but nodded politely, still trying to imagine nuns and priests having brothers and sisters. Con looked nervous.

She took his hand and examined it gently, pressing softly on the swelling. He winced.

'Good lad, Con, is it? I'm sure you got worse on the hurling pitch! That's sore, I can tell but you're lucky, it's a clean break so I'd say I'll just strap it up and no moving it for a week or two and you'll be good as new. My things are below in the infirmary so I'll take him down there. Father, we'll be back in a few minutes.' And with that, she ushered Con out of the room leaving Liam alone with Father Aquinas.

Without really preparing it, he blurted out.

'Father, how come Mrs Kinsella came and told Mammy that Daddy wanted to go away with her so, that she and Daddy were...?' He reddened with embarrassment but how else was he going to find out? One of the boys at school told him months ago how babies were made and at the start, he didn't believe him, it seemed so ridiculous. There was no way his parents ever did that, but then he asked Daddy. They were walking home from a match after winning and they were splitting a bag of chips between them to celebrate. Liam asked him straight out if what the boys in school had said was true. Daddy stopped and sat down on a bench beside the river and told him all about it. He explained it was a very special and lovely thing between two people who were married and there was nothing bad about it, but he still found the whole thing perplexing, and he looked at everyone he met who had children in a whole new light. Was everyone in the world doing that mad thing with their private parts? It seemed unbelievable but apparently they were. He was sure of one thing; he'd never do it with anyone in his whole life.

Father Aquinas was silent, and Liam feared he was going to get a clout for having the cheek to ask. Eventually he spoke.

'I don't know why she said it. But I do know that she is not well. Not like the flu or chicken pox or something, but she isn't well in her head. She thought she was in love with your father and she believed he felt the same about her. None of it was true, Liam, that's the important thing, none of it. It all happened in her head.'

'But I don't understand...' Liam was more confused than ever.

'I know, Liam, it seems very hard to take in. I realise this is very difficult for you all, but it's very important for you, and for your whole family that you believe him when he tells you that he didn't do anything wrong.'

Every night in bed, Liam relived that terrible night three weeks ago. Mrs Kinsella knocked at the door when he was in bed and Mammy and Daddy were having their tea by the stove. As usual, he was half dozing and half listening to them. He couldn't hear what they said but hearing their voices, still made him feel safe and happy. Daddy still had no work and he was talking about going over to England again, but Mammy wasn't keen on the idea. They were just about to go to bed, he heard Daddy locking the back door when there was a knock on the front. He heard Daddy answer it and then Mammy's voice in a loud whisper. 'Mrs Kinsella! It's nearly midnight. What on earth do you want at this time of night?' She sounded very cross.

'I want Seán,' was all she kept repeating over and over, louder and louder.

Then she started screaming. 'Seán, you have to come away with me now, we can go away, you and me and Marion, we could have our own family. I can make you happy, we can be together. You know it's what we both want!' She was crying then. Con woke at the noise and sat up in bed and then he crept out to the top of the landing, with Liam following behind. Kate was already there and the twins appeared moments later. He remembered watching his older brother and sisters' faces register shock and horror at what they were hearing.

'Yerra get away out of our house now, disturbing us at this hour of the night with all your old nonsense, God love you and your foolish notions. My husband is going nowhere with you or with anyone else.' Mammy was ushering her out the door.

'Tell her, Seán,' Mrs Kinsella screamed. 'Tell her the truth. It's me he loves, not you. Not you.' She spat the last words into Mammy's face. Her hair was all hanging down in front of her face and she sounded drunk, slurring her words. Tears were coursing down her cheeks and her make-up was all smeared, she looked frightful.

Mammy turned to look Daddy in the face. 'Well, Seán? What have you to say for yourself?'

They couldn't see their father, he was standing at the kitchen door, directly below where they were sitting, but they could hear him. When he spoke, he sounded shocked.

'Mary, I swear on our children's lives I don't know what she's talking about. I never touched her, I swear to you.' Liam willed his mother to believe him and wished Mrs Kinsella would just drop dead and all of this horrible thing would never have happened.

There was silence, only broken by Mrs Kinsella's sobs. Mammy looked back the hall, straight at Daddy.

Then she turned to Mrs Kinsella and said in a voice Liam didn't even recognise, 'Listen here to me, you, my husband has shown you nothing but kindness, we all have. And this is how you repay us, coming in here, making all sorts of wild accusations in the dead of night and upsetting me and my family? You are never to darken this door again, do you hear me? I don't care if the roof falls in or if the place is overrun by rats; my husband and *my* children's father will not be coming to your rescue. You must think I'm some kind of a simpleton, I've seen what you've been trying to do, with your, "Oh Seán, help me with this, and Oh Seán, that thing is broken," but I've the measure of you, lady. You have a child to rear and this is the example you are setting her? You aren't fit to be her mother! I don't know what you did with your own man if you ever had one, nor do I care, but you won't be having mine. Now, get yourself out of my home before I fire you out by that stupid peroxide head of yours.'

Mrs Kinsella changed then; she stopped crying and was livid. 'Are you going to let her talk to me like that, Seán? Are you?' She was screaming now. Liam felt Kate put her arm around him and hold him close to her.

'You heard my wife, Laura, it's time you left. There is nothing between us, there never was. I don't know where you're getting this from, but I've never given you a reason to think there was anything going on between us as you well know. Now, go on home before we have the whole street in on top of us.' Daddy sounded calmer than Mammy but his voice didn't sound like his normal one either.

Liam watched his parents usher her out the door and noticed the lights from several neighbours' houses reflected on the path outside. Everyone heard what had happened, it would have been impossible not to with the racket she was causing.

The front door was closed and the Tobin children watched their parents stand, not touching, in the hall. They were unaware of the audience they had at the top of the stairs.

Daddy tried to put his arms around Mammy but she pushed him away. Kate beckoned them back to their bedrooms. Mammy and Daddy's room was downstairs, and the girls had the big room upstairs since there were three of them. Con and Liam went back to their room leaving the door slightly ajar.

'Mary...Mary, look at me!' Liam heard his father plead. 'You can't seriously think there's anything in what she said. Dear God...you do, you think I was carrying on with her.'

'I don't know what to think.' His mother's voice was quiet. 'You were in there often enough.'

'The only reason I was in there at all was to make a few bob doing odd jobs. How else are we supposed to live?' Seán was reasonable.

'I'd rather starve than take her money. I'd rather beg on the street than be paid by that hussy for the use of my husband.' Liam was terrified, he never heard his mother speak like that.

'The use of your husband! For God's sake! Would you listen to yourself, woman? I was painting, hanging doors, fixing things as you well know. I've been telling you for weeks I'll have to go to England, but you won't have it. Tom O'Mahony from the dockyard can get me a start. Well, let me tell you something for nothing, if my own wife doesn't trust me, and we are on the brink of starvation since I'm out of work, I might as well go now then, hadn't I?' Daddy was shouting.

'Seán, keep your voice down, the whole street will hear you,' Mammy spat.

'And that's all you care about, is it? What the narrow, small-minded attitudes of the people of this place have to say? You care what they think but not what I think, is that it? You'd prefer to believe the auld tittle-tattle out of people with nothing better to do than believe the word of the man you married, who never gave you one reason to doubt him in all the years. Is that what our marriage means to you, is it?'

Daddy stormed into their bedroom and, moments later, the front door slammed with such force it shook the whole house. Liam tried unsuccessfully to hold back the tears. He could hear Mammy crying downstairs, it was horrible. Liam lay awake for the rest of the night and relief flooded his body when he heard his father come home around dawn.

The atmosphere in the days that followed was awful. The following Friday night, after the incident with Mrs Kinsella, Daddy sat them down and told them he was going to England for work and he'd be gone for a few months. He explained that the family needed the money and that he didn't want to leave them but it was only for a while, until things got better in Cork. Liam tried to hold back the tears but failed. His father hugged him tight and told him that he loved him very much and asked him to be a good boy. The following morning, he was gone. Things with Mammy were bad when he left, they were speaking but not the way they always did. Liam would never forget the stiff way she stood as Daddy hugged her when he walked down the street to get the Innisfallen over to Wales. He was going to get a bus to London and then another train to Dagenham. She didn't want him to go, Liam knew she was trying to pretend everything was fine, but her eyes were red from weeping and lack of sleep. Mrs Lynch from across the road called in most evenings and the two women chatted quietly by the range.

Liam couldn't bear it anymore. He didn't want to ask his mother, she seemed so sad, but he was afraid his father was never coming home again. In desperation he asked Kate, 'Daddy is going to come home, Kate, isn't he?'

'Ah Liam, it's too complicated for you to understand,' she said. 'Just leave it, will you?'

He persisted though and eventually she explained exasperatedly though it didn't really make sense.

'Look, Daddy didn't do anything with that tart next door but Mammy was mad at him because he was in there so much and now all the neighbours are talking about us, gossiping that he did do something with her, and so because she didn't trust him at first, he got very cross and went away to work in England.'

'And does Mammy know he didn't do anything wrong?'

'Yes, of course she does, are you happy now?' Kate was impatient.

Liam wasn't one bit happy, but he knew that was the only explanation he was likely to get.

Father Aquinas seemed to know more about this situation than anyone and for some reason he wasn't being as scary as he normally was.

'So Daddy is definitely not gone off with Mrs Kinsella?' Liam desperately wanted the priest's reassurance.

'Liam Tobin, I am a priest so I'm not allowed to tell a lie. For a priest to lie is way worse than a lay person, and I promise you that your father is not anywhere with her or any other woman, for that matter. She is somewhere where she can get help with her problems and your father is in Dagenham working in a car factory. And let me tell you something else, there are people who gossip, and there always will be. But anyone who knows your father knows he is a decent God-fearing man who is devoted to his family so don't mind anyone who says otherwise.'

'But why was Mammy so cross then, if he did nothing wrong?' he asked.

'Look, Liam, that night, the night Mrs Kinsella called, well, your mother got a shock and she reacted, we all do when we've had a shock. Mary Tobin is a very good woman and a devout Catholic so she takes marriage vows very seriously indeed. I'm sure once your father comes home and things pick up here, everything will go back to normal. Now, what about you? You're coming up for the end of sixth class, have you thought about going up to the secondary?' The priest changed the conversation.

'I don't think so, Father, we can't afford it.' His voice was flat.

'Well, would you apply for a scholarship? There are a few available every year to lads who show promise but whose families wouldn't be in a position to pay the fees. You might get one if you tried really hard.'

Liam was amazed at this new side to Father Aquinas, he seemed almost like a normal person. Since everything happened, Liam had given up all hope of going to the secondary. 'I...thought about it but you have to be really brilliant at tests and I'm not, so...' Liam answered truthfully. 'Anyway, I wouldn't fit in, I suppose...and with everything going on at home...'

The more he thought about it, the more he realised it was probably a stupid dream anyway. All the other fellas would be from rich families and he'd be so different, and now that everyone was talking about his family, it would be even worse. The thoughts of going somewhere where, not only was he the poor boy, but also the boy whose father ran off with the neighbour filled him with nauseous dread. He'd heard from other fellas that the scholarship lads got a hard time, not just from the students but from the teachers, too. Liam knew that to be true, he saw it with his own eyes. The priests in the primary were not as hard on the sons of the richer fellas. They were not especially bad to the Tobins, who were definitely not rich, but not the poorest of the poor either but some of the fellas from the lanes, living in real squalor got an awful time from them altogether. Not all the priests, to be fair, but some of them were right snobs.

'Well, you have to do an exam in Mathematics, English, Irish, and Latin. You have to get over 90 percent in each one and if you do, then you are eligible.' Father Aquinas said it as if it were simple to do. Liam usually got around 70 percent in English, Irish, and Latin if he stayed up all night learning, but he struggled with Maths. He'd never get 90 percent in a test.

'I don't think I could do it,' Liam admitted.

'Well, you certainly won't if you decide you won't before you even start,' Father Aquinas said sternly. 'Nothing that is worth achieving is done without effort. You are bright enough, not a genius as I recall, but you have the capacity to learn. The information needed is in your text books, it's simply a matter of learning it and regurgitating it on the day of the exam. Now, I'm sure your mother will be wondering where you both are, so you better get going. No doubt, news of the brawl will have reached her by now,' he added drily.

'Yes, Father, thank you,' Liam answered; the meeting was clearly over. He wondered if he should wait for Con or go home and face his mother alone. On balance, he decided he might fare better without Con; he usually did in these situations.

CHAPTER 5

'Absolutely not. Not under any circumstances, so you can just stop talking about it right this minute.' Liam opened the back door to hear his mother laying down the law to someone.

'You can't stop me, I'm over eighteen. I don't need your permission,' Kate shouted in frustration. 'It's a great opportunity, and I'm legally an adult, you can't tell me I can't go, just like that.'

More arguing. He was sick of it. Their family never used to be this way, they all got along, stuck up for each other and even if they were getting on each other's nerves, someone would intervene, and soon they'd all be laughing again. It seemed like a hundred years ago that they sat around eating dinner and chatting and laughing. Daddy was the peacemaker, that was the problem, without him, all anyone did was fight. He tried to slip unnoticed through the kitchen when Mammy spotted him and his cuts and bruises.

'Holy Mother of God! What happened to you?' She ran over to him, almost knocking Kate.

'Nothing,' he replied.

'Well, it doesn't look like nothing! Are you after getting beaten up? Who did this to you, Liam?' His mother raked his face for a clue, he couldn't lie to her and she knew it. Her voice was cracking with the emotion of it all.

Kate was now looking at him as well. 'Mam, someone is bullying him because of the situation with Daddy...'

To Kate and Liam's horror and, moments later, the bandaged Con who arrived in the middle of it all, their mother collapsed onto a kitchen chair and wept. They had never seen Mammy cry, even when Granny died, or when Daddy went off to get the boat to England, and to see it now was shocking.

'Mam, I'm sorry, I didn't mean it.' Kate was kneeling beside her mother, in tears herself.

'This is all my fault. I know it is, but I'm not keeping him away, I swear to ye, I want him home just as much as ye do.'

Liam was bewildered. *Did Kate think Mammy was keeping Daddy away from them? Wasn't he working in England, wasn't he coming home when he got a bit of money saved up? Father Aquinas told him that Daddy was working in England so it must be true. Why wasn't Kate saying it wasn't Mammy's fault?*

Mammy then looked up and saw Con. Seeing him with his bandaged hand and cuts all over his face seemed to stop her crying at least.

'Con! What happened? And I want the truth.'

Con glanced at Liam as if to say leave the talking to me. Liam knew from bitter experience that such a course of action would end badly, loads of people saw what happened so she'd hear about it soon anyway. Con would only make up something stupid that Mammy wouldn't believe in a blue fit so he jumped in, 'I was walking past the monastery when John-Joe Murphy started picking on me because of Mrs Kinsella and Daddy, and then he started thumping me. Con jumped in and saved me from them because all his gang were with him. Then Father Aquinas came along and put the run on John-Joe and gave him a clatter. He took us into the monastery and cleaned us up and he told me that no matter what anyone says Daddy has nothing to do with Mrs Kinsella and that she isn't right in the head and that Daddy is in Dagenham making cars in a car factory and she is in a place, not England, getting help for whatever is wrong with her that makes her make up mad things about other people's husbands and fathers.' He ran out of breath and he knew he was babbling, but it was the only way to stop Con jumping in and he also wanted to talk to his mother about it. Nobody in the family mentioned it and it was so tense and strange, at least now it was out in the open.

The silence in the kitchen was palpable. The clock ticked on the dresser as the family tried to digest what Liam had just said. The twins appeared at the door, drawn in by all the commotion.

Mammy sat in silence, planning what she was going to say. From her face, she looked stunned that Liam knew about everything, her eyes went to each of her children in turn, searching their faces for how much they knew.

'Sit down. I should have spoken to ye about this before, but I just...' she said quietly, gesturing that they should all sit at the kitchen table. For once, there was no arguing over who sat where. Usually nobody wanted to sit near the dresser because whoever sat there always had to get a glass or get the salt or get the twenty other things the person who was supposed to set the table forgot. The twins sat inside beside each other as usual, Kate sat in Daddy's seat and Con and Liam sat outside.

'So, ye all know what happened?' It was more of a question than a statement. They nodded.

'We were on the top of the stairs when she came in that night,' Annie said quietly.

'Right. I see.' Mammy was quiet again. 'I'm so sorry ye had to hear that, I was wrong to get so cross with Daddy. I know people are saying he went off with her, but your father is a decent and honest man, who never told a lie in his whole life. I should have believed him right away. I did believe him, but I was annoyed with him for being kind to her. She read something into nothing, and I should have...I'm sorry, I wish...' She wiped her eyes on the corner of her apron. 'I received a letter from him saying that there might be some work in the new tyre factory coming up soon and if there is, he'll be home the minute he gets a new job. He misses us all, and he really wants to come home. We want him home as well, don't we? Now, I know it's hard to listen to gossip about your family but you know the truth so do what Daddy would want if he were here, hold your head up and just ignore it. Can ye do that? Daddy did nothing wrong, nothing at all, but people might be saying bad things.'

Again Mammy looked uncomfortable. 'Now I don't know what you've heard at school, Liam...' she began.

'I know all about babies and where they come from and all that,' Liam proclaimed proudly.

'Well, you wouldn't want to put too much store by what big eejits above in the brothers have to say about anything...' she began.

'No, it was Daddy who told me,' Liam said confidently.

'Right,' she said again, struggling to digest yet more new information.

'So, as Father Aquinas told Liam and Con today, Mrs Kinsella isn't right in the head. She thought she was in love with your father and he with her, but it was all in her head. Now I think she is in a hospital for people who believe things that aren't true, and they're going to make her better.' Her voice was hard to hear as she was speaking so quietly.

'Is that why Daddy's gone to England?' Con asked. For once, he wasn't trying to be the know-it-all man; he wanted to know what was going on as much as everyone else did.

'No, pet, of course not. He went to England for work, you know that,' Mammy looked heartbroken.

'But he didn't have work before Mrs Kinsella said what she said, and he stayed here, so how come he went after she came in here that night?' Molly wasn't going to let it go.

'Look, there's no point in lying to ye. Maybe if we hadn't had that fight, I could have convinced him not to go, but he was talking about going for a long time and I always said no. He was cross with me afterwards, and he was right to be, but I've apologised to him and he's forgiven me. I suppose I was hoping something would turn up but things were just getting worse and worse. Sure ye know how little money there was. Your father was not a man for signing on the dole but it was going to be inevitable if he stayed, we had no money at all.

We were trying to keep it from ye, how bad things were, we didn't want ye worrying, but maybe we should have explained. Ye are growing up so fast,' her eyes rested on Liam. 'But anyway, what happened happened, and your dad and I are fine. I'm praying so hard that the job will come up in the tyre factory, and we'll have him home. Daddy loves you all very much, he's always saying it, and there's a letter on the sideboard for each of you, they just arrived today.' Liam was delighted at the thought of a letter just for him from his father but his mother's voice was worrying. She sounded sad.

Con and Kate exchanged glances; clearly they blamed their mother a bit. A part of them still believed that if the fight never happened, he'd never have gone.

She went over to the sideboard and opened a big envelope addressed to herself, taking from it five letters.

'Where's yours, Mammy?' Liam asked as each of the Tobin children took their letter.

'I read mine this morning when the postman came,' she said, rubbing his cheek as she handed his over.

'Take it out to the yard to read it in peace if you want to. I'm just going up to Murray's to get carrots.'

Liam sat in the yard and stared at the letter with his name on it. He never got a letter before and though this one wasn't strictly written to him with his full name and address—it just said Liam in Daddy's straight writing—it still felt very important. He sat on an orange box beside the hen run and opened the envelope.

Dear Liam,

I hope this letter finds you well and in good spirits. I miss you very much. I'm working over here in a car factory, making new motor cars. I'll send you a picture of them in my next letter if I can get one. There are loads of men from Cork here so I'm not too lonely. Actually, that's not really true; I'm very lonely for my family. I live in a house with ten other men and there's a woman who owns it called Mrs Keyes—she is kind but a terrible cook. I'm used to Mammy's lovely cooking so I'm nearly being poisoned here!

I know this situation must be confusing for you, Liam, but I need you to understand that no matter what anyone says about me, I did nothing wrong. Mammy knows it too, but people will gossip all the same. I miss going to matches with you and Con, and slagging Kate about Elvis, and testing the twins on their homework. I miss it all. I hope and pray we will all be together soon. I never stop looking for jobs in Cork.

Take care and be a good boy and help your mother,

Love,

Daddy

LIAM SAT on the box and cried. Daddy sounded so sad. Something was very wrong in his family, but he had no idea how to fix it. The back door opened and Con came out.

'Well, what did yours say?' he asked.

Liam didn't want to tell him. After all, it was his letter, sent to him privately, but he felt he had to.

'He said he missed us, and he missed going to matches, and that he was working in a car factory. He never said when he was coming home but that he was looking for jobs here all the time. What about yours?' Liam hoped that Con's letter might shed some more light on the situation.

'More or less the same,' he said, picking up a hurley and pucking the sliotar off the back wall. The leather ball made a thud as it hit the various Xs Con had put on the wall to get his shooting at goal more accurate. It had been Daddy's idea.

'How much longer do you think before he comes home, Con?' Liam asked.

His brother shrugged. 'I think he wants to come home but now he's got work over there, he'll be slow to give it up. Things were getting bad here, moneywise. I'm only an apprentice, and Kate hasn't much to spare either. Daddy wants to provide for us.'

'Do you think he would have gone anyway or was it because he was cross with Mammy?' Liam sensed that this was the only conversation Con would have with him about it.

'I don't know. I suppose Mammy blamed him at the time for the business with that mad tart next door even though he did nothing wrong, but he thought Mammy held him responsible or something, said that if he wasn't in and out to her the whole time, none of this would have happened. That's what Kate reckons anyway, I dunno.'

Liam was unaccustomed to talking as equals with Con and was afraid that anything he might say would relegate him into the baby category again, but he had to know more.

'Was there something going on, do you think?' He prayed silently for the right answer.

'Nah, he'd never do that. And anyway, your wan is half-cracked, she made the whole thing up, but she,' he gestured with his head towards the kitchen, 'should have given him a chance. She should have backed him, not blamed him.'

Liam sat on the box, watching as his brother swung the hurley and hit the small leather ball off the brick wall of the yard.

CHAPTER 6

The following weeks were spent in a haze of study. Things were better at home now that everything was out in the open. The new tyre factory was going ahead and so there was an optimistic air in the Tobin household for the first time in months. Liam was working every chance he could even though the others were perplexed. He decided he'd have a go at the scholarship. If Father Aquinas thought there was hope, maybe it was worth a shot, but he decided to keep it quiet from the rest of the family. There would be enough time to tell them if he got it.

'It's only the auld summer test, ya big dope, and aren't you going into the hospital with Kate soon? You'll be running around the place with files and letters and all that stuff, so nobody's going to give a tuppenny damn about the tests of sixth class,' Con would say regularly, often dumping his books on the floor, or throwing bits of paper at him while he was trying to study.

Father Aquinas gave him extra lessons after school and the exam was a week after school broke up. Mammy was making do with the money Daddy sent from England. Things were certainly better, but there wasn't enough for school fees. Liam was afraid if his father heard about his plans to stay at school, he might put off coming home, thinking he could make more money over there. On top of that, he knew how disappointed Mammy was when Con left school, so he didn't want to get her hopes up only to have them dashed once again.

His siblings were totally caught up in their own lives and hardly noticed him and if Con found out, well, he'd get an unmerciful slagging, so he just pretended all the study was for the end of term tests. Mammy still said the rosary every night, but Liam sometimes saw the twins secretly reading a magazine while absentmindedly answering the prayers. Mammy was shattered by everything that had happened, and she knew the others still blamed her a bit for Daddy leaving, so she didn't correct them as often as she used to for fear of starting another row and a round of accusations. Daddy was gone six months now.

Kate had convinced Mammy to let her go nursing in England where there was more money to be made, better experience, and better everything, according to Kate. In the end, Mammy just gave in. She left Cork without a backward glance. Liam remembered Mammy hugging Kate tightly at the quayside and his sister joking that she was only going to England not to the moon. Kate couldn't wait to get away, the bright lights of London were calling and all sorts of adventures awaited her. Mammy was quiet all the way up the hill afterwards. 'It looks like it's just you and me now, Liam.' She sighed.

Con was at work and the twins were doing a secretarial course—they were the fastest in the class at shorthand and typing and had been offered jobs already even though they were just fifteen. Molly was going to the civil service, which was a brilliant job apparently, and Annie was going to work in the Harbour Commissioners. Liam was surprised they agreed to work in two different places; he assumed they would insist on being together like they were since birth. Kate joked that they could have great variety if they wanted since they were impossible to tell apart. Molly could easily go to Annie's job and vice versa. They giggled at the idea over the dinner table the other night. Though Liam thought it was a stupid idea, he joined in; it was the first laugh they'd had in ages.

The day of the exam dawned bright and sunny. He got out of bed and knelt beside it. Con had gone to work early—he and Willy were in with a local builder who had the contract to build loads of new houses outside the city. Liam couldn't understand anyone who would want to live so far out, but it seemed that they did.

He blessed himself and thought about what prayers he would say. He began with Our Father followed by the Hail Mary and the Glory Be as he usually did. He then said the Memorare—a special prayer to Our Lady that was to be used sparingly since it was really a begging prayer. Then he said a prayer to St Joseph of Cupertino—never known to fail in an exam. He tried one to St Jude, as well—patron saint of hopeless cases—and eventually resorted to pleading directly with God to let him get the marks.

He knew it was stupid but he decided that if he got the scholarship, he would write to his father and he'd come home to see him go to secondary school, even if he didn't have a job.

He got a sudden pang of guilt about lying and thought about telling Mammy about the exam as he was leaving the house but decided against it. It was Saturday morning and school was broken up for the holidays. He told her he was going to a match with some of the lads from his class so she wouldn't worry, but he hated deceiving her.

All the way up the road, he went over his revision notes in his head. Algebra, quadratic equations, sin, cos and tan, geometry. Then Latin declensions, the Irish short stories, the poetry of John Milton, *Hamlet*—the list of things to remember was endless. The idea that he could write four A-standard papers one after the other over an eight-hour period seemed an insurmountable obstacle. Maybe he was wasting his time, he thought as he walked in the gate. He opened the door of the exam hall and took his seat.

The priest announced that every boy was to place his bag at the back of the hall and bring two pens and a mathematical set to the allocated desk for the exam. Maths was first, which Liam was relieved about since it was his weakest subject. He glanced around the room to size up the competition. The priests never made it clear how many scholarships were available but surely some of these boys were going home empty-handed. There were at least thirty fellas in the room, some he recognised from his class and even from last year's class, but a lot of them were faces he'd never seen before. He assumed it was only open to his primary school, but he must have been wrong.

Sitting in the desk beside him was Patrick Lynch, his neighbour. He finished school last year and was working in a warehouse of a big shop downtown. Mr Lynch definitely couldn't pay for secondary education since every penny he earned continued to be handed over the bar of the Glue Pot. Mrs Lynch did her best, she did a bit of cleaning in the big houses in Sunday's Well and she took in laundry, but things were very tight in their house. Mammy always said she and Mrs Lynch were great friends. She always gave her the twins' clothes and shoes when they outgrew them. Mrs Lynch had a two-year-old girl called Connie and another on the way. He hoped Patrick got a place; he was a nice fella and was on the same hurling team as Con. He was really good, and he never got much of a chance with his dad being like he was. All the girls were mad about Patrick, Con told him, especially all the shop girls he met at his work. Even though he was only a year older than Liam, he looked much older. Daddy always said that Joe Lynch was a fine looking man too in his time—something he found hard to believe, bloated and scarred as Patrick's father was now.

Daddy always defended Joe, which surprised Liam given how abstemious his father was compared to Patrick's.

'You shouldn't judge a person until you've walked in their shoes, lads,' he'd often warned as he dried the dishes after dinner. 'Joe was a nice lad and a gifted hurler, but the demons of his childhood caught up with him. The only place he got any relief was in the bottom of a glass.'

Liam got a lurch of loneliness for his Daddy. He'd love to have had him there to walk him up to the gate this morning.

'Good luck,' he whispered.

Patrick half-smiled back. He looked pale, like he was going to vomit. 'You too, Liam,' he replied.

A priest Liam never saw before rang a bell and a group of older fellas started giving out the papers. Liam looked down and glanced over it. Thank God, it was all things he had revised and he felt confident starting it. The time flew by, and he managed to finish the entire paper. He thought most of it was right; if it wasn't, he didn't know any better, so with relief, he handed it up.

'There will be a thirty-minute break before the Latin paper. Please reassemble in your allocated seat at 11:30. There will be Mass after the Latin exam in the school chapel at 1:15. Attendance is expected.' The priest left the hall and the level of chatter rose instantly.

'How'd you get on?' Patrick asked as he gathered his pencils and mathematical set.

'All right I think. I thought question six, the angles of the triangle, was hard though. How about you?'

Patrick seemed more relaxed than before the test. 'Was it a scalene triangle?' Patrick asked.

'Yeah, that's what I said, anyway.' They chatted easily as they left the hall into the bright sunshine.

Liam turned over the shilling in his pocket his father had sent with his last letter. He never had money, but Daddy had taken to sending them each a shilling when he wrote. Even better than the money was that Daddy always asked about Mammy and urged him to help her and be a good boy. Whenever a letter would come, she would hand each of the children their own and then slipped one into her apron pocket with a smile. He prayed each letter would tell them when he'd be home.

'I have a shilling, my dad sent it to me,' Liam began. 'Do you want an ice cream?' He reddened immediately as he said it; maybe Patrick would think he was showing off. Though they were neighbours and had known each other all their lives, they didn't mix in the same group. Patrick was older and played on the under-sixteen hurling team where most of the others were fifteen or even sixteen so he always seemed a bit more sophisticated than Liam.

Patrick smiled broadly, 'But you should keep that money for yourself, maybe for books if you get the scholarship.'

'Books are included in the scholarship, I asked Father Aquinas,' Liam replied. 'So, what do you think? A penny wafer each in Murray's to celebrate the fact that we can identify a scalene triangle?'

'If it was a scalene triangle.' Patrick laughed. 'Right so, two ice creams it is. But I won't be able to get you one back.'

'That's grand,' Liam replied. 'I never have money usually, it's just my dad sent it.'

They walked companionably down the hill to Murray's, chatting about the maths paper and the upcoming Latin. Mrs Murray was quiet in the shop so she asked them what they were doing. Mammy always said Mrs Murray was silent as the grave if you told her something. Nobody ever knew who got stuff on tick or whose line of credit had run out. She was the soul of discretion. When they told her about the exam and warned her to keep it to herself, she gave them extra big ice creams. They explained that they didn't want everyone knowing they went for it since there were loads of fellas trying and they probably wouldn't be picked. Normally, Liam wouldn't dream of telling the neighbours anything he didn't want repeated over the whole street, but everyone knew Mrs Murray was discreet. Daddy always said it was the sign of a great business person to be able to keep their gob shut.

'Tis a pity a few more round here wouldn't practice a bit of discretion when it came to other people's business,' he'd often say as Mammy was telling him the latest news as she put out his dinner in the evenings.

'I bet your mam is saying novenas at home for you, though,' Patrick remarked as they licked their ice creams, their faces up to the warm sun.

'She would be if she knew I was going for the scholarship, but she doesn't. Things have been a bit hard lately, she's enough to be dealing with.' Liam wondered if Patrick knew about the big scandal. He assumed he did since the whole place knew about it. He waited for his new friend's reply, hoping he wouldn't say anything bad.

'Mine don't know either, not that my da would care either way, and it would just be another thing for my mam to worry about. Your dad is great, I remember watching ye all on a Sunday going down the park to a match and walking home with chips. My auld fella was only ever in the pub. You must miss him.'

'I do,' Liam said, relieved that Patrick had said something nice about his dad. He was great, and he was glad someone remembered that.

'Maybe he'll be home soon. Everyone says there's work in the new factory and there's talk of another one opening soon. A few of the fellas that work with me in the warehouse are going for jobs there.'

'I hope so. He's not in England with Mrs Kinsella, you know.' Suddenly it was important that Patrick knew this.

'Course he's not. No one with half a brain thinks that he is. Sure, isn't she as daft as the crows, you'd know that by looking at her. Her daughter is gone to live with an aunt I think, that's what my mother heard anyway. She's just a bit younger than us, isn't she, the daughter? What's she like?'

Liam smiled happily, pleased that Patrick knew the truth.

'I don't know really. She was quiet, just played on her own out the back most of the time, I think. She was too young for the twins, and anyway, they are so stuck together they've no time for anyone else.'

'They were a class ahead of me in the infants room. There're really brainy, aren't they?'

Liam sighed and threw his eyes heavenward.

'May God forgive me, but they are a right pain in the arse.' He felt bad saying arse, but he wanted his new friend to like him. 'They're such know-it-alls and sure they hardly ever even talk to me, they're so high and mighty. What about your sister?'

'Well, there's just me and her, she's small so she's cute still, and one on the way, and my mam. She got a bit of a fright, when she found out she was expecting Connie, I think she thought I'd be the only one and now another one. It's going to be grand, but my auld fella, well, you know what he's like, you've heard him often enough. He hits us sometimes.' Patrick's voice was quieter now.

Liam wondered what to say. He had told Patrick about Daddy and now Patrick was telling him about his awful father. He wanted to say something that would make him feel better about it all. He knew exactly how Joe Lynch was, Daddy had to intervene sometimes if he was getting violent, and often the guards took him away.

'Well, I bet you get this scholarship and get a big job somewhere and then you'll be able to buy your mam and your sister a nice house, and you can get a big dog and train him to bite your da if he looks like he's going to hit anyone.'

Patrick burst out laughing and, for a moment, Liam felt stupid for making such a suggestion.

'That's a brilliant idea, Liam, a massive dog who is nice to everyone except my da when he's drunk. He's all right sober, you know?' Patrick was kicking a stone with the scuffed tip of his shoe.

'My dad always said he was, and that he was a great hurler when he was young and that he's got a great singing voice,' Liam added, instantly regretting the last bit since Joe Lynch reserved his singing to the small hours of the morning.

'Oh yeah, the whole street knows about his singing all right,' Patrick said ruefully.

They walked back to the hall, testing each other on Latin verbs as they went.

The rest of the exams went in a blur. Patrick and Liam went to Mass at lunchtime, and Liam prayed hard to his team of saints for inspiration. The best would be if both he and Patrick got the scholarship and they could be best friends in school. By the end of the day, he was exhausted but pleased that he had done his best. After the last exam—Irish—the priest in charge told them that their parents would be notified by post within a week if they were successful or not. Liam was determined to watch the postman like a hawk to intercept any letter. There was enough time to tell Mammy if he got it. She'd be pleased, he knew that, and proud to have a son going to secondary, but he worried that she might be relying on his wages a bit more now, so maybe it wasn't going to be the best news. He was due to start in the hospital in two weeks' time but the thought filled him with dread. He desperately wanted to go to secondary, especially now if Patrick was going too.

A week later, he opened the front door laden down with shopping that Mammy asked him to pick up in town. He had planned to go on the bike but Con had taken it.

There was a girl Con was keen on over on the Southside and there hadn't been a sign of him for weeks. He told Liam he wanted to take her to a dance in the City Hall so he was taking all the overtime he could to make enough for the tickets and a new rig out. Liam couldn't see why he wanted to go to a dance in the first place, let alone why he'd waste money on a shirt and a suit when he had loads of work shirts and at least two good shirts for Mass that Mammy had turned the collar on only a few weeks ago, but Con insisted. He had put away a charcoal suit and a shirt and tie in Matt Murphy's Gentleman's Outfitters in town and was paying it off by the week. He gave up going to matches and he bought nothing. He handed up half his wages as rent to Mammy, and the rest he spent on the clothes and this girl. Her name was Hilda, and she was the most beautiful girl in the world according to Con. The Royal Showband was playing and this Hilda was mad about them. He even caught Con practicing jiving, a kind of dance, in their bedroom when he thought everyone was out. Liam thought he looked like a right eejit but when he pointed this out to Con, he got a clatter.

He pushed the door open with his foot since both his arms were full. There was the bicycle in the hall; he could have used it after all. Frustrated with his brother, he fought the urge to kick the bike. The kitchen door was closed, which was unusual, and he sighed in exasperation that he'd have to put down the bags to open it. Dropping the bags, he opened the door and saw his mother, Molly, Annie, Con, and Kate standing at the stove. *What was going on? Why was Kate home? Nobody said she was coming home.* The silence was deafeningly eerie. Instantly, Liam knew something was wrong.

Mammy turned and looked at him with tears streaming down her face.

She pulled him into an embrace. He wriggled free. 'What? What happened?'

There was silence as everyone stared, unable to speak. Liam watched Kate take his hand and lead him to a kitchen chair. He normally would have shaken her off, but something was very wrong.

'It's Daddy, Liam. An accident, he was killed. An accident at the factory, something fell on him...' Kate tried to go on, but the words wouldn't come.

Time seemed to slow down. This was ridiculous, they were making it up. This wasn't really happening. Blood thundered in his ears, and he felt sick. Mammy was gulping for air as if she couldn't breathe.

Kate put her arms around him, but he pushed her away. 'No! You're lying! He's coming home! He is! Mammy said he was! Con too! He's not dead! He's not!' Liam screamed, he felt pounding in his head, this wasn't happening.

Con came towards him, and Liam pummelled his chest as his brother restrained him.

'It's true, Liam. Kate didn't want us to get a letter from the factory so she came on the boat last night. You'll have to be a big fella now and be strong for Daddy, all right? That's what he'd want.'

'Shut up, you! You're trying to be a big man yourself and you're not, Con, so stop telling me what to do! You don't know what Daddy would want. I want to see him! I want my daddy!' Liam knew he was acting like a baby, but he didn't care, he just wanted his daddy.

Mammy came towards him and as she did, Kate stood between her and Liam.

'This is your fault,' Kate spat. 'He would never have even been in England if it wasn't for you. If you had trusted him and stood by him, instead of being so worried about what the neighbours would say. You broke his heart, do you know that? He never got over you thinking there was something between him and that lunatic next door. If it wasn't for you, none of this would have happened.' She finished with a sob.

'I know...do you think I don't know that? I should never have...' Mammy's voice was barely audible.

'She's right,' Con said dully. 'This is down to you. I hope you're happy.'

'Stop this, stop shouting, all of you!' Liam screamed so loudly he didn't recognise his own voice. He threw himself into his mother's arms, sobbing.

'It's not your fault, Mammy, it really isn't,' he said over and over.

'I wish you were right, Liam,' she said quietly, rubbing his hair but then letting him go and leaving the room. The five Tobin children stood in silence in the kitchen, trying to absorb what had happened. Their beloved father was never coming home.

CHAPTER 7

The neighbours held a fund raiser in the local hurling and football club to gather the money to get Seán Tobin's remains home. People came and went in the house in the week that followed. It took ages for the English authorities to release the body though nobody was able to adequately explain why. Mammy sat dry-eyed beside the stove, dressed in black, silently saying the rosary for the repose of the soul of her husband while her neighbours brought trays of cakes and pots of stew.

Liam was in a daze of misery. He went to sleep each night remembering when he was small and used to listen to Mammy and Daddy chatting downstairs. He tried to remember that feeling of safety and love. Sometimes he could just about recall it, but more often, it felt like that time was like something he read about in a story, something that had happened to someone else. He tried hard to picture in his mind's eye the scene he witnessed years earlier, his Mammy sitting on Daddy's lap as he rubbed her hair and they stared into the fire together. He tried to block out everything that had happened and turn the clock back to when they were the happiest family in the whole wide world.

Every morning when he woke, just for one second, none of this had happened. Daddy was gone to work, and he was going to Mass with Mammy and the twins and everything was as it used to be. He willed his mind to hold on to the image but reality forced its ugly way into his consciousness even if he refused to open his eyes. He would lie there, silently begging his old life to come back, but it was pointless.

Today was the day. Daddy was finally coming home. The Inisfallen, the boat they watched so often leave Cork port together, was now sliding into the quayside and somewhere on it was a box with Daddy in it. It seemed unbelievable. Liam used to love sitting on the grassy bank of the River Lee with Daddy and Con after a match in the park and watch the huge ship pass by, so close you could almost shake hands with the people gathered on deck to get the best view of the city as she docked. Now he hated that boat. That was the boat that took his father away and now it was bringing him back to them dead. He wished it would sink and then instantly regretted that thought. If it sank, the other people whose mammies and daddies and families were on board would be as sad as him and what would be the point of that? He dragged himself downstairs; Mammy would need him for jobs.

'Mr O'Connor is meeting the boat and will take charge from there.' A tall man in a black suit was talking to Mammy in the kitchen as he entered.

'Oh right. That's fine,' she said as if she were in a trance.

The man turned as Liam opened the door and extended his hand. 'Hello, I'm James Cantillon, I'm so sorry for your terrible loss. I work for Mr O'Connor, the undertaker; I'll be helping you and your family today. What's your name?'

'Liam,' he answered. He didn't care if it sounded rude; he wanted him to get out of their house.

'Well, Liam, if you need anything today, or if you want any help with anything over the next few days, you just call me. Is that all right?'

Liam knew the man was trying to be kind, but he just stared at him as if he were mad. The only thing he wanted was to have Daddy back, surely this man knew that.

'Thank you, Mr Cantillon...' Mammy began.

'James, please,' he interrupted. Liam supposed he was only a bit older than Kate, around twenty maybe.

'James, thank you, James,' she said, still in that dreamy faraway voice.

'The car will be available at around four to take you and the family to the church if you wish,' he said. 'But since it's so close, would ye rather walk?'

'We'll walk,' Liam said, but his voice came out as a squeak. He was embarrassed and felt his face redden.

'Fine so. I'll be back then if you don't need anything else?' James asked kindly.

'No. No, thank you, we're fine for now...' Mammy said.

Con appeared at the door. He wasn't there when Liam woke so he must have been up for ages and had gone out somewhere.

'That's fine, James, thanks,' he said. Liam looked at Con; he seemed older, dressed in his new suit that he was supposed to wear to the dance in the City Hall. He was shaving now, and he looked like a man, not a boy anymore.

'Do you want tea, Con?' Mammy asked.

'I'll make it myself,' he replied curtly. Neither Kate nor Con had spoken properly to Mammy since the night they were all together in the kitchen. They still blamed her for what happened, and the twins were following their lead. Liam felt sorry for Mammy, he could see she was heartbroken, but he hadn't the words to make her feel better. The only thing he could do was be as nice to her as he could and try to make up for the hostility of his siblings.

'Do *you* want a cup of tea, Mammy?' he asked.

She looked at him with shining eyes, his words breaking her reverie. 'No, thank you, pet, you're very good. I think I'll go over to the church and say a prayer.'

'Will I come with you?' he asked.

'That would be lovely. We'll light a special candle for your daddy and say a prayer to St Michael the Archangel to take him safely into heaven.'

As they crossed the road towards the church, Liam tried once more to make sense of it all.

'But Mammy, sure isn't he in heaven long ago, he died last week?' Liam wished he understood things better. Adults were always saying confusing things. He was older now, and knew more about things, but he didn't feel wiser at all. His twelfth birthday was last month but even though the family tried to make a fuss of him, and Mammy even made a cake—the first one in ages—it was all a bit flat. Daddy was in England then, and he thought that was the worst it could be. He never dreamed it could be this, Daddy dead.

'That's right, love, he is. He's up in heaven looking down on us and keeping us safe because that's what the dead do for us. They watch over us.'

'But how come someone wasn't watching over Daddy, so? Like Nana and Granda or someone like that? If the dead mind us, how come nobody was watching over Daddy keeping him safe?' The pain was bubbling up through him again, like acid burning him inside.

Mammy stopped and turned to him, holding both his hands in hers. 'God needed Daddy. It's as simple as that. He needed him to go home to heaven, and we'll just have to manage without him because God's need is more important that our needs.'

This was making no sense. 'But God has loads of dead people in heaven, everyone that ever died since the start of time, surely one of them could have done whatever he needed Daddy for. Why did he have to take my daddy?' Tears coursed down his cheeks again.

'I don't know, Liam. I wish I did. But it's not for us to question the will of God. We must accept it.' Mammy tried to reason with him, but Liam was past understanding any of this.

'I hate God! I hate him! I hate him for taking Daddy and for making Mrs Kinsella and for making the Inisfallen and I hate England and I hate everything.' He was screaming, he knew it, but he didn't care. People were watching, and then he was running, running as fast as he could up the hill. He could hear his mother calling him back, but he just wanted to run and never stop.

He ran as fast as he could, his heart pounding in his chest. Tears ran sideways from his eyes and still he ran. The wall of black that met him was a shock, and he barrelled into it with full force. He felt strong arms encircle him and hold on to him even though he struggled hard to escape.

'Easy, Liam, easy.'

He stopped struggling and looked up into the face of whoever was restraining him. He was outside the monastery.

'Easy, lad. Just take it easy now. You're grand. Now, I'm going to let go of you, but you must promise me you won't run off again. I'm too old to catch up with you.' Father Aquinas kept hold of Liam by the upper arms but crouched down so they were face to face.

'Promise?'

'Promise,' Liam agreed. His chest hurt from running so hard, he doubted he could run even if he wanted to, anyway.

His mother was walking quickly towards them and eventually she stood beside him.

'Thank you, Father, I'm so sorry about this...' She was puffed out as well.

'No bother at all, Mrs Tobin. I'm very sorry for your loss.'

'Thank you, Father,' Mammy panted. 'Would you say a prayer for him please?'

'Indeed I will, in fact, Mass in the monastery chapel was for the repose of his soul this morning. Seán Tobin was a good man, he is resting at the right hand of the Lord, you can be sure. I know his body is coming home later today and that's going to be hard for you all. Now, if I'm not intruding, might I make a suggestion? I have a few things inside that I need help moving, schoolbooks and the like, now that the term is over. Maybe if Liam had a spare few minutes he might give me a hand. I have young Lynch in here as well, but we need another pair of hands, so if it's not too much trouble?'

Mammy held the priest's gaze for a moment as if something unspoken was passing between them and she replied, 'Of course,

Father Aquinas, I'm sure Liam wouldn't mind helping. Seán...I mean Seán's body is coming at four, but we were just going to the church to say a prayer when...'

'That's very kind of you, Mrs Tobin,' he interjected. 'I'll send him down before four, you have my word. Now, Liam, let's go and find Patrick and see what can be done, shall we?'

Liam caught his mother's eye and she nodded and smiled weakly. He followed the priest into the monastery. The last thing in the world he wanted to do was sort out books, but there was nothing else to do either. He wanted to run away from himself, from his thoughts, the reality of his horrible life.

Patrick was standing in the middle of the hall with long tables set up all around, heaving under the weight of schoolbooks, copies, jotters, and pencil cases.

'The hardworking parents of this city do everything in their power for their offspring to have all they need for school and this is the regard those young bucks have for them. These books have been found around the school during the year. Our job is to catalogue them, see what we have and then, er, redistribute them to people who might have a bit more respect for them. So, Liam, Patrick is gathering up all the English books; you can gather all the Irish and pile them on that table over there—Maths and Science on the other side, and Latin and French under the window. Anything else ye can put over by the door, and we'll go through them when we've time.' With that, the priest swept out of the room, leaving the two boys alone.

Liam stood motionless in the rectangle of tables when Patrick came over. They'd not seen each other since the day of the exam, over ten days ago.

'I was going to call over, but I didn't know if I should...' Patrick began.

'It's all right. I wasn't really...' Liam didn't know what to say.

'Yeah, I...it's terrible about your da. My mam got a Mass said.' Patrick was trying, Liam knew, but just like himself he had no idea what to say.

'We better get these books sorted before he comes back and

murders us.' They smiled in shared complicity, both knowing that the priest would do nothing of the kind.

He did arrive back after about half an hour but with lemonade and cake. He made a makeshift table out of the piles of books and called them from their work.

'Now, Mr Tobin and Mr Lynch, all that sorting is thirsty work,' he smiled, handing them each a bottle of lemonade. The bubbles fizzed in Liam's mouth, and he took an iced bun from the plate. Patrick did the same and, to their astonishment, Father Aquinas followed suit. They never in their wildest dreams imagined a priest would drink lemonade, or eat a sticky bun. The three sat munching companionably and Liam felt the closest to normal he had felt since he heard the news.

'I suppose ye are wondering why ye got no letter about the scholarship?' he said between bites.

Liam had wondered before Kate told them about Daddy but since then, it never entered his head. He knew though by looking at Patrick that he thought about nothing else. Both boys remained silent, unsure of what to say.

'Well, Liam, you've had enough to be thinking about, I suppose, but anyway, the reason ye got no letter is because I wanted to tell ye myself. Ye both got it.' He took a big slug of his lemonade.

Liam and Patrick looked at each other. Could it be true? Were they going to secondary school together? Patrick's face split in a grin as wide as Cork harbour and Liam couldn't help but smile too. His father would be so proud, would have been so proud, he corrected himself. Daddy would only be able to see him from heaven. Patrick was so happy, he could hardly contain it. He looked from the priest to Liam repeating, 'Oh wow! I got it! I got the scholarship!'

Finishing off his lemonade, the priest dug into his soutane pocket and pulled out a sheet of paper.

'The first year booklist. Ye better get back to those tables and collect the best ones before the free-for-all next week. Now I've to go, but Liam, make sure you're home by three in time to get cleaned up and everything. It's going to be a very hard few days for you and the whole family, so be patient with people and tell your mother about the scholarship when the time feels right. Maybe Patrick could hang around with you over the next while to keep you company. Funerals can be lonely times even when loads of people are around. Ye are both scholarship lads now, and I won't lie to ye, some of the others attending St Bart's will look down on ye because ye don't come from the backgrounds they do but don't mind them and stick together, and ye'll be grand. The best of luck to both of ye.' He stood up and shook each of their hands before turning on his heel and sweeping out of the room once more.

CHAPTER 8

The rosary around the closed coffin, the removal from the funeral home to the church the following day, the endless flow of people through the house, the cups of tea, the uneaten sandwiches, and the cakes piled high on the kitchen table—it all passed in a blur.

The morning of the funeral, Con helped him tie his black tie, and he wore long trousers for the first time in his life. They were an old pair of Con's he got when he first started working. The fabric felt strange on his legs as he walked across the road with his black-clad family. Patrick was sitting in the church when they arrived, about ten rows back from the coffin, which had lain overnight in the Church of St Teresa. The Goldie Fish on top of the steeple glittered in the sunlight as the community gathered to pay their last respects to Seán Tobin. Liam wished he could sit with his friend rather than in the front row with Mammy and the others where everyone would come and shake his hand and tell him they were sorry for his trouble. He never knew what to say so he said nothing. He couldn't come to terms with the reality that it was Daddy in the coffin.

Usually when someone died, the coffin was open for the first part —the rosary—but because Daddy died so long ago, they couldn't do that. He never got to see him in his coffin. Patrick said maybe it was for the best, better he remember him the way he was when they were all happy. But Liam tried to explain it was like he couldn't make his brain believe it. His strong father, whom everyone liked, the man, who was strong as a horse but gentle as a lamb, was dead and lifeless in a wooden box. That's how Mrs Lynch described him when she came to pay her respects the other night. Liam never thought of Daddy as either a horse or a lamb, but he knew what she meant.

He sat beside Mammy because he knew none of the others would. They were polite to her in front of people and they put on a show for the neighbours, but he knew how they really felt. He tried to ask them to be nicer to her, Molly and Annie especially, but they just said that Kate and Con were right, it was Mammy's fault and they couldn't forgive her. Molly was really mean to him and said he was only sucking up to Mammy because that's what he always did and that he was just trying to be her pet. Annie told her to shut up and said it wasn't Liam's fault and that she shouldn't take it out on him, he didn't understand. He wanted to scream at them that he did understand but he knew he'd never win against the two of them so he just left it.

James, the undertaker, came up and asked him if he'd like to shoulder the coffin. He never thought they would let him because he was too small, way smaller than the other men who were carrying his father to his grave.

'Am I not too small?' he asked.

'Of course not,' James replied. 'No pressure, only if you want to. We can have four men at the four corners and Con can be opposite you. Your shoulder won't touch the coffin, but you can balance it with your hand.'

'I want to,' he answered.

The funeral Mass went in a blur. Father Aquinas, Father Mac, Father O'Donnell, and Monsignor McGregor from the school concelebrated. Liam knew it was a great honour to have so many priests on the altar. Father Mac did most of it, talked about Daddy like he knew him well, which of course he did. He talked about him as a young man growing up in Blackpool, playing hurling for Cork, meeting Mammy and all of the family coming along. He talked about how Seán Tobin was abstemious, and though Liam wasn't too sure what that meant, it sounded like a good thing. How he was a great neighbour and friend to everyone he met. Liam could imagine some people nudging each other when he said that, nodding spitefully. 'Oh, he was all that, especially to young pretty widows,' he imagined them saying. He forced those thoughts from his mind and tried to focus once more on Father Mac.

The choir sang some hymns. Nothing Liam particularly liked, and he wondered who picked them, Mammy probably. At the end, Kate went up to the lectern and Liam watched as she composed herself to speak.

'Dear Lord in heaven we ask you
To bless this home of ours,
To guide us and protect us,
Beneath Heaven's shining stars.
To protect your faithful servants
As we travel near and far,
We worship and adore you Lord,
Beneath Heaven's shining stars.'

Hearing his sister recite the final prayer of the Tobin family's nightly rosary removed the last bit of composure he had. Molly and Annie clung to each other and fat tears flowed unchecked down Con's face. Liam squeezed his mother's hand and tried to reach her, but she was miles away, drowning under waves of crashing, painful grief.

The priest then came down and as he was swinging the thurible over the coffin, he said the prayers Liam had heard thousands of times before as he served funeral Mass as an altar boy. The smell of incense wafted around the church.

'Into your hands O Lord we commend the spirit of our brother Seán. Acknowledge we humbly beseech you, a sheep of your own fold, a lamb of your own flock, a sinner of your own redeeming. Receive *him* into the arms of your mercy, into the blessed rest of everlasting peace, and into the glorious company of the saints in light. *Amen.* May *his* soul and the souls of all the departed, through the mercy of God, rest in peace. *Amen.*'

The undertakers gathered round and ushered Liam towards the coffin. He was placed in front with his Uncle Willy who was also short. Con was behind him with Daddy's brother Tony, and the final pair were another two uncles. They lifted the coffin and Uncle Willy put his hand on Liam's shoulder. He could feel the coffin almost touching his other shoulder though he didn't bear the weight, he wasn't tall enough. He put his arm on Uncle Willy and his free hand on the front of the coffin in case it slid forward. Once James was satisfied it was being carried securely, they began to walk slowly down the aisle. People wiped their eyes on either side. The church was packed, and there were even more people outside. Liam felt proud of his father; the knowledge that so many people liked Daddy and came to his funeral meant something to him.

He spotted Patrick out of the corner of his eye, and his friend gave him a nod of encouragement. It was unusual to see Patrick so serious but then this was a very serious occasion, Liam supposed.

The coffin was placed in the hearse and more people came forward to express their sympathy. He walked over to the back of the hearse and put his mother's arm in his. Con stood behind them with the girls on his arms, and behind them were the rest of the family—aunts, uncles, cousins, neighbours, and friends. It struck Liam how well they organised themselves in rank of closeness to the family without anyone telling them where to stand. People just seemed to know.

They walked behind the hearse all the way to the graveyard. Daddy was going to be buried with his parents, and the idea gave Liam some comfort. Nana Tobin and Granda were really nice and before they died, they used to visit often, bringing sweets and cakes. He was glad Daddy was going to be with them. Nana died three years ago, and Granda died within six months of her. Mammy was fond of saying that he died of a broken heart. Mammy was right, Granda didn't like living without Nana. He hoped his mother didn't die of a broken heart now. That would be too much to bear.

He never noticed the figure standing at the graveside as the funeral cortege approached. It wasn't until they stopped right beside the big black hole that he saw her. Everyone was silent and people stared. Mrs Kinsella was dressed in a black coat, but she had a bright red scarf around her neck and was wearing a lot of makeup. She was dabbing her eyes with a black lace handkerchief, much more glamorous than the white cotton ones the other women carried.

She stood on the far side of the grave alone as the crowd gathered round. Despite the hundreds of people, nobody stood near her. Liam felt Mammy stiffen and stare at her. Nobody knew what to do, she wasn't welcome here, surely she knew that. No one had seen her since that terrible night when she screamed and begged Daddy to go with her.

Mr O'Connor, the undertaker, whose funeral parlour was only a hundred yards from the Tobins' house knew the whole sorry tale and so decided to intervene. He walked around the grave as Father Mac and the other priests were putting on their vestments and preparing the aspersorium full of holy water to be sprinkled on the coffin. Liam didn't want to watch what happened next. Instead he focused on the familiar actions of the priests. They didn't wear the alb and chasuble that they wore at Mass, the floor-length garments were too cumbersome to wear outside, and it was considered undignified for a priest to disrobe in front of the congregation so they just brought the stole and placed it around the neck over the long, black everyday soutane. Priests could wear a black, white, or purple stole and on this occasion, Father Mac was wearing white to symbolise hope.

He was trying hard to focus on the priests, but it was impossible. Mrs Kinsella was shouting at Mr O'Connor. 'Get your hands off me! I am entitled to be here. This is a graveyard, not a private house, I am a free citizen and I'm allowed to go where I like.' Her voice kept rising in volume as she warmed to her theme.

Mr O'Connor was now red-faced and was trying to usher her away from the graveside, but she wouldn't go. Then Con stepped forward and crossed the grass at the bottom of the hole the gravediggers had dug.

'Mrs Kinsella, please leave my family to grieve for our father. We need this time, so I'm asking you politely to leave us now.' He seemed so dignified, so calm, not at all like the Con Liam knew. The Con he knew would have hit her a clatter.

'But I loved him too...' she wailed as black makeup smeared all over her face.

Mammy stood without moving. Molly, Annie, and Kate were transfixed in horror as the scene unfolded. Instinctively, they took their mother's arms. Then Liam spotted Father Aquinas talking to two of the Murphys—the huge older brothers of the dreaded John-Joe. They nodded and walked purposefully towards her and, without any discussion at all, picked her up, one on each side, and lifted her body out of the graveyard as she screamed, 'Seán, Seán, don't leave me,' all the way out.

Liam felt empty as his father's coffin was lowered into the ground. That was the bit he was dreading the most but in the end it was all right. It didn't matter where Daddy's body was; his soul was in heaven with God and all the saints and Nana and Granda and everyone who had died.

After the funeral, everyone came back to the house where even more food and drink had arrived. Mrs Lynch seemed to be coordinating things and everyone was eating and drinking within minutes.

Patrick came and stood beside him.

'You don't have to,' Liam said flatly.

'Have to what?' Patrick seemed genuinely confused.

'Mind me like this, I know Father Aquinas told you to but I'm not a baby.'

'I wasn't minding you. I just thought you might need a friend. Sorry,' he said, and moved away down the hall and out the front door.

Instantly, Liam felt bad. Patrick was a great friend and here he was being horrible to him. Glancing around, he realised no one would miss him if he left. Con was talking to Uncle Willy with a girl beside him. She was small with dark hair and she looked nice. Maybe she was the famous Hilda. Kate was packing her things upstairs because she was getting the boat back to England tonight—the place where she worked had been more than generous with time off, but she needed to get back to work. The twins were nowhere to be found as usual, and Mammy was sitting beside the stove, surrounded by her relatives.

Liam took his jacket from behind the door and went out into the street. It was dusk now, and everyone was either at the Tobins or at home in their own houses. He walked in the direction of Patrick's house to apologise. He knew Mrs Lynch and Connie and Baby Anna, who'd been born ten days previously, were at his house so Patrick probably was at home on his own. He reached the door and was about to knock when he heard shouting from within. Joe Lynch was home and he was plastered again. The funeral of Seán Tobin was the excuse this time though he didn't ever need one. He didn't bother to come to Mass and Liam suspected Father Aquinas or some of the neighbours kept him from the house. Liam had overheard another of the neighbours saying that Joe Lynch was insisting on coming to pay his respects, shouting that 'Seán Tobin was the only man around here who treated him with respect.'

He wasn't allowed in anyway, and Liam was glad. The carry-on with Mrs Kinsella was bad enough without having Joe Lynch roaring and making everyone nervous as well. Liam wondered why Patrick's father should feel that way, especially since it was Daddy who had to get involved so often when Joe was drunk and dangerous. He remembered how kindly his father spoke of Joe Lynch and it made sense. Daddy never spoke to him the way other people did as if he were worthless. No matter how bad he got, and sometimes it was very bad, Seán intervened but always kept Joe's dignity. He knew that Joe had had a hard life and Liam supposed he felt sorry for the man.

Who was he shouting at now? Mrs Lynch and the girls were at his house so it could only be Patrick. Nervously he went to knock, maybe the distraction would stop the shouting, but the door was off the latch and pushed in when he knocked. The scene in the narrow hallway made him want to run home. Patrick was lying on his back on the ground and Joe Lynch was about to hit him with a hurley he had raised over his head. The noise of Liam opening the door caused Joe to turn around and face him.

'Who the hell are you?' he roared at Liam. 'Get the fuck out of my house now!' His face was swollen and had cuts and gashes in various stages of healing as if he'd been in several fights; his clothes were dishevelled and filthy. He stank of stale porter and his greasy grey hair hung down over his collar, but the top of his head was shiny and bald.

Patrick took the opportunity to get up and grabbed the hurley from his father's hands.

'Jesus Christ, you little fu...' he screamed in rage, bearing down once more on Patrick. He was not a big man, but he was wiry and strong and now he had Patrick by the throat against the wall. Liam acted without thinking. He picked up the hurley that Patrick had dropped and hit Joe Lynch as hard as he could on the head with it, just like Daddy had shown him when he wanted to get mileage out of the ball if he got a puck out in a match. The metal strip that banded the bottom of the stick caught on some skin and immediately blood pumped from his head. Joe registered shock and then slumped lifeless to the ground, the blood stain growing quickly on the threadbare carpet.

Both boys looked in stunned silence for what seemed like ages and then looked at each other.

'Is...is he dead?' Liam whispered.

'I don't know. I hope so, because if he's not, we will be when he wakes up,' Patrick replied, still in shock.

'What are we going to do? What if your mam comes back?' Liam was trying to think straight.

'We should get a doctor. Do you know a doctor?' Patrick asked.

'How would I know a doctor? I know Dr Wells has a surgery up the road, but I only went to him once. We haven't money for doctors and anyway we're never really sick.' Liam was starting to panic. 'What about an ambulance?'

'How do you get them to come? Doesn't the doctor call them? We could get the guards.' Patrick didn't sound sure.

'The guards,' Liam was terrified, 'but what if they think it was me, and he is dead then...' The panic was rising.

'Okay, okay. No guards. Let me think,' he paused. 'Father Aquinas. He'll know what to do. He came back to your house after the funeral, but he's saying late Mass this evening so he's above in the monastery,' Patrick sounded confident, and Liam agreed. The priest had been kind to them in the past so he might help them now. And he was good in a crisis, look how he handled Mrs Kinsella today. The other alternative was to run and get Mrs Lynch, but then she'd want to know what happened and everything...no, Father Aquinas was a better option. They ran out of the house and closed the front door, leaving Joe Lynch on the ground, possibly alive but also very possibly dead.

They ran up the hill and battered the door of the monastery. Father Xavier, principal of the secondary, opened it and looked in disgust at the two dishevelled boys before him. Everyone said he was horrible.

'What on earth do you mean banging on the door like that..?' he began indignantly, glaring at the pair in front of him. He was one of the priests that only liked the rich fellas.

'We need to talk to Father Aquinas, please Father. It's an emergency,' Liam panted.

'Father Aquinas is at prayer and cannot be disturbed,' he answered imperiously and went to close the door. Patrick quickly placed his foot in the door to stop him. Father Xavier looked in horror at the audacity of the gesture and spoke coldly. 'Remove your foot immediately or I will call the guards.'

As Patrick went to remove his foot, they heard the voice of Father Aquinas behind Father Xavier.

'What's going on?' He opened the door wider. 'Patrick? Liam? What in the name of the Lord is happening?'

'These boys were attempting to force their way in here, Father Aquinas...' Father Xavier began, his voice dripping contempt.

'Thank you, Father Xavier, I'm sure they're sorry for disturbing you. I'll deal with this.' He ushered them away from the door and followed them outside. He stared at the two of them for a moment and then said curtly, 'Over there,' indicating a bench in the monastery gardens, far enough away from the door so as not to be heard.

They blurted out the entire story, words tumbling over each other, finishing each other's sentences, and eventually they stopped.

'Are you telling me that your father is lying in your house in a pool of blood and that Liam Tobin is the cause?'

'Yes, Father,' they chorused miserably.

'Right.' He strode off in the direction of the gate, the boys following behind, jogging behind him to keep up until they reached the Lynches' door.

Father Aquinas pushed the front door open with the two boys behind him. The hallway was empty. The hurley lay abandoned on the floor and the large bloodstain was darkening to black on the cheap old carpet.

'Well, he's not dead anyway. If someone had discovered him, the place would be swarming with guards by now,' the priest said with a relieved sigh. 'We better find him, though. He can't have got far.'

They continued down the hill to the river until they spotted him on a bench beside the quay wall, holding something up to his head. As usual, Father Aquinas was right. Joe Lynch was sitting still, looking into the murky waters of the River Lee.

'Stay here and keep quiet,' the priest instructed Liam and Patrick. As he approached him, they ducked down behind a post-box just feet away from where they could see and hear everything.

'Good evening, Mr Lynch,' the priest greeted him as if it were perfectly normal for a bleeding drunk and a priest to have a chat. 'That looks nasty, what happened to you?'

Even in this condition Joe Lynch was more reverential than he was with non-clergy members.

'Hello, Father, I em...I...' Patrick and Liam looked at each other. Maybe he forgot?

'Well, you know what might just be the thing for that now? A medicinal drop of whiskey. You just rest yourself there, and I'll be back in a moment.'

Joe Lynch did as he was told and stayed on the bench. The boys watched on in amazement as Father Aquinas, a pioneer of total abstinence, walked regally across the road, his soutane flapping around his ankles, to the Swan Bar and Lounge. He emerged moments later carrying a brown paper bag, which he brought back to the bench. Opening the bottle, he handed it to Joe.

'Now then, that might take the edge off that pain and sure please God you'll be feeling better in the morning.'

Leaving Joe Lynch a full bottle of the strongest whiskey money could buy, he walked back up the hill, gesturing that the boys should follow him. Once they were around the corner, he stopped, 'Now, Patrick, go home and clean the carpet as best you can. Liam, you go home to your mother, she has enough to contend with at the moment. If anyone asks, just say you were with Patrick, which is the truth. Hopefully, if he drinks the full bottle, which I'm sure he will, your father won't remember a thing about tonight or where he got the cut from by tomorrow. I know I don't need to tell ye, but this never happened, all right? Now, goodnight to ye.'

He walked away from them, never once reprimanding them for their actions or mentioning the fact that their predicament meant he didn't turn up for evening Mass.

'Will it work, do you think?' Liam asked Patrick.

'I'd say so; he doesn't usually have enough money for that much drink so it will probably make him forget everything. I hope it does, anyway, though what we'll have to put up with all that inside him, I don't want to think about.'

Liam thought before he spoke, 'Is he often like that, y'know, the way he was earlier?'

'Yeah. It's not too bad if it's me, or even Mam. It's when Connie gets upset, that's the worst. He wakes the baby with his roaring, but Connie is so scared of him. I hate him, I really do. I know it's a sin and everything, but a bit of me was disappointed that he didn't die tonight. I know we'd have been in desperate trouble and everything but at least he'd be gone and my Mam and me and the girls would have some peace for once.'

Liam didn't know what to say. He'd give anything to have his father back and Patrick wanted his dead. Life seemed so unfair, that someone as nice as Daddy would be lying in the cold ground and someone as horrible and awful as Joe Lynch was walking around, not a bother on him, making people miserable.

Patrick went on, 'It's not fair, you know? You had a really nice Dad, one who didn't drink or anything and he died, and my auld fella is a bastard and he's still going strong.'

Liam looked at his friend. He didn't usually curse, so to hear him using that word about his father was a shock. Still though, he echoed Liam's own thoughts. And he was definitely right about Daddy. They walked back up the hill, going over everything that had happened.

'Father Aquinas was great, wasn't he?' Liam said. 'I hope he doesn't get in trouble for not saying Mass.'

'Yeah, especially if that long string of misery Xavier had to do it. He gives me the creeps. He's always watching everything, y'know? He and Father Aquinas are as different as two people could be. Imagine we used to be so scared of him when we were small lads doing the communion. If someone would have told me that he would actually go into the pub and buy a bottle of whiskey for my da, just so that he'd forget what we did, I'd have said they were cracked.' They were still marvelling at it as they walked in companionable silence back up the hill.

What a day, Liam thought. In a way, the madness with Joe Lynch took his mind off the fact that they had buried Daddy today—for a while, anyway. Eventually, they came to the corner. Liam's house was at the end of the terrace, that's why their yard was a bit bigger than the others on the terrace. Patrick's was halfway up on the other side.

'Night, Liam, and thanks...y'know, for everything. I'm glad you didn't kill him for your sake, but the fact that you hit him with a hurley to save me...well, thanks.' Patrick was kicking the kerb, eyes downward, clearly uncomfortable.

'No bother, you'd have done the same for me. Night.' Liam smiled as he opened the front door and leaned back against it. It felt good to have a best friend even if everything else was horrible.

Liam heard murmured conversation in the kitchen but decided to go up to bed. He hadn't the energy for conversation; he just wanted his home to feel like home again. He doubted that it ever could be now that Daddy was never coming back to it. Did everything happen today? The funeral. Mrs Kinsella turning up. Hitting Joe Lynch with a hurley and leaving him for dead. And then Father Aquinas sorting it all out. Questions tumbled over themselves in his mind. He wished he could just switch it off like a radio, but it seemed like today was neverending. As he went up the stairs, Mammy opened the door into the kitchen.

'Ah, Liam love, I was getting worried. I kept you some dinner.'

Liam sighed inwardly and came back down. He wasn't hungry, but Mammy would only fret if he didn't eat. Everyone but Mrs Lynch was gone. Patrick's little sister was asleep on the chair by the stove with a coat over her, and the baby slept in a crib that Liam recognised as being from their attic. They were so young; Liam hated the thought of Joe Lynch hurting them.

'I was with Patrick,' he answered. He hated lying by omission, but Father Aquinas had told him to, so he felt it was probably all right this once.

'Kate wanted to see you before she left, but she couldn't find you. You look exhausted, pet,' Mammy said wearily, placing a plate of food in front of him.

He began eating, tasting nothing. He'd totally forgotten about Kate. 'Where's Con?' he asked.

'He's staying with your Uncle Willy for a while. It's closer to his work so it's easier.'

Liam knew the real reason Con wasn't living at home anymore. The same reason Kate was gone back to England. He wanted to shout at them that what happened wasn't Mammy's fault. She loved Daddy with all her heart and she knew that he would never even look at another woman. She would give anything to have him here tonight, drinking cocoa and talking, but she would never have that again. He wished more than anything that he could make it better, but there was nothing he or anyone else could do.

CHAPTER 9

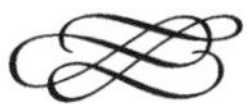

Liam walked in through the huge gates of St Bart's College on that first morning feeling like a fraud. He half-expected someone to tap him on the shoulder and ask him what on earth he thought he was doing. Patrick was to meet him at the bottom of the road, but he sent a young fella off the street with a message to say he had to go in earlier for some reason so he'd see Liam there.

Everyone seemed to know everyone else, and the accents he heard were not like anything he was used to around his street. Mammy had said a lot of boys from the country, who had plans to join the priesthood, go to St Bart's—it being a seminary. She was so busy fussing over him that morning he couldn't wait to get out the door. Ever since she heard about the scholarship, she had been like a hen with an egg. Nothing would do but getting him a brand new uniform in town, a fountain pen, even a real leather satchel. He would never forget the look on her face when he told her the news. It was the first time she smiled in weeks but then almost immediately she broke down in tears, saying how proud Daddy would have been of him. She hugged him until he feared he'd suffocate and told him over and over how wonderful she thought he was.

She had a small sum, given to her by the factory as a gesture of goodwill after Daddy's death, and she decided to spend it on getting Liam kitted out for school. He tried to tell her that because he was a scholarship boy there were uniforms available, ones other fellas were finished with, just like the books, but she vehemently refused to even entertain the idea. He was going to force the point but when he raised it, she got all emotional and started crying again.

'Your father would have been so proud, Liam, so proud of you going off to the seminary. And without a word from anyone, you just went off and did it all by yourself. The least he would want is for me to spend a few bob on kitting you out properly so you'll be the match of anyone going in there.'

He didn't bother trying to explain that he couldn't care less about new clothes and that no matter what she did, he would still remain a scholarship boy and therefore not the match of everyone. He thanked God once again for the opportunity and even more for allowing him to have the opportunity with Patrick. He wished he was beside him now as he made his way to the big hall where he had sorted books on the day his father's body had come home from England.

That was two months earlier, but it felt much longer. He still cried most nights in bed, but he was at last accepting the reality that Daddy was never coming home. Now, when he woke, he knew he was dead and it was just him and Mammy. Kate was still in England and had written to say she was doing a line with an English lad. Mammy worried that he was a Protestant, but she didn't dare ask. Things were very prickly with her and Kate and her infrequent letters home were factual but lacked any real affection for their mother. They were addressed to both Mammy and Liam. He hated reading them because of the look that came over Mammy's face when she read about Kate's new life in England. Con was still living with Uncle Willy. He'd got him a job in the new tyre factory, and he was spending all his spare time with Hilda. He came up for his tea every Friday, and he talked mostly to Liam about matches and things like that. He answered Mammy when she asked him questions but that was all. He said he was thinking of going to England with Hilda once she finished her bookkeeping exams. Kate said there was loads of money to be made over there and loads of craic to be had as well. In the past, he knew Mammy would have expressed horror and outrage that he would consider going somewhere with a girl and not so much as an engagement ring between them, but she didn't say such things now. It was as if she was grateful he called at all, and she didn't dare give him an excuse to stop. Liam tried to talk to Con, to persuade him to be nicer to their mother, but he said he was so angry with her that he couldn't forgive her. The best he could do was turn up for his tea every Friday and count the minutes till he could go. He didn't actually say the last bit, but Liam knew it was what he felt.

The twins were both in the Civil Service now, both having passed the exams with flying colours, of course. They were offered positions in Cork but refused them at the last minute choosing instead to take jobs in Dublin. They were living in digs with a Mrs Finnegan in a place called Gardiner Street. They loved it. Molly was in the Department of the Taoiseach, and she said Mr Lynch was a gentleman, and even though he was very busy running the country, he had a word for everyone. The twins wrote to say that the Taoiseach remembered Daddy from his hurling days, and he sought Molly out when she started working to say he was sorry for her loss. Mammy and Daddy had great time for Jack Lynch, being a local man and a hurler, so that letter had cheered up Mammy a bit.

Annie worked in the Department of Justice and to hear her you'd swear it was she who was writing the new Criminal Justice Bill. She'd sicken you with the name dropping as if she mixed with barristers and solicitors her whole life. Mammy read their letters over and over, not because she was that interested in the Probation Act or what heads of state were visiting, but for a trace of affection from either of her daughters—some inkling that they were softening in their attitude towards her. There never was one, or an invitation to visit. Liam knew Mammy would have loved a trip to Dublin, or even to England to visit Kate, but such a trip was never suggested.

As they sat each night with a cup of tea or cocoa after dinner, his mother confided to Liam her hopes that one Friday Con would bring Hilda home, so that she could meet her properly. They met during the funeral, of course, but it wasn't the same thing—that whole time was a blur. Liam suggested this to him, but he just said she worked late on Fridays. Liam was going to say it didn't have to be a Friday, but he knew Con wouldn't bring her home, not with things the way they were. Liam wondered if there was any way to encourage his siblings not to lay the blame for their father's death on their mother, but he couldn't think of anything. Daddy would have said that time is a great healer, so maybe it was just a case of waiting, but he hated the fact that Mammy felt so isolated and rejected, especially since it wasn't her fault at all. Liam had to try, not for the first time, to quell the murderous thoughts he had about Mrs Kinsella. If this was anyone's fault, then it was hers.

Most of the boys attending St Bart's were boarders, so Father Aquinas warned them that they would not only be scholarship boys, but also two of the very few day pupils. They had spoken to him one day when they went up for a look around before the school opened. He never mentioned the night of Mr Lynch or the whiskey and neither did they. Patrick's father had gone missing for a few days after that incident, much to everyone's relief, but like a bad penny he turned up again, with no recollection of having ever turned up at Seán Tobin's funeral. In fact, it was a source of rage to him that his wife hadn't informed him of the death of his neighbour. Liam knew he was back when he found Mrs Lynch in their kitchen with his mother applying a cold compress for a black eye and a cut lip.

Father Aquinas brought them into the monastery and once again gave them tea and fruit cake as they chatted easily about the coming years. He taught in the junior school, of course, but all the priests and brothers lived together, so he told them who would be teaching what subjects.

Liam hid his disappointment when he heard that Father Xavier would be teaching Maths. Firstly, because he found the subject so difficult but he also remembered the superior attitude of the priest the night he and Patrick had come looking for help when he thought he might have murdered Mr Lynch. Father Xavier had light blue eyes and very pale skin. He had one of those silly hairstyles where he combed a long dark oiled piece from the side of his head over the bald top in an effort to make it look like he had hair, but the reality was it looked ridiculous. Everyone knew he only liked the wealthy people's sons, and he was unashamed in his favouritism. Liam and Patrick were both trying to avoid him as much as possible.

Daddy used to annoy Mammy by saying, 'Isn't it a right oddity that they find plenty of vocations up the long avenue, not so many in the cottages.' Liam didn't know what he meant but when he asked him one day as they were walking home from town, he explained, 'Not all of them, Liam, but some people in the Church are very fond of money and fond of people with money, so sometimes I wonder if they are more interested of making nuns and priests of wealthy people's sons and daughters than those children of the poorer people. Your mother wouldn't hear a word said against the Church, and I'm a good Catholic, who goes to Mass and all of that, but I'm not blind either. That's all I meant.' Liam knew from the tone he used that that was the end of the conversation. Liam had a feeling that Father Xavier might just be the kind of priest Daddy was talking about. Still, Liam had been brought up to believe that you judge a person by their words and deeds not by their address or any other trappings of wealth, so he held his head high as he passed a group of boys a little older than himself. They were resplendent in navy blazers with royal blue piping and grey flannel trousers. Their shirts were crisp and white and their black leather shoes gleamed with newness.

Liam was wearing a pullover. 'You didn't have to have a blazer,' the man in the shop had said when he came in with Mammy—the uniform was either a pullover or a blazer. There were two full pounds difference in price between them so despite Mammy's misgivings, Liam insisted on getting the pullover.

He realised now that he was the only one without a blazer. As he entered the hall, his eyes scanned anxiously for Patrick. Relieved, he spotted him and walked over to where he stood, also in a blazer.

'How come you had to come in early?' Liam asked.

'I needed to get a blazer. The day I came in looking for a uniform, all the blazers were from fellas who were finished school so they were huge. Father O'Keeffe, he's in charge of uniforms, sent word that I was to come in early and get fitted.' He looked older, Liam thought, in his nearly new uniform. Mrs Lynch had let the trousers down since the ones he got were too short and she pressed them around a hundred times so the original crease wouldn't show—well not unless you were examining them anyway. She turned the collar and cuffs of the shirts he got, marvelling at the fact that nobody had done it before, and with his striped tie, Liam thought his friend looked very grown up and sophisticated. He'd grown over the summer, as well, so he was a good head taller than Liam. He fought the urge to wish he had a blazer too, knowing his father would expect him to rise above such silliness.

Other boys their age filtered into the hall slowly, most of them in pairs or threesomes, though one or two looked forlorn and lonely. The hubbub of chatter that seemed so loud outside was subdued by the presence of several black soutaned priests, who were standing on the stage at the top of the long room. Most boys held suitcases, presumably containing their belongings for a whole term spent at school. He tried to imagine what it would be like to live in the school and felt sorry for one lad standing alone, who was trying unsuccessfully to hold back the tears. Liam nudged Patrick and nodded in his direction.

'Shall we ask him if he wants to stand with us?'

Patrick grinned, 'Do sure, he looks like the cows we used to see waiting in line to go into Slattery's slaughterhouse! Though he looks fairly well-heeled, so he mightn't want to be seen with two paupers like us.'

Liam walked across to where the apple-cheeked boy stood. He was slightly chubby with blond curls and looked like an angel that you'd see in holy pictures. He was what his mother would have called a nice soft boy, who showed all the signs of being well-fed and well-minded.

'Do you want to come over near me and my friend rather than stand on your own?' Liam asked, feeling kind of foolish and slightly regretting his decision.

The boy looked at him as if he were a terrifying animal.

'We're new as well, and we don't know anyone either,' he added, hoping to relax the boy.

'All right,' he replied and followed Liam back to where Patrick stood waiting.

'I'm Liam Tobin, and this is my friend, Patrick Lynch. We're from Chapel Street, just under the Goldie Fish, and we're here on a scholarship.'

They had made a decision soon after getting the scholarship that they would tell everyone their status right away. Patrick said it would take the power away from anyone who would try to put them down about it if they said it loud and proud. Liam had smiled when he said that, it was just like something Daddy would have said.

They waited for him to reply and after a few seconds he did. 'My name is Hugo FitzHenry, and my mother is paying for me to come here though I fervently wished she wouldn't.' His voice sounded very posh to Liam's ears.

'Why not? Why don't you want to come here?' Patrick was curious. Hugo observed them for a moment, his china-blue eyes unblinking. Then he spoke again, in the strange accent.

'Well, for several reasons really. Firstly, I loathe school in all its forms. I had a governess, then a tutor, and eventually I was sent to the village school, all uniformly dreadful experiences. Secondly, I have to leave my pony, who hates it if I go away even for one night, and thirdly, I like sleeping in my own bed and all the comforts of home. Cook makes me creamy porridge and a boiled egg with toast soldiers every morning, and she warms my socks and vest in the oven before I put them on in case I get a chill. I don't feel I am to be regarded with the same level of adoration here.' He smirked at the last bit as he glanced around the austere hall, and his accent sounded almost English. The boys couldn't imagine what kind of a background he came from but if he had a pony of his own, they must have land and therefore he must be rich. They didn't know any rich people so this Hugo FitzHenry was a novelty.

Liam and Patrick exchanged a look that said, 'Listen to your man,' and smiled conspiratorially. At least he had cheered up and he seemed happy to be with them. Liam wondered if he was in the wrong place, he was definitely gentry and they were all Protestant—the descendants of the English invaders.

'Sorry now, but you do know this is a Catholic school, don't you?' he said, anxious that the poor lad wasn't in the wrong school.

'Mama...er…my mother converted to Catholicism to marry my father and now she's more devout than those born to the faith, certainly more than he ever was. It really is most trying. And the most tragic result of her passionate indoctrination into the Church of Rome is her only child being locked up here for the foreseeable.' He sighed dramatically.

'Converted from what?' Liam asked confused. Hugo's vocabulary was like nothing he'd ever heard before.

'C of E of course, she's from Berkshire. My grandparents nearly went mad, they didn't want her to marry my father in the first place, but to relinquish her faith in favour of papacy, well that really was the definitive blow.' He winked conspiratorially. 'Though they weren't particularly devout either, but they didn't know any Papists, which was a fact more by design that by accident if you know what I mean.'

Patrick and Liam were dumbfounded. They didn't even understand half of the words he said, it was like he swallowed a dictionary.

'So your mother is a Protestant?' Patrick was incredulous.

'No, that's what I've explained. She *was* Church of England then she met my father. In Paris, I think, sometime shortly after the war. He was a writer and she fell in love with his bohemian ways. Though the fact that he also was heir to a large estate in County Waterford probably oiled the wheels of romance.' He grinned. 'Anyway, he was Catholic and so the only way they could marry in the Catholic Church was for her to convert, and he couldn't inherit if he married outside the faith, so she did. The funny thing was my father wasn't interested in religion at all; he used to say she only did it to annoy her parents, which is entirely believable if you met her. But, much to the incredulity of all concerned she became quite zealous, daily communicant and so on. Papa was just pleased she found some way to fill the days at Greyrock. She's charming and lovely, of course, but a little, shall we say, flighty and utterly infuriating.'

Liam didn't know what to say. He never heard anyone speak about their family like that. He was like someone he'd read about in a story, not a real person who would be in his class in school.

'So, you chaps are here on scholarships, are you? You must be frightfully clever in that case, so I would be delighted to strike up a friendship if it was agreeable to you both. Where did you say you hailed from?'

Patrick stifled a laugh. 'Well, Hugo, we're locals. I'm from a street at the bottom of the hill there and my friend Liam lives across the road and down a bit. We haven't a pony, or any land, and I've no idea what toast soldiers are. I never met anyone who had been to Paris and I never spoke to a Protestant before, so there you have it.'

Hugo pealed with laughter and slapped his thigh theatrically. 'You are a hoot. Perhaps this place isn't so bad after all. Though I see I will have some work convincing you that I'm not any kind of Protestant, worse luck. They are altogether less enthusiastic about all of this religion stuff, but what Mama wants, it seems Mama must have, so here I am.'

'What does your father think about it? Did he pick this school?' Liam asked.

A cloud passed over Hugo's cherubic face and his eyes were downcast. 'My father died just six months ago. He was wounded at El Alamein in 1942; he was there with Monty putting a stop to Rommel. He came home though so many didn't, but he was never strong. He had some shrapnel buried in his chest. The doctors said it could kill him if they tried to remove it so it was better left where it was. He met mother at a dance when she was visiting some friends in Paris in the late forties and that was that. They met in Paris and a few years later, married in England, and then came to live back at Greyrock—that's home, outside Lismore. They waited a long time for my arrival but along I came in 1955. He got pneumonia last winter and he died.'

Liam recognised the pain behind the words. Gone was the jokey, almost pantomime performance, and all that was left was a boy who missed his father.

'My dad died too, three months ago—in an accident at work.' Liam's voice cracked with emotion.

'I'm sorry. Did you get along with him?' Hugo asked.

'Yes. He was the best father in the whole wide world.'

Silence passed as each boy was lost in his thoughts.

'What about yours, Patrick? Is your father alive?' Hugo asked curiously.

'Oh yes, very much so, more's the pity, though Liam did a fairly good job of trying to finish him off a few weeks back. I'm hoping he'll have better luck next time.'

Now it was Hugo's turn to be shocked and his face caused Patrick and Liam to collapse into uncontrollable giggles. After a moment, Hugo joined in, and Father Aquinas looked on with satisfaction from the stage to see the three friends happily laughing together.

CHAPTER 10

The weeks flew by and Liam got to grips with all the schoolwork he was given every night. At least the house was quiet, and he had moved into the girls' bedroom since there was more space. Mammy had bought him a desk, a chair, and a lamp from the second-hand shop on Blarney Street and even got someone in to put distemper on the walls. She made him a lovely patchwork quilt out of old clothes that the girls left behind. Sometimes, Patrick came over to study with him before a test, and he always remarked how cosy and nice it was. Mammy always made them scones or soda bread with jam and tea and delivered it up to the room. Patrick teased him that he was as well-minded as Hugo.

Some of the boarders and even one or two of the priests made the odd snide remark about them being poor but mostly everyone was nice. The only one they really hated was Father Xavier. He regularly made references to those who are going places and those who were not. He frequently worked into the conversation the names of the wealthy and powerful families in the city and their connections to the school. He ignored Liam but seemed to really take a dislike to Patrick, often mentioning the behaviour of drunks and undesirables while looking straight at him. Funnily enough, he never brought Hugo's family up, and they sounded more refined than even the merchant princes of Cork.

At least, they got to go home each evening. Poor Hugo was stuck in there every night and Father Xavier slept in the boarder's section so he was always around. Liam and Patrick suspected that Hugo hated the fact that he had to board and they could go home. Hugo quizzed Liam each morning as they shuffled into morning prayers.

'What did you have for dinner last night?'

Liam would throw his eyes to heaven in exasperation, but he answered him honestly, 'Bacon and cabbage.'

'And floury potatoes with butter?' Hugo would add hopefully.

'Yes, spuds with butter and salt and the top of the milk,' Liam would say with a sigh.

'And what did you have for pudding?'

'I've told you a thousand times, we don't call it pudding,' Liam would say chuckling.

'All right, all right, afters then, dessert, whatever you want to call it,' his impatience bubbling to the surface.

'Let me think,' Liam would deliberately hesitate. 'Can you remember, Patrick? You came for your tea yesterday, didn't you?'

'Oh yes, Liam, it was gorgeous, so it was. It was rice pudding with sultanas and cinnamon and cream, or was it ice cream?' His green eyes would dance with devilment.

Hugo groaned in agony.

'I think we had both, Patrick, now that I come to think of it, yeah, and then there was chocolate biscuits after with the tea,' Liam would add with a giggle.

'I know you pair delight in torturing me, but honestly, you have no idea the slop we are given in this place. It is simply intolerable, and to think that my two so-called friends are living it up and being fed like prize pigs not two hundred yards from here, well, it's too much, simply too much.'

It was true that Hugo had lost some of his chubbiness in the first weeks at St Bart's. All the boarders complained about the food but none so often or loudly as Hugo did.

'Liam, I am just going to come right out and say it. I've been dropping such heavy hints in recent weeks it's a miracle you are not limping, but all to no avail, so I am left with no option but to beg.' Liam was confused.

'I know I cannot go to Patrick's house due to the nature of Mr Lynch's proclivities around whiskey.' Patrick had told him about his awful father. 'So you are my only hope. Please, dear Liam, if you care anything for my well-being, you will bring me home to your sainted mother and she will feed me and love me as I should be loved.'

Liam looked at Patrick. Was he serious? Hugo FitzHenry of Greyrock Estate with his own pony and a cook and God alone knew what else, wanted to come to his house for a meal? His friend just shrugged and smiled.

'But, Hugo, our house is tiny, we don't even have a garden or anything, and we're just, well, we're not rich or anything,' Liam began.

'I could pay if it's a question of that,' Hugo interrupted.

Liam was horrified, 'No, Lord no, that's not what I meant at all. It's just it wouldn't be what you're used to.'

'Frankly, Liam, what I am used to is cold lumpy porridge made on water, cold lumpy spuds as you so charmingly call them, and gristly meat, and the highlight of the week is a tiny, soft plain biscuit on a Friday night. Seriously, I'd love to come to your house. Not just for the food, though I won't lie to you, that's a huge part of it, but to sit by the fire, to chat to your mother, to feel more like a person and less like an inmate even for one evening.'

Liam and Patrick suddenly felt so lucky. Mrs Lynch worked in the big houses in Sundays Well most evenings and she took his little sisters with her, so Patrick often had dinner with Liam and his mother. He was sure she wouldn't mind if he brought Hugo home, though he'd have to explain about the Protestant thing ahead of time. Come to that, he'd have to explain about Hugo, though that was another story altogether. He was different, he didn't care about hurling or girls or any of the normal things lads talked about. His primary topic was his aching hunger, followed by his pony. He regularly had Patrick and Liam perplexed and bewildered by his tales of life at Greyrock. He had no idea what his mother would make of Hugo FitzHenry.

Liam wasn't that interested in girls either, but they were all mad about Patrick. He was definitely the best looking, tall with shiny black hair and a fine physique. He was on the under-sixteen school team even though he was much younger than his teammates and was making a name for himself around the school. Liam liked hurling too but although he made the school team, he wasn't tall or bulky enough to be a star. Still, he was quick and that was a help. Hugo even hated to watch the games let alone participate. The other boys didn't know what to make of him and called him 'The Squire' behind his back. Patrick and Liam knew that their presence during the day insulated Hugo from the worst of it, but they both dreaded to think what happened in the evenings. Some days, Hugo was so quiet he'd hardly say a word, and he sometimes had bruises that were never explained. Patrick had asked him who was bothering him and promised that he would deal with them, but Hugo changed the subject.

He constantly bemoaned his blond curls and one evening, he took a scissors to them himself. He looked a fright with bits sticking out everywhere so Liam did his best to even it up. Even with his shorter haircut, there was something fragile about him. Some of the other boys teased him mercilessly but never when Patrick and Liam were around. Liam suspected that life was hard for him in the evenings when they were safe at home.

'Would they let you out?' Patrick asked.

'Well, I believe Liam's mother needs to write to Father Rafael and invite me. He's the keeper of the keys and if he deems her to be of sound mind and character and unlikely to draw poor innocent me into ways of sin, he will give his permission.' He had it all worked out.

'I'll ask her so,' Liam agreed, trying hard and failing to visualise Hugo in their small kitchen.

As he suspected, she was thrilled to be asked. 'Mammy, the only thing is he's a bit weird. Like he talks all posh like someone from England, and Patrick and me don't know what he's on about half the time. His mother used to be Protestant and then she married his father who was a Catholic and she converted and promised to bring him up as a Catholic. They live in a huge mansion, with horses and servants and everything but don't let it put you off him. He has no interest in most of the stuff lads like, and he's always going on about food. He's really funny and he's very kind, too. He gets loads of pocket money, and he's always buying sweets for me and Patrick in school when the tuck shop is open. He reckons the priests are starving them so he makes me tell him what I had for my dinner every single day, and he nearly drives himself mad then thinking about it.'

'He sounds like a right character. Do his mother and father come to visit him at all?' she asked as she kneaded the dough for the soda bread.

'No, his mother never comes, and his father died a few months back. He was in the British Army and he got wounded fighting Rommel in Egypt, so then he was never strong after that. He died of pneumonia.' Liam got sad even thinking about it.

'Ye're well met, so.' Her eyes glistened for an instant. 'Does he like it above, apart from the food?'

Liam and Patrick caught each other's eye. 'I don't know, he doesn't say much, but he's so different from the others up there, and from us too, but for some reason he gets on with us. Some days, though, you can tell he's been crying, but anytime we ask him, he says he's grand.'

'I told him I'd sort out anyone that was giving him a hard time, but he doesn't want that either,' Patrick added.

'Well, whatever ye do don't go getting yourself into any trouble, do ye hear me? Now, Patrick, you'd never go out for a bucket of coal for me, would you? And Liam, run up to Murray's for butter. I suppose you're coming for a feed too, Mr Lynch?'

'You know me, Mrs T, never say no to a plate of grub.'

'Right, I'll give you a note tomorrow for Father Raphael, Liam, and sure can't this Hugo FitzHenry come down with ye after school on Thursday. That'll give me time to get the place straight. I'll make corned beef maybe, and a jam sponge for dessert. Would that be all right, do you think? '

Liam jumped up and kissed his mother on the cheek. 'Mammy, that would be *stupendous* as Hugo FitzHenry might say.'

She smiled, one of the rare ones since Daddy died.

The dinner was a triumph according to Hugo. Liam told his mother about a hundred times to stop fussing about the house—he wasn't coming to do an inspection. She made homemade vegetable soup from bones she got in the market that had been boiled for hours, and it was absolutely delicious, served with thick slices of fresh baked soda bread slathered with butter from the creamery up the hill.

That was followed by corned beef with boiled potatoes, carrots and parsnips mashed with cream and salt. Liam thought Hugo was going to faint with delight. He chatted endlessly and admired and praised everything he saw, heard, and ate. Mrs Lynch popped in to meet the famous Hugo and was equally charmed by him. He told Mammy how cold it was at night in the dorms, and she told him she would knit him some bed socks. Liam and Patrick watched in amusement as Hugo FitzHenry worked his magic on their mothers. After dinner, they sat by the stove tucking into jam sponge and cups of tea, and he regaled them with tales of life at Greyrock, about his father and his war record, his mother and her fervent Catholicism, and his entire life story so far. Liam had warned him in advance not to say anything derogatory about either his mother or the Catholic Church and he'd get on fine. He left to trudge back up the hill laden down with scones and brack and all sorts of goodies to keep him going.

That began a pattern of Hugo coming to Tobin's house every Thursday. Mammy looked forward to it, and the feedback for her efforts was the exact opposite of Con's on a Friday night. No matter how much trouble she went to for him, making his favourite dishes and packing up extra for him to take back to Willy's, he never showed even the slightest gratitude. He made it clear that his visits were out of a sense of duty and to see Liam.

One evening as he was drying the ware while his mother washed, Liam raised the subject.

'Is he ever going to be like he was, do you think?'

'Who pet?' Mammy asked.

'Con, you know, the way he used to be, joking and messing and always up to mischief.' He didn't say anything about Daddy.

'I don't know, love. He's very cross with me. He thinks that I shouldn't have let your Dad go to England that time. Maybe he's right. I don't think they'll ever forgive me.' She stood looking out to the yard washing the same plate over and over. Tears started rolling down her cheeks.

'But he was going to come home, to the tyre factory. I just don't understand why they are so bitter against you,' Liam said quietly. He hated upsetting her, but he wanted to know the truth.

'He was. It was all set up. His last letter was all about how he got the word that there would be a job for him. I was delighted—having home was all I cared about. He knew how much I loved him, and how sorry I was for the way I reacted. I shouldn't be talking to you about this, but sure, you know it all anyway. That business with your one next door, well, it hurt me. I asked him time and again not to be going in there so much, people were talking, but he just wanted to help her. That's the kind of man he was, he didn't care what people said. He thought she was vulnerable, I suppose, and well, I was jealous. She was so pretty and always done up to the nines, and I felt like an auld dishrag beside her. When she came in that night, screaming and all of that, I was so ashamed. I knew that the neighbours would be nodding their heads and wagging their fingers, 'Didn't I tell you there was something? Seán Tobin isn't as innocent as he looks!' And all of that.' She wiped her eyes with the corner of her apron.

'Tell me,' Liam encouraged her.

She sighed, and it seemed to come from her toes, 'Then the job was gone in the dockyard only a few weeks after. Sure, it was touch and go there for years before, 'tis a miracle it lasted as long as it did, to be honest. There was nothing then, everyone was idle, no work anywhere. I don't think he would have gone on the dole even if things had been good between us, he'd have hated it. But since things were bad, we weren't talking, not the way we used to, and he decided to go to England. I should have stopped him, I know I should have, but he wanted to go. He wanted to get away from me, I'm sure, but he wanted to provide for ye all, as well. He hated leaving ye, though. You must remember that, Liam. I thought it was just going to be for a few weeks, he'd come back, and we'd patch things up. We were both angry, I was upset because I thought he'd drawn all this on us, and he was angry because he felt I should have trusted him. I did trust him, Liam, of course I did. I was just cross with him for getting us into that position in the first place. I honestly thought it would blow over, a bit of time apart and we'd be fine.'

'Did you ever think he...you know, went after, with Mrs Kinsella?' Liam asked tentatively, squirming with embarrassment but knowing this was the last time they would ever have this conversation.

She laughed ruefully, 'No, love, I never thought that. I knew she was in a hospital up the country. People round here put two and two together and make seven, short of things to talk about, your Daddy used to say.'

'So did ye work it out, you and Daddy?'

'We did. I wrote to him in England and said I was sorry for the way I reacted, that he was right, that I was destroying my marriage based on the idle gossip of people with nothing better to do. I told him that we all missed him, and I asked him to come home.'

Liam could see that talking about him was breaking her heart. 'And what did he say to that?'

'He said he was sorry, too. That he should have respected my wishes. He said he had a lot of time to think and if the situation was reversed, he wouldn't have liked it. If there was some single man living next door and I was in and out to him, even if it was totally innocent, he wouldn't have been happy about it. He wrote every week, just about how much he was working and how much he missed us all. Then the last letter, he said that the job had come through in the tyre factory and he missed us all so much and wanted to come home but that the man that got him the start in England had gone out on a limb for him so he wanted to give him two weeks' notice. If it wasn't for that, he told me, he'd be on the boat home that night.' Her voice cracked, and the tears came in earnest now.

Liam let her cry. He just sat there, holding her hand, feeling a lot older than his fourteen years.

Eventually her sobs subsided.

'I...he wrote that letter on the third of April, he died on the fifth.'

The unfairness of it all swept over Liam like a wave—the tragedy of his father's death, the fact that his generosity and kindness had led to that whole thing with Mrs Kinsella, and the fact that Kate, Con, Molly, and Annie still blamed their mother—it all seemed so wrong.

'But if you told Kate and the others this...' he began.

'They know,' she said flatly, wiping her eyes.

'But how can they blame you so?' he began.

She put her hand on his again, 'Because they need someone to blame. They can't blame that...' She tried to find a word for her, 'Person next door, they can't blame God, they can't blame each other, they can't blame Seán, so they blame me. It's the cross in life I have to carry, as well as losing my husband. That's how they see it; I shouldn't have reacted the way I did to that woman coming to my door.' She was resigned.

'But if they knew he was coming home, he planned to, but he didn't want to let the man down,' Liam was insisting.

'Kate knows. She went for dinner with him the night before he died. He told her he was coming home.' His mother was trying to control her emotions.

'And still she blames you...' Liam shook his head in disbelief.

'Not really, not deep down, but she's grieving, and that's her way of doing it. The others are just following her lead. She'll come round, I hope. I pray every day that she will and if she does, the others might follow. They're grieving and they're angry, it's to be expected. Being angry with me is the safest option; they know I'll always love them no matter what. In the meantime, I don't know what I'd do without you,

Liam. Ever since you were a baby you've been my pet, you know that. And I'm so proud of you, up in the Seminary, and I know your Daddy would be too. You've never been an ounce of trouble to us, Liam, not once.' Her voice sounded far away, wistful.

They sat together in front of the fire, and Liam vowed that he would never do anything to hurt his mother. She'd had such a terrible experience. He tried to stop vicious thoughts about Mrs Kinsella crowding his mind, telling himself over and over she was sick, that she couldn't help it. He remembered the night he went in to set the mouse trap and the bottle of stout on the table, obviously for his father. She set her cap at him, despite the fact that he had a wife and children and he was only trying to help her. He wondered about a God that allowed such a terrible thing to happen to a good family that only ever tried to serve him.

CHAPTER 11

Hugo felt his teeth with his tongue. They were still there for now. The huge hands that were forcing his face deeper and deeper into the mud of the school field felt like vices. He struggled to breathe, his mouth and nose full of mud. A knee into the small of his back sent spasms of pain through his body.

'Don't think we don't know how close you are to that pair of tinkers Tobin and Lynch,' a voice hissed in his ear. 'If you say one single word, just one, twill be the last thing you ever say, d'ya hear me, ya little faggot?'

Hugo tried to respond but no words came out. A ferocious kick hit his groin, and a sound emerged from him that he didn't recognise. The Clancy twins had roughed him up several times before but this time they seemed determined to kill him. They were Father Xavier's nephews so they were untouchable. All Hugo could feel was pain and death was appealing. 'Please God, just let me die now, let them kill me and all of this will be over,' he pleaded and prayed.

'Our uncle said he saw you deep in chat with Aquinas earlier and he has a message for you. You are a filthy stain on this school, you are disgusting, and everyone wishes you were dead. No wonder your father died and your mother packed you off here, instead of having to live with the shame of having a faggot for a son. You get what you deserve, sure you probably love it, you filthy queer, but if you ever mention a word about anything, you *are* dead. Do you understand?'

Hugo managed to nod and thankfully they left.

He lay in the dark for a moment, the cold wind soothing his aching body. His pyjamas were wet and covered in mud, but he couldn't move. This was the worst beating he'd had since arriving at St Bart's but not a week went by that something didn't happen to him. He'd have to get up, get inside and get cleaned up before the bell rang for mass. He longed to tell someone, anyone who could make this stop, but there was no way. He hated Xavier but knew that he wasn't the only boy who was subjected to his night-time visits. It was awful, painful, and Hugo burned with shame to even think of what happened. The priest never said a word, he just came in, did that awful thing and left. Hugo cried tears of humiliation and agony into the pillow. He once wrote to his mother, telling her what was happening, but he tore it up before he sent it. All mail in and out of the school was censored, he'd be sure to be caught. He could tell Patrick or Liam, or even Father Aquinas, but he didn't want them to know, the disgrace would be too much. Patrick and Liam had no power, anyway, being scholarship boys. If they had rich fathers, maybe someone would be able to do something, but as it were, they were seen as vermin by Xavier and his cronies. Father Aquinas would be horrified, but Hugo knew that he must have done something to make Xavier pick him. He would never try anything with Patrick or Liam so it must be him. The Clancy twins were right. If anyone found out, they would think that he liked it. Xavier was clever too, he covered his tracks well, no bruises that anyone could see, he never treated him differently in school, he was cold and dismissive.

Each night afterwards, Hugo spoke to his father, begging him to do something. To strike Xavier down from heaven, to have him hit by a car, or have a heart attack or something, but still it went on. Hugo knew that his beloved father would help if he could hear his only son, so one night he stopped praying. The abuse went on for four months in Hugo's first year at St Bart's. Then abruptly it stopped. He never knew why, and Xavier never looked in his direction again. Father Jerome took over the night duty and he only ever saw Xavier in the corridors.

CHAPTER 12

June 1971

The three boys were sitting on the grass, preparing for the last of the summer tests. Liam and Patrick were determined to do well and justify their scholarships but, as usual, Hugo couldn't give a hoot and wanted to chat.

'Why not? I've been to your house often enough,' Hugo was determined.

Patrick sighed in exasperation and snapped his Latin book shut.

'Arrgh! You're driving me mental, Hugo! I have to learn this *Latin in the Modern World* for tomorrow so if I answer you now, will you just go off and think about croquet or cucumber sandwiches or something and leave me alone? Why won't we come to your house? I'll tell you a hundred reasons why not, for starters, because Liam and I would be like a pair of muck savages in Greyrock Mansion or whatever you call it. Because your mam would have a stroke if she saw the pair of us coming up the avenue, because we haven't even proper clothes to wear—the best thing I have is my uniform, and I'm hardly going to wear that now, am I? Because we don't know the front end from the arse end of a horse, need I go on?'

Patrick was lying on his belly and took a cigarette from Hugo's packet. Two more exams in the Intermediate Certificate to finish and then the long summer stretched ahead. They were finishing third year and the holidays beckoned. Liam's eyes were stinging from the cigarette smoke, but he didn't complain. Patrick was a year older than him, and Hugo and most lads his age smoked. Having said that, if they got caught by the priests, they were dead.

'Xavier caught Johnny Cleary smoking after class last week, and he got a desperate hiding altogether,' Patrick said as he exhaled.

'Well, wouldn't you think that's a good reason to give the filthy things up then?' Liam said as he wafted the smoke away from his face. 'Don't be drawing him on you.'

The headmaster was a viciously violent man, and they all agreed it was best to stay out of his way. He taught them Maths, and Liam always had his homework done and paid attention in class. It was the worst class of the day. He walked around with the metal-studded leather strap dangling from his belt, everyone hated him. Liam noted once again that when the priest was mentioned, Hugo clammed up. Patrick noticed too, and they tried to talk to him about it, but any efforts to draw him out failed.

Luckily for Hugo, he was in Brother Martin's Maths class. He was old and kind of doddery so Hugo got away with murder.

Changing the subject back to the visit to Greyrock, Hugo went on. 'What do you say, Liam? Do you agree with the cigarette thief here?' Hugo asked as he struck a match.

'Well, I suppose he's right, we would look a bit out of place,' Liam conceded.

'Oh, really? And that's a problem, is it? You two don't exactly fit in here with your patched trousers and second-hand books, but I don't see either of you giving up. Being so intimidated, hmm? I thought you were braver than that.' Hugo gave Liam an almost imperceptible wink. He knew Patrick would rise to the suggestion that he was scared. 'If it would make you feel more at home Patrick, I could have you woken at five o'clock each morning for you to go down and muck out the stables.' Liam stifled a chuckle.

'How would we even get there?' Patrick asked. 'It's miles away.'

'By motorcar, my dear fellow. You've surely seen them, four wheels, steering wheel, runs on petrol? The one my dear mama will send for me in two days' time. Oh, for goodness sake! I know all you Cork boys imagine there is nothing beyond Midleton, but honestly, if you two are to make anything of yourselves, you will have to travel the world a little bit. Waterford is a good start.'

Liam and Patrick exchanged a look.

'I'll ask,' Liam agreed.

'All right, all right,' Patrick sighed, raising his hands in defeat.

'Excellent!' Hugo declared. 'I'll telegram her now.'

Two days later, Liam found himself travelling in a very luxurious motor car, driven by a chauffeur. The only other time he'd been in a car was when Daddy's friend used to take them to a match, none of the neighbours had a car. He looked out in amazement at the sea as they travelled along the South Coast of Ireland. They stopped in the seaside town of Tramore, and the three boys ate ice creams as the sun set over the Atlantic. There was a large dance hall near the beach and girls were queuing up outside to get in. Liam was glad his mother wasn't there to see the outfits, which were very tight, and some of the skirts were very short. He could imagine her disapproval.

He wondered if Annie and Molly dressed like that when they went out in Dublin. They probably did. And God alone knew what kinds of things Kate got up to. The longer she stayed in England, the more different she seemed. He wondered if Cork would ever again be glamorous enough for his sisters. Patrick thumped him on the arm.

'Oi! Don't you know that all girls are nothing but occasions of sin?' he teased.

'I wasn't looking at them,' Liam reddened, embarrassed that

Patrick thought he was looking lustfully at the girls when he had been thinking about his sisters.

'Oh yes you were, Liam Tobin, you can't lie to me! I don't blame you either, though. Look at the one in the yellow, she's a cracker.' Patrick craned his neck to get a better look. Hugo was busy sucking ice cream out of the end of the cone, and Patrick threw his eyes heavenward.

He gave Hugo a kick on the ankle to direct his attention, but he was too busy eating his ice cream.

'Ow! You ruffian! Always so violent, you working class.' He smiled.

'I don't know what we'll do with you, Hugo. There's a whole gang of gorgeous women not fifty yards away and you are too busy stuffing your face to notice them. Anyone of them would be thrilled to bag the lord of the manor, though your mama probably has some nice, horse-faced young one lined up for you.' He nudged Hugo who nearly choked on a blob of ice cream.

'God forbid!' he announced spluttering. 'Utterly mystifying creatures. No, I shall be steering well clear of any such entanglement, thank you very much.'

'Ah, but you do want to get married, don't you? When you grow up?' Liam asked. 'Like, it's what you do, unless you go for the priesthood.'

For a reason Liam couldn't understand, his two best friends collapsed into hysterical laughter.

Hugo wiped his eyes eventually, 'My dear Liam, there are few guarantees in this life, death and taxes, my father was fond of saying, but another is that I will never, ever, *ever* even consider in my wildest dreams—no scratch that—wildest *nightmares,* consider becoming a priest.'

'Really?' Liam asked. 'What about you, Patrick? Would you think about it? The priesthood, I mean?'

Patrick gave Liam a sidelong glance. Hugo was watching curiously, awaiting his answer. While St Bart's was a seminary for the education of priests, plenty of boys never expressed an interest in a religious life.

'No, Liam, I think I like girls too much to give up that whole thing. How about you?'

Liam spoke quietly, he hadn't intended blurting out his dearest wish. 'If God calls me to the priesthood, I'll go. I'd love to have a vocation, but it's probably too early to tell if I have one yet or not.'

The great thing about Patrick, Hugo, and himself was that even though they laughed together all the time, they never laughed at each other. He knew by their faces that they thought he was mad to even consider it, but they wouldn't laugh at him.

'Well, if you do feel a vocation coming on, resist it for a while at least. We've a lot to do before you shackle yourself to Holy Orders!' Hugo grinned as he threw his arm around Liam's shoulders while they walked back to the car. Patrick laughed and kicked a lemonade bottle along the path in front of him.

The journey continued, and his friends dozed off as the setting sun streamed in the windows. Liam thought about what it would be like to join the priesthood. The overriding feeling he got when he thought about it was the joy he could bring to his mother. She'd had so much pain and heartbreak in her life, and she had been so devout in her faith. Her favourite son to become a priest of the Lord would make her so proud and happy. He had more trouble trying to work out what Daddy might think about it. Though he never said it outright, he suspected his father didn't see the church as the faultless paragon of perfection his mother did. Whatever happened, he hoped his father would be proud of him.

He had no interest in girls, not the way Patrick and Con were always going on about fashion models and the actresses in the pictures. Hugo wasn't into girls either, but then as Patrick pointed out, he was too in love with himself to have room for anyone else. Liam smiled at the memory, Patrick was always teasing Hugo, but they were fond of each other under it all.

Liam was nervous about visiting Hugo's home despite his assurances that they would be welcome. Both his and Patrick's mother had spent the previous two days darning and ironing clothes for the adventure. Someone like Hugo would most likely have been sent to one of the really posh boarding schools up the country if his mother hadn't decided that Cork was far enough. There were lots of fancy schools, even for Catholics, that played rugby and cricket but, for some reason, she decided St Bart's was the place for him. Liam always got the impression that Hugo played down how rich his family were—the car and the chauffeur certainly weren't like anything he'd ever experienced before. He wondered how much Hugo had told his mother about them, did she know that they come from small terraced houses in a working-class part of the city? Did she know about Daddy dying in England or about Patrick's father being a drunk? He had no idea how he should behave, though Mammy kept warning him to mind his manners and not make a show of her—he hadn't a clue what manners she was on about. He suspected that neither did she.

Con had burst out laughing when he told him about the upcoming trip. He called last Friday for his tea as normal when Mammy was getting his suitcase ready for Liam's first ever holiday.

'Off mixing with the quality, are ya boy? Sure you won't even look at us by the time you come back, you'll be so full of airs and graces,' he said, putting on a silly posh voice.

Mammy snapped at him, 'Hugo FitzHenry has sat at this table more times than I can count, and a nicer boy you couldn't meet. Don't you be making Liam feel like he's getting notions above his station by being friends with him.'

'I was only messing,' Con replied sullenly.

Mammy instantly relented. 'Ah, I know you were, love. I shouldn't have snapped at you. It's just we are all nervous. Liam doesn't know what kind of a set-up he's going into down there.'

'Sure won't he be grand? Patrick Lynch will be with him, and your man Hugo is sound out, for all his talking like he has a boiled spud in his gob!' Con nudged Liam, and he chuckled.

'You're no better or worse than anyone else, Liam Tobin, just remember that, and you'll be fine. That's what Daddy would have said to you. Now, Hilda wants me to go to an anniversary Mass for her grand-aunt so I better make tracks. I'll see ye, and good luck in the castle, Liamo! Bye, Mam.'

Things were still a bit frosty, but Liam sensed a thaw in the relationship between his mother and Con of late. He was different to the girls; he couldn't hold a grudge forever. Con then did something he hadn't done since Daddy died, he kissed his mother on the cheek. It was just a peck, Con would hate it if anyone made a big thing of it, but Mammy went red with pleasure and ran out after him with an apple sponge she had made for him, all wrapped up in greaseproof paper. She caught up with him in the hall as he was putting on his coat.

'Thanks, Mam, Willy and I would have nothing nice after dinner if it weren't for you,' and he left, whistling down the street. Liam felt relieved, at least one of the family was being nice to Mammy. He prayed each night after he said his usual prayers that the girls would soften their hearts too in time.

Eventually, the car turned off the main road and drove through a set of very ornate gates. On the left of the gates was a large red-bricked cottage, which Hugo pointed out as the gatekeeper's lodge. 'Though of course there's no need for a full-time gatekeeper anymore, so the estate manager lives there now. His name's Tom Courtney and his daughter Martha. She and I used to play together as children but she works in the house now so it's not the same. She says she likes it, but it feels strange for me. Still, it's impossible to get people for that sort of work nowadays; nobody wants to live like this anymore, servants and so on. You can't blame them, it's 1971 not 1871.'

Liam and Patrick nodded knowledgeably as if the hiring or otherwise of people to open gates or iron newspapers was a daily part of their lives. The car jolted as they drove over cattle bars sunk into the ground. Hugo noted their looks of alarm and explained, 'There is a herd of deer on the estate, as well as cattle, been here for years, my father hunted as a boy, so mother keeps them for posterity. I think she hopes that I might go out one day and get pleasure from shooting the poor beasts, but she is, in this, as in most other things when it comes to me, utterly wrong.'

The car drove on for what seemed like ages and eventually the avenue snaked around to the left and the most incredible house was revealed. Liam had only seen pictures of houses like this in books, he never saw one in real life and the idea that his friend lived in such a place was amazing.

'I knew it would be big and fancier than our places but I never imagined...' Liam panicked. There was no way he and Patrick could go into that huge mansion as guests. Hugo's mother would know straight away what kind they were. He looked down at his hand-me-down shoes—painstakingly polished by his mother—his darned socks, and his patched trousers, and a sudden sense of inferiority threatened to overwhelm him. He caught Patrick's eye and knew he felt the same.

Hugo tapped on the glass between them and the driver and asked him to stop. They were about a hundred yards from the house. He turned to his friends and with a sigh said, 'You both look like you'd rather write out Latin declensions for the next week than go any further.'

Liam wanted to reassure him, 'It's not that, Hugo, sure it's so good of you to ask us, but it's just, well you've been to our houses, and we...'

'We don't know how to behave or what to say...' Patrick finished, unusually vulnerable.

'Look, I know it's different, not better, just different. When you both let me join you that first day, it made me think maybe I could bear it at St Bart's and I have. I never really had friends, not being really English or really Irish, and then the whole C of E and Catholic thing, well, I never fitted in anywhere, but I feel like I fit in at St Bart's and that's because of you two. Liam, your mother makes the most marvellous dinners, and we chat by the fire for hours, and your mother, Patrick, making me cakes and biscuits to keep me alive in between visits. I...well, I think I'd have gone insane these past years without that. You and your families saved me. I know it sounds dramatic, but honestly, you did. Going back there on Thursday nights with my belly full and a bag of cakes and buns, putting on my bed socks or wrapping myself in the lovely knitted quilt you mother made me, Patrick, well, it made me feel like someone cared about me. I can't describe...well...I won't ever forget it. To you it may not seem like much, but to me, that kindness meant the world. I just wanted to repay your hospitality a little bit, I suppose. Please don't feel intimidated, it's smaller than St Bart's and you walk around there as if you own the place, don't you? So, just treat Greyrock the same, all right?'

Liam and Patrick tried to relax. Hugo really wanted them to enjoy the trip, and he was such a decent lad even if he was as posh as anything. Liam felt a huge rush of affection for him; he had visited their homes and wanted his friends to visit his.

The imposing grey stone facade was gleaming in the late evening light. Being June, it wouldn't get dark until after ten so the lovely, yellow buttery light made the house seem more welcoming. There were at least fifteen windows across the two upper floors, and the entrance was via a bright red door with a huge doorknob and knocker —double the width of Liam's front door—accessed by a set of carved stone steps. The red of the door was the only relief from the grey cut stone of the house, though in front of the entrance were carved lions and beneath them stone troughs full of bright red flowers. The house looked down over a huge garden with ornamental trees and a pond and, in the distance, a huge belt of trees to the right. The entire place had an uninterrupted view of the ocean. The car drew to a halt on the gravel driveway in front of the house and immediately the front door opened. A man in a dove-grey-and-black uniform appeared and Liam wondered who he was. Hugo's father was dead so maybe he was a relative. Behind him appeared a glamorous woman, with ash-blond hair pinned back from her face. She was thin as a rake and was dressed like she was going somewhere very fancy in a pink and scarlet dress and red high-heeled shoes. She wore a lot of silver jewellery that caught the sun as it shone. She waited for the man to open the car door and as they gathered their belongings, Hugo turned to them.

'Welcome to Greyrock,' he said with a half-apologetic smile.

'Er, right.' The normally confident Patrick was bemused.

The man held the car door open and Hugo got out first.

'Welcome home, Master Hugo,' he said in a deep voice. He stood aside to allow the woman to hug her son. Liam couldn't believe this woman was Hugo's mother. She looked like one of the models out of the magazines the twins were always stuck in. Mothers were generally thin or fat, but they always looked like mothers, he'd never seen one so beautiful.

'Thank you, Patterson, it's good to be back,' Hugo replied warmly.

'Hugo, darling! I thought you would never get here! Honestly, you'd have been home from England quicker—that dratted road. And now, you must introduce me,' she trilled in a strong English accent.

'Mother, these are my friends, Liam Tobin and Patrick Lynch. Lads, this is, as you've probably guessed, my mother, Lily Auden-Fitz-Henry.' He took out his handkerchief to wipe lipstick off his cheek as he introduced them.

Liam put out his hand to shake hers as his mother had instructed him. She'd even consulted with Father Mac about how to greet people of the gentry so she was fairly sure that's what you did. Before he knew it, she had moved forward and was offering her cheek so he almost punched her in the stomach. She smelled of flowers and something else, something spicy, and he was confused for a moment. She seemed to think he should kiss her. He leaned forward awkwardly and gave her a peck on the cheek, reddening as he did so. He rarely kissed his own mother let alone someone else's. Patrick followed his lead and looked equally uncomfortable, Liam noted with relief.

Mrs FitzHenry fixed them both with a gaze for a split second as if she were sizing them up and making a judgement. Liam noticed her eyes, they were almost transparent as if they would change depending on where she was. He couldn't put his finger on it, but there was something strange about her. She definitely wasn't like anyone's mother that he knew, but it was something else. Mentally chastising himself, he tried to push those feelings from his mind. His mother and father brought him up not to judge people before you knew them, so perhaps, it was just that she was different from anyone he had ever met before. Hugo was a great lad and she reared him, so she couldn't be that bad. He wondered what his parents would make of this place. Mammy would probably be tongue-tied, nervous as he was, but Daddy would take it all in his stride. What he would give to be able to go home and tell him about the butler and the big avenue and everything. With a pain that was almost physical in its sharpness, Liam realised once again that he would never get to go home and tell Daddy about anything. Every time he forgot his father was dead, though over three years had passed, the realisation came upon him like an icy-cold wave of misery crashing over him, almost drowning him.

'Patterson, take the boys' things to their rooms and we shall take tea in the morning room, I think. Despite its name, it's the nicest room for the evening sun, isn't it, Hugo?' She took Hugo's arm and led them into the house. She kept up a stream of prattle as they walked through the hallway, the walls of which were adorned with huge oil paintings of people from long ago. Their feet sank into the deep pile runner, which covered the polished mahogany floor. In the recesses of the walls, ornate vases and pieces of sculpture sat on carved plinths. There was even a full suit of armour. Hugo's mother must have noticed the boys staring in amazement because she stopped at one of the portraits.

'Dreadful, aren't they? So dark and dreary, but William, my late husband, wouldn't hear of them being removed. There are over a hundred portraits in total so I'm afraid there's no avoiding them. I have tried to dilute the effect with some nice watercolours and so on, but it's an uphill climb. They are all members of the FitzHenrys since they came here in the 1600s. My late husband was inordinately proud of them, especially him.' She smiled, indicating a painting of a man dressed in a long cloak with an ermine collar and carrying a huge sword.

'They apparently resisted every attempt made by the British crown to force them to convert from Catholicism to Protestantism. They were threatened with their lands being confiscated and all sorts but ultimately the crown knew that the FitzHenrys were both powerful and popular and to alienate them would do more harm than good. Besides, they're intermarried with almost all the titled families in

Ireland so they never wanted to open that particular can of worms. But I'm sure Hugo is always going on about his ancestors, he and his father would spend hours discussing this one and that one. I switched off to be honest.'

Liam and Patrick caught Hugo's eye. They knew he was wealthy but this was beyond their wildest imaginings.

'Not really, Mother, it's not the sort of thing one talks about at school.' He smiled, glad to have the upper hand for once. Usually, it was Patrick or Liam explaining how things were to Hugo. No wonder he found their way of life so confusing, this place was so far removed from Chapel Street it might as well have been on another planet.

'Really?' She seemed surprised. 'You and Papa did so love discussing it I would have thought you'd have your friends bored senseless with the FitzHenrys and their exploits.'

As they carried on past rooms, Liam spotted a grand piano and a huge fireplace in one and a massive dining table in another, set for loads of people. They passed a girl about their age, dressed in the same grey-and-black uniform of the other man. She stood back into an alcove to allow them to pass, her eyes downcast.

Hugo stopped beside her, 'Hello, Martha,' he said with a smile.

'Good afternoon, Master Hugo, and welcome home, sir.' She curtseyed.

Hugo winked at her, and she smiled conspiratorially.

Liam suddenly felt very foolish thinking about his mother's efforts to make their house look nice when Hugo came, having good cutlery or using paper napkins. He must have thought, well, Liam couldn't begin to imagine what he must have thought.

At the end of a corridor, Hugo's mother opened another enormous door and entered a room decorated in various shades of yellow and gold. Huge windows overlooked another garden, full of roses this time, and heavy drapes on either side were held back with what looked like golden ropes. Hugo was right that St Bart's was a little bit bigger but that's where the similarities ended. Everything in St Bart's was worn and sparse, hard surfaces and functional furniture. This place looked like a palace that he had seen pictures of in a story book.

On a side table was a silver tea pot and delicate china cups and a huge plate of pastries and sandwiches. Hugo descended on the plate happily.

'Mrs O'Brien's scones, oh how I've missed them,' he said, slathering one in butter, jam and cream before even the tea was served.

The man they called Patterson appeared and poured.

'If you were this slow at St Bart's, you'd go hungry!' Hugo teased them as they stood, unsure of what to do.

The scones and little sandwiches were delicious and the tea was welcome after the long journey. The butler gave them each a plate and they helped themselves.

'Thank you, Patterson. So, Liam, you first, tell me all about yourself.' Mrs FitzHenry fixed him with a quizzical eye. Liam couldn't help but feel he was being tested to see if he was a suitable friend.

'Well,' he began, determined to give a good account of himself. He tried to imagine his father was sitting beside him, the thought gave him confidence. 'I'm from Cork city, I live just down the hill from school, we both do,' he added, nodding in Patrick's direction. 'I live with my mother, but I do have an older brother and three older sisters. They've all left home now, though.'

'And Hugo tells me that your father sadly has passed away, also?' she asked.

'Yes, he was over in England, working, and he was in an accident.' Liam still found the words hard to say.

'That's dreadful, how tragic for your family. You must miss him. And how about you, Patrick?' She smiled, turning her attention away from Liam. It felt like a bit of the light was gone from the room.

'I live across the road from Liam, his mam and mine are friends. My father is alive, more's the pity,' Patrick added sardonically, and Liam watched Hugo's mother for a reaction.

She burst out laughing. 'Oh, Patrick, you are funny! Hugo did mention something about him in one of his letters.' Hugo went puce with embarrassment. Bad as Mr Lynch was, he didn't want Patrick to think that he discussed his friend's private family business in his letters home.

Patrick didn't mind. Everyone knew what Joe Lynch was like anyway, there was no point in trying to hide it. He gave Hugo a grin to indicate everything was fine.

'And your mother?' she went on. 'What is she like?' She leaned forward in her chair, anxious to hear the latest instalment from the Lynch family.

Patrick seemed to relax then, Mrs FitzHenry seemed fascinated with him.

'Ah, Mam is great, she's got a lot to put up with, but she does her best for us. She works very hard,' he added.

'Well, your father may be a little trying at times, but he must be a handsome man to have produced such a son.'

Patrick held her gaze as she smiled a funny smile at him. Liam was bewildered with what was going on, but one thing was clear, Patrick was definitely Hugo's mother's favourite of the two new visitors. He knew Patrick was better looking than him; females of all ages it would seem were drawn to him. Sometimes, Liam wished he looked more like his friend, tall and muscular with almost-black hair and skin that tanned easily in the summer. His dark-green eyes held Hugo's mother's gaze. Liam would have been mortified if she'd looked at him like that, but Patrick was used to it. The girls always stopped to look at them, whispering to each other as they walked home from school, and Liam knew for certain it wasn't him they were interested in. Patrick smiled and flirted with them a bit, though if his mother knew, she'd murder him. He even met up with a girl called Josie Quinn down in the park a few weekends ago. Liam listened to the details of the kissing that went on with mixed emotions. On one level, he was fascinated by the whole idea, but he couldn't help feeling that he was losing his friend to a world he knew nothing about. Apparently, a friend of Josie's thought he was nice, according to Patrick anyway, but Liam wasn't interested. He couldn't understand what was so great about girls. Con, and now Patrick, seemed to be always going on about them, and who was nice looking and who wasn't. Anyway, he'd have no idea what to say to one, and as for the kissing business, that filled him with terror.

Mrs FitzHenry chatted on, mostly to Patrick and Hugo while Liam took in the surroundings. He knew from the way he went on that Hugo was in a whole other league from them, but this house was beyond even the regular speculation he and Patrick indulged in before the visit. Everyone at St Bart's wore a uniform and while Hugo's was brand new and not a hand-me-down as his and Patrick's, everyone looked more or less the same. Hugo always had money for the tuck shop as well and was really generous to his two friends, buying them exactly what he got for himself. He seemed so grateful for the weekly visits to Liam's house and was thrilled when Mrs Lynch could come in after dinner on her way home from her cleaning jobs to have a cup of tea with them before Hugo went back to school. He chatted so easily with them all, fascinated with the details of their lives and never once looking down his nose. It seemed incredible that he would come from a place like this. He even started peppering his speech with Cork slang, calling his mother his mam and adopting the sing-song accent of the city. Liam noticed it often but, unlike Patrick, didn't tease him about it.

Liam watched Hugo soak up the atmosphere of the home he so clearly loved. He saw his gaze land on a framed photograph on a side table as his mother chatted with Patrick about the priests in St Bart's. It was modest in its proportions unlike the other huge portraits and hunting scenes, and it was of a man in a military uniform. He was undoubtedly Hugo's father—he had the same baby face and blond hair—and even though he looked serious in the photo, his vivid blue eyes and the laughter lines on his face still made him look cheerful. He could see the pain in his friend's eyes as he looked at the photo and knew exactly how he felt. He'd love a photo of Daddy in a frame like that. Mammy said it was her only regret that they couldn't afford a photographer on their wedding day. Especially now, after everything that happened. He wished Mammy had a lovely picture of Daddy to put on the mantelpiece. No one in the family had a camera so there were none in existence except a group one at a wedding a few years ago. Daddy and Mammy were in the back row so it was hard to distinguish his features. Liam kept it beside his bed anyway, it was better than nothing.

Mrs FitzHenry rose to go. 'Now, gentlemen, I'm so sorry, but I must leave you. I have to attend a village committee meeting about fundraising for the church roof. If William were alive, he'd just write them a cheque, but one has to be so careful not to tread on toes and suchlike. He was so much better at dealing with people than me. But then, he was Irish and understood them better. I don't think I have quite the same touch. Still, one must try. Hugo, I'm trusting you to be the perfect host, show the boys around and Patterson will ensure you have everything you need. If there's anything we can do to make your stay more comfortable, please don't hesitate to ask. Hugo has often told me how kind you both have been to him and how your mothers have shown him such hospitality. I really am grateful. Perhaps we could all meet the next time I am in Cork. It would be lovely to put faces to the names as it were.'

Liam and Patrick must have looked appalled at the prospect of Lily Auden-FitzHenry visiting the small terraced houses under the Goldie Fish because Hugo started laughing.

'Excellent idea, Mother, we'll arrange it,' he said with a grin, enjoying his friends' discomfort.

She kissed each of them on the cheek once more and swept out of the room.

Left alone in the morning room with his friends, Liam relaxed for the first time since he left home.

'I can tell you now, Hugo boy. If you ever bring your mam to my house, my mam would need an ambulance for the shock so don't do it to her!' Patrick was only half-joking.

'Don't worry, she never goes to Cork. She's biding her time till I get back here to run the place, and she'll be off back to London. She's a city girl, my mother, hates country life and while she has done her best, out of respect to my father, she can't wait to escape.'

'Well, I hope you're sure because no amount of polishing or cleaning would bring my place up to standard. Jays Hugo, this is some gaff you have!' Patrick joked. 'We knew you were loaded, but we'd no idea that you really were the Lord of the Manor! I can't imagine what you must think of our houses, coming out of this place. We'd never have asked you if we'd known, sure we wouldn't, Liam?' Patrick nudged him to play along.

'Lord no, and there was my poor mam pulling out the good forks for Hugo was coming! Seriously though, are you really a lord or something?' Liam smiled.

'An earl, actually, it's a hereditary title so I became Earl of Drummond when my father died. Not something that I want bandied about school, though. They think I'm enough of a posh git, as you two might say, already.' Hugo smiled. 'Now, do you two want the tour of the old pile or not?'

They followed Hugo into more rooms than they could count, each one decorated beautifully and filled with antiques and paintings. Then he took them outside to the stables where horses looked suspiciously out of their stalls.

'Would you like to have a go?' Hugo asked.

'Of what? Riding them?' Patrick was incredulous, but Liam could see he would love to. He hoped that Patrick wouldn't want to and then they could just take a walk, they looked huge.

'If you like. What do you think, Liam?' Hugo asked.

'I dunno, Hugo. I never was even near a horse before. They look a bit...' Liam didn't want to look like a sissy in front of his friends but he was terrified.

'I'll give you Delia, she's lovely, and she won't run away on you or anything. I learned to ride on her and never fell off, not even once.'

Hugo led them into a room that was full of shiny leather things for saddling horses. One by one, he handed all manner of straps and saddles to the boys and proceeded to expertly put them on the three horses. The grey one, called Delia, while the smallest of the three was still gigantic. She stood quietly while Hugo tacked her up. He gave them each a pair of boots into which Liam and Patrick tucked their trousers as Hugo showed them. Leading the horse over to a low wall, he instructed Liam how to get up on the horse's back. He scrambled up, trying to hide his terror and once he was seated, he realised how far away the ground was.

'Don't worry, Liam, we'll go very slowly and, honestly, she's a sweetheart, just grab a bit of her mane as well as the reins and keep your heels down and your legs around her and you'll be fine.' Hugo chuckled at his discomfiture and went to set Patrick up on a big black horse that kept doing something strange with his nostrils, like he was trying to blow his nose. He wasn't as happy as Delia to stand quietly so he pranced and whinnied as Hugo got all the things on him. Patrick didn't look one bit scared and Liam wondered, not for the first time, at their friendship. They were thrown together by the scholarship, and the whole experience of school had cemented their relationship, but Patrick was so much tougher, braver, and more adventurous than he was. He supposed he had to be, with his father like he was. Mrs Lynch didn't watch him the way Mammy watched him, and sometimes he envied all the freedom his friend had. He did well at school and was determined to get a good job and get himself and his family away from his father, and Liam knew he would do it. For all his bravado though, Patrick was kind, he often talked about Daddy and how great he was, and he always included Liam when he was chatting to older lads or even girls. He was kind of a hero in school since they won the Harty cup, all due to Patrick's winning point in the dying seconds of the game. Liam was on the team, as well, and he did his best, but his ability was born out of sheer slogging rather than natural flair. Daddy always said that one day Patrick would be a brilliant hurler, just like his father was before the drink took hold of him, Liam remembered, smiling with satisfaction as they lifted the cup—his father had been right.

Eventually, Patrick was up on his horse, and he walked him over to where Liam and Delia stood.

'What ya think of this, Liam boy? Aren't we a right pair of toffs up on our horses?' He was laughing with the exhilaration of it all.

'I'm scared stiff. I haven't a clue what to do. If this thing takes off, I'll lose my life.' Liam didn't need to pretend around Patrick.

'Sure, I'm the same but 'tis a bit of craic, yerra we'll go slow and sure what's the worst that can happen? You'll fall off! You've had more belts and flakes playing hurling. You'll be grand.'

Hugo came up beside them, having leapt up effortlessly on an even more enormous grey horse that kept going backwards and then forwards. Hugo seemed oblivious to it though and chatted easily. Liam thought he had never seen a more malevolent looking creature in his life.

'Righto, are we ready?' Hugo seemed so relaxed, so at home in the saddle. 'I think we'll go down via the pleasure gardens and round through the woods. Try to stay on the path as we go down though because the gardener will go mad if there are hoofmarks on the lawn. Once we get to the woods, we can do what we like. There might be a few old trees down if you want to try a jump or two.'

Liam's horrified face at such a prospect caused the other two to burst out laughing as Hugo went out in front, followed by Patrick, and finally himself. The horse walked calmly enough and once or twice Liam even looked up to see where he was going. He tried to remember all the instructions, to keep his heels down, his hands on the withers, which he learned was the end of her neck where it met her back, and his legs around her belly, but not too tightly because apparently that's the sign to the horse that you want to go faster, which he absolutely did not. The lawn was an expanse of the greenest green Liam had ever seen. There were flower beds with riotous colour dancing on the breeze all around the perimeter of the gardens and a few ornamental trees here and there. Beyond the lawns was the expanse of ocean, filling the vista from left to right. He thought it was the most beautiful place he'd ever seen.

On they walked and eventually they were in the woods, where the sun dappled the leaves and created shadows through the canopy.

'My father and I would come here all the time when I was younger,' Hugo remarked as he fell in beside Liam.

'Here, Hugo, this horse wants to go faster I'd say, he's pulling mad to go on, will I let him?' Patrick yelled back.

Hugo laughed and called out, 'Let's start slowly, shall we? You've only been up on him five minutes. There's a meadow through the next gate on the left, you can go in there but keep him at a trot.'

Liam watched amazed as his friend raised one hand in the air like they'd seen in the *Lone Ranger* comics and took off down the path.

'Will he be all right?' he asked Hugo, trying to hide his worry.

'Well, Diablo doesn't like rough handling so if he's unhappy with Mr Lynch's approach, he won't hesitate to make sure they part company. He'll be fine on the straight, it's the corners where you can take a tumble. Don't worry though, he'll be fine, that's a soft meadow with nothing to injure him if he does fall.

Liam and Hugo walked on and stopped inside the gate of the field. There was Patrick, and while he looked tense, he seemed to be managing. As he approached the corner, Liam could hardly bear to look, Diablo cantered on and Patrick wobbled. His foot came out of the stirrup and they watched with concern as their friend grabbed round the horses neck. Amazingly though, he didn't fall off but righted himself and raised his arm in a whoop of delight. Patrick was clearly cut out for horse riding.

'Well, he's not exactly graceful but I think Diablo and he have an understanding. Do you want to get down for a bit? Have a look around? There's a little beach over there,' Hugo suggested.

Liam was relieved to get off Delia, despite her docile nature, and dismounted as Hugo showed him. His legs felt strange as he walked to the secluded small beach through the trees.

'Imagine having your own private beach and a wood and all those gardens, you're so lucky, Hugo!'

Hugo led him to a seat overlooking the sea. No building could be seen and the only sound was the warm breeze in the trees and the odd caw-caw of a seagull.

'I suppose so, but it's just what we always had. Martha and I, you met her, used to play here all the time, swimming and jumping off those trees up there. My father made us a swing and we used to swing out over the water as far as we could and then we'd jump in. He helped me make a camp as well, further up the woods, I spent a lot of time in there, on my own, just thinking about things. I remember sitting there for hours after Mother told me I had to go to St Bart's. I know it could have been worse, I suppose, most chaps like me end up in England at school, but I was terrified and miserable. I just wanted my pap...my father,' he corrected himself, embarrassed.

'It's okay, I called my father Daddy, you called yours Papa. It's fine. I suppose if they'd lived, we'd be grown out of it by now, but they didn't so I always think of him as Daddy and you should go on thinking of yours as Papa if that's how you remember him. What was he like?' Liam was absentmindedly building a tower of the small pebbles on the beach.

'Nice, kind, funny. Always joking and laughing, with Mama especially. He could make her laugh so much. She gave up a lot to marry him, you know? She came from an even grander place than this, don't tell Patrick for goodness sake, but my grandfather on my mother's side is a marquis and staunch Church of England, of course. When Mama said she wanted to marry an Irish Catholic they nearly went mad, even though Papa had a title as well. He was Earl of Drummond, it's the name of this area. Papa always joked he never knew which part they hated more, the Irish part or the Catholic part. Anyway, she defied her father, and none of the family really speaks to us. When Papa was off fighting in the war, they wrote once I believe, wishing him well and maybe there was a bit of an olive branch there, but Mama can be quite trenchant, and she didn't forgive them for their rejection of her and vicariously, of us. Then Papa came home. But as I said, he was never really well after being injured during the war, so he never really went back to his regiment, but they ran the estate here together and looked after the people that relied on us for their livelihoods. They were so happy together. I thought it would go on forever. When he died, Mama just went to pieces.'

Hugo's voice was so sad, Liam knew exactly how he felt.

'Mine were the same. When I was small, I used to listen at night and hear them talking and laughing downstairs. My daddy was very funny too, and he could make Mammy laugh even if she was cross over something. One time, I remember creeping downstairs and looking in and seeing them, Mammy sitting on Daddy's lap, and they were just staring into the fire. He was rubbing her hair and they looked so happy. I keep that image in my mind. I told you before about the trouble with the woman next door, things could have been so different.' Liam surprised himself; normally, he didn't talk about it at all.

'I'm sure they loved each other to the end, Liam. Your mother always talks so fondly of him.' He paused, 'Do you think you'll ever get married?' Hugo stared out to sea as he spoke.

'No. I don't think so, anyway,' Liam answered.

'Why not?'

'I don't know. I just can't imagine it. I...I just can't see how I'd want to...' Liam struggled to put words on how he felt.

'Get married or have a girlfriend? I know. Though Patrick seems to have loads of girls after him.' Hugo smiled and looked sideways at Liam.

'Yeah, he does, he's always going on about girls these days, and my brother Con is the same. I don't know. I'm just not that interested. I think maybe I have a vocation, and then God takes away that bit of you that wants to go with girls.' Liam knew it probably sounded stupid, but he didn't mind in front of Hugo.

'Well, if it's what you want, I think you would make a truly splendid priest. I definitely don't have a vocation, and anyway, someone needs to take over this place. I've known that was my destiny since I was born. I hoped that maybe I'd get a few years to be free, you know? To live my life, somewhere far away from here, but there's nobody else, so that's not going to happen. Mama does her best, but she's just holding the fort as it were, watching the calendar until I come home and release her. Then I'll be here, all on my own.' Hugo sounded like he had the weight of the world on his shoulders.

'But you, with all this, and you're a nice person too, you'll have girls queuing up to marry you, surely?'

Hugo looked at him, his face a mask. He looked deeply into Liam's eyes as if weighing something up. The seconds ticked by, and Liam was about to apologise for interfering in his friend's private life, maybe he shouldn't have assumed he could speak freely.

Hugo's voice broke the heavy silence, his voice cracking with emotion as he spoke quietly. 'That's the problem, Liam. It's not girls I'm interested in.'

'So what do you mean?' Liam asked, perplexed. He didn't want to be a priest and he didn't want to get married, what else was there?

The silence crackled between the two friends.

Hugo's eyes glistened with moisture as a possibility dawned on Liam. They locked their gaze, and Liam could see the pleading there. Hugo was begging him not to reject him, not to turn away appalled.

As he tried to process what he thought Hugo might mean, Liam was shocked. He couldn't believe that Hugo would just come out and say it. Maybe he got it wrong, he'd heard whispers from older lads in school about boys who went with other boys, or men, but surely Hugo wasn't like that?

He knew it was a mortal sin, that to engage in any carnal activities, even with girls, was an occasion of sin, but to have intimate relations with another man was a most grievous sin. In fact, when he first heard about it, he was sure they were making it up. What on earth would possess a man to want to be with another man in that way? He had never really allowed himself to think those thoughts, knowing that God could see into your mind and knew instantly what any person was thinking.

'I've shocked you,' Hugo said quietly.

'No. Well, I don't really know...I don't know anything about it, but...' Liam was torn between wanting desperately to reassure his friend but to distance himself from the conversation. He felt his face redden with embarrassment. What Hugo was telling him contravened every law Liam knew, the law of the land, the law of society and, most importantly, the law of God.

'You won't say anything, will you?'

'Of course not. No, of course, but...well...how do you know? That you're not like other lads...I mean maybe you're not...I don't really know what Con and Patrick are on about with girls either, but I'm not...'

'That I'm one of those? I've always known. I don't think you become homosexual.'

Liam flinched at the word as Hugo went on, his voice choked with emotion.

'I think you're born like that, I've prayed and begged and pleaded with God to take it away. I don't want to be like this, but I can't help it. I just can't. Maybe, it gets passed on in families. I have an uncle, my father's brother, my uncle Piers lives in Paris, nobody really mentions him, but Papa kept in touch with him. When Papa died, I read one of the letters he wrote, telling about his friend. He lives with a Frenchman. To the outside world they're flatmates but...I think, reading between the lines, he might be...'

Liam could feel his heart beating in his chest and sweat prickled his skin. He had no idea what to say. He knew he should tell Hugo that these thoughts were the work of the devil, that the devil was working within him and that he must cast him out, but he couldn't make the words come out. Hugo and Patrick were his best friends, as different as chalk and cheese, but he loved them both dearly. He couldn't hurt Hugo by saying he thought he was a sinner, but could he condone the way of life Hugo described?

'But...that's not the life you want though, is it? Like, not really?' Liam was doing his best to stay calm, but he was floundering.

'I don't know what kind of life I want. I don't know if I want to live at all to be honest.' Hugo was barely audible.

The statement shocked Liam. Surely Hugo couldn't be considering taking his own life. Trying to put aside his horror and doubts, he looked at his dear friend. He had to stop him even going down that line of thought.

'If you didn't have to take this place over, if you could live another life, is that what you'd want?' he asked gently, hardly believing they were having this conversation.

'If...if...if. Life can't be lived on if, can it? To live that life, I don't know, apart from the sin, it's illegal, so you'd live like a fugitive, and it would break my mother's heart. The estate would fall into rack and ruin, so no, I'll marry someone suitable, I suppose, but I hate the thought. The idea of living here, with a woman, having a family, well…it makes me shudder. And some poor girl, getting stuck with me, thinking she was getting someone normal, who would love her properly and have children and all of that, but instead she gets me. I don't think I can do it to someone.'

Liam heard the anguish in Hugo's voice and watched with horror the tears flowing down his face. He wondered what his father would do in this situation. He would have been kind, he decided, he wasn't as religious as Mammy was in the sense of following the priests blindly, he would have tried to understand. Liam put his arm around his friend's shoulder. Hugo cried and his body shook with the pain of it all, and Liam just comforted him. When the sobs subsided, he reached for his handkerchief and handed it to Hugo who blew his nose and wiped his face roughly. Hugo then got up and dipped the handkerchief in the sea and wiped his face with the cold salty water. When he was finished, he came back and walked straight towards his horse.

Patrick was on the path ahead of them when they remounted. Hugo trotted on masterfully, his head bowed so Patrick wouldn't see the evidence of his tears, and Liam and Delia plodded away. He wished he could catch up to Hugo, just to reassure him that his revelation didn't affect their friendship, but he had no idea how to make Delia go faster, and anyway, he was afraid to try.

'Ah lads, this horse riding is great craic!' Patrick announced, falling in beside Liam. 'I nearly came off a few times, but I managed to stay on. I could get used to this, Liam boy! Maybe yourself and myself will get a couple of auld nags and tie them up to the church railings, what d'ya think Father Mac would make of that?' He laughed. His good humour was infectious and soon all three friends were chatting happily again.

The two-week visit to Greyrock was an endless stream of new adventures, billiards, deer stalking—though they never shot anything—boating and swimming, archery, and they even tried fencing—activities Patrick and Liam only saw in books. They ate quail and venison and were stuffed to within an inch of their lives with cake and desserts of all sorts. No wonder Hugo was traumatised by the basic fare at St Bart's, Liam thought as he reluctantly turned down another helping of Tiramisu. He couldn't wait to describe everything to his mother, she'd never believe it. They parted for the summer with heavy hearts. Hugo was going to London to join his mother, from where they were embarking on a 'Grand Tour of Europe' as he called it, visiting various cities and meeting up with other families like themselves.

Patrick and Liam were going home to Chapel Street.

CHAPTER 13

1974

The boys sat transfixed in the sunlit classroom oblivious to the distant sounds of a hurling match outside, all eyes were on the guest speaker. The huge Brother Aiden in his brown robes and sandals was keeping the entire class captivated as he spoke about his village in Mali. In advance of the talk, Brother Jerome had asked each boy to locate Mali on the map in their geography books. The order ran a school out there and each year St Bart's ran a big fundraiser, so the name of the village of Sangha was as familiar to them as Chapel Street or Blarney Street, but to see pictures, and to hear firsthand what life was like in this place so far away was mesmerising.

'...after the rainy season we have to replaster the walls of the huts, they are only covered in a mud mixture so the rain washes it away.' The brother pressed a button on the new slide projector and the image was beamed up onto the white wall of the classroom. Tiny huts, it seemed inconceivable that whole families could dwell within.

'This is a picture of the council building, the village chief and the elders meet there to discuss various matters but as you can see, there is only room to crouch. It means if anyone gets too angry, he'll bump his head and that will knock the fury out of him…' The class laughed and urged the boys in the front to keep their heads down.

'…this next one is of the chief. He's a very nice man, and he lives almost all his life in his house, the villagers supply him with food and anything else he needs. He is the spokesman for the community, and he also settles disputes. It's a hereditary position so his father was chief, and his before that, and his son will take over when the chief dies. It's a hard life out there; the chief is only in his forties, I would think, though he looks much older…'

The boys were fascinated as they gazed at the photograph of the chief who was squatting down outside another of the mud constructions. His face looked like the pictures the brother had shown of the dry river beds during the times of drought in the village. He had a silver beard and wore a very ornate pillbox-style hat, and what looked like pyjamas. Brother Aiden spoke with such enthusiasm and passion for his village it was infectious.

He showed them pictures of a place called the circumcision cave, where only men and boys entered for the annual circumcision rite. The entire class winced as he explained the process. He explained how important the crocodile was to the people of the village, how they believed that a crocodile led the first settlers there when they had searched for water. Antelope, hyenas, elephants, gazelles, all were features of the amazingly dry and flat landscape, as different from the lush green fields of Ireland as it was possible to be.

Liam could have listened to him all day. It sounded so exotic and so exciting. He tried to visualise himself out there, converting Africans to the word of God but also helping in practical ways, setting up schools, medical clinics, and making life better for the people of Mali. He was gearing up for his Leaving Certificate Exam in a few weeks and had made up his mind to apply for the priesthood. He prayed every night that the Lord would send him a sign of his vocation, but he still wasn't sure. Not that he was unsure if he wanted to dedicate his life to the service of God and his church, on that he was absolutely convinced, it was just that he felt so ordinary, so unsaintly.

All the priests he knew seemed to exude a kind of goodness, a peace, something otherworldly, and he felt such a mere mortal.

Brother Aiden was finished with the photos and was opening the floor for questions. Hugo raised his hand immediately.

'Brother, how do the local people take to Catholicism when what they are used to is a very different system?'

The priest paused for a moment as if weighing up if the question was impertinent or was in some way disrespectful to the Catholic faith. He was mistrustful of Hugo's accent but his innocent open face, blue eyes, and blond curls, which had not faded as he grew older, convinced the priest that the question was genuine.

'Well,' he began, 'the people of Sangha are grateful that we have brought the word of God to them, and they see the error of the pagan beliefs of the past. As well as building a church, we have set up a school, a well, and a medical clinic, so they know that our intentions are honourable and good. They did, at first, cling to the old ways, the worship of animals and the movements of the sun and the moon, and other ignorant beliefs, but we have brought them into the light of Christ's love, and for that, they are eternally grateful. Any other questions?'

Several boys raised their hands, and the brother patiently answered their questions about how they got around the village, if he ever saw a lion, and why they wore such unusual clothing.

Liam glanced at Patrick, who had lost interest in the talk and was more interested in the hurling match outside by now. They were playing a Munster colleges final at the weekend so it was all he could think about. There had been some problem with Patrick's selection for the team a few weeks ago. To everyone's amazement, Patrick seemed to have been dropped even though he was the best player the school had.

When Liam read the team from the school notice board the week before, he went to find his friend.

'What's going on? Are you injured?' he asked Patrick when he eventually found him in the library.

'Nope. It's Xavier. I knew he'd wait for the exact moment it would hurt me most, and so he has,' Patrick said bitterly

'What? Why? I don't understand. Why would he drop you, sure you're the best we have, we won't stand a chance against Midleton without you. Sure, everyone knows that.' Liam was perplexed.

Patrick led Liam outside to the handball alley behind the library, where he lit a cigarette.

'Remember when we were in First Year?'

Liam nodded, 'Yeah, what about it?'

'Well, remember Hugo used to come in with bruises and some days we knew he had been crying?' Patrick looked into the distance and exhaled the cigarette smoke slowly.

'Yeah, we thought the Clancy twins were bullying him, but he'd never say...'

'It wasn't just the Clancy twins,' Patrick said. 'And it wasn't just bullying.'

'What are you on about? How do you know?' Liam was confused.

'One of the fellas on the team, he left since, remember Colm Kelleher? Well, he left because Xavier was interfering with him; he used to come into the dorm at night. Anyway, Colm, he told his old man, and they took him out of the school. Well, before he left, he told me that Xavier was doing the same to Hugo.'

The silence hung between them, heavy and loaded. Liam felt sick, how could this be true? Poor Hugo.

'Are you sure? Like, I heard before, and Daddy kind of warned me about anyone doing that to me years ago, but Xavier...the principal of the school...I can't believe it.' Liam was shocked and horrified.

'Well, believe it. I didn't know what to do. I knew Hugo would deny everything if I asked him, so I waited for evening study and I stayed behind afterwards. I was going to tell Father Aquinas, but he's a priest too and I didn't know him all that well back then. I know he helped us when you battered my auld fella with the hurley, but that was different. Xavier was just packing up to go, and I went up to him and said that I knew what he was doing and that if he didn't stop, I'd tell.'

Liam was speechless. The bravery of his friend astounded him. Xavier was terrifying and, to add to it, Patrick was a scholarship boy. Xavier didn't think he even had a right to attend St Bart's.

'I'd never have had the guts to do that,' he said quietly.

'Well, I was bricking it, I thought he might throw me out but it was a gamble. The business with Colm Kelleher had only just happened so maybe he was on a warning from the bishop or something. Anyway, I couldn't bear to think of poor Hugo having to put up with that.'

'Did it stop?' Liam whispered, horrible images crowding his mind.

'Yeah, I think so, he gave up doing the night duty in the school the next day. I never said it to Hugo, and you mustn't either. He'd hate it if we knew. Sometimes, I think I should have told on him, gone to Father Aquinas about it, but no one would believe me.'

Liam considered the revelation Hugo made that first summer they went to Greyrock. They never discussed the issue again, but Liam wondered if the experiences he had in St Bart's made him think he was a homosexual. He shuddered with revulsion at the thought of poor Hugo being interfered with by Xavier. It wasn't the first time he'd heard of it, but he couldn't believe that someone in such an important position as a school principal and a priest of God would behave in such a debased way.

'So, he bided his time, waited till he could get his revenge, and now he has. He knows I really want to win the cup, on my last year, he knows how hard I've worked and kept up with my studies, as well, and this is how he's going to hurt me.' Patrick sounded heartbroken.

'But why isn't he still afraid you'll tell?'

Patrick shrugged, 'I suppose he thinks it's all over and done with, it was years ago, and anyway, as I said, who's going to believe me? Hugo would probably deny it, and Colm Kelleher is long gone. If I said anything now, he'd just make out I was bitter at being dropped from the team, and I was making it up.'

Liam felt sorry for his friend. He'd worked so hard. Even though he had natural talent, he was always the first to training and the last to leave. He was captain, so he made sure that every lad played to his best ability. Even the latest in his long line of girlfriends had to take a back seat. The past few weeks had been very hard on Patrick, his mother was in the hospital—she was saying she slipped down the stairs, but he confided in Liam and Hugo that his father had come in drunk and assaulted her. Patrick was at training at the time, he would never do it if his son was at home, and the girls had been terrified. They slept in Liam's house while Mrs Lynch was in hospital. Liam talked Patrick out of finding his father and giving him such a hiding he'd never recover. While he could understand his friend's frustration and rage, he convinced him that the only person to be hurt would be Patrick himself. And now, to be denied his chance to win, all because he was brave enough to stand up for Hugo seemed so unfair.

'Maybe it is Xavier you should be threatening to batter, not your father.' Liam smiled ruefully. 'Though you'd only hurt yourself in the end.'

'Oh no, Liam, you're wrong there, he'd be hurt. If I was left at him now, either of them, in fact, they'd definitely be hurt,' Patrick said darkly.

Liam watched his friend gaze out the window at the team putting the finishing touches to their training for the big match at the weekend. Nothing would convince Xavier to let Patrick play. He was the main selector and the principal, the decision was the talk of the school, and nobody would dare challenge Xavier.

The brother finished his talk and the boys packed up their bags to go to afternoon study. Normally, Liam was studious, definitely the most diligent of the three of them, but today he couldn't concentrate. He looked at Hugo, who was doodling on his page, lost in a world of his own. He wondered if they would ever discuss what had happened, it seemed unlikely, but Liam understood so much more about his friend now.

It was, as Hugo pointed out regularly to Liam when he admonished him for poor grades, irrelevant what he got in the Leaving, his future was marked out anyway. He had no choices, he couldn't decide to go out and help the poor people of Mali, or to study medicine and save lives, or do engineering and build bridges, or whatever, his future was Greyrock and marriage, and that was all there was to it. Hugo loved his home and felt proud to be the next in line to take care of it, but the fear that he would be the last Earl of Drummond weighed very heavily on him. Whenever they had the conversation, Liam could see the despair hidden behind his friend's devil-may-care attitude. He wished there was something he could do, some way of easing the huge weight Hugo felt was on his shoulders, but it seemed he was right, that was going to be his future, like it or not.

Father Xavier was supervising study, and the attitude he had towards Liam and Patrick hadn't shown any signs of improvement over the years. Liam never knew the reason he kept the worst of his wrath for Patrick until last week. He never lost an opportunity to make Patrick feel small and constantly referred to his scholarship status, frequently explaining to him in front of the whole class that it was only due to the kindness of the order that he was allowed into the school at all. Despite the constant needling, Patrick never rose to the bait and accepted all the jibes, though Liam knew inside he was seething. Knowing what he knew now, he admired Patrick's forbearance even more.

The constant singling out of Patrick had made Liam feel worse because he was a scholarship boy as well, but Xavier didn't seem to have such a set against Liam as much as poor Patrick. He knew his friend could come across as cocky and a bit of a messer sometimes, but he wasn't like that really. He was loyal and honest, and he and Hugo were the best friends anyone could wish for. He wondered if Patrick suspected anything about Hugo believing he was a homosexual, but if he did, he never said. However, he had stopped teasing him about the 'lord and lady' stuff he used to go on with. In so many ways, Liam hated the idea of leaving St Bart's, not seeing Hugo and Patrick every day, not having lessons. He would miss them so much. He knew he'd see Patrick around the place, he was hoping to get a start in an accountant's office in town, maybe do exams at night and train as a bookkeeper. There was no question of higher education for him, the money wasn't there.

Liam prayed fervently that he would be accepted as a scholarship student to the seminary in Maynooth. It took seven years to train for the priesthood, and there was no way Mammy would have the money to pay for that. She just had the widow's pension, and Con and the girls gave her what they could as well. Over the years, things had improved with his siblings. They no longer blamed her for Daddy's death, though they rarely came home to visit. That time when they were a united, happy family died with their father, and it would never again be the same. The twins were both going out with fellas in Dublin, and they seemed all right when they brought them home one time to meet Mammy, but a bit brash and loud. Then, Liam thought, so were Molly and Annie. All makeup and short skirts, Mammy nearly choked when she saw the cut of them, but she daren't say anything in case all the bad feeling flared up again. Liam knew she was mortified at the state of them though as they got done up to go dancing with the boys, hating the thought of the neighbours seeing how they turned out. Kate was still in England and she wrote once a week, telling them about her job in the county council over there and the girls she shared a flat with. She was still doing a line with the same English fella, but they'd never met him. Mammy loved receiving her letters and when one arrived, she'd make a pot of tea and a plate of whatever she'd baked and they'd sit down and read it together.

It was all going to be different, living away from home if he got in. Mammy would really miss him, he knew that, but the idea of a son training for the priesthood would take the edge off her loneliness. He hadn't told her yet that he applied, in case he didn't get in. She'd had enough sadness and disappointment in her life, he thought. There was a scholarship exam straight after the Leaving, and he had to have several interviews with different members of the hierarchy to see if he was a suitable candidate. Most importantly, he had to be recommended by the seminary. Father Aquinas would try his best to put in a good word for him, he knew that, but Father Xavier was the principal of the seminary and he'd have the final say.

His reverie was interrupted by the arrival of Father Aquinas into the study hall. He rarely entered the secondary school, so his arrival caused a stir of interest among the gathered boys. Father Aquinas spoke to Father Xavier for a moment.

'Liam Tobin, get your bags and things please,' Father Xavier said. All eyes turned to Liam. What had he done? There was only one reason a priest came to get a boy out of class or study and that was if they were in trouble. Reddening under sixty pairs of curious eyes, he threw his Irish book and copy into his bag and followed Father Aquinas out the door.

A thought struck him, maybe something bad had happened at home. Since Daddy's death, Liam was acutely aware of how life can be sailing along and then destroyed unexpectedly. If something bad had happened, they would send Father Aquinas. He was a constant presence in their lives, checking in to see how they were doing and calling to their mothers as well. He took a personal interest in Liam and Patrick. The night of Joe Lynch and the whiskey was never mentioned again but since then, Liam trusted him implicitly. He really saved their bacon that night. Liam didn't want to criticise Patrick's actions regarding Hugo, but he would have gone to Father Aquinas. Walking behind him out of the hall, he wondered how much Father Aquinas knew.

His heart was thumping loudly in his chest as he followed the priest to the entrance of the monastery. He'd not been in there since the day he and Patrick were told to choose their books for first year and had lemonade and apple tart. That was nearly six years ago.

The priest opened the door and held it open, 'After you,' he said.

Liam stepped inside and the same aroma assailed his nostrils, instantly transporting him back in time. He stood in the hallway, with its statues in alcoves and fine, polished furniture standing on the dark parquet floor.

'I think the study is free, let's sit in there.' Father Aquinas seemed distant, angry even. Not his usual chatty self at all.

Liam followed him once more, racking his brain thinking why the priest had summoned him, dread filling him.

The study was sumptuously decorated with bookshelves on every wall, wing backed chairs around the fireplace as well as two Chesterfield couches either side of a coffee table. Several vases of fresh flowers were dotted on side tables, and a large oil painting of the founder of the order loomed down at him from over the fireplace. If he wasn't so worried, Liam would have smiled at the sight of the television in the corner, remembering when he told his family about it when he was small. Father Aquinas indicated that he should sit.

'I'm sorry for tearing you away from your studies, especially with the exams so close,' he began, his sonorous tones filling the small room. 'I wanted to discuss something with you.'

Liam wasn't sure if he should speak or not, so he remained silent. Unperturbed, the priest went on, standing with his back to the room, looking out over the grounds. The huge width of his back almost filled the window and his soutane was a little short. It was the longest one available, Liam supposed, not many priests were over six foot four or five. He wondered at the sheer bulk of the man, some adults seemed to shrink as Liam got older and taller, but not so with Father Aquinas, he was huge when they were kids and he was huge now. No wonder he struck the fear of God into the small lads.

'What are your plans?' he asked, turning to face Liam.

'Well…I...em…I was thinking, well hoping really, t-to go for the priesthood.' He stuttered and stammered out of nervousness. Relief slowly seeped through him; it wasn't about something bad happening to Mammy or the family.

'I thought so. We got a letter last week from the admitting office of Maynooth, from a Canon Sheehan, asking if we thought you would be a suitable candidate having received your letter of application. How is it that you never expressed an interest in the clerical life up to this?'

Liam thought for a moment, knowing whatever he said next was going to have a serious influence on his future plans. Honesty was the only option.

'I didn't want to get my mother's hopes up, Father. I'd have to be accepted first, and then I'd have to get another scholarship as well as a nomination from here, so I'm not sure that I'll be able to go. I didn't want her getting all excited about it and then for it not to happen,' he finished in a rush.

'So you want to join the priesthood to please your mother?' Father Aquinas asked imperiously.

'No, Father. I want to be a priest. I pray every night for Jesus to strengthen my vocation, to let the people who need to see it see the potential in me. I want to serve God and his church. I want it more than anything, but I'm afraid I'm not good enough.'

'Why do you want to be a priest? Really, why? You'd have to give up so much that young men nowadays seem to enjoy, socialising, working a job and having a wage, going to dances, meeting girls. Why would you turn your back on all that?' Though the questioning was serious, Liam thought he heard softness in his tone.

'I don't care for any of that, Father. I don't go to dances now and I could if I wanted to. As for a job, well isn't serving God and the people of his church a job? I never had much growing up, so the poverty bit won't be a problem. I've known since I was in first year, but I was afraid to say it…'

'In case those other two buckos you knock about with laughed at you?' The priest was hiding a hint of a grin.

'No, Father, honestly they wouldn't. Neither Hugo nor Patrick wants the religious life, and I suppose they don't understand why I do, really, but they would never mock me over it, they'd support me. I know they would,' Liam spoke with conviction.

'Ye'er an odd partnership that's for sure, but ye seem to be thick as thieves all the same. I wasn't sure young FitzHenry would fit in here at all but he did, and young Lynch is going to make a go of himself as well by all accounts despite the father he has. But you, Mr Tobin, what are we to do with you?'

Liam was unsure what the priest was asking.

'You know there are only academic scholarships available for Maynooth, don't you? And well, Liam, I might as well be honest with you, your teachers aren't confident that you'll make the grade to qualify. I know you've been working very hard and really doing your best, but whether you'd get a scholarship or not, well, I don't know. Father Xavier asked me to talk to you ahead of the interview in Maynooth. I suppose there's no point in putting a young man forward for selection if he hasn't the wherewithal to pay the fees, do you understand?'

Father Aquinas looked uncomfortable. Liam knew he hated

being the one to deliver the bad news. The clock ticked on the mantelpiece as what the priest was saying sank in. Xavier was behind this, he knew it. He probably thought that Patrick and he were in cahoots about the Hugo thing so he was going to punish Patrick by dropping him from the team—no doubt, he wouldn't get much of a reference either—and he was going to block Liam's entry to Maynooth.

'So, Father, does that mean that St Bart's won't recommend me for the priesthood?' he asked quietly, willing the priest to dismiss such a terrible notion.

'Liam, it's not a question of you not being suitable. Personally, I think you'd make a fine priest indeed, but it's not up to me. You haven't the money, or any way of getting the money, so there is not much point in applying and getting your hopes up, and your mother's hopes up. There are scholarships for the brightest and the best, of course, and the order does fund some students, but this year we already have several candidates that the board think might be…' The priest had the good grace to look embarrassed.

'Not scholarship boys, you mean? I see.'

Liam didn't trust himself to say anymore. All his hopes and dreams, everything he prayed for just vanished, it wasn't going to happen. He should have been grateful to get a secondary education; most lads he'd been in the primary with were out working for years or had emigrated. He'd been lulled into a sense of false security by the scholarship, thinking that this life was possible for someone like him, from a background like his. Daddy was right, they were only interested in the lads with plenty of money. Liam knew some of the farmers' sons—with a few bob behind them—would be proposed for the funding, that was just how it worked. The prevailing feeling must have been, you got your secondary education for nothing, don't come with the begging bowl again. Liam knew how Father Xavier thought, and he could almost hear his dismissal. He was too cowardly to deliver the news himself though, sending Father Aquinas to do his dirty work for him.

'Liam, I'm so sorry, I am...maybe the brothers... I know some monasteries in England you could consider, the White Friars in Bristol, for example, they're always looking for young men to join.'

Liam knew that the words sounded hollow. Joining a monastic order of brothers was not the priesthood, but it was the best a boy from Chapel Street could expect.

'I...I'll think about it, Father, thank you.' He fought back the hot tears of bitter disappointment and willed his voice not to betray him. He longed to get away, to run out the door and down the hill and into the city, to run and keep running away from St Bart's, the place that built up his hopes, that made him believe it could really happen, only to crush him.

CHAPTER 14

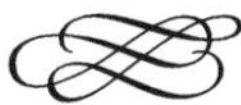

'There he is,' Patrick said. 'Liam! Where've you been? You missed extra Latin. Father Tim is raging; I told him you went home sick...'

Hugo and Patrick plonked down either side of him on the bench beside the River Lee. It was low tide and the muddy riverbed was exposed, showing its haul of twisted metal and tree branches and lots of other unrecognisable detritus gathered by the river as it made its way to the mouth of the harbour. The shadow of St Teresa's Church, with its majestic Golden Fish on the spire, cast its spell as the summer sun hung low in the sky and settled over the city.

'So why didn't you turn up?' Hugo finished.

Liam didn't answer, and he noted the glance shared between his two best friends, something was wrong.

'Liam, what's wrong? Did something happen? Why did Father Aquinas want you?' Patrick asked.

Not trusting himself to speak, he merely nodded. He longed to let it all out, to sob like a child, but he couldn't. The realisation that he would never become a priest washed over him in waves, each one deepening his despair.

'Come on, Liam, you're worrying us now...' Hugo sat beside him and craned to see Liam's face. 'You can tell us, whatever it is.'

Slowly, he told them of his meeting with Father Aquinas. Each word hurting as he spoke.

'Father Xavier won't put me forward, so that's it,' he finished miserably.

Patrick's face said it all, this was Xavier hurting them again, anger and frustration filled the air around him. He caught Liam's eye. They knew they could never say in front of Hugo that Xavier had it in for them because he would be sure to question why, so Patrick changed the subject.

'This is the bench, do you remember? The night we thought we killed my auld lad? Father Aquinas saved our skins that night; he's all right, under it all.' They had shared the story with Hugo but nobody else. 'Isn't it typical of Xavier, though, to send him to tell you, that oily fecker wouldn't even have the guts to tell you himself. 'Twas the same when he dropped me from the team, he got poor old Father Barry to put the notice up. The fellas they're putting forward for Maynooth are his nephews, the Clancy twins, that pair of eejits. I heard them talking about it in the dressing room yesterday, thinking they were alone. I didn't know if you'd be put forward as well so I never said anything.'

Liam noticed Hugo flinch at the mention of their names. The Clancy twins were notorious in the school as bullies, but they were untouchable having Father Xavier as their uncle. Their father was some big shot as well so they were loaded.

'And that other fella, Daly, y'know with the foxy hair? He's a right lick-arse too, no wonder they put them forward. They said his father donated a stained glass window to the monastery so that's why he's getting it.'

Hugo was fuming, 'I hate him. I know it probably shocks you, Liam, but I really do hate Xavier, I always have. How dare he impinge on your desire to serve God? He knows nothing of Godliness, absolutely nothing.' Liam had never seen Hugo so angry.

Patrick added, 'The order could easily pay for you, sure they're loaded, living up there in that huge mansion, like little kings, and there's someone like you, who wants to join, and you'd be bloody good at it as well, and they won't let you into their cosy little club because your father isn't a solicitor or a doctor or a rich farmer. They'd make you sick so they would. My father, waste of space that he is, is right about one thing; Jesus himself was born in a stable. They've certainly moved a long way from there, haven't they? Bloody snobs, that's what they are, and then the cheek of them, suggesting you go off to the brothers in England so they can look down their snouts at you, prancing around in their hand-stitched soutanes...' Patrick was livid at the unfairness of it. He thought Liam was being punished vicariously for Patrick's own action of confronting Xavier, and that stung more than his own rejection from the hurling team.

Liam was touched by his loyalty, though he felt Patrick shouldn't criticise the clergy like that. Why should they pay for him to train? There was nothing special about him.

'Was the money the only reason? Did he say anything else?' Hugo interrupted Patrick's rant.

'I think so. He just said that the teachers didn't think I'd make the grade for an academic scholarship so there wasn't any point in putting me forward, getting my hopes up for nothing...' he answered mindlessly, throwing pebbles into sludge of the riverbed.

Patrick calmed down a bit and tried a different tack. 'Liam, maybe it's for the best. I mean, it's a tough old life, I know you get to live like a lord and all that, but no wife, no children, never having a home of your own, never getting your wages and deciding what to spend it on, maybe you're as well off.' Patrick was trying to look on the bright side. Even if he thought Liam was mad even considering taking holy orders, he did know how much it meant to him.

'What if you were to find the money?' Hugo interjected.

Liam and Patrick stared at him as if he were mad.

'Find it, of course, why didn't we think of that? Have a look around there, Liam, in case someone dropped a couple of hundred quid on the street there, you know what people round here are like, dropping big wads of cash everywhere.' Patrick chuckled, hoping to raise the glum mood.

Liam tried to smile at Patrick's joke but failed miserably.

'There's no way, Hugo, none at all. It's four hundred pounds a year for seven years when you count accommodation, tuition, food, and books. Mammy could save up for the rest of her life, and scrounge off Con and the girls and everything, but we'd never even come close. I thought that if I got the scholarship for the fees, maybe Mammy could make me a suit and maybe someone in the sacristy could maybe make me a stole, even then it would be financially near impossible, but maybe it could have been done, but without the fees for tuition and accommodation covered, it might as well be millions.' His friends were trying to cheer him up, but he didn't want hope, there was no hope, and thinking there might be was only prolonging the agony.

'I don't mean find it like that, you dingbat. I mean if he was to get it from somewhere, from someone.' Hugo was thinking.

'From who, exactly? Who do we know who has that kind of money just to splash out on Liam's education?' Patrick asked.

'Me,' Hugo answered simply.

Patrick and Liam just stared in stunned amazement.

'Hugo, that's such an incredibly kind suggestion, but I could never ask you to...' Liam immediately dismissed the idea.

'Why not? And anyway, you didn't ask, I offered. Look, you've been to Greyrock, my father and generations before him managed the estate very well, I can afford it, and I want to do it. If one good thing comes out of me having to go back and take over and get married and all of that, if it means I got to do one thing that *I* wanted to do and was able to do because of my position, then it makes it worth it. I know you two think my life is a charmed one, and yes, we are wealthy, there's no point in pretending otherwise, but my whole life is based on expectations, what my family need me to do, and this is something *I* want to do so if you'll accept my help, then I'll pay your fees. Xavier can't stop you applying as a fee-paying student, can he?'

'No, I don't think so, the recommendation I need is only for the scholarship. But Hugo, I'd never be able to pay you back, I'd have to take a vow of poverty, and I'd have no way of repaying.' Liam was trying to make his friend see how implausible his suggestion was.

'It's not a loan, it's a gift. I know to you it sounds like a lot of money, but honestly, it's not, not really. Anyway, I'd love to see Xavier outmanoeuvred so I'm not being totally altruistic.' Hugo was nonchalant, and his friends knew he wasn't showing off—he was merely stating a fact. Through all their years in school together, Hugo played down his background, he wasn't overly flash with his cash and while he was very generous to them both, buying sweets and paying for outings when they had a Sunday off together, he never bragged about his wealth.

'But what about your mam? Won't she say no?' Patrick asked.

Hugo shrugged. 'No, of course she won't. Firstly, she'd be thrilled to have a pet priest. She really has embraced the Papist faith most enthusiastically for a blow-in.' He grinned and winked at Liam, knowing how his descriptions of Catholicism exasperated his friend.

'Seriously though, she'd be fine about it, and anyway, I'm eighteen now, so I run Greyrock. She's more than happy to hand it over lock, stock and barrel. I doubt she'd even notice if I didn't tell her, which of course I will. This day couldn't come soon enough for her, she is much happier in London. I expect she'll spend a lot more time there now, she has lots of friends, and we have a townhouse in Mayfair so she's secretly thrilled to break out of the Greyrock shackles though she wouldn't admit it. She doesn't love the place the way I do, the way my father did. She hates being there without him.' He paused. 'So, Liam, will you accept my help? And I just want you to know before you decide, whatever decision you come to, it changes nothing between us.' Liam caught Hugo's eye, and the look that passed between them spoke volumes.

Liam found it hard to speak, to get the words out of his mouth. He wanted to say so much, but nothing came forth.

'Have a think and let me know,' Hugo said, clapping Liam on the back and getting up from the bench. Patrick tousled Liam's hair, something that always drove him mad, and grinned. 'Told you it was a good idea to befriend little Lord Fauntleroy, didn't I, Liamo? Stick with me, kid! You will take him up on it, won't you?'

'I don't know. I need to think it over. It's so much money, and what if I don't make the grade?'

'You'll be great, you work hard, and you have a way of knowing what to say to make things better for people. Look how much your mam relies on you; look how often you stopped me beating seven kinds of you know what out of my auld fella? That's what makes a good priest Liam, you'll be great, you just need the chance and Hugo's giving it to you. And to add to it all, Hugo gets one up on Xavier so everyone's happy.' To Patrick it was simple.

'Maybe, it's really kind of him, amazing really. I'll have a think. I've to go to Roches Store for thread for Mam, anyway, so I'll do that now.'

'Right oh—I'll call over later, and we can try to remember the declensions again. That Latin is breaking my heart, boy, I won't be sorry to never have to look at it again after next week.'

'Labor ipse voluptas.' Liam smiled.

'Don't tell me,' Patrick racked his brain. 'The pleasure is in the work itself!' he announced triumphantly.

'You see? You've a better handle on Latin than you think.'

'Nah, boy, I'll leave all that auld gibberish to you!' And he ran to catch up with Hugo, leaving Liam alone with his thoughts.

'That was a good thing you did back there,' Patrick said as he caught up with him. 'It will mean the world to him.'

'I just hope he'll accept it,' Hugo replied, burying his hands deep in his pockets against the evening chill. Despite the fact that it was early June, the weather had not yet improved, everyone said the sun comes out the day the Leaving Certificate starts. The smoke from the fires in the houses on the hill combined with a light mist to create a smell that was uniquely Cork city. He took a big lungful, knowing his days in the city were over soon.

'Will you be sad to leave?' Patrick asked, lighting up a cigarette and offering one to Hugo, who accepted. Liam constantly berated them for smoking, but they were oblivious to his admonishments. They stood in the protection of a doorway, and Patrick cupped the match flame with his hand against the stiffening breeze.

'Yes. Amazingly, I've come to think of St Bart's really fondly. I thought I'd hate it, I probably would have if not for you and Liam, so yeah, it's going to be a wrench to leave.' Hugo inhaled and blew out a long line of smoke. The edges had been knocked off his accent after six years in Cork and while he didn't sound like Liam and Patrick, he blended into their world a lot better than he used to.

'But you'll visit, won't you? I mean, it's not like you'll be working, only sitting around all day getting your portrait painted and stuffing yourself with quail's eggs.' Patrick grinned and nudged him playfully.

'Well, that's right, I mean a two-thousand-acre estate with cattle and bloodstock and crops and a large house with several staff just runs itself. I plan to spend my days fencing and playing the lute.' Hugo knew better than to rise to Patrick's well-meaning teasing.

'Seriously though, you will come back, won't you? For the odd weekend? Sure you could stay in Liam's place, his mam would love that. Mine would too, but we can have nobody in my house with the way that fool of a father of mine goes on. We can go chasing women together below in the Arcadia and between your money and my charming good looks, we'll have them eating out of our hands.' Patrick chuckled.

Hugo stopped walking, and Patrick looked back to see what was the matter.

'What?' Patrick asked.

Hugo considered now would be the right time to tell Patrick his secret, but he just couldn't get the words out.

'Nothing.' He grinned. 'Just taking a breather, this hill is ferocious.' He took a deep breath and walked on, feeling despondent that he lacked the courage to confide in Patrick. Telling Liam was one thing, but Patrick was a whole other prospect. Hugo hated himself for it, but he just couldn't say it.

'Of course I'll come back. Though chasing women may be something you'd have better success at alone. You seem to be doing fine in that department so far.' He laughed, though it sounded hollow in his own ears.

'Ah, you're just a late bloomer, sure once you get out of the jail above and start living your life, you'll have the cream of the crop battering down your door, I'm telling ya!'

'If you say so, Romeo.' Hugo smiled.

CHAPTER 15

Dear Patrick and Hugo,

I'm not being lazy writing to you both together, but I'm afraid that I'll miss out on telling one of you something and think I told the other or vice versa. That probably doesn't even make sense but, anyway, ye know what I mean! There's an old typewriter here in the rec room, and I've managed to procure some much sought after carbon paper so I'm laboriously hammering this out with two fingers, so ignore the mistakes because I can't start again. I don't know how girls do it. I was in the clerical outfitters last week and this young woman was battering away on a typewriter and not even looking where she was putting her fingers, I was mesmerised. Of course, and I can only tell you two this, she thought my fascination was with her not inconsiderable charms, if you know what I mean, rather than her typing skills so I had to fend off some fairly heavy flirting. I was absolutely mortified, especially as a lad from my class was also in the shop, fierce serious chap from County Louth or somewhere. You'd think that if I was in there buying a rig out for a priest, she'd realise she was barking up the wrong tree but no, she was quite determined. She wanted me to take her to see a film, some romantic thing, I'll tell ye it took all my powers of persuasion to convince her that I wasn't what she was after. Of course, if I was trying to get a girl, I wouldn't stand a chance probably. One of the lads here heard about it and wondered if she wasn't a plant by the college to see if we'd be tempted down the route of sinful assignations with the opposite sex, but I doubt it.

I miss ye both. And St Bart's and home and Mammy's cooking and my own bed. I'm finding it harder than I thought to be honest. The lads here are nice enough, but a good few of them all came from the same schools and know each other already so I'm at a bit of a loss. I'm sure I'll make friends though. I joined the hurling team, I wasn't that good in St Bart's, but that was up against the cream of Cork, the best hurling county in Ireland, so maybe I won't be too bad here. We've had a few training sessions, and I'm not the worst and at least it gets me chatting to some of my fellow students. I know ye both are dying to know what life is like here, so I'll try to explain it.

I mentioned that I was in the clerical outfitters when your one took a shine to me, well I was getting a soutane if you don't mind! All students here dress as clerics from the first day. It feels wrong somehow, but it's the law. (There are about a thousand laws, a lot of them to do with smoking, I don't mind telling you, so you pair of chimneys would be in right trouble.)

There are 600 seminarians here altogether, 106 in my class all walking around in soutanes and white collars, we even wear them over our jerseys and togs when we're training or playing a match. We don't play in them in case you're imagining a load of hurlers in full soutanes, but we tog off on the side-lines. We must look a right sight. Apparently, when the college plays matches against other universities, like UCC or UCD or wherever, all the girls come to support their team and wear jerseys and college scarves, while we've only priest supporters. Some of the fellas find the fact that it's all men here a bit hard to take, I don't mind though, I'm used to it from St Bart's, I suppose. The only females in the whole college here are the women who work in the kitchens and serve the grub, and they're not likely to be considered an occasion of sin if you get my meaning.

Most of the lads are country fellas, and maybe a bit innocent if anything, but I don't know about one or two of the others. They seem very interested in the ladies for lads training for the priesthood. There's a big mix here, I suppose.

We study hard, I've picked English and History, I suppose to be a teacher maybe, and then us lads interested in going abroad have extra classes in things like language and culture in Africa and India and places like that. I'm really hoping to go on the missions. Remember that time Brother Aiden came to the school with the slides of Mali? Well, ever since then I thought I'd love to go somewhere like that. Imagine me, Liam Tobin from Chapel Street out in one of those foreign places.

None of it would be possible without your help, Hugo, so don't think I ever take your generosity for granted. I remember when Daddy and I, God rest his soul, used to go down the docks to see the big ships tied up, and he used to bring a little book with all the flags of the world in it. We'd see what flag was on the fore and aft to see where she'd been or where she was going to. I can't believe that someday, if I study hard and don't mess it up, I might get to go to some of those places and spread the word of the Lord.

Speaking of which, we do have prayers every day and Mass, of course, but the emphasis is all about getting the degree it seems, at first, anyway. I thought we'd be doing theology, learning the trade as it were but no, it's all Shakespeare and the Tudors and those lads. I enjoy it though, and I even like doing the assignments. The library here is amazing, about ten times bigger than St Bart's so you can find out anything you want to know. Wait till ye hear this, you don't even have this in Greyrock, Hugo. There's a heated swimming pool! Of course, I can't swim, a fact some of the fellas here find incredible, but trying to explain that swimming lessons were not exactly the norm in Chapel Street and you'd want your head read to swim in the river, is a waste of time. Some fellas used to out by the Shaky Bridge, remember? But Mammy always said they were very rough so I was never allowed down there, the precious little flower that I am!

Once again, I find myself surrounded by fellas from much wealthier backgrounds than mine but without my two best friends to make me feel less of an oddball. It's strange, but I suppose I'll get used to it. I avoid the Clancys, which isn't very priest-like I know, but honestly, they are exactly the same here as they were in school, throwing their weight about. They ignore me, thankfully, probably mortified that someone as poor as me went to the same school as them. Whatever the reason, I say a prayer of thanks that they behave like I don't exist.

There are a few lads who are musicians and a good few nice singers as well so there are often music sessions in the rec room, where I'm writing this now. Other nights, we just sit around chatting, with cups of tea and often a cake that some lad's mother sent in, but the debates at those nights often get a bit heated, especially with the fellas from the North, going on about civil rights and the IRA and all that. If they're not talking about that, it's about the curse of emigration. I don't really have strong feelings about that kind of thing, politics and all that, but you'd be eaten alive if you said that of some of the more radical fellas here, I don't know what kind of priests they'll make, but probably more dynamic than me anyway.

The first week we were brought to the chapel and told to meditate. I hate to say it, Hugo, but maybe I'm wasting your money up here. All I could think about was how Mammy gets her brown cake to be so nice compared to the dry old sawdusty stuff they give us here. I fear I don't have the necessary piety to be a priest, but I'm trying as hard as I can. It's just when I'm supposed to be thinking elevated holy thoughts I can't stop my mind filling with brown cake and hurling matches and missing the craic we had in St Bart's.

I can't believe I'm not going to see ye until Christmas. You aren't really allowed out of here, well you are, but it must be for a very sick parent or something like that. Unfortunately, skites with pals don't class as an emergency in the eyes of the dean. So we'll have to wait till then to be back under da Goldie Fish! Write back straight away with all the news. How's the job going, Patrick? I hope you're not spending all your money entertaining the ladies! And Hugo, what's it like being back at Greyrock? Is your mam gone back to England permanently like you thought she would? I hope you're not too lonely, it must be strange after living with all the lads in St Bart's, with not a square inch to yourself, to be rattling around your mansion all day! Just joking, I know you're very busy.

And, Hugo, thanks again. I have to pinch myself some days to make sure this is really happening.

God bless,

Liam.

CHAPTER 16

'Master Hugo, the farrier is here and he needs to speak to you about Delia.' Martha's voice cut through his daydream as he gazed out of the drawing room windows at the green fields, speckled with munching cattle that eventually gave way to the pounding Atlantic Ocean. He was contemplating once again how such an expanse of land and sea and sky could be so restrictive. He felt again the familiar conflict. He loved his home and he felt privileged to be its custodian, but mostly, he felt trapped.

He frequently recalled a conversation he had with his father shortly before his death. Being home made him feel closer somehow. He sat with him in his room in the afternoons just talking, and when his father was too weak, Hugo would read the racing results out of the paper. He cherished those memories. One day, his father told him to put away the paper and to sit beside him.

'You are only twelve, Hugo, and I wish I could stay around to help you grow into this position that you have by birth, but it's looking increasingly unlikely. You will do wonderfully when the time comes, I know you will, I see it in you already, the love of this place. But remember this, you don't own the land, the land owns you. You have a duty to protect it, nourish it, and support all those who rely on it for their livelihoods.'

He died a week later.

Hugo blinked back a tear, surprised at how the memory could affect him so many years on. He would never leave Greyrock, he knew that, even if he could. Despite all his trappings of wealth and privilege, he was as stuck as the Friesians in the fields below. His fate as determined, as immovable.

'Oh, Martha, yes I'm sorry, of course, send him up.'

Martha withdrew, and Hugo was once again alone. He had long ago become accustomed to this arrangement though at first it did not sit comfortably. There was only a matter of weeks between Hugo and Martha in age, and it seemed hard to imagine when she was serving at table in her uniform that they had grown up together, the entire estate their vast playground. Martha's mother died when she was only five and so when Hugo's father died, she understood. They would talk for hours in a tree house they made when they were much younger. His parents never minded his friendship with Martha though he knew from conversations with the children of his parents' friends that it wasn't the proper thing to be friends with someone from the lower orders. His parents never gave a hoot about those kinds of conventions. Hugo remembered his mother giving them lots of treasures from Greyrock for the tree house. Hugo smiled at the memory; it must have been the only treehouse in the world decorated with ancient silk rugs and fine bone china.

He remembered how he'd reacted to the news that Martha was going to work as a maid in the house. Hugo was so cross with his mother for thinking that his only childhood friend should be a maid. He couldn't understand how she could have done that.

Hugo recalled his mother's hurt when he confronted her in anger.

'Hugo, what would you have me do? Allow her to take the boat to England like so many others? Of course, we would have paid for her to go to secondary school, but Tom is a proud and stubborn man and he wouldn't hear of it, anyway, I don't think she really wanted to go. It was the best option for her, it was what *she* wanted, and she's happy to be working here. You are the only person with a problem.'

The first summer he came home she met him in the tree house, though not when she was supposed to be working. Mrs Duggan, the housekeeper, was a stickler for efficiency and would tolerate no tardiness or lack of application from any of the staff, even if they were best friends with Master Hugo.

'Look, Hugo,' Martha explained reasonably, 'I know this is weird for you, it is a bit for me as well, but you know as well as I do that I hated all those old sums and verbs and all that rubbish. I know I could have gone to the secondary if I'd really wanted it, my Dad said he'd take the money from your mother if it was what I really wanted, but I honestly didn't. I love working here, it's my home, where I grew up, and sure, don't we all have to work somewhere? You'll be working running this place one day, and I'll be working downstairs, and Daddy works in the yard and Mrs Duggan works as a housekeeper, Mrs O'Brien is a cook, what is it really, only geography.'

She could always make him laugh, and he realised, not for the first time, that despite her lack of interest in school, Martha Courtney was a very smart girl.

And so they settled into their roles at Greyrock, all awkwardness gone. They met most days in the corridor or the dining room and exchanged a few words, but they were both conscious of how it would look to everyone else so they kept it brief.

His thoughts were interrupted by her reappearance with the farrier behind her, his cap in his hands.

He looked at her now, thinking how little she'd changed. Unruly blond curls corkscrewed around her face despite her uniform cap, and her blue eyes sparkled. She was such a tomboy, better than him at climbing trees, riding the horses faster than him; she could gut fish and help cattle when they were calving.

'Thank you, Martha,' he said as she withdrew, leaving him alone with the farrier who'd been coming to Greyrock for decades.

'Ah, Mr Cotter! How nice to see you,' Hugo crossed the room to greet him.

'Hello, Master Hugo, I'm sorry to disturb you now, sir, but there's a problem with the mare, Delia. I looked in on her this morning, just to make sure the new shoes were all right on her, she's pushing on the years, like us all. But anyway, she's not right at all, Master Hugo. I'd put my house on swamp flu, I'm sorry to say.'

Hugo's heart sank. He'd learned to ride on Delia, so gentle you could put a baby on her back and it would be quite safe. He had a flashback to the terrified face of Liam on that first visit to Greyrock, and how Delia carried him so carefully. Swamp flu was an equine disease that spread rapidly and any infected animal would have to be destroyed immediately.

'Will we get McGregor, sir?' Mr Cotter asked.

'No, Mr Cotter, he's in Lismore lambing today and tomorrow, we can't afford to wait for him. Anyway, you know more about horses than anyone so if you say its swamp flu then that's what it is. I'm very fond of her, that's the trouble, but we'll have to put her out of her misery. I'm right in saying there's no cure?'

Hugo hated the prospect of putting her down but his father always did the really unpleasant jobs himself and Hugo would do the same.

'No, sir. Nothing to be done and I'm sure that's what it is. Will I do it for you, sir? If you don't want to…or Tom could.' The old farrier was kind and knew Hugo since he was a baby. He knew that to kill anything was against his nature.

Hugo sighed and got up. 'Thank you, Mr Cotter, that is kind of you to offer, but I'll do it myself. My father showed me how. We might as well go down now, there's no point in letting her suffer. '

Both men went downstairs and round to the stables together. Tom Courtney was in the yard, shotgun slung over his shoulder, and he walked silently with them to the stable.

Hugo knew the moment he saw poor old Delia's eyes that she was in pain, she barely raised her head when he entered the stable. The farrier and Tom watched on as Hugo spoke gently to her and kissed the white star between her eyes.

Hugo rested his head on the big old horse, brushing her forelock from her big brown eyes.

'I know you are in pain, my love, don't worry it will be over soon,' he whispered. Delia whickered weakly. 'Thank you, Delia, thank you for being so lovely, goodbye, my old friend.' He kissed her gently and rubbed her muzzle, wiping a tear from his eye.

'Are you all right with this, Master Hugo?' Tom asked. 'I'll do it if you want.'

Hugo cleared his throat. 'Thanks, Tom, I know you would, but I'll do it myself. I remember Father teaching me when a young filly broke her leg in two places when we were hunting. There was no vet so he showed me what to do. Draw an imaginary cross between ears and eyes and where they intersect, aim one half inch above that. It goes right into the brain and death is instantaneous and painless.' He spoke as much to himself as them, ensuring he would cause the animal no further distress. Tom cocked the gun and handed it to Hugo.

He took it and spoke soothingly to Delia as she looked trustingly into his eyes, her long lashes closing softly. Nobody rode her anymore, she was too old, but she had a lovely retirement with the best of care. She trusted Hugo completely, and he knew what he had to do.

He took a breath to steady himself, all the time murmuring softly to the mare whose legs seemed so stiff she could barely move; she whickered in distress. Hugo felt her big brown eyes, pleading with him.

He did it in a moment, in the exact spot, and Delia fell instantly to the ground. Hugo leant beside her to ensure there was no sign of life and then he closed her eyes, kissing the blaze on her sweet face as he did so. Handing the gun back to Tom, he walked out of the yard, not trusting himself to speak.

He spotted Martha coming out the kitchen door as he approached the main entrance. She must have heard the shot.

'Hugo?' she asked as he walked past her, head down. 'What's the matter? What happened?'

He looked up, ashamed of the tears that shone in his eyes. His father loved animals and was always kind to them but he was stoic about what needed to be done. Hugo had done the same today, but it broke his heart.

'Come on, I'm finished now anyway, it's my half day.' Martha coaxed him away from the house in the direction of the small copse of trees where they had built their tree house so many years earlier. Wordlessly, he allowed her to lead him through the trees and eventually they reached the huge copper beech. The treehouse was a bit battered but was still there, so they hauled themselves up and in the door, six feet off the ground. Amazingly, it was dry inside, all of their childhood things dusty but untouched. Martha opened the wooden chest that contained rugs and pillows in plastic bags. Hugo remembered his mother insisting they put everything in plastic for fear of becoming damp; she was terrified of him getting sick. He smiled at the memory.

As they made themselves comfortable, they realised it was the first time they'd had any real time together since Hugo had come home for good. They chatted about general things every day but always in the house and often with other staff milling about. Suddenly, Hugo felt strange, panic set in. Why did Martha bring him here?

'So, what's wrong?' she asked directly, plonking down on a cushion.

'Delia, she got swamp flu, I had to put her down.' His voice sounded leaden to his ears.

'Oh Hugo, poor you, and poor old Delia, that's awful.' Martha knew how much the old mare meant to him. 'Do you remember when your dad taught us to ride on her? That must have been horrible. I couldn't have done it, that's for sure.'

'I don't know, I hated doing it, but she was in such pain, and McGregor is in Lismore all day so she'd have had to wait…' his voice tapered off.

'Sure McGregor wouldn't have been able to do anything anyway, only put her down, and your father showed you, so you did the kindest thing. He'd have been proud of you today, Hugo.' She nudged his foot with hers, smiling, trying to raise his spirits.

'Oh I doubt that, Martha.' The words came out as he thought them; it shocked him to hear them out loud.

'What? Don't be silly, you're doing such a great job here, and taking care of the place, and all of us so well, of course he'd be proud.'

'You don't understand,' he said quietly.

Loneliness and the need to connect in a meaningful way with someone overwhelmed him. He missed Cork so much, the companionship of Liam and Patrick, the welcome of their mothers. Even though his nature still preyed on his mind constantly, having loving and accepting friends was enough. Well, maybe not enough, but as good as he could expect. Back in Greyrock, he felt alone, isolated, and it felt like the strain was killing him, slowly.

'Understand what?' Martha asked, eyes focused him.

'I'm not who you think I am,' he said with a sigh.

'What are you talking about? Not who I think you are, I've known you my whole life.' She was bewildered. 'What's the matter, Hugo? You can talk to me, you know.'

Her head was tilted to one side, questioning.

Hugo felt that old familiar fear of telling someone what he really was, tempered with the desperate need to confide in someone. Maybe if Martha knew, it would alleviate some of the awful pressure that was building in his head every day. He knew that everyone, the church, the law, everyone said that he was nothing short of an abomination, and he was filled with waves of disgust and revulsion. He thought about Xavier and what he did. Tortured himself with questions about how Xavier knew about him. That must have been the reason he was chosen, and then he would think of Liam. He accepted him, he didn't turn away. He thought of his uncle in Paris, living happily with a man. Maybe it was a way to live somewhere far away like Paris. It certainly was never going to be an option in Ireland, anyway. He'd heard of pubs in Dublin where men like him went. One of the stable lads used to work in a shop across the road from this place where men could meet. He overheard him telling the others in disgust and their ribald jokes made him wince.

Maybe Martha would understand. Then again, maybe she

wouldn't, and would go straight to her father, who would tell the parish priest and then he'd have Father O'Flynn up here casting out demons or something. Tom Courtney was a devout Catholic and the most implacable man Hugo had ever met, he would never in a million years understand. The permutations of confessing to Martha filled him with dread, but he was going to explode if he didn't talk to someone.

'Whatever it is, Hugo, we can solve it. We always did, didn't we? Is it a girl?' He detected a hesitation in her voice.

Hugo turned to face her, looking straight at her.

'No, it's not a girl. I don't know, I want this life, running Greyrock, but getting married, having children. I don't want that,' he said, knowing he sounded like a petulant child.

'Why not?' Martha was perplexed. Hugo was always going to come back and run Greyrock, get married, hopefully produce the next earl. That was always the future, what had changed?

'Maybe I'll leave, go to Paris or something.' The words sounded stupid to his ears.

'Paris in France? It is in France, isn't it? I was always hopeless at geography.' She giggled. 'What's so great about Paris? Why would you leave here?'

'Martha, I'm going to tell you something, and I hope you won't tell anyone.' He tried hard to swallow.

'Of course I won't, I never said anything that time you stole the brandy and got drunk in the stables, or the time you let all Ryan's sheep into Joanie Dunlea's garden to get back at her for drowning the kittens. I'm like the grave, Hugo, you should know that.'

He took a deep breath. 'I don't like girls in the way other chaps do. I don't want to kiss them or…' He could feel his face reddening.

'Do you want to go for the priesthood? Is that it?' Martha was flabbergasted.

'No. I don't want to be a priest, I…I like men, I'm a homosexual.'

The breeze buffered the leaves of the huge trees outside causing them to rustle, a moorhen screeched in the distance, and they sat in silence. Instant regret flooded through him, wishing he could turn the clock back two seconds. Eventually Martha spoke, 'Jesus, Hugo. Don't be daft. Like that's not…well it's not…the church, everyone, the guards, everyone…you might think you are...but that's just because you've never...' Martha struggled to find the words and failed.

'I'm sure. I've always known.' He tried to maintain his composure, but his heart was thumping wildly.

They sat in silence, just trying to absorb the revelation. Eventually Martha spoke again and there was a determination in her voice that Hugo recognised. She was always the braver of the two of them. Once she got an idea in her head, there was no stopping her.

'Hugo, we had a great upbringing, but I suppose it was strange looking back, just us, no other kids. Maybe, you just feel nervous about girls, y'know what to do. Maybe, if you went with a girl, then you'd realise...'

She was moving closer to him. Dread, panic, and revulsion threatened to engulf him. His heart felt like it was going to leap out of his chest. Maybe she was right, maybe all he needed to do was be with a woman, and then he'd like it and all of this would be gone.

Martha wound her arms around his neck and began to kiss him. He made himself encircle her waist and responded as best he could. Every fibre of his being felt like it was wrong, but he persevered. Maybe this would cure him if he could just endure it. Still kissing him, she peeled off first her clothes and then his. She was pretty, he knew that, and he trusted her. Somehow, he managed to do what was required of him. He's heard enough in a boys' boarding school to know what to do, even if it felt awful. Martha was gentle and loving and kind and he knew her motives were honest. More than him, she had a sense of order about her world. She was not trying to inveigle her way to being the next Mrs FitzHenry. She was a friend, trying to show him what he was missing. The entire experience was an ordeal and, afterwards, he had to use every ounce of strength he had not to run.

Martha pulled a rug over them and held him to her breast.

'There, now that was nice, wasn't it? You just need a bit of practice. Nobody need ever know about this, Hugo. I don't want you thinking

I've notions of you, I just wanted you to see...well, what you were missing really, I suppose.'

'It was. Thanks, Martha.' He barely trusted himself to get the words out. He dressed as soon as he could, and they walked back towards the house.

'Have you done that...you know...before?' he asked, curious now at her expertise.

'Once. It was last summer, remember Finbarr? The groom that was here for a few months? Well, we were...well, I thought we were going out together, but he left. I found out afterwards he was with at least two other girls at the same time.' She sounded sad.

'I'm sorry.' He couldn't think of anything else to say. The canopy of trees cast shadows on the ground as they walked, totally alone in the woods.

'It's okay. I wish I hadn't done it with him because he turned out to be such a rat. You're different, though, I hope you feel better now, Hugo. Y'know about all that other stuff...'

Hugo couldn't let her think she had cured him or converted him. He couldn't live with yet another lie. It felt like he was being crushed by the weight of the secret he had to keep. He stopped and faced his oldest friend.

'I'm sorry, Martha, I'm so sorry, and please, it's not you, you are lovely and so...so kind to do what you did for me, but it doesn't change anything. I wish, you've no idea how much, I wish with all my heart that I could have just realised after making love with you, that I just...but I can't. I'm the way I am, and there's nothing anyone can do about it.'

'It's okay, Hugo.' She put her arms around him, and they stood together in the forest, each lost in their own thoughts.

He'd have given anything to have someone to talk to, Liam, Patrick, or his father. Liam was out of bounds by the seminary. They wrote every week, but he couldn't explain in a letter. In contrast, Patrick was getting on so well in his job, he had a girlfriend he was crazy about, and much to his family's delight and relief Joe Lynch seemed to be on the missing list. Nobody had seen him in weeks, and

Patrick said they lived in hope of the knock on the door from the guards saying they'd found his body. Hugo knew better than to admonish his friend for such unchristian thoughts. Patrick's house didn't have a telephone; very few private houses did so even though there was one at Greyrock, which was useless apart from allowing him to speak to his mother in their house in Mayfair. Anyway, Patrick still didn't know what the Lord of the Manor really was, but it would have been nice just to hear his voice. He thought about going to visit Mrs Tobin, but he was afraid—she was a very astute woman, and she would know something was wrong. He couldn't bear to even think about how she would react to a revelation of homosexuality. No, he'd have to stay away.

He and Martha walked back to the house in silence and parted in the stable yard. He wanted to find the right words, something to make her realise that he was grateful, that he appreciated what she had done, but nothing seemed right. She smiled ruefully and went in the servants' door.

Hugo looked into Delia's stable, but she was gone. Tom would have arranged to have her moved and buried quickly.

'I'll put her above in the pet cemetery.'

Hugo turned around, Tom stood behind him, pipe between his teeth.

Hugo thought of all the hamsters, kittens, ponies, and dogs that had been buried in that special plot over the years. The best loved animals of the FitzHenrys were there for centuries, on a hilly spot looking over the ocean. Each animal had its own little headstone; Delia would have hers, too.

'Thanks, Tom.' Hugo tried to keep his voice level. Tom was kind but gruff, a man's man and couldn't bear any emotional rubbish as he called it. Apparently, even when his beloved wife died, he shed not a tear. The man was granite all the way through.

In the weeks that followed, Hugo walked the estate and worked sixteen- and seventeen-hour days. Tom Courtney urged him to pull back a bit, but he didn't want to. Physical work exhausted his body so when he went to bed, he slept a deep, dreamless sleep. On the rare occasions he did dream, he dreamed he was back in St Bart's and Xavier was walking the corridors. He would wake in a sweat, his heart pounding. On those nights, he started drinking brandy to make him sleep, he woke in the morning with a pounding headache but at least he slept. The alternative was the endless nights of pain and self-loathing. He never felt lower.

CHAPTER 17

'Mr Lynch, there's someone here to see you.' The young secretary entered the office Patrick shared with two others. He still was trying to get used to being called Mr Lynch by someone his own age. She was very pretty as well, which made it even stranger. They chatted often during their coffee breaks, and she was extremely nice. Not his type though, she wasn't into clothes and makeup the way the girls were down in the Arcadia. She played camogie and was much more of a tomboy and though Patrick secretly didn't rate the girls' version of hurling as being up to much, she was actually on the Cork team so she must be handy enough at it. They used to joke about who could score from a sideline cut from the farthest out, and she said that someday she'd show him how it was done properly. She might have been a nice match for Liam if he wasn't hell-bent on the priesthood he'd often thought, she was kind and gentle like he was.

'Thanks, Helen,' he replied, wondering who could want to see him at work. His clients, the small businesses for whom he did the accounts never called to the office. He usually went out to their premises once a month, gathered up all the invoices, receipts, petty cash chits, and so on and took them back to the office where he did up the monthly accounts. It wasn't the most fascinating job in the world, but the pay was good, the hours reasonable, and the man he worked for, Jim O'Neill, was a decent sort. He had been there since he left school and was studying for his accountancy exams by night. Or at least he was supposed to be, most nights he was cycling out to Blackrock to see his girlfriend, a cracker called Jackie. Jackie, short for Jacqueline, just like the late American president's wife, and she was every bit as gorgeous, too. His mam was forever giving out about his spending all his time and most of his wages on her, but she was a high-end girl. She expected regular presents and nights out, she wasn't going to stick around waiting for some fella with his head in the books every night of the week. Mothers didn't understand that, though.

Hugo seemed impressed when he'd shown him her picture, but then Hugo wasn't the best judge of these things, he supposed. He was probably more into the pearls and twinset kind of woman with an accent that would cut butter. He wondered what Liam would make of Jackie, he'd probably say she looked very glamorous or something, but he wouldn't have a clue. Patrick often shook his head at how uninterested in women his two best friends were. It was a mystery to him, he loved going dancing, seeing the girls in their dresses, and big hairdos and makeup. The more dolled up the better as far as he was concerned.

He walked down the dun brown corridor, off which lay offices with men working on sets of accounts behind doors of frosted glass. The mustard linoleum caused his shoes to squeak as he walked towards the reception area. He thought about where he would take Jackie on Saturday night. There was a good showband playing in the Arcadia, The Clippers, and they played all the American stuff, but it was three and nine to get in, multiply that by two, plus drinks, it was an expensive night out. Jackie had hinted that if Patrick wasn't going, a lad from the post office had offered to take her, so he was going to have to shell out or miss out and see his best girl on some other lad's arm.

He pushed the door with the frosted glass to enter the reception and was alarmed to see two Gardaí standing there. Immediately, he thought, *It's my father, they've found him.*

'Mr Patrick Lynch?' the older of the two policemen asked.

'Yes, I'm Patrick Lynch.' A thousand emotions churned up inside him, relief, fear, dread, joy. It was hard to process.

'I'm Detective Inspector Donal McMullan and this is Garda John Holland. Is there somewhere we could talk?'

Mr O'Neill came out of his office, the main one adjoining the reception, obviously having overheard the guards' arrival.

'Use my office if it's convenient. I hope everything is all right,' he said with concern on his face.

'Thank you, sir. That would be fine.' The younger guard gestured to Patrick to enter the office, followed by both officers.

'Patrick, I'm afraid we have some bad news for you. You might want to sit down.' The detective's voice was grave. Patrick knew what was coming, he was ready, he'd been ready for years.

'I'm very sorry to have to tell you, your mother has been killed.'

Their faces swam in front of Patrick's eyes. They had it wrong; it was his father that was dead, not Mam. Sure, she was at home with the girls. She'd be putting his tea on now; he'd be home in an hour.

'No, it's my father who is missing. He's the one who...' Patrick knew he wasn't making any sense. 'What...what happened?'

'We're not too sure yet, son. Some of the neighbours heard shouting and screaming, your little sisters ran out to a Mrs Tobin, that's where they are now, but by the time we got there, your mother had passed away. She had been assaulted. As I said, we're not sure what happened yet, but...'

'My father. It was him.' Patrick knew with a conviction that went deep into his bones. His father had finally murdered his mother. He'd come close so many times, he thought back to the time he thought Liam had killed him. His father's rages were unstoppable, he knew that's what had happened. He came back, from whatever hole he was hiding in for the past few months, and laid into his poor mother, and the girls looking on. He tried to maintain his composure, squeezing his eyes shut and breathing deeply.

'Have you got him?' he asked.

'Your father? No, well, if it was him, he fled the scene. Though your sisters did say it was him, and we'll pick him up the moment he's spotted. Every guard in the city is looking for him.'

'Where is she now? My mam?' Patrick knew he was in charge of the family now. He had to keep it together.

'An ambulance took her to the Mercy, but a doctor pronounced her dead at the scene.' The older guard's tone was kind, but he obviously thought the only way to deliver news like this was straight, with no frills or platitudes.

'I want to see her, my sisters will be all right with Mrs Tobin. She knows not to let them out of her sight.' He drew a ragged breath. 'I'll just get my jacket.'

The younger guard explained quickly what had happened to Mr O'Neill, who offered his car to drive Patrick wherever he needed to go.

'I'm so sorry, Patrick, take as much time as you need. If there's anything we can do, anything at all...'

Patrick nodded his thanks and took the jacket Helen was holding for him. She squeezed his hand in sympathy, and he followed the guards out to the squad car.

He stared out the window as they drove through the city centre towards the hospital, located on the other side of the river from their home.

He was directed and accompanied to the morgue where he formally identified his mother's body. Her face was purple and puffed up, her lip cut; a chunk of her hair had been ripped from her scalp. He barely recognised her.

He couldn't get the words out, he just nodded and whispered, 'That's my mam.'

The older guard put his arm on his shoulder, and Patrick let the tears flow.

'Let it out, lad, you're all right,' he said soothingly as Patrick's body was wracked with sobs. 'We'll get him, don't you worry, and you'll do right by your little sisters now.'

What seemed like hours later, Patrick was brought to the Tobins' house, his own in darkness across the street. Detective Inspector McMullan went in with him.

The detective knocked on the door. Patrick was relieved to see Liam's mother, she opened the door and wrapped her arms around him, and there they stood for a few moments. Then he looked up and saw Liam standing there.

'How did you get here?' he croaked. 'I thought ye weren't allowed out?'

'Special circumstances, Mam got the guards to ring the college and there was someone driving down anyway. Patrick, I'm so sorry…' Liam's voice shook. Mrs Lynch was so nice, she worked so hard for her family. Against all the odds, they were great kids, and then for this to happen. All the way down in the car, Liam railed in his mind against a God that could allow this to happen.

'It was him, you know?' Patrick said bitterly.

'I know.'

Before they could say anymore, Patrick's two little sisters appeared at the top of the stairs.

'I put them to bed. They were exhausted, poor little pets. I stayed with them till they slept but they must have woken again.' Liam's mother was trying to reassure Patrick that his sisters were being taken care of at least.

He opened his arms, and they ran to him. Connie was nine and Anna only six. They buried their heads in his chest.

'Daddy…Daddy did a bad thing…' Anna began, sobbing.

'I know, pet, I know, he's a very bad man. The guards are going to lock him up forever and ever so he can't ever come near us again,' Patrick soothed their sobs. The girls looked at the detective, and he nodded.

'We will, I promise,' he said solemnly.

'When is Mammy coming home?' Connie asked. Patrick caught Mrs Tobin's eye. She obviously hadn't told them.

Patrick sat on the stairs, a sister on each knee with Mrs Tobin and

Liam on either side. He took a deep breath and tried to keep his voice steady.

'Mammy is gone to heaven, she's gone up to see Nana and Granda and Auntie Kit, and she's having a lovely cup of tea up there with them all. She wants us to stay here for a bit, and I'll be minding ye with Mrs Tobin to help, and we'll be grand.'

The children tried to absorb what their brother was saying.

Liam's heart was breaking for the three of them, sitting together on the stairs.

'I don't want Mammy to be dead,' Connie said in a sad, little voice.

'Won't she ever come home, Patrick?' Anna whispered, her eyes locked with her brother's.

'No, pet, she won't,' he answered.

There were no screams or wailing, just the unadulterated sound of pain and anguish in a little child's voice—children who had seen too much violence and fear in their short lives. Liam was preparing to help Patrick with the barrage of questions, but they were exhausted from crying so they just sat on their brother's knee and cuddled into his chest as he rubbed their heads.

Later, when they had fallen asleep and the detective had left, Patrick and Liam lifted them up to the double bed in what had been Liam and Con's bedroom. Mrs Tobin had retired, as well, shattered by the day's events. Mrs Lynch had been her closest friend. Liam knew that when all that business blew up with Daddy and that woman next door, years ago, it was Mrs Lynch who helped them through it. She loved to have Liam, Hugo, and Patrick for tea and scones when she was sure Joe was on a skite, and she worked so hard for her children. Liam knew he was supposed to believe that this was all part of God's plan, but that seemed hard to accept tonight.

He sat at the fire with Patrick, reminiscing about their childhood. Patrick talked about how proud his mam had been when he got into St Bart's and then when he got the job in O'Neills. Patrick told him how she said she wished she had a camera the day he went off to work, in his shirt and tie. Liam urged his friend to hold tightly to that memory, like a snapshot in his mind, and always remember the joy he and his sisters brought their mother. He must block out the image of her on the cold slab below in Mercy.

'It's not that easy, Liam. I…I hate him, I've always hated him. God knows I begged her to leave him, especially now that I'm working. We could have got a little house somewhere, changed the locks, and she'd have had some peace, but she's just not that kind. For better or worse, and all that rubbish. He's been missing for weeks now. I was sure when the guards came to the office, it was to tell me they found him. I was trying to make sure I reacted properly, like Mam would want us to and not do what I felt like doing, which would be whooping for joy. I was sure, and when they told me it was my mam, I…I…just couldn't take it in, y'know? Why did God do that, Liam? You're supposed to be learning all about his mysterious ways and all that, what was he thinking? My poor mam put up with so much, and then that bastard gets in and beats her to death. How can that be right? Where was God when that useless excuse for a man was battering my mother for the last time?'

Liam wished he could find the words to comfort his friend, to have an answer for why a merciful God would let this happen, but he couldn't. Why did Daddy get killed, why did he land such a difficult cross on poor old Hugo? He found the more he thought about it, the more questions were raised and the fewer answers he had. He wondered once again if he was cut out for the priesthood. A major part of his job was going to be this, helping families who were bereaved, and what had he to offer? Nothing, absolutely nothing at all.

Patrick stared, unseeing, into the dying embers as the wall clock ticked in the silence.

'Did you tell Hugo?' Patrick asked eventually.

'Mam asked Father Aquinas to phone him from the monastery.'

'I can't believe it, Liam,' Patrick said for the hundredth time. 'My mam, she never hurt a fly. She went to Mass, she was a good person, Liam. She put up with him, worked so hard, and where was God, Liam? Where was he?'

Liam had never seen Patrick so distraught. He searched his mind for some theology, some wisdom, anything to ease his friend's pain but found nothing.

'I don't know, Patrick, I really don't. All I can think is that there's a divine plan, something we have no knowledge of, where God has decided he wanted to call your mam to heaven now, at this time.' The words sounded hollow to his ears.

'But, even if he wanted her, how could God's need be more than Connie and Anna's? I'll be okay, I'm able to fend for myself, but they're just little girls, they need their mammy...' His voice choked with emotion. 'And why did she have to have such a brutal death? Years of battering and then to die at the hands of someone that God created as well. I'm sorry, Liam, either there is no God, it's all lies, there's no divine plan, or if there is, he's one evil bastard. Either way, I want nothing more to do with it.' He stood up. 'I need to get some air.'

Liam watched helplessly as his friend walked out into the dark night. He sat by the fire thinking. Maybe Patrick was right. Why would God give us people to love, people we need, and then take them away? Why did Daddy have to die? Hugo's father? Why Mrs Lynch? If he created Joe Lynch in his own image and likeness, why did he turn out to be so bad? Why did he give Hugo that huge cross to carry his whole life? None of it made any sense. Faith, that's all you were told. Have faith and everything will work out fine in the end, but Daddy had faith, Mrs Lynch was devoted, so much so she wouldn't leave her abusive husband because she took a holy vow, and where did it get them? Six foot under, that's where, and left the people who needed them bereft.

Every day, Liam learned in the seminary about the divine grace of the Lord. Of how he loves us and looks after us, but tonight, in a little terraced house in Chapel Street, Liam had to admit God seemed a very remote prospect indeed.

The days that followed went as funerals always do, in a blur, while simultaneously seeming interminable. Hugo came from Greyrock, and the three friends spent a lot of time together talking and reminiscing. On the night of the burial, they polished off a bottle of brandy between them, sitting around the range in Liam's kitchen. Father Aquinas had been coming and going. Mrs Tobin had been busy trying to feed everyone, and all the neighbours pitched in with food as they always did. That last night though, as Connie and Anna slept upstairs, it seemed to be understood by everyone that the boys who'd been inseparable since they were twelve years old, needed to be alone with each other.

They cried, and they laughed, and they were comforted by each other's presence.

CHAPTER 18

'Ah, Mrs Duggan, what can I do for you?' Hugo asked pleasantly as the housekeeper appeared in the morning room. He's not spoken to her in weeks. Since the funeral of Mrs Lynch, Hugo had been travelling back to Cork more frequently to see Patrick and the girls. They loved to see him coming, always laden down with gifts, and he found his new purpose of cheering them up meant he had less time to wallow in his own misery. He was surprised that she'd requested a meeting with him. She and Patterson handled most of the details of the running of the house, and Hugo was very grateful that they didn't need to consult him on every little thing, so her request struck him as a little odd. He hoped she wasn't leaving, she had been running Greyrock since he was a child. She was formidable and stern, but she was a kind-hearted woman under it all. He remembered she always turned a blind eye when they were children and the cook gave him and Martha buns before their dinner. One time, he managed to keep a pet rat in his bedroom for months without his mother knowing, thanks to her, so he knew she was on his side. Her iron-grey hair was perfectly set in waves and her black uniform seemed to be made of something stronger than mere fabric.

'Good Morning, Master Hugo, thank you for seeing me. I'll get right to the point...well, there's been a staff development you should know about.'

'Really? What?'

'It's Martha, sir, Martha Courtney. She's gone, sir.' Mrs Duggan was making no effort to hide her disapproval. She was always of the opinion that Martha was altogether too flighty and far too familiar with Hugo.

Hugo was confused. 'Gone where? Have you asked Tom? Perhaps she had an errand to run or...'

'No, sir, I don't mean she is unavailable at the moment, I mean she has left Greyrock, for good, it seems.'

Hugo was incredulous. 'There must be some mistake. Martha wouldn't just go off without telling anyone, she would have told her father, surely? What does he say?'

'I've not spoken to Tom, sir. He's not been in the house and when I sent one of the girls to fetch him, he wasn't available.' Her tone indicating that she didn't believe that story for one minute.

He rang the bell and Patterson appeared.

'Ah, Patterson, please fetch Tom for me, tell him it's urgent.'

Turning back to Mrs Duggan, he resumed his questioning. 'What makes you think she's gone for good?'

'Well, sir, her things are gone from her room, and she swore young Florrie to secrecy when he met her in the yard at around four o'clock this morning. He was checking on the new foal, so he slept in the barn. She was obviously trying to slip away unnoticed.' Mrs Duggan pursed her lips in disapproval. Loyalty to the FitzHenry family was paramount for the staff of Greyrock to her way of thinking. Anything less was intolerable.

Tom Courtney knocked and entered.

'Tom, Mrs Duggan here tells me that Martha is gone. What's going on?'

Tom was his usual taciturn self. 'She's gone all right. To where I don't know.' He didn't raise his eyes.

Hugo had a flashback to the day in the woods three months earlier. He'd been so busy with the funeral, and going up and down to Cork, he had barely five words of conversation with Martha since then. He no longer ate in the dining room, it seemed stupid to go to all that trouble just for him, and he kept such long hours that he instructed the cook to leave him something on the sideboard, and he ate it when he came in. During the day, he ate with the workers in the yard, and he hardly ever ate breakfast, sometimes because he was hung-over from the brandy, other times because he wasn't hungry. Because of this, he rarely ran into her. He reluctantly admitted to himself he was relieved, he was embarrassed about that day, and perhaps it suited him not to have to talk to her, but he never imagined for a second that she would ever be anywhere but Greyrock.

'Did she give any indication? Any reason to think there was something wrong?' Hugo was worried about his friend.

Mrs Duggan glanced in Tom's direction. 'Well, sir, she had seemed rather distracted these last weeks, not herself.'

'Is that true, Tom? Is there something wrong?'

Tom looked up and stared directly at Hugo. Something unspoken in his eyes. After several seconds, he spoke, but didn't answer the question.

'Martha has left Greyrock. I don't expect you to keep her position open for her, and I don't know when or if she'll be back. It might be best if you advertise the position.'

Hugo was about to argue that he couldn't care less about the job but that he wanted to know why Martha had left, but something in Tom's demeanour stopped him. Suddenly, a thought struck him. Maybe she was so appalled at the thought that she had sex with a homosexual that she couldn't bear to stay. Maybe Tom found out about it, maybe somebody saw them in the woods. Tom Courtney knew where she was, of that there was no doubt in Hugo's mind.

Hugo forced himself to speak.

'Well, I must say I am saddened to hear it, but Martha is her own person and perfectly entitled to go where and when she wishes. I hope she returns to us, Tom, and if you do hear from her, please tell her I said that. Her job and home here is hers for as long as she wants it. Now, if you'll excuse me...'

Hugo left the room and walked back to his own bedroom. He needed to be alone to process what had just happened. Sitting on the bed, he spotted a note on his bedside locker, it could have been there earlier when he got up, he overslept that morning and had a meeting with a tenant so in his haste to get out he could have missed it.

There was no name on the envelope but once he opened the one sheet of paper, he recognised the writing as Martha's.

Dear Hugo,

I'm sorry about this, but I'm leaving Greyrock. I know I should have told you face to face, but I'm not as brave as you. I'm fine, I just need to get away, please don't worry. Live your life, Hugo, whatever way you want. I hope we meet again someday.

All my love,

Martha xxx

PS. Please keep an eye on my dad. I know he's a grumpy old git, but he's all I've got. Also, I got Jenny the scullery maid to drop this note for me so don't tell Mrs Duggan or she'll make her life hell.

Hugo folded the letter. What did she mean needed to get away? Away from whom? Him? He was sure she was repulsed by what they'd done and needed to distance herself. It was the only possible explanation. It was 1977, maybe she realised that there was more to life than being a maid. She was right; she was bright and funny and could do anything she wanted. He had no right to ask her to come back; he could offer her nothing but a job from the last century and his friendship. It was clearly not enough. He'd have to face it, Martha was his only friend at Greyrock, and now she was gone.

CHAPTER 19

Days turned into weeks on Chapel Street, and it was soon going to be Christmas. Patrick and Mrs Tobin were doing their best to make it a nice one for the children, but it was hard.

Only that morning, little Anna blurted out as he was trying to brush her hair, 'Ouch! You're hurting me, Patrick. Mammy does it without hurting. I hate Daddy, I wish he were dead and not Mammy.'

He decided that even though they were only small, they were better off knowing the truth. They'd seen enough of it, anyway, every time he'd come home drunk.

'I do too, pet,' he said, bending down on his hunkers to look straight into her eyes. 'I hate him, too, and he is the one that should be dead, not Mammy. Mammy was kind and good and loved us, and he's a terrible person. We will never again look at his face or speak to him as long as he lives.'

'But what if he comes back?' Connie asked fearfully.

'He won't. He knows the guards are after him, and he's a coward so he'll stay away. I promise. And anyway, I'm here at night and Mrs Tobin collects ye from school and gives ye ye'er dinner so ye're safe.'

'But what about when you are out at dances with girls? Who'll mind us then?' Anna's little face was worried.

Patrick knew his days of dances and courting were over for now, he had more important responsibilities. Jackie had come to the funeral, all dolled up with loads of makeup on and hugged him, but he hadn't seen or heard from her since. He hoped she would come to his side immediately when she heard the news, but she didn't. He supposed there wasn't much future for her in a fella who stayed in babysitting his little sisters every night and who had to use his wages to run a house.

Helen from the office had called a few times, she even brought dolls for Connie and Anna and took them upstairs to play house when the house got too full during the funeral. She brought cakes and a shepherd's pie even though the house was groaning under the weight of food. Why did people think that when you lose someone all you want to do is eat? Still, they meant well, he knew that. She was nice, Helen, easy to be around, she wasn't too loud or always looking for attention. Some evenings, she'd call and they'd just sit and drink a cup of tea and not say much at all. Other times, they'd talk about hurling, she even took the girls training with her at the club, and they loved it. Patrick bought them little hurleys and a ball out of his wages, and they were forever pucking the ball against Liam's mother's back wall, just like he and Liam used to do as kids. Life passed into the humdrum of the ordinary in the weeks that followed. He didn't go out anymore but went to Liam's mam for his tea after work. The girls would have theirs eaten and their lessons done and would be delighted to see him. He set the fire in the morning in his house and put a match to it before he went over to the Tobins for his dinner, so the place would be warm for the girls when they all trooped across the road. He had literally no idea what he would have done without Helen and Liam's mam. They kept him going, helped him get their own house back to some kind of normal. He used Seán Tobin's tools, still in the shed in his yard, to fix up most of the damage that was done the day his father came back. Father Aquinas even helped and was surprisingly handy with a hammer and nails. They painted it all inside. Mr O'Neill bought the paint and they even got some new furniture. Hugo said they had lots of things in storage that they didn't use at Greyrock so it all arrived in a big truck one day, much to the excitement of the whole street. Patrick had to laugh when he realised that the furniture that graced the living room and the bedrooms of a small terraced house on Chapel Street was probably worth more than the whole street put together. He accepted all offers of help gratefully, people really did want to help, and Patrick was determined that Connie and Anna would have a comfortable and safe place to live. It was the least they deserved after everything they'd endured. It still looked a bit higgledy-piggledy as Connie said, but it was safe and warm.

He was walking back from dropping the girls to school, they'd been off for the first few weeks after the funeral, but Father Aquinas said it would be best for them to go back, be with their pals and try to get a bit of normality back in their lives. Patrick asked Mrs Tobin, and she agreed but said to tell the teacher that if they were ever upset they were to send someone down for her and she'd go and collect them. He never asked Mrs Tobin if she'd look after the girls on a permanent basis but it was a given. She missed Liam so much, now that he was in the seminary, and she had time on her hands. Connie and Anna loved her. Mam would have wanted Mrs Tobin to do it, they were best friends, and it had allowed him to go back to work. Jim O'Neill had been great, telling him to take as much time off as he wanted, but he wanted to get back. It wasn't good for him, sitting around the house all day, brooding. The lads from the hurling team tried to get him to come out to a dance, but he wasn't in the form, it was too soon, and anyway, his sisters started to fret if he didn't get back at six on the dot.

Patrick was lost in thought and almost collided with Father Aquinas as he came out of the tobacco shop across the road from the monastery. Hugo used to go there to buy contraband cigarettes when they were in school, much to Liam's disapproval.

'Ah, Patrick, how are you?' The old priest was kind. He had retired from teaching earlier in the year and was taking on a more pastoral role in the community. Patrick and Liam felt a huge debt of gratitude to the man they feared so much as boys, without him they would never have entered the hallowed halls of St Bart's.

'Hello, Father, I'm all right, you know yourself,' was the best he could muster.

'It's very hard for you, that's true, but you are made of tough stuff, Mr Lynch, always were, you'll do well. How are the little girls getting on back in school?'

'Well, the first few days were tough, but they're settling now. Anyway, everyone said it was best for them so...' Patrick dug his hands into his pockets against the skinning December breeze blowing up the hill from the river below.

'Lord, but it is perishing, isn't it? Will you come in for a cup of something hot?' Father Aquinas asked, 'or have you something to do?'

'Thanks, Father, I'd love it. I have loads to do, I suppose. I've the day off, and I was going to try to clear out the yard behind a bit. When we cleared out the house, everything got dumped out there and come the summer, it would be nice for the girls to have somewhere to play, but I just can't face it...'

The priest patted him on the shoulder and said kindly, 'Yerra, the whole world looks a bit brighter after a cup of tea and a bun, I always think. It is nothing that can't wait, I'm sure.'

As Patrick followed him up the avenue to the monastery, the priest chatted about the new students and how strange it felt not to be facing a whole class of small lads this year. Patrick relaxed in his easy chat and marvelled at how Liam and he used to be terrified of him when they were small.

'I was talking to Liam when he was home for the funeral; he seems to be getting along fine in Maynooth,' Father Aquinas said. 'I'd say ye miss each other though, do ye? Yourselves and young Hugo FitzHenry were as thick as thieves. A right unlikely bunch ye were too...' He chuckled as he opened the door and squeaked down the polished hallway in his rubber-soled shoes.

Hugo had a theory that priests wore different shoes to most men so that they could sneak up on fellas smoking.

They entered the big, warm kitchen, with its welcoming aroma of baking.

'Sister Catherine is at Mass, she brings the older priests to ten o'clock. She's a saint that woman, a walking saint, the way she puts up with us and looks after us. Her apple tart is one of the great wonders of the world. I'm a divil for sweet things. I'll have to cop on now in the new year, but Christmas is no time to be thinking of the waistline, sure it isn't. Your mother, God rest her, was a lovely baker as well, I used to call to her on the odd occasion, and she'd always have the scones or a bit of brack. Sure I'm desperate altogether for the sweets.' He smiled, patting his stomach. He always used to be tall and skinny, but Patrick saw a bit of a paunch where there never had been before.

As Father Aquinas busied himself with kettles and rooted around in a tin for cake, Patrick took in his surroundings. He'd not been in this kitchen since the day Aquinas brought them in to tell them they were going to St Bart's and gave them lemonade and sticky buns.

Father Aquinas set the tea things out and produced a fruit cake.

'How is young Hugo? Enjoying being Lord of the Manor, I suppose?'

'He's grand, Father, grand out. I saw him a few weeks back, he gave me a load of antiques out of Greyrock for the house, worth a fortune, I'd say. My poor mam couldn't have dreamed we'd ever have things so nice, even if they do look a bit mad in our tiny terraced house.' Patrick smiled. 'I might take my sisters down there for a short holiday over Christmas. Hugo is always inviting us, Mrs Tobin as well. 'It is some place he has, like a small castle or something—land and cattle and horses and the whole lot. It is a million miles away from here, I can tell you. I remember the first time Liam and I went down there, we were like eejits not knowing what to say or do, but sure Hugo's fairly normal under it all.' Patrick joked but then became serious. 'To be honest, Father, I don't know how we'd have managed without him, y'know. He lent me the money for the funeral and everything, and he calls up and down all the time, takes us out for drives in his car. The girls are mad about him, and he spoils them rotten.'

'He's a grand lad, Hugo, and it isn't easy having a life like that foisted on you even if it looks very glamorous from the outside, you know, no more than yourself, Patrick. He never had a choice, only to go back there and take over from his father, God rest him, and sure maybe he'd have wanted a different kind of a life, but he can't have it. Isn't life strange that the three of ye, so close as ye are, all had to cope with the death of a parent very young? Liam losing his father the way he did and keeping his mother going after, and your poor mother, and you having to become a family man before your time, and Hugo's father leaving him with all that responsibility whether he liked it or not.'

Patrick was slightly taken aback. Why wouldn't Hugo want to run Greyrock? He loved the place. It struck him as an odd thing for Father Aquinas to say. They chatted and ate for an hour. It was nice to talk about hurling and the weather and greyhound racing, Father Aquinas's secret vice.

As he left, the priest shook his hand warmly.

'That girl, Helen, she was a great help to you over the last while, wasn't she?'

Patrick was surprised the priest noticed a girl, he wasn't even sure he would recognise one. Female people, apart from nuns, didn't feature at all in the life of the priests of St Bart's.

'Er...yes, Father, she works in the same place as me. She calls up a few times a week and she's been very nice to the girls, has them playing camogie and all. They're delighted with her.'

'Well, you could do worse,' Father Aquinas said with a smile.

'Ah no, Father, she's not my…' He felt intimidated even using the word girlfriend in front of a priest. All they had ever been taught by the priests was that girls were nothing more than occasions of sin in a young man's life, and the best thing was to steer clear if they wanted to keep their soul pristine.

'She's just a friend from work,' he finished lamely.

'Well, Patrick, I do know your mother was worried about the kind of girls you were knocking around with, so I just wanted to say I think she'd like Helen very much. I know you're young, but maybe it is time you thought about settling down. You need to provide a stable home for your sisters now, and it is a hard thing for a lad to do on his own.'

Patrick was shocked. Was Father Aquinas seriously suggesting he get married? To Helen? He was only going to be twenty next month.

'Ah, Father, I've no notions in that direction for a while yet,' he joked, albeit a little nervously. Talking to a priest about girls in any way, shape, or form was alien territory.

'I'm not saying you should get the banns read this weekend, Patrick. I just think that if the Lord sent a nice, kind girl like Helen into your life when you needed a bit of a dig out, you should sit up and take notice. That's all.'

He bade him goodbye at the door, and Patrick walked back down the avenue. Maybe the priest was right, Helen was a lovely girl, and Connie and Anna really liked her. Maybe when things settled down and he was feeling a bit better in himself, he'd ask her to come on an outing with them, to the pictures or something.

He returned to his house and got a start on breaking up the remains of the old furniture in the yard. Even though the cold was biting, it felt good to be doing physical work. The time flew and before he realised it, it was time to collect the girls from school. He'd told Mrs Tobin that he'd do it today.

Mrs Tobin knocked on her window as he passed, beckoning him into her house. Connie and Anna's coats were hung up on the banister at the bottom of the stairs.

'They're inside having their lunch, don't worry,' Mrs Tobin spoke quietly to him in the hallway, closing the door behind her so the girls couldn't hear them.

'How come they're home? Did something happen at school?' he asked.

'I was looking for you to let you know,' she began.

'I was out the back chopping timber, I probably didn't hear you knocking, sorry,' he said, deeply concerned now.

'Well, apparently, Anna started screaming at school saying she saw your father out the window of the classroom. Now, she was probably only imagining it. God knows what the poor little mite's been through, but the teacher sent an older girl down for me, and I collected them.'

The guards still had no luck in finding Joe Lynch. He had evaded capture for over a month now, despite their best efforts. Every few days, Donal McMullan visited Patrick to let him know of their progress in the investigation but so far nothing. There was a chance he took the boat to England before the alarm was raised, but it was unlikely. The sailing of the Inisfallen out of Cork on the day of the murder was two hours after Mrs Tobin raised the alarm. By then, the ports were being watched. Patrick assumed he must have got a spin in a van or a lorry down to Rosslare, the port in Wexford, and left from there. The guards scoured the city, the usual places, the down and outs hung around, but nobody had seen him. Donal told Patrick that no stone was left unturned, they even rounded up all the tramps and petty criminals and brought them in for questioning, but it was as if Lynch had vanished into thin air.

Patrick went into the kitchen and the girls ran to him, jam smeared on their faces.

'I saw him, Patrick, I promise I saw him. He was looking in the window of the school. There was a man with him, a huge tall man with red hair…' Anna began to sob. Connie's eyes were bright, but she was trying to be brave. Patrick knew both girls were terrified of their father.

'I believe you, Anna,' Patrick said, catching Mrs Tobin's eye. Anna didn't lie. If she said she'd seen him, then she had, which meant he never went to England, or else he was now back. Suddenly a thought struck him. A place, a horrible, old half-house-half-pub his father used to go to years ago. The fella that owned it must have been over six foot, and he used to deal in stolen property. He had a big head of red hair. Patrick never told anyone, not even Liam, but his father used to make him rob houses when he was four or five. He'd shove Patrick in through the windows and tell him to grab as much as he could. Once he got too big to fit through, he was off the hook but even then he knew it was wrong and he hated doing it. They would bring the stuff out to this place and the fella with the red hair would give them money for it, which Patrick knew his father would drink and then come roaring and shouting and breaking the place up again. Patrick was fairly sure the guards wouldn't have checked that place; it looked derelict the last time he passed it. There was a slim chance that his father was there, and he knew he should call the guards, tell them of his suspicions, but he wanted to be sure he was right first.

'I have to go somewhere. You'll keep them, won't you, till I get back?' he asked.

'Of course, but back from where? Where are you going, Patrick?' Mrs Tobin was worried.

Patrick didn't answer her. He didn't want to lie, and he knew she'd worry if he told her the truth. He just wanted to check, it was probably empty but just in case, he wanted to see for himself.

'Nothing probably, I just need to check something. I'll be back in a couple of hours. Thanks, Mrs T.'

He walked up the hill into the biting cold December wind as dusk settled on the city. Smoke from the chimneys of the terraced houses swirled into the dark sky. The smell of turf and wood combined with the odour of the low tide was so familiar to him it should have given him comfort, but tonight it didn't. He strode on determined to find Joe Lynch. The exercise was keeping him warm as he climbed the hill out of the city. It was getting dark and his jacket wasn't providing much resistance to the sharp wind. People were scurrying past, their Christmas shopping in bags, heads down against the skinning gusts that carried sleet and the threat of snow as the night went on. As he walked, Patrick racked his brain for memories, anything that would help him find his father. He desperately wanted to tell Connie and Anna that they had nothing to fear, that he was out of their lives for good. It was the only way to rebuild some of their trust that had been shattered by the loss of their mother.

His father had a few drinking buddies. He called them his associates, but they were no more than a bunch of drunks like him. That place—where the red-haired man was—consisted of one room with a sour smell and a few broken chairs. He tried to visualise it in his mind. It was out past the city boundaries, two or three miles out into the country, in the direction of Mallow. The guards wouldn't have made any connection between there and Joe Lynch though. His father was nothing if not cunning. He had never been arrested for robbery or anything like that, even though he'd done plenty of burglaries.

He walked on, thinking all the time. The lights of the city faded, and he found himself on a narrow country road, unlit except by the occasional passing car. The houses seemed to all be back from the road so fields stretched on either side of the road away into the infinite, inky night. Eventually, he was across the road from the pub. To the outside, it didn't even look like a proper pub, more like a ramshackle old house, but one crooked Guinness sign hung limply from the gable. There was a light inside, shining weakly out into the complete darkness. The paint was peeling off the walls outside, and weeds and briars grew in profusion all around it. A less inviting place would be hard to imagine. Patrick crept around the side and hid in the brambles and blackberry bushes that pushed against the walls. He spotted a window slightly ajar with heavy curtains drawn almost closed hanging inside. The right hand curtain was hanging limply, having lost some hooks, so a slice of the room was visible. He crept under the window and waited, his heart thumping so loudly in his chest he was sure whoever was inside would be able to hear it. Rustling in the briars behind him made him shudder, rats probably. He tried to concentrate on the sounds coming from inside the building. There were definitely voices inside, but they were indistinct. Suddenly, the murmured hum burst into a crescendo of raucous laughter and the clink of glasses sang out. Someone was having a great time. Taking advantage of the noise, Patrick stood up and peeped in through the chink in the curtains. Sure enough there he was, Joe Lynch, and he was holding court inside, surrounded by a bunch of men in various states of physical degeneration. The tall red-haired man was exactly as Patrick remembered him. He was leaning on a makeshift bar, observing everything. Joe was mid story, he always fancied himself as a raconteur, and the gathered audience hung on his every word.

Again the voice dropped in volume, making it impossible to hear what his father was saying, but Patrick watched incensed as his father carried on his story without a care in the world.

Joe Lynch looked so much older than his forty-five years, but a lifetime of hard drinking, fighting, falling, and poor nutrition meant he was a battered-looking specimen. His hair was long now, balding on top but growing past his collar, and straggly grey. He was unshaven and filthy looking, in clothes Patrick didn't recognise. Patrick shuddered at the thought that that creature was his father. The laces were missing from his boots, and he looked like a tramp that you'd see hanging around the quays in town. Even though he was horrible to her, Mam always made an effort with his clothes, trying to have him turned out as nicely as possible. People were quick to judge a whole family based on the husband's appearance. It was almost an unwritten competition, who's got the nicest house, the best turned out family, the best coat at Mass on Sunday. It was ridiculous really when nobody had very much, *tuppence ha'penny looking down on tuppence,* his mam used to laugh. The wave of pain and anger washed over him again, his mam was gone, died a terrible brutal death, and that monstrous tyrant was still alive.

'And then sez I,' his father roared, obviously at the climax of the tale. 'What do you mean you weren't expecting me home, you stupid fat bitch!'

The gathered crowd laughed, and Joe slapped his knee. He was making fun of Mam, Patrick couldn't believe it. Even though he knew his father was a cold-blooded bully, he didn't imagine how anyone could make up stories about how he murdered his wife for the entertainment of these degenerates.

Joe stood up and accepted their applause and laughter as if he were on the stage of the Opera House. Eventually, as the reaction subsided and another round of drink arrived, Joe made his way unsteadily out of Patrick's line of vision. To his left, he heard the door open, Joe was coming out. Stealthily, Patrick crept around to the front of the building, staying low and in the shadows. Luckily, the overgrown bushes provided cover as Patrick watched his father chuckling and muttering to himself as he steadied himself against the wall, stumbling almost into the briars. The bar had no toilet, and the customers did their business outside against the ditch. Someone inside roared at Joe to shut the door after him, and Patrick heard it slam.

His father tripped again and muttered some obscenity to himself as he half-walked, half-fell towards the ditch, ham-fistedly attempting to unbutton his trousers as he went, and a cigarette clamped between his teeth.

As Joe stood with his back to the road, humming some indistinguishable tune, Patrick was immune to the bitter cold, feeling nothing but blind fury. How could he sing and tell jokes, laugh at the horrible death he gave his wife? Patrick saw the white-faced terror of his little sisters, his mother unrecognisable on the slab in Mercy hospital, the years and years of torture at his father's drunken hands, and something inside him snapped. Without thinking, he attacked him from behind and grabbed his straggly grey hair while simultaneously kneeing him in the lower back. Screaming with pain, Joe fell like a sack of potatoes to his knees.

He turned in stunned disbelief to find his assailant, rheumy pale blue eyes trying to focus.

'Wha...da...fu...' Before he could say another word, Patrick crashed his fist into his father's face.

'You bastard, you murdering bastard, you killed my mother and now you're telling stories about what a big man you are? You're the big strong Joe Lynch, are you? So brave you only attack women and children. Well, you know what? That's the last time you'll ever hurt anyone. I'm going to kill you, you worthless fucker. I wish I'd done it years ago.' Patrick spat as the blood pumped from Joe's broken nose. Patrick dragged him up and hit him again and again and again, until his father fell down on all fours, vomiting.

Patrick kicked him in the ribs, the satisfying sound of cracking bones registering. Joe rolled in agony onto his back, covering his head with his bony arms. Patrick sat astride his father's puny chest as he groaned in agony.

'You listen to me now,' Patrick hissed into his father's face. 'I wish to God I did this years ago. Liam and I should have finished you off when we had the chance, but I want you to look closely into my face, you pathetic, idle, useless drunk.' He spat each word slowly. 'I hate you. Connie and Anna hate you. Mam would have hated you if she wasn't such a good person and if it wasn't a mortal sin, and now look at me. This is the last human face you are ever going to see because you are going to burn forever in the fires of hell for what you did to us.'

Panic filled his father's eyes. Despite his confused state, he realised what was happening, and he opened his mouth to speak. His arms and legs flailed despite his diminishing strength as Patrick put his hands around his father's skinny neck and squeezed as hard as he could, never taking his eyes off Joe's for a second. He wanted his father to die seeing the unadulterated hate in the eyes of his only son. Blood thundered in his ears, he knew what he was doing, he wouldn't deny it, and nothing was going to stop him.

Time stood still, Joe's eyes bulged and eventually his body stopped moving. Tentatively, Patrick released the pressure from his father's throat and no sound came. His tongue hung loosely from his mouth of broken yellow teeth. Joe Lynch was dead.

Nothing happened. The raucous laughter erupted in the pub once more. There was nobody passing on the road. That crowd inside wouldn't even think to come looking for Joe. In that world all you needed was a drinking partner, not a friend. Any one of them would sell the other out happily for their next drink.

He stood, disgusted for a few moments, looking at the sight of his father, broken and bloody on the ground.

He looked up to the star-filled sky as the reality of what he had done was sinking in.

'I'm sorry, Mam. I know you wouldn't have wanted this, so I'm sorry if I upset you, but I'm not sorry for killing him. I swear I'm not, I'd do it again if I could.' He knew he should say an Act of Contrition, seek absolution from the Almighty for this most grievous sin but in order to do that, he had to be sorry, and he wasn't.

He stood up, leaving the body of his father where he lay. The sleet had turned to snow and Patrick trudged back the way he came.

CHAPTER 20

'All right, start again and tell me slowly what happened.' Hugo was trying to stay calm as Patrick sat on his couch with his head in his hands.

It was almost dawn. Luckily, he'd been up and heard someone outside. He instinctively grabbed the shotgun from the case and went out into the dark, starless night.

Patrick was on the doorstep, looking dishevelled. Something was very wrong, but he didn't speak. Hugo brought him in and gave him a brandy, which remained untouched on the side table beside him, and wrapped a blanket round his friend's shoulders. He was freezing cold.

'How did you get here?' Hugo began, hoping to ease into the reason for the visit.

'A lorry going to the port in Rosslare, he dropped me at the end of the road there,' Patrick replied, his voice sounded almost robotic.

'All right, and it's great to see you, obviously, but…' Hugo began.

'I had nowhere else to go.'

'Patrick, where are Connie and Anna?' Hugo was really getting worried now. Patrick was the toughest of the three of them; he'd never seen him so distraught.

'They're grand, Liam's mam has them. Don't tell Liam I'm here, Hugo, okay? He's a priest, he can't be seen to be...he wouldn't understand.' Wild bloodshot eyes fixed Hugo.

Hugo tried to stay calm. 'Okay, Patrick, if that's what you want, but I do think we should call Liam. He's calling here today as it happens on his way home for Christmas, he'll be here this morning sometime. I said I'd send the car, but he said he'd get the bus.' Hugo was bewildered, but whatever it was, it was bad.

'No, Hugo. Tell him he can't come, I can't see him.' Panic and desperation caused his voice to tremor.

The shrill ring of the telephone startled them both as their eyes rested on the phone.

'Hello?' Hugo said, racking his brain as to who would ring at six thirty in the morning.

'Hugo? It's Father Aquinas.'

'Hello Father...em...'

'I'm sorry for ringing so early, but Mrs Tobin has been up and she's worried about Patrick. Is he with you by any chance?'

Hugo saw the haunted look in his friend's eyes across the room.

'Er...yes he is, Father, he just arrived...'

'Hugo, listen carefully. Joe Lynch's body has been found outside some kind of a pub not far from here and Patrick is missing. The guards are on their way there now. The sacristan passed the scene on his way in to prepare for early Mass, that's how I know. Apparently, Lynch has been murdered. One of the drunks in the bar said he saw someone fitting Patrick's description walking away.'

The priest's words washed over Hugo like ice. This must be some kind of nightmare.

'You need to get him back to Cork as soon as possible, otherwise there's going to be a man hunt for him, and he'll be arrested as the main suspect. Will you do that?'

'Yes, Father, I'll see what I can do.'

'Good, we'll speak later on.'

Hugo stared at Patrick for a long second.

'That was Father Aquinas. Did you kill your father last night, Patrick?' Hugo couldn't believe those words were coming out of his mouth.

Patrick slumped in a chair, his head in his hands. He raised his head and fixed his bloodshot eyes on Hugo, his normally neat hair standing on end.

'That's why you can't get Liam. He's a priest, he couldn't understand, he shouldn't be near someone like me.'

'Patrick, Liam is on his way here this morning anyway. He's your best friend, and he will want to help you, as do I.' Hugo was trying to be reasonable.

'No, no he wouldn't, how could he understand, he's good...a priest for God's sake, and I'm a...I'm a murderer.' Patrick was distraught. 'You can't let him come here, if he comes, I'm going. I have to...' Patrick stood up, making for the door. Hugo had to make him stay, but Patrick was much bigger and stronger.

'Patrick, listen, I won't let Liam come if you really don't want to see him, but I know Liam is not going to judge you, I know it, don't ask me how I know, but I just do.' Hugo tried to hide the desperation in his voice. He needed Liam to convince Patrick to give himself up.

'You don't know, how could you know? I've murdered someone, actually killed them, committed the worst mortal sin ever. How can a priest ever accept someone like that?'

'Because he accepted me, and I'm a sinner,' Hugo said quietly.

'What? You've never done anything wrong your whole life, Hugo. No, if Liam is coming here, then I'm going to go. I don't want him dragged into this, putting him in a terrible position,' Patrick said, dismissing him.

Taking a deep breath, Hugo used the only card he had.

'Liam accepted me when I told him I'm a homosexual, and even though every law in the country, church, and state says I am beneath contempt, Liam was my friend. That's how I know you can trust him, Patrick,' Hugo pleaded with his friend, looking deep into his eyes and grabbing him by both arms.

Patrick opened his mouth to speak but no sound came out.

'Why did you never tell me?' he asked eventually.

Hugo sighed deeply. 'Because I was afraid. I was scared you'd be disgusted, that you'd think I was only friends with you and Liam because I was attracted to you or something. I was afraid you would reject me,' Hugo answered sincerely.

'I wouldn't have.'

'Well, now you know. That's why I don't want to go after girls and why some horsey duchess isn't sniffing round as you so often put it. Anyway, it doesn't matter at the moment, we've got bigger problems. But, Patrick, we do need Liam. So can I phone him?'

'But murder, Hugo, he's going to be a priest. They might throw him out if they knew he was friends with someone like me,' he whispered, tears in his eyes.

'We three are friends before we are anything else. You and he are inseparable. He will want to help, and we really need him. If we ever needed him, Patrick, we need him now. Can he come?'

Patrick nodded.

Hugo lifted the receiver of the telephone, asking the operator for the seminary. Liam had explained that personal phone calls were not really allowed, but this was an emergency.

'Good morning St Patrick's College, how may I help?' An officious female voice answered on the first ring.

'Good morning, this is Hugo FitzHenry, Earl of Drummond, I wish to speak with Liam Tobin, please.' Liam mentioned that the receptionist was very interested in people of Hugo's class and had been very impressed when Liam's first tuition cheque had been signed by Hugo. It endeared Liam to her that he moved in such exalted social circles.

As he suspected, it worked, and the obsequious tones replied, 'Certainly, your Lordship. It may take some time to locate him. May I call you back once I have found him?'

'That would be most kind,' Hugo replied. Normally, if the boys heard him speaking in that accent, there would be no end to the slagging, but needs must. He gave her the number for Greyrock and explained that it was a matter of some urgency, and she assured him that she would find him as quickly as possible.

True to her word, the phone rang after ten minutes.

'Hugo? Hugo, it's me, is everything all right. I'm getting the nine o'clock bus...' Liam began but before he could continue, Hugo interrupted.

'Liam, shut up and listen. Patrick turned up here this morning; he's in a dreadful state. I can't go into it over the phone, but...'

'Can't go into what, Hugo? Is he hurt?' Liam was whispering and trying to figure out what was happening, but the secretary was clearly listening in. She seemed very excited to tell him that the Earl of Drummond was on the line.

'No, not hurt, not physically at least, just get here as fast as you can, will you?'

'Oh Lord, all right, I'm on the way. We'll sort this out whatever's happened; the bus isn't for another two hours.'

'It's all right, I'll send the car to collect you. Ring your mother, wait, she has no phone. It's okay, I'll ring Father Aquinas from here, just get here as fast as you can.'

'Fine, see you soon.' Liam hung up and smiled his thanks to the secretary, who he knew would have loved to have been told what was going on.

Hugo lifted the phone again and this time dialled St Bart's monastery. He could visualise the black Bakelite phone ringing in the polished hallway, holy pictures adorning the walls, and a thick pile rug in heavy Axminster in the centre.

'St Bart's Presbytery,' a dour man's voice answered.

Hugo felt winded. Colour drained from his face. Suddenly, he was twelve years old again. He swallowed down the lump in his throat and prayed his voice would come out normally.

'Good morning, my name is Hugo FitzHenry, I wondered if I could speak to Father Aquinas please?' He tried his best to sound authoritative but inside he was shaking.

'Ah, Mr FitzHenry. Father Aquinas is in the refectory having his breakfast.'

Hugo thought quickly. Every second on the phone to Xavier was torture, but he had to get to Father Aquinas.

'I appreciate that, but I do need to speak to him as a matter of some urgency. Failing him, I will have to go to the bishop.'

Silence on the line. Hugo waited, hoping the gamble would pay off. Xavier may not have rated the complaints of a child but if that child, now an adult, were to reveal the nocturnal activities of a priest, surely there would be consequences—especially if that child was now an earl. Hugo could never do it, not because he wouldn't like to see Xavier pay for what he did, but to tell anyone filled him with such deep shame and disgust. Xavier didn't know that, though.

'Just one moment.'

Hugo heard the phone receiver being placed on the table and the sound of footsteps moving out of range.

After what seemed an interminable wait, Father Aquinas came on the line.

'Hugo?' he asked.

'Yes, Father, it's me. Liam is on his way here, and we'll look after Patrick and get to the bottom of it, but could you go down to Mrs Tobin's? She's minding Connie and Anna and they must be upset worrying about him. Can you just reassure them that all is well and that Patrick will be home soon?'

There was silence on the line for a moment.

'I will, Hugo, though how true that is I'm not sure. Get him back here as soon as you can, I'd say.'

'We'll try, Father,' Hugo said, and hung up.

'What did he say?' Patrick asked.

'Just that he was going to go down and reassure the girls you were okay and that you should get back to Cork as soon as possible.' Hugo was trying to be gentle.

'They know it was me then.' It was a statement more than a question.

'Well, they suspect you. That's what he thinks is the case, but he's only going on gossip. Apparently, someone like you was seen leaving the place where the body was found.'

Hugo turned on the wireless. It was a minute to eight; the news would be on soon. Maybe there would be a report on the finding of a body. Perhaps, he wasn't dead. Hugo knew very well from Patrick and Liam how rumours and gossip spread in the lanes and terraces under the Goldie Fish. Maybe Patrick just beat him up, that would be understandable, surely a judge would forgive that.

No mention of the alleged murder. That must be a good sign. Hugo listened to the rest of the bulletin and when the weather forecast came on, he looked over at Patrick whose head was resting on the back of the chair. He was sleeping. He was going to wake him up. How could he sleep at a time like this? But then Hugo remembered how traumatised his friend looked, how absolutely shattered he was and thought better of it. Best let him sleep. Liam wouldn't be much longer, and they might get some sense out of him together.

He left Patrick on the chair and covered him with a rug. He did his morning duties distractedly, running through everything that needed to be done with Tom as they did every day.

'Hugo, is everything all right? You seem a bit...I don't know...' Tom noticed.

'What? Sorry...yes, I didn't sleep well last night. I'm fine, just a bit tired.' Hugo lied.

'You're doing well, you know? It seems a lot to take on, I know it does, but you're managing fine.' Tom obviously thought running Greyrock was getting on top of him. How Hugo wished that was the case. He was totally out of his depth if what Father Aquinas said was true. But he and Liam would have to try and sort it out themselves. The strangeness between him and Tom in the days after Martha's mysterious disappearance had dissipated somewhat, but Hugo knew her father knew more about her departure than he was letting on. Tom was a great manager of the estate, but he wasn't a man to confide in, and anyway, the fewer people who knew that Patrick was even here at this stage the better.

Shortly after ten, the car pulled up on the gravel outside, and Hugo went out to meet Liam. By now, the house was buzzing with staff, tradesmen, and deliveries, so it was vital to remain calm, give no cause for gossip or speculation.

Wordlessly, they went to the morning room.

'Shhh,' Hugo nodded in the direction of the sleeping Patrick.

'What's going on, Hugo?' he asked as soon as Hugo shut the door and they were alone.

'Liam, sit down for a moment.' Hugo quickly relayed what Father Aquinas had said.

Liam was as shocked as Hugo had been when he first heard the news.

'He couldn't have, Hugo! I just can't accept that Patrick...would do...'

'Wouldn't kill his own father?' Patrick finished the sentence for him as he rubbed his weary face with his hands.

The three young men sat in the bright sunny room decorated in yellows and creams, warm from the bright winter sunlight outside and the log fire crackling in the grate, despite the freezing temperatures outside.

'Well? Did you?' It was Liam who asked.

'I did.' Patrick's expression was unfathomable.

'How?' Hugo asked. Liam and Hugo sat at either end of a sofa in front of the fire, and Patrick perched on the edge of the sumptuous armchair opposite, his head in his hands.

'He was in a pub. Well, he first came to Anna's classroom window and looked in; it terrified her, and she said this fella was with him. I always thought he'd gone to England straight after...after he killed Mam, that's why the guards couldn't find him, but the way Anna described this fella, well then, I knew where he was. He used to go to this place, out the Mallow road, when he used to make me rob houses when I was small, four or five, and the fella Anna described, well it was his place. So then, I thought maybe, that's where he was. I went out there, just to check it was still there. I swear I had no intention of doing anything else. It was years since I was there, and I didn't want to send the guards on a wild goose chase. Anyway, I looked in the window, and he was laughing, like, laughing his stupid head off, and then I realised he was telling them how he'd killed my mam. Like it was a big joke...' Patrick's voice cracked with emotion. He took a deep breath and continued, 'There was a load of auld tramps and fellas no better than him there, and they all thought it was great gas altogether. Then he came out to have a piss, there's no toilet in that place, it's a right kip, and he was absolutely paralytic drunk, staggering and swaying, and singing...and I just, I just laid into him, I couldn't stop. I didn't want to, to be honest, I just... Once I started, I couldn't stop. I...well I did it, and that's all there is...'

Silence descended in the room as each of them was lost in his thoughts, trying to process what had happened.

'So now what?' Liam asked eventually.

'Well, what are the options?' said Hugo, trying to be practical. 'Firstly, you could go to the guards, give yourself up and claim, I don't know, that you were just...' he fought to find the right words.

'Just so mad, so filled with rage and hatred and violence that I beat up an old drunk and then throttled him with my bare hands?' Patrick finished. 'Because that's what happened. There are no mitigating circumstances, apart from the fact that he murdered my mother, and I don't regret it, so I won't lie and say that I do.' Hugo had never heard that steely edge in Patrick's voice before, and it chilled him.

'Well, we could tone down that line of chat anyway, Patrick. Have sense would you? At least express regret. You could say you'd been drinking.' Liam was grasping at straws.

'What, like him, you mean? No, Liam, I definitely won't be saying that.' Patrick was adamant.

'Anyway, he was with your mother right before he went to find Joe Lynch so she'd have to lie and say he was drunk,' Hugo reasoned.

'Well, there's no way she'd do that, anyway. Nor should she,' Liam felt the need to add.

This really was a mess. What on earth were they going to do?

'You could go to England, I suppose, but then what about the girls?' Liam couldn't believe he was suggesting it.

'Either way, he's going to be leaving them, a life on the run or a life behind bars.' Hugo was trying to see a positive side but was failing miserably.

'I am actually still here.' Patrick half-smiled for the first time. 'I'll have to turn myself in. I can't be on the run, sure they'd find me eventually, anyway, and at least this way…'

'But what about Connie and Anna?' Liam asked.

'I know. They're all I've been thinking about. Do you think your mother would look after them? I couldn't have them being sent to an institution, and there's nobody else. Mam would never forgive me. Oh Jesus, what have I done?' Suddenly, he was shaking and sobbing, and his two friends looked on helplessly.

They sat with nothing to offer but companionship. They both knew he was right; there was nothing else but to turn himself in.

'We'll come with you,' Liam said, though in what way that would be helpful, he had no idea. It might make the process a little easier on Patrick.

'Will ye? But what about your vocation, like, I killed someone, Liam. Maybe, you'd be better off staying out of it.' Patrick looked much younger than his twenty years.

'You are my best friend and a good person. I'm still trying to let all this sink in, to be honest, but nothing will change that, Patrick, nothing. Do you understand? I'm going to stick by you through this, you're not alone.' Liam was adamant.

'Me too, if you want me…' Hugo began.

Patrick got up and walked over to where Hugo stood.

'I'm sorry you thought I wouldn't react well to your...news. Maybe, I wouldn't have either, I don't know, but in the light of recent events, I'm in no position to be judging anyone, am I? I just know I can't face what's to come without both of ye, so thanks.'

Liam looked enquiringly at Hugo.

'I told him. He thought you would be too torn, he didn't want to tell you, and I convinced him you'd be all right. You've got a track record of accepting friends in the habit of committing mortal sins.' Hugo smiled ruefully.

'God help me if I ever become a bishop, I'll have to have ye excommunicated.' Liam grinned. 'Look, I'm not saying it's not terrible, but let's get some perspective here. Joe Lynch was a horrible bully, and now he's dead. Patrick shouldn't have killed him, that's obvious, but nobody would be shedding any tears if he was hit by a bus now, would they? I know I'm training to be a priest and I must follow the commandments and everything, but I refuse to see the death of Joe Lynch as a tragedy for anyone, except Patrick. I wish I could turn the clock back, but for your sake, Patrick, not his. So I'm not conflicted, you shouldn't have killed him, but he had it coming.'

'It will be a tragedy for Connie and Anna when I get put in jail and they end up in an orphanage.' The fate of his little sisters weighed heavier on Patrick than his own.

'Patrick, we both know my mam, there's no way on God's green earth she'd stand by and let Connie and Anna go into care, you know that. Between us all, no matter what happens, we'll look after them.' Liam spoke with confidence.

'But we've no family, Mam only had her sister Kit and she's dead. The rest of them disowned her years ago for marrying him. I've no idea about any of the Lynches, not that I'd leave them with any of his family, anyway,' Patrick replied.

'You might not have blood family, but you've got us. And as Liam says, we'll take care of the girls, whatever it takes. Money's no problem, Liam says his mam...'—the three smiled at Hugo's use of the word, so often they teased him about calling Lily, mother or mama when he was younger—'will have the girls. When you go to court, and we hope you don't, obviously, but it seems inevitable at this stage, I'll make sure you have the best defence team money can buy. The girls will be loved and cared for, you can rest assured of that,' Hugo said. 'So, are we going to Cork?'

Patrick sighed and nodded sadly. Liam put his hand on his friend's shoulder.

'Are you hungry?' Hugo asked. 'God knows what's facing you, so you should eat something.'

'Nah, let's just go. I'm not hungry, anyway.' Patrick spoke and Liam could hear the weariness. The past months had been so hard on him, dealing with the brutal murder of his mother, then trying to tend to the needs of two small girls in his grief, trying to be big brother, father, housekeeper, and everything they needed. He could understand how his friend just saw red when he heard Joe Lynch laughing, there but for the grace of God went anyone. Surely a court would see that and make allowances. Connie and Anna needed Patrick, they loved his mam, Liam knew that, but Patrick was their idol. He couldn't begin to imagine the effect his removal from their lives would have.

Now, he thought, mentally steeling himself. The three friends were going to have to be practical and strong.

'I wonder would they make a few sandwiches for the car? Hugo's right, you do need to eat.'

Hugo was on the phone to his legal man in Dublin but nodded to Liam and indicated that he should ring the bell to summon Patterson. Liam felt silly doing it, but the kitchen was miles away and this was the fastest way. He rang and moments later the butler appeared. Hugo was still speaking to the solicitor and so Liam took over.

'Ah, Mr Patterson, hello.' He always felt awkward speaking to the servants at Greyrock as if he was pretending to be someone he wasn't.

'We're going to Cork by car in a few minutes, and we won't have time to eat, so I was wondering if there was a way that maybe you or the cook or…' Liam hated this, but he ploughed on, 'someone could make a few sandwiches or something here, and maybe a flask of tea for us to take with us?'

'Certainly, sir,' Patterson responded, casting a worried glance at Patrick, who was now staring out the window, his hands deep in his pockets, lost in thought. 'I'll ask the cook to do it right away, it will be in the car for you when you're ready to leave. Do you think Master Hugo will need an overnight bag? If so, I'll ask the valet to organise it.'

'Er, maybe, I'm not sure, best have a bag though just in case.' Liam hoped he was doing the right thing. Hugo was on another call now, and Liam didn't want to interrupt him.

'Fine, I'll let him know.' And Patterson withdrew.

Hugo finished the call, and he and Liam shared a glance that asked how on earth did they get into this. They tried to look cheerful for their friend's sake.

'Better get going, I suppose,' Liam said, more to break into Patrick's reverie than anything else.

Patrick turned, 'Will they let me see Connie and Anna, do you think? Before…before they arrest me or charge me or whatever?'

Hugo answered as he replaced the receiver for the phone in its cradle. 'Right, the first call was to my solicitor O'Kelly. He's a good man, though criminal law isn't his area.' Even the use of the word 'criminal' to describe Patrick seemed ludicrous. 'He said they will most likely take you into custody, but we can apply to the court for bail. You'll be brought to the district court and then the judge will send it forward to the circuit court. You don't need to say anything or make a plea or anything like that. O'Kelly says to say nothing until he gets there. He's leaving Dublin on the next train. He's going to meet us at the Garda station, and he'll be with you so you'll have someone on your side at least. As regards bail, they may or may not grant it, but he's going to be with you when you go to the court. They'll probably hear the bail application then, either that or tomorrow, he thinks. He's working on getting someone to represent you, a barrister, he has someone in mind but apparently he lives in the South of France and only chooses a small number of cases each year. According to O'Kelly, this Geoffrey d'Alton is the best counsel there is, and maybe, that he'd be working for me, or my title or something, could be the thing that would swing it. Seems like a ridiculously snobbish attitude, but we'll use whatever we've got. All O'Kelly has to do at the bail hearing is explain that you're not a flight risk and that this was an exceptional instance of violence on your part, previously of good character and all that. That last call was my mother. I told her the story, I hope you don't mind, but she'll hear about it soon enough, anyhow. It was a long shot but she knows everyone, so when I mentioned the barrister's name, believe it or not, she knows this d'Alton character and is going to use her considerable powers of persuasion on him, as well. She sends you both her love by the way.'

'What are my chances of getting bail?' Patrick asked.

Hugo smiled in what he hoped was an encouraging way. 'Around fifty-fifty,' he said.

In fact, O'Kelly had said bail was unlikely given the seriousness of the offense, but there was no point in making matters worse by telling Patrick that.

CHAPTER 21

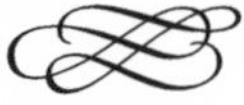

Delivering Patrick to the Garda Station was the hardest thing Liam ever had to do. They were promptly dismissed by the desk sergeant once Patrick had been taken into custody. The solicitor was there when they arrived, but he explained to Hugo that the bail hearing wouldn't be until the next day so he arranged to be in court for that. He was going to be with Patrick when he was interviewed later. There had been no further communication from this d'Alton so they were just praying he'd say yes. Hugo was confident that if anyone could convince him to take the case, it would be his mother. At least that was some chink of hope in an otherwise catastrophic day. Hugo's solicitor spoke of him almost in whispers, like he was some kind of a legal demi-God. Apparently, he was Irish, though you wouldn't know it to hear him speak, but he was renowned for his cases in the Old Bailey, the Palais de Justice in Paris, and even in America. When he was involved with a case, the press gathered and people clamoured to get into the public gallery to see him perform. It all seemed a bit surreal. Liam wondered at how much someone like that would cost and thanked God once again for Hugo. Left to their own devices, Patrick would have had to have someone appointed by the court to represent him, given that they couldn't afford even a normal-priced legal team, let alone the wondrous Geoffrey d'Alton.

Out on the footpath outside the Garda station, Hugo lit up a cigarette and exhaled slowly. 'Well, he's the best money can buy, and that's what Patrick's getting. Apparently, according to my solicitor, the barrister is a snooty pompous ass but aside from that, he's a legal genius.'

'We'll put up with him, whatever it takes. You're very good, Hugo. He does appreciate it, I'm sure, we all do. Without you, and your money, well I just don't know...' Liam began.

'Stop. I mean it. Just stop. I don't want to hear another word about this. I love you two and your families like my own. In fact, you are my family, I only have my mother and you lot, so it's what families do, isn't it? Help each other when needed? I don't want people thanking me like I'm some random stranger bestowing my great wealth on the population. Patrick is like a brother to me, and I'll do whatever it takes to get him out of this.' The strain of the day was showing and Hugo's eyes were bright with tears.

Detective Inspector Donal McMullan crossed the road on his way into the station, presumably to interview the suspect. Liam recognised him as the man who broke the news to Patrick about his mother, and he remembered Patrick telling him of the detective's kindness at that time. If he was involved in this case, that was a good omen. He stopped beside Hugo and Liam. They had a brief chat, and he asked how the girls were doing. He also explained that a social worker was being assigned to the case, given that the girls' only next of kin was now in custody. The children should technically be taken into the care of the state. Liam explained that his mother wanted to look after them, and they would be much happier with her. The detective was understanding and said he'd try to make sure that case was put to the relevant authorities and there would probably be a hearing to determine the best interests of the children. Liam was glad the detective seemed to be on Patrick's side, even though he couldn't say so in as many words.

'They would be happy with my mam, they really would,' Liam pleaded. The detective stood outside with them in the freezing cold air and accepted a cigarette from Hugo.

'Sure, Liam, I know that. You can see how she is with them, I've seen it myself when I was keeping Patrick informed of the progress of the case to locate Joseph Lynch, and please God, the courts will see it that way too. Those poor little girls have put up with so much in their short lives, the best chance of having a normal childhood, or as normal as they can have, is with someone as kind and loving as your mother. I've had plenty of dealings with Joe Lynch over the years, a right nasty piece of work he was, too. You didn't hear this from me, but that fella is no loss to the world. It's just a pity Patrick had to be the one to do for him. God knows he got into plenty of scraps over the years with fellas over drink and money and all the rest of it. It's just bad luck it wasn't one of them gave him a clatter. Now, as regards the girls, I'll do my best, Liam. I'm not promising anything, though; I've seen some mad things happen in court. It depends on who you get to be honest.'

'I know you will, Inspector. We really appreciate your help, and I know Patrick does too.' Liam smiled.

'If he'd only sent us up there rather than taking it on himself, now I better get on,' he said, stubbing out his cigarette and turning back into the station.

Hugo checked into a hotel in the city. He was exhausted, having been up most of the previous night. He could have stayed at Liam's house, he knew, but he needed access to a telephone to try to get this d'Alton.

'I'll check in and try to get my mother on the phone, see if she's had any luck with this barrister. I don't even know how she knows him, but she has lots of friends from different walks of life. I'll see you in the morning.' Liam gave him a quick hug, something they didn't normally do, and Hugo smiled ruefully.

'We'll get him out of this, won't we, Liam?' he asked.

'Well, if we can't, it won't be for want of trying.'

Patrick sat quietly on the hard tubular steel seat. Opposite him was the detective, Inspector Mc Mullan. Patrick was glad to see him, he had been kind the day Patrick learned of his mother's murder and they'd got to know each other as the search for Joe Lynch dragged on. The inspector kept Patrick informed each week of the progress, or lack of it. He was a decent man and Patrick trusted him.

Mr O'Kelly was sitting beside him and had spoken to him for a moment before the interview, advising him to tell the truth but not to answer any questions he didn't want to answer.

The detective took a clean tape out of its box and inserted it into a reel to reel recording machine. It clicked and whirred as he pressed the record button.

'Interview with Patrick Joseph Lynch, 19th December 1977.' He looked at his watch, 'Two twenty-three p.m. Detective Inspector Donal McMullan interviewing. Solicitor Brian O'Kelly also present.'

'So, Patrick, can you tell me in your own words what happened yesterday? Start off in the morning and try to be as accurate as you can.' Patrick swallowed and glanced at Mr O'Kelly, who nodded, encouraging him to speak.

'Well, in the mid-morning up to lunchtime, I suppose, I was at the monastery talking to Father Aquinas. He's my old teacher and a friend of the family, you could say. When I left him, I went back home. I was clearing up the yard, and I was just going to get the girls from school at three o'clock when Mrs Tobin called me. She's my neighbour and my late mother's friend. She's been helping with my sisters since Mam was killed. Anyway, she told me that Connie and Anna, they're my little sisters, were inside her house. Anna was upset at school so they sent for Mrs Tobin. Anyway, I went straight over there, and Anna told me that she'd seen our father looking in the window of the classroom and that there was a tall man with red hair with him. Anna doesn't tell lies, so as soon as she said it, I remembered a place—it's kind of a pub, not even a pub actually, more of a dosshouse for down and outs, out the Mallow Road where my father used to go when he was robbing. The fella there had a big head of red hair, and he was huge, six four or five, I'd say. My father used to take stolen goods for him to sell. All dodgy people went there; no respectable people ever went into that pub, I'd say. Well, we thought he was gone to England, my father, but then I just thought I'd check this place first.'

'Why did you not come and tell the guards of your suspicions? Why did you take it on yourself?' McMullan interrupted, though his tone wasn't aggressive.

Patrick paused, 'Well, I wasn't sure if it was still there, and ye were so good when Mam died. I just thought I'd check the place out and if I found anything, I would let ye know. Stupid, I know now looking back, but that's what I thought.'

'All right, carry on. You left the girls with Mrs Tobin and then what?'

Patrick told the whole story, his voice choked with emotion as he recounted Joe's cackling laugh. When he finished, leaving out no details he could remember of the assault, he sat back in the chair, suddenly exhausted.

'Did you set out to kill him, Patrick?' McMullan asked gently.

Patrick didn't need to look at Mr O'Kelly.

'No, I didn't. I was so angry when he was laughing about my mam and calling her names and when he came out, he was plastered drunk, staggering and all that. He was chuckling away to himself and singing, like he hadn't a care in the world. I thought about Connie and Anna and how scared they were all their lives of him, and what he did to Mam... I just...I don't know, I wanted to hurt him. I did do it, Inspector, I did kill him, and I won't pretend that I'm not glad he's dead, but I didn't plan it, it just happened.'

'That's all for now, Patrick, thank you. Interview terminated two thirty p.m. D.I McMullan attending.'

Standing up, he ejected the tape and labelled it. Patrick was unsure of what he should do. Noting his confusion, the detective sat down again.

'Right so, Patrick, you'll now be taken into custody and given prison issue clothing. You did right to come forward, that will help your case. Everything will be taken from you, so I suggest that you give anything of importance to Mr O'Kelly here, then you'll be assigned a cell and as soon as possible, you'll be brought before the district court.'

'What happens then?' he asked, trying to hide his terror. He knew on some level he was going to be locked up but to hear the word prison made his stomach lurch.

'Well then, you'll meet with your legal team, and the judge will send this forward to the circuit court. They don't deal with crimes like this in the district court. Then the prosecution will prepare the book of evidence and a date will be set for the trial.'

'Will I get bail?' He knew he sounded like a kid, but he couldn't help it.

Mr O'Kelly spoke, 'Ideally yes, Patrick, but there's a possibility the judge would see you as a flight risk, so I'd prepare yourself to be in prison until the case comes to trial.' His voice was kind, he knew how hard this was.

'I'll give ye a few minutes there so.' The detective left the room.

'How long could that take?' Patrick asked dully.

Mr O'Kelly placed his hand on Patrick's arm. 'Patrick, the best that we can hope for here is that the prosecution brings a charge of manslaughter rather than murder. They'll decide that based on the book of evidence. You'll be pleading not guilty to murder, but I'd advise, and I think your barrister will agree when he gets here, that you should enter a guilty plea to the lesser charge of manslaughter, but as I said, we'll have to wait and see. Either way, Patrick, you will be going to prison. I'm sorry to be the one to tell you, but it's best if you know the truth.'

Patrick didn't trust himself to speak, so he just nodded and willed back the tears that stung the back of his eyes.

'If I do get found guilty of murder...' Patrick began.

'Hopefully, it won't come to that.'

'But if it does, how long will I be sent to jail for?'

Patrick could hear the clock ticking on the wall. It was the only thing on the drab sludge-coloured walls.

'If you are found guilty of murder, you'll be facing life in prison,' O'Kelly said quietly.

The words hung in the air, and Patrick was finding it hard to breathe. The solicitor's face swam in front of him, and he thought he might throw up. Mr O'Kelly told him to put his head between his knees and try to take slow, even breaths. After a minute, he felt a bit better and stood up. Mr O'Kelly knocked on the door and a younger guard opened up. He bade Patrick goodbye, and Patrick followed the guard down a corridor in the direction of the cells. As the door closed behind them, Patrick looked around the bare room. There was a bunk with a grey blanket and a thin pillow, a bucket stood in the corner, and that was it. Patrick lay down and stared at the ceiling, terror and despair threatening to overpower him. He tried to visualise a hurling pitch, green grass and blue skies, but it was impossible.

The familiar aromas of stew and soda bread and clean laundry filled the small kitchen, and Liam was glad to be home despite the terrible circumstances.

'Oh Liam, what in the name of God is going on?' His mother had been out of her mind with worry, he could tell. As briefly as he could, he told her what had happened in low tones so as not to alert the girls, who were playing with their dolls on the stairs.

'Where's Hugo?' she asked.

'He's gone to a hotel. He said to tell you he knows he could have stayed here, but he's trying to get a barrister for Patrick with his mother's help. Some Irish man who lives in France but isn't inclined to take cases here so much anymore for some reason. Anyway, he needs a phone to organise it all so that's why he's gone to the Metropole.'

'Right, thank God we have him anyway. We couldn't afford legal bills. He's a great lad. Are you hungry?' his mother asked.

'Em...yes, something to eat would be nice. We had some sandwiches in the car but, to be honest, we were so upset I couldn't eat. You should have seen poor Patrick, Mam. He was in an awful state.'

Liam sat at the table as his mother put out cutlery and a plate.

'So what happens now?'

Liam wished he could tell his mother something other than the truth.

'He'll be held in the Garda station overnight and transferred to prison in the morning,' Liam replied as Mrs Tobin placed a steaming plate of stew in front of him.

'The solicitor told us that he'll have a preliminary hearing in the morning to determine if he will get bail or not, and for the judge to send on the case to the circuit court. And then the book of evidence will be compiled. It's a slow process, and Patrick could spend several months on remand awaiting trial.'

'Did he admit he did it?' she asked.

'Sure, I suppose there's no future in saying he didn't, Mam. He said he did it, that he didn't intend to kill him, but that when he saw him laughing about his mother, something inside him snapped and he did what he did. He's telling the truth, which is the only way forward here.'

Mrs Tobin nodded in agreement. 'I suppose you're right, but

what's to become of those two little girls? They've been through so much already.'

'Well, I had a quick word with the detective, remember him? The man who told Patrick about his mother.'

'Yes, Detective Inspector McMullan. He's been keeping Patrick informed about the search for Joe Lynch, he's been very good.'

'Well, he was the one questioning Patrick at the station. Anyway, I asked him if he could use his influence to suggest that the girls stay with you rather than going into care. That was all right, wasn't it?' Liam ate his delicious stew, he didn't realise how hungry he was.

'Of course, I couldn't have them taken away. Will they let me keep them, do you think? Until Patrick is released.'

Liam put down his fork.

'Well, maybe Father Aquinas could help with that, as well. I know he deals with the children's services through his work above in the school. I know you love them, but Mam, you have to understand, there's a really good chance that you'll have them for years if Patrick gets convicted. It's a big undertaking.' He knew his mother wouldn't hesitate, but he wanted her to be fully aware of what she was getting herself into.

'Kathleen was my best friend. She'd do the same for me. I love those little girls and if I can give them a home for as long as they need it, I'm very happy to do it. I'll talk to Father Aquinas in the morning and see if we can arrange to do whatever needs doing. Please God, Patrick won't have to go to jail, but I know he's after landing himself into serious trouble. We'll just have to wait and see if Hugo can get this miracle man from Dublin or France or wherever he is and see what he'll have to say about it.'

'We'll have to tell them.' Liam nodded in the direction of the hall.

'Finish your dinner, and we'll do it together.' His mother squeezed his shoulder.

They cleared away the plates and called the girls into the kitchen. He was dreading this, but it had to be done. There was no point in lying to them, they would find out anyway and it was vital that Connie and Anna trusted them. Mrs Tobin held Anna on her lap, and

Liam put his arm around Connie. They left out the gruesome details and tried to paint Patrick in as positive a light as possible, focusing on the fact that their father was dead and could never hurt or frighten them again. They seemed relieved but kept asking for Patrick.

Liam looked at his mother, unsure of how much they should be told. She gave him an imperceptible nod, they had to be told something and a diluted version of the truth was the only option. They had had so much pain and sorrow in their little lives already, how could he tell them the person they loved and relied on most in the world might be locked up for years?

'Girls, the thing is, Patrick was very cross with your father for hurting your mammy and for frightening you. All he wanted to do was protect you. He got so cross that he hit him and when Patrick did that, well, your father died. Now the guards don't want people going around hitting other people and making them hurt or die, so Patrick will have to go into a court and a man called a judge will decide if Patrick should go to jail or not for doing it.'

As the words he spoke registered on their faces, Liam never felt more inadequate.

'But Liam, the guards won't take Patrick away from us. He's the good one, isn't he? Daddy was the bad man not Patrick. They won't put Patrick in jail, will they, Liam?' Connie's eyes filled with tears while Anna clung to Liam's mother.

Liam pulled her onto his lap and stroked her hair. 'I hope not, pet, but even if they do, me and my Mam and Hugo will look after ye, so try not to worry. We are doing everything we can to help Patrick, I promise you that. Hugo is getting a very clever man from France to come and explain to the judge that Patrick is very good. We just have to pray that the judge sees that.'

Eventually, the girls fell asleep, and Liam sat up in the kitchen with his mother, thinking about the last twenty-four hours. They tried to stay positive, but the outlook was bleak. As they were about to go to bed, there was a gentle knock on the front door.

Liam went out and was surprised to see Hugo shivering on the doorstep. It had begun to snow heavily again and Hugo only had a light coat.

'Hugo, God Almighty, come in, it's freezing.' He led his friend inside and shut the door on the blizzard outside. 'I thought you were staying at the Metropole?'

'I was,' Hugo replied shivering as he took off his jacket, now covered in snow. Mrs Tobin appeared with a towel for his hair and led him to the range before putting on the kettle.

'I had to come and tell you. My mother managed it, after about fifty international phone calls. This d'Alton initially refused the case. He doesn't like working in Ireland. Apparently, not good enough for him or something. Anyway, whatever the reason, she's managed to convince him. She said they had a mutual connection, and she has met him once or twice so she spoke to him this evening, and he's finally agreed to take the case as a favour to her.' The relief shone out of Hugo's eyes.

'Oh, Hugo, that's marvellous! Well done!' Liam felt some of the earlier despair dissipate, maybe there was hope after all.

Mrs Tobin hugged him. 'Thank you, Hugo. I don't know where we'd be without you, honestly I don't, you're a Godsend.'

'Mrs Tobin, just as I was telling Liam earlier, please don't thank me. I want to do it, you're all like family to me, I'll do whatever I can to fix this.'

'I know you will, pet.' Mrs Tobin held his hand. 'We all will. And you're dead right, we may not be related by blood, but we're family all the same. Not another word, I promise. Now, a cup of tea and a slice of fruit cake? Or would you rather a rasher sandwich or I've got a bit of stew left over.'

Hugo chuckled for the first time in weeks.

'Just like when I used to come down on Thursdays and I'd eat enough for ten men and leave with my pockets full of cake. You kept me alive all those years, you know? A rasher sandwich would be lovely, and maybe a bit of cake for after? I meant to eat in the hotel, but I was so busy on the phone I forgot. Gosh, I didn't realise the time,' he said glancing at his watch. 'Perhaps I should have left it till the morning.'

Mrs Tobin kissed him on the top of his head. 'You're as welcome here as the flowers of May, Hugo FitzHenry, you always were and you always will be. Now, sit down there, and I'll get your food. There's no way you're going back out in that weather, so settle yourself down there by the fire. Liam, run upstairs and get him some dry clothes, he'll catch his death in those wet trousers. It might not be as fancy as the Metropole, but I won't have it on my conscience that you get pneumonia so you'll stay here tonight.'

'Well, that's telling you.' Liam grinned as he went to get Hugo something to change into. When he came back down, Hugo was warming himself by the range. He took the hand-knit sweater, shirt, and the corduroy trousers gratefully and ran upstairs to change.

'You look less like a drowned rat now, at least.' Liam smiled as his friend came back.

'Thanks, Liam. I was soaked through. How are the girls, did you tell them?'

Liam filled Hugo in on the conversation as he devoured an entire plate of rasher sandwiches followed by half a fruit cake.

'Where do you put it, Hugo? You could eat for Ireland but there's not a pick on you,' Mrs Tobin wondered with a smile. 'You were always the same, though you were a pudgy little lad when you came here first.'

'I forget to eat, Mrs Tobin. I think that's it, some days I eat nothing at all and then realise it at ten o'clock at night. The cook is probably fit to strangle me though she never says. I'm rather like a camel, I believe, stock up and then go for ages and ages.'

'What you need is a good woman to mind you, doesn't he, Liam?' Mrs Tobin joked, ruffling Hugo's hair.

'Mam, like myself, Hugo needs a woman like he needs a hole in the head, sure haven't we you? Wouldn't some young one only be pecking at him and he footloose and fancy free?' Liam caught Hugo's eye behind his mother's back and gave him a wink. Hugo smiled and despite the awfulness of the situation, felt a warm glow of love for these people.

'Sure, you've plenty time yet anyway, I suppose. We'll have to focus on Patrick now, and on these little girls. I'll pray hard tonight and ask Seán and Kathleen to intercede with Our Blessed Mother for Patrick.' She kissed both of them on the head and went up.

They chatted for a while and eventually Liam yawned.

'Shall I just stretch out on the couch, Liam?' Hugo asked. 'I know you have a full house now with the girls, as well.'

'Well, Mam cleared the bed in the girls' room for me. It's a double if you don't mind sharing. There are boxes and things up there but at least we'll get some sleep.'

Hugo looked uncomfortable. Knowing, even accepting a homosexual friend was one thing, sharing a bed with one was quite another. He hated the idea of Liam feeling awkward.

'But you better not snore, or I'll give you the treatment Con used to give me if I disturbed his sleep, right? A hobnailed boot into the head!'

Hugo smiled but considered making up a reason he had to go back to the hotel. Liam was being so kind but surely the idea of sharing a bed with Hugo, now that he knew what he was, was abhorrent. Before he could object, Liam went upstairs and Hugo had to follow.

In the bedroom, boxes and cartons were stacked everywhere. Like every house where the children were grown up and gone, all of the things that they accumulated that were too important to throw out but not important enough to take with them were gathering dust in their mother's home. He smiled at the Elvis posters on the walls and the remains of makeup in a drawer. It seemed like a million years ago when he, Kate and Con and the twins all lived here, when he would creep downstairs at night to see Mammy and Daddy chatting quietly by the range, and everything seemed so perfect.

Hugo cleared his throat. 'I...you don't have to do this...I'll sleep on the floor, and you can...'

Liam looked at him.

'Hugo, if it doesn't bother you, it doesn't bother me, all right? I'd say we've had more than enough to deal with for one day so let's just try to get some sleep, shall we? As you said, we're as close as brothers, closer actually, so I don't think you're going to jump me in the middle of the night or whatever...' Liam took off his trousers and jumper and slept in his shirt and underwear.

Mammy had placed hot jars in the bed earlier so it was lovely and warm and the weight of the woollen blankets that smelled of Daz washing powder transported him back to a time when life was simple. Hugo climbed in beside him and lay on his back.

'This is the first time I've shared a bed with a man,' he said into the dark. 'Probably the last too, but I'm glad it was you, Liam.'

'It won't be the last. At least I hope it won't be for you, I mean. For God's sake, Hugo, it was He who made you, He's the one that made you what you are. I know what people say, but how can something that's part of you, part of who you are, be so wrong? It's not like you chose it, you just are the way you are. You don't want to hurt anyone, you're a good person. Love is love. I think you should find it and keep it and remember God made you, and He also made men like you, so you're not alone.'

'But isn't it against everything you believe or are taught by the church.' Hugo was amazed.

'I won't lie to you, Hugo. I've wrestled with it, but...I don't know, this isn't probably a very theological way of looking at things, but Jesus was all about love. That was his main message. For us to love each other. And I love you and I love Patrick and no matter what happens, or how ye live, that won't ever change. Just go, Hugo, go to Paris, visit your uncle, whatever it takes. Even if it's just now and again, for a visit, nobody needs to know. You only get one life, you know? Losing my father, yours, Patrick's situation, should teach us that.'

'Thanks, Liam. I love you, too.'

Hugo lay with his hands behind his head most of the night, wide awake despite being shattered with exhaustion. Liam was sleeping peacefully beside him. Hugo realised he was right. What was he going to do, sit in Greyrock forever, trying to deny to himself and everyone else what he was? He would do it. As soon as all this business with Patrick was resolved, he'd get in touch with his uncle. His father always said he'd be happy to hear from him. He might visit him, maybe even have an experience. Even if he didn't, he couldn't imagine the relief of living just for a while as he was, rather than how the world expected him to be.

CHAPTER 22

Liam and Hugo stood on the steps of the courthouse the next day, waiting for it to open. D'Alton was on his way from France, by aeroplane. He was due to land in Cork Airport within the hour.

At the other end of the building, Liam noticed a woman standing alone. Every time he glanced in her direction, she caught his eye. She was dressed in a dark wool coat and hat, her blond hair was clipped neatly back and she looked like a respectable kind of girl, uncomfortable in her surroundings. There were lots of people milling about, stamping their feet and stuffing their frozen hands in their armpits for warmth.

'Do you recognise her?' he asked Hugo, who was sucking on a cigarette as if it were his last breath.

'Who?' he exhaled.

'That girl there at the other side with the navy coat, she looks familiar,' Liam nodded in her direction.

'No, I don't think so, why? Should I?'

'No, it's just she keeps looking over at us...' Liam began.

Hugo smiled. 'Well, she's barking up the wrong tree if she's set her cap at either of us.'

Before Liam had time to reply, she walked towards them.

'I'm sorry,' she began. 'I just wondered, aren't you Patrick Lynch's friends?'

It was freezing cold and sleet was breaking through the heavy dark clouds. Liam noticed her hands were gloveless and almost blue with the cold. She gripped her handbag tightly.

'Yes,' he replied. 'Do you know Patrick?'

'I'm Helen Dunne, I work in O'Neills with Patrick, and we're friends. I've been calling to his house recently, just to see how he and his sisters were getting along, but a neighbour told me he's been arrested, and… Well, I just wondered how he is.'

Liam and Hugo remembered Mrs Tobin talking about a girl who worked with Patrick. He and Hugo saw her at Mrs Lynch's funeral, but they didn't have a chance to speak to her because she was looking after Connie and Anna. By all accounts, she was a great help and support. Liam's mam said that she and Father Aquinas had been hoping a romance might blossom out of it once Patrick recovered a bit from the shock of his mother's murder.

'Of course, I remember you, Helen. We didn't get a chance to be introduced at the funeral, but my mother said you are a wonderful help with the girls, they're mad about you. Why don't we go to that little café across the street? It's freezing out here. We can sit in the window and watch for the court opening. It probably won't be for twenty minutes and by then, we could be dead from hypothermia,' Liam suggested.

'Well, I don't want to intrude…' she began.

'Nonsense,' said Hugo. 'I'm Hugo FitzHenry, and this is Liam Tobin. Now, we'll be perished if we have to stand out here for another second, so let's have a cup of tea and we can fill you in.'

They chatted over tea, and the men warmed to Helen. She clearly had strong feelings for Patrick, but they doubted that he knew that. She definitely wasn't his usual type, no flashy clothes or makeup, but she seemed a really nice person.

'The vultures are circling,' said Hugo, pointing to the steps of the large limestone courthouse. People were trying to get into the building through the crowds, who'd appeared in a steady stream in the past half hour. Murders were rare, so there was a ghoulish interest in this one and once it became known that Geoffrey d'Alton was taking the case, public interest intensified. The story made all the national newspapers and even some in England. Hugo didn't know how that information had become public but somehow it had.

So often they had passed the iconic Cork Court House building over the years never imagining for a moment that it would ever feature so heavily in the story of their lives. People surged forward in increasingly large numbers as the doors opened, some carrying flasks and wrapped-up sandwiches. The macabre nature of someone who attended murder trials as a hobby was something Liam found deeply distasteful. Hugo was more circumspect.

'It's big news, a murder, so people are bound to be curious. I'd say everyone supports Patrick though since the whole city is buzzing with the story. Now, shall we go over and meet this Mr d'Alton and see if he is a mere mortal or really the magician he's lauded to be?'

'Well, thanks for the tea…' Helen began.

'Come with us,' Hugo offered. 'I'm sure it would cheer him up to see friendly faces in the audience or gallery or whatever it's called.'

She smiled and her face was transformed into a picture of beauty. She was a lovely girl, and Liam wished that for her sake and for Patrick's things could progress between them. Before anything like that could even be considered, however, they had the gargantuan task of getting him off a lifelong prison sentence for murdering his own father in cold blood. It seemed an impossible task, but to Liam it was black and white. Sure, the sixth commandment said *Thou shalt not kill.* However, he felt that maybe he should have more of a moral dilemma on his hands, but he didn't. It would have been so much better if Patrick had gone to the guards with his suspicions about Joe's whereabouts, and of course, he should not have killed him. But should Patrick, a kind, loving man have to spend his life behind bars because he rid the world of a thoroughly evil man? The church says there is hope for everyone to be redeemed and that could even be stretched to include Joe Lynch, but the past is the best indicator of the future, and

Liam seriously doubted Lynch's capacity for redemption. Should Connie and Anna be denied the loving care and protection of their brother for years and years because of this? He was certain they shouldn't. They'd suffered enough, Mrs Lynch suffered enough, and Patrick suffered enough. It was time for it to end. Let the dead rest in peace and let the living live. That's what he'd say if he could take the stand, but unfortunately, nobody cared what he thought.

The press with their big cameras ran out of a big van and spotted them as they crossed the road.

'Lord Drummond, why are you involved in this murder trial?'

'Lord Drummond, does your friend Patrick Lynch intend on pleading guilty?'

'Lord Drummond, were you there on the night on the attack?'

'Lord Drummond, why did Lynch flee to your estate, Greyrock, after the event?'

Hugo set his face in a stern line and battled his way through, studiously ignoring them as he, Liam, and Helen made their way into the building. It was the most dreadful feeling of being under siege, and Liam wondered how famous people did this every day of their lives. Cameras clicked and the questions kept coming as well as entreaties for a photo.

'He's here!' someone shouted.

Like a flock of starlings, the rabble moved down the steps once more.

Suddenly, there was a flurry of activity as a very tall and incredibly handsome man was chauffeured to the courthouse in a black Mercedes. Obviously, the famous Geoffrey d'Alton. More reporters had appeared out of nowhere, there was even a television camera, and further crowds were gathering.

'How did they know he was involved with this case? Or that the hearing was today?' Liam asked, perplexed.

'I've no idea, I certainly didn't tell anyone,' Hugo replied, equally curious.

Liam watched as d'Alton emerged from the back seat and stood up straight. He was tall and slender and was probably in his early forties though he could have been older. He was well-maintained as his mother would have said. He wore a wig and a gown and his longish silver hair shone as it curled over his collar. His perfectly arched eyebrows rose in disdain in response to the haranguing tones of the reporters as if he deemed them unworthy of a response. His skin was tanned golden brown and intelligent sapphire-blue eyes took in the scene at a glance. He looked out of place on a cold drab winter morning in Cork, like a peacock in a flock of pigeons, Liam thought. He swept up the slush covered steps, his gown billowing out behind him, issuing instructions to a suited man beside him as he went.

Mr O'Kelly came to Hugo's side as they observed this most theatrical of entrances.

'That's Archbald Fenton with him, his private secretary,' O'Kelly told them in a murmur.

The idea that someone like d'Alton would defend the son of a drunk from a small terraced house in Cork had captured the public's imagination. The fact that a member of the gentry was also involved added even more spice. Patrick was clearly not d'Alton's typical client but the Earl of Drummond was.

Brian O'Kelly drew them into the foyer of the courthouse, past the security desk, followed by several members of the public and, eventually, by d'Alton and his secretary, who recognised Mr O'Kelly. The pair approached, ignoring Liam and Helen, and once they were gathered, Fenton spoke in reverential tones to the barrister.

'Mr d'Alton, may I introduce Lord Drummond.'

Liam smiled. Obviously, they were lesser beings and were undeserving of an introduction.

'I'm pleased to make your acquaintance, your Lordship,' d'Alton said with a bow of his head. His accent sounded like the men you'd hear on BBC. Patrick would have said he sounded like he'd a boiled spud in his mouth.

'Good morning, Mr d'Alton, and thank you for coming. I appreciate it. These are my friends, Liam Tobin, Helen Dunne, and of course, you know my solicitor, Mr O'Kelly.'

Liam was always slightly surprised when Hugo went into what

Patrick called 'Lord Mode'. His accent changed slightly, and he seemed more aloof and confident.

'My secretary does, I believe,' d'Alton cast a dismissive eye over Liam and Helen, giving them an almost imperceptible nod. Then he turned his full attention to Hugo, explaining what would happen next. He ignored the rest of them, but Liam couldn't care less how senior counsel d'Alton felt about him as long as he got the best deal possible for Patrick.

After a few moments, the court clerk approached d'Alton's secretary and whispered something to him, which he in turn relayed to d'Alton. Several young legal people were gathered, waiting for the great man to speak. He was a celebrity in the legal world and held their rapt attention.

'The case is being called,' he announced. Hugo rolled his eyes at Liam behind the silk-clad back, and the little group followed behind the majestic sweep of black that bellowed out in the wake of Geoffrey d'Alton Senior Counsel.

They settled themselves as best they could into the narrow benches of the public gallery and looked down on the court. Helen sat between Hugo and Liam. Detective Inspector McMullan was in the body of the court along with several other Gardaí, but he did glance in their direction and gave them a brief smile.

Patrick stood in the dock with his back to them, a guard standing behind him. It was hard to tell how he was from his body language as he couldn't turn around. Hugo had arranged to have a suit and shirt and tie sent into the prison. It was important he made a good impression.

'All rise, the court is now in session, Judge Eamonn O'Duibhir presiding,' the clerk announced aloud.

The judge was also in a wig and gown and looked around two hundred years old. He banged his gavel for order and there was lots of activity of solicitors, barristers, Gardaí, and clerks as they gathered papers and took their positions. Eventually, the judge spoke, his strong voice belied his frail appearance.

'Patrick Joseph Lynch, you are accused of the murder of Joseph

Thomas Lynch on the eighteenth day of December 1977 at a location known as Tinker's Cross, Mallow Road, Cork. How do you plead?'

Patrick's voice was clear. 'Not guilty.'

The judge nodded slowly.

Mr O'Kelly had explained that the state was pressing for a murder charge because they felt they could prove it was premeditated and by Patrick pleading not guilty, on d'Alton's instructions, the case would now go to trial. Patrick was going to say he did it, but that there were extenuating circumstances, and d'Alton was going to argue that what happened was, in fact, involuntary manslaughter. The hope was that if d'Alton managed to present Patrick as the victim of this dreadful man, not the other way round, and the prosecution then saw that he had swayed the jury, they would offer to accept the lesser charge of manslaughter. The good news was that with d'Alton on their side, there was a possibility of getting off on the murder charge. The bad news was that Patrick was still going to be sentenced because he did it.

The judge spoke in almost bored tones as this was just another day's work, not somebody's life in his hands.

'I am sending this case forward to the circuit court to be heard. I understand there is an application for bail?'

The prosecution stood up. 'We would seek to have bail denied, your honour. The defendant may be of good character, but we determine that he is likely to abscond, given his lack of ties here and the seriousness of the offence.' The young barrister seemed nervous and sat as quickly as he could.

'I see. I will need to hear from the arresting officer,' the judge ordered. More shuffling and muttering below the bench and then D.I. Mc Mullan took the stand and was sworn in.

'Has this man come to your attention previously?' the judge asked.

'The defendant is previously of impeccable character and has never been in any kind of trouble with the Gardaí before.' The prosecution looked annoyed. McMullan was supposed to be on their side.

'Hmmm...I see. What about you, Mr d'Alton? I presume you are making an application for bail.'

There were some barely audible communications between the bench and the detective and some transferring of papers when d'Alton addressed the court. Suddenly, all the noise stopped and you could only hear the sonorous tones of the barrister.

D'Alton stood and spoke. 'Yes, milord. My client is not a flight risk and is ordinarily of impeccable character. The Earl of Drummond, of Greyrock, Co Waterford is willing to stand surety for him.' You could cut his accent with a knife.

The judge deliberated for a moment and then spoke, 'While I accept that a reoccurrence of his violence is not likely, you do not imagine that a young single man with access to considerable funds through his friend the earl, recently accused of a heinous crime, would not attempt to abscond?' The judge looked imperiously at d'Alton over his half-moon spectacles.

'No, my lord, I don't.'

'I wish I shared your optimism,' the judge said, and the opposing council smirked.

Liam and Hugo shared a look.

'On balance, I think it's best that the defendant remain in custody until the trial. Bail denied.' He banged his gavel.

'All rise,' the clerk called, and the attendant crown shuffled to their feet. The judge left the bench and went into his chambers and that was that.

Patrick turned around and caught their eyes for a moment. They tried to smile encouragingly, but his face betrayed everything he was feeling. He was going to jail, he'd spend Christmas there at least, and maybe a lot longer.

They shuffled out, not speaking. Once outside, d'Alton moved to walk away when Hugo ran after him, grabbing his arm and almost spinning him around.

'What the hell just happened? I thought you were going to get bail for him?' Liam had never seen his friend so incensed with rage.

D'Alton gazed at his arm where Hugo had grabbed the sleeve. Hugo let him go, and d'Alton spoke as if to a recalcitrant child. 'Your lordship, I understand you are upset, but the judge was not going to grant bail as I had my secretary explain to your solicitor earlier. I said I would try, and try I did.' D'Alton was as silky as his gown.

'Try? Try? You call that trying? I could have done better than that myself,' Hugo barked. 'If this is a portent of what is to come, I fear your reputation not only precedes you but also exaggerates your prowess.'

D'Alton was icy. 'If you do not wish me to represent your friend that is entirely your prerogative. My bill for services to date will be compiled and sent to you. Good day.'

He turned on his heel and walked off.

'Hugo, go after him,' Liam pleaded. 'I know he's a bit of an eejit but without him, Patrick has no chance. Don't let him go.'

'I'm paying that oily bastard to get Patrick out of this and so far all he's done is swan around like he's some kind of God, being snobbish and condescending to everyone he meets and has achieved nothing!' Hugo was raging.

'I know that, but we also know we are banjaxed without him, it's as simple as that. We don't want him deciding he's not going to do it, then where would Patrick be? He only took the case because you are who you are, it adds to his already gigantic ego to have a peer on his client list, so play him along. Charm him, invite him to Greyrock, whatever it takes.' Liam was trying to coax him out of his black mood.

'He's such an arrogant...' Hugo began. 'He only wants to win so that he can be seen to win. He couldn't care less about poor old Patrick.'

'I know that, but why does it matter what his motivation is so long as he gets him a lighter sentence? He's pleaded not guilty. D'Alton advised him to do that, and we'll hopefully go for manslaughter since it wasn't premeditated. And maybe, with extenuating circumstances and all that and his previous good character, things might not be so bad. Either way, we need d'Alton a hell of a lot more than he needs us so sickening as it is, and I know this is costing a fortune, we have to keep him with us, okay?' Liam put his arm round his friend's shoulder. He knew Hugo to be one of the most generous people he ever met, but he was stubborn as well and if he took a set against something, it was usually permanent.

Hugo sighed. 'Fine, I'll apologise.' He was still seething but followed the barrister and his secretary to the car where they were just about to leave. Crowds surged towards him and journalists were everywhere. The press would love an altercation between the earl and the barrister on the side of the street.

'May I get in?'

'Certainly, your Lordship.'

As the chauffeur pulled away in a hail of flashes and microphones, Hugo settled himself into the back seat beside d'Alton. His secretary sat in the front.

'I shouldn't have said what I said. I apologise,' Hugo said, staring right ahead.

'Apology accepted. It is important to consider the bigger picture, your Lordship,' d'Alton explained.

'Hugo, please,' Hugo said.

'Very well, Hugo, the thing is, your friend did kill his father, so I've got an onerous task ahead of me. I'm not a bookmaker so I won't give you odds, but I will do my best. I'll ask you to allow me to do it as I see fit. Otherwise, I'm afraid there's no point in proceeding.'

Hugo felt like he was in the principal's office for some misdemeanour, but something made him trust this man.

'Very well. I understand this is your area. I was, am, very worried about him, and I just want…' Hugo tried to explain.

'I know. Now where can we drop you?'

Hugo indicated that anywhere was fine, and he found himself almost ejected onto the street. This was certainly not a case of he who pays the piper calls the tune. D'Alton was definitely calling all the tunes.

Liam and Helen stood outside the courthouse in the bitter cold.

'You must be perished. Can I get you a drink to warm you up? Liam asked kindly.

'No, no thanks, I'm fine. Poor Patrick, he looked so upset being led away like that, like he was some kind of criminal.' A tremor shook her voice.

'I know, it's horrible to see him like that, but we're doing all we can,' Liam reassured her.

'I wish there was something else I could do, to make it a little easier…'

Suddenly Liam had an idea. 'Well, if you want to help, you could maybe take the girls for an afternoon? My mam is doing a wonderful job with them, but she could do with a break, and sure they like you very much. Maybe you could take them into town for tea and a bun or something?'

'Do you think your mother would mind?' Her eyes lit up at the prospect of helping in a practical way. 'I could take them into Cash's to see Santie Claus.'

Liam smiled at her enthusiasm for the first time that day. 'I'm sure my mam would be thrilled, and sure Connie and Anna are mad about you. And they've never been to see the big man, I'm sure of that. Mrs Lynch, God rest her, would have loved to be able to do something like that for them. Why don't we go up to my house now and arrange it, there's no more point in waiting around here, I suppose. Do you think they've taken him up to Cork Prison?'

'I suppose so. I wonder if we can visit,' Helen said.

'Well, we can get Mr O'Kelly to check on that. For now, let's just hope Hugo could get the words out to apologise. If he doesn't, we are in even deeper trouble.'

They began the walk together back up the hill to Liam's house, chatting about the case. They passed Hugo's car, his pride and joy, an amazing light blue sports car.

Liam pointed it out to Helen.

'My mother nearly had a stroke when she saw it. Poor Mam's been saying novenas since that he won't be killed in it.' Liam grinned.

'He's certainly a very...em...larger than life character,' Helen said diplomatically.

'Ah, he's normal really, for an earl. Actually, he's the only earl I know so maybe they're all like normal people. But honestly, he's great, and God knows where we'd be without him,' Liam added.

'Yes, Patrick often spoke about you both. Ye really are best friends, aren't ye? I'm sure he appreciates everything ye are doing for him, but then, that's what you do, isn't it?'

As they walked, they chatted easily, and Liam remembered Patrick saying that he thought she would be a good match for him ages ago if he wasn't hell-bent on being a priest. Liam could see what he meant, she was funny and kind and not kind-of-scary the way the ones that are all done up with makeup often are. He sometimes wondered what it would be like to have a girlfriend, but always found himself dismissing the idea. He didn't miss that part of life, he really didn't, he had his friendship with the lads and his relationship with his mother and, to a lesser extent, his siblings, and it was enough for him. That part of being a priest didn't unduly worry him; it was his somewhat hazy attitudes to God's law that were the most troubling part. His best friends were both in contravention of the law of the church, yet he would defend each of them to the last. What did that say about his future as a priest?

Liam heard voices in the kitchen as he opened the door. Father Aquinas was in the kitchen, his hat and coat hanging on the banister, and he and Mam were chatting about the events of the morning.

'Ah, Liam, how are you?' He stood up and put out his large hand to shake. 'That was a tough old morning for you all.' He noticed Helen standing behind Liam. 'Hello.' He smiled.

'Hello, Father, this is Helen Dunne, a friend of Patrick's.'

'Sure, we've met before, at the time of the funeral, how are you, Helen?'

'Fine, thank you, Father.' She smiled.

'Mam, Helen wants to take the girls out for the afternoon, give you a break. She's going to take them into town to see Santie.'

Mrs Tobin smiled at her son. He knew her so well and was so considerate always.

'That would be lovely for them, and sure they're mad about you, Helen. I'll call them now. They'll be thrilled since the alternative was sitting here with me for the afternoon. You wouldn't put a milk bottle out in this weather!'

She went off to call them and get them ready, and Helen accompanied her. Squeals of delight came from upstairs; the news had obviously been delivered. It was nice to do little things to cheer them up after everything.

'Well, how did it go?' Father Aquinas asked.

'Bail was refused, so he'll be in jail for Christmas at least. Your man d'Alton is a bit of an eejit, to be honest, the carry-on of him. But apparently, he's the best. That's what we've been told anyway, so...' Liam poured himself some tea.

'That seems to be the case all right. One of the brothers above is interested in the law. Now, how are you all bearing up?'

'Ah all right, at least it's the Christmas holidays. I don't know if I'd have been let out of the seminary to go to my best friend's trial who is accused of murdering his father. It's not a conversation I'd like to have with the dean, put it that way.' Liam smiled ruefully.

'I could see that all right. There's a few above that feel the same,' he said, casting a glance in the direction of the monastery. Liam smiled inwardly at the relationship that had developed between him and his old teacher over the years, friends and confidantes.

'Most of the brothers, though, are praying for Patrick. He is such a grand lad, and he's had so much to put up with. I'll tell you what, he'd be lost without your mother.'

Liam nodded. 'Mam's been just brilliant. She loves those girls like they were her own and they feel safe with her. The detective said that he was going to speak to the social worker about what's to happen with them while the case is going on at least. Do you think you'd have any influence? They need to stay here with my mam.'

'Of course, that's where they should stay. I'll get onto them this afternoon. I deal with the children's services from time to time, for school-related matters. I'm sure we'll be able to organise that.'

'Thanks, Father.' Liam smiled gratefully. 'Please God, it will only be short term.'

The priest didn't share his smile. 'I don't want to seem pessimistic, Liam, but I think you and your mother should prepare for it being more than that. Father Kevin, the legal mind above, said he'll have to serve some jail time even if the charge is reduced. The fact of the matter is, rightly or wrongly, he did kill him.'

The words hung heavily in the air between them.

The girls burst into the room, looking adorable in matching red coats and hats.

'Well, aren't ye the picture!' Liam smiled.

'Hugo bought them some lovely things, he's a great boy so he is, always was. He'll make a great daddy himself someday, please God,' Mrs Tobin said with a wistful smile.

'We're going to see Santie.' Little Anna's eyes shone with excitement.

'Ye're not! I can't believe it!' Liam gasped. 'Can I come, too? And sit on his lap, and ask him for new rosary beads?' The little girls giggled.

'No, you can't,' Connie chuckled. It was good to see them so happy. 'You're too big. Santie only comes to children.'

'And anyway, he's too bold,' Mrs Tobin joked.

Anna, who took everything literally, was dismayed. 'Liam isn't bold, and Patrick isn't bold, the only bold one is Daddy. And Santie wouldn't bring him anything anyway because he's the boldest person ever.' Tears filled her eyes.

Helen went over and gathered her up in her arms.

'He was bold, and now he can't hurt you anymore. But you and Connie are the very best girls in the whole of Cork.'

'Ireland,' Connie interrupted.

'Of course! Silly me! The very best girls in the whole of Ireland, and I bet Santie will have something lovely for ye, but we better hurry in case he has to get back in his sleigh to go home to the North Pole!'

Instantly, the excitement was restored, and Liam and his mother exchanged a look. If only this hadn't happened. Patrick needed someone and those girls needed a mother. Helen was the obvious choice. But now, everything was up in the air.

Father Aquinas put his hand in his pocket and produced two shiny half crowns. The girls' eyes glittered.

'Now, this is for a sticky bun after ye see the big important man in the red suit, and maybe ye could get a cup of tea for poor Helen as well after?'

'Ah, Father, there's no need...' Mrs Tobin began.

'Not at all, sure they deserve a little treat,' he said with a smile.

Liam, Father Aquinas, and Mrs Tobin watched in admiration as Helen took their hands and the happy trio skipped down the hill.

CHAPTER 23

'Helen has been wonderful, she takes the girls whenever she can, spoils them rotten, of course, and they just are stone mad about her.'

Liam and Hugo were sitting on the hard bench across from Patrick. In the weeks after the refusal of bail, they tried to keep everything as normal as possible for Connie and Anna. Santa had brought them more presents than all their other Christmases combined, and they made lovely cards for Patrick, which he was allowed to have in his cell as a special dispensation from the governor. They asked when he was coming home all the time, but Liam's mam told them that Patrick had to help the guards. They trusted her completely so they were happy with that.

'It would be great if we had a date for the trial, wouldn't it? It's been weeks and nothing doing.' Hugo was trying to stay positive but frustration was creeping into his voice.

'I don't know...do I want it to happen tomorrow, or not for twenty years, you know?' Patrick said. 'It's horrible in here, but things are better if you're on remand rather than a convicted prisoner, with visits and all that. And the warders are all right, they all know my story and so they treat me well enough. But there's just a cell with four walls, and I'm only allowed one book. I'm dragging it out, trying not to read too much because you're only allowed one visit to the library a week. Having Anna and Connie's Christmas cards up is great, though. I can see their little drawings, and it makes me feel a bit less lonely. Ye've all been so good. Father Aquinas called yesterday, and Helen came in last week. At first, it was a bit awkward, you know, I don't know her that well. She was around since Mam's funeral and a few times since, but I was all over the place then. She's nice. We had a good chat, well, considering where we were, she told me all about how Connie and Anna were getting on with your mam, Liam. Honest to God, I don't know what I'd do only for ye. I'll never be able to repay ye for everything ye've done for me, especially you, Hugo. A fella in here told me how much your man d'Alton is costing...'

Liam looked at Hugo. He knew what was coming.

'I said it to Liam and now I'm telling you. Stop. I don't want thanks. In fact, it rather offends me. We are like brothers us three, closer than most brothers I know, in actual fact, and that makes us family in my book. We'll do everything we can, and I don't want to hear another word of thanks, is that clear?'

Hugo looked so stern, the other two grinned.

'Jays, Hugo, you looked so scary then you'd nearly fit in around here!' Patrick teased.

'A huge prison full of men, God I'd hate that,' he quipped with a wink, and the three of them descended into helpless laughter.

The months dragged on and D.I McMullan kept them updated in as much as there was anything to say. They all visited Patrick as often as they could. The girls went back to school, and life took on a kind of normality. They missed their brother terribly, but everyone decided it was better not to take them to see him. The sight of the prison would only frighten them. Hugo was busy with Greyrock; Tom Courtney had taken a bad fall and was in a wheelchair. The doctor told Hugo that there was no real progress, he wasn't healing as well as had been hoped so the full burden of the estate fell on Hugo. He considered hiring a new farm manager, but he didn't want to dishearten Tom and, anyway, it would take so long for someone to become familiar with the whole place. Maybe Tom would be back on his feet by the time the new person was competent enough to be left alone. Hugo missed Martha. Before she left, and before the night when *it* happened, he still found it hard to even think about it. They often met in the corridors of the house and had a chat. She knew he found running the estate overwhelming and though she had no solutions, it was nice to have a friend. Hugo knew how much Tom did before his accident, but the reality of the added workload was exhausting. He got back to Cork as often as he could get away, and he'd had a few letters from d'Alton's secretary detailing any little developments. Mr O'Kelly explained that the prosecution seemed to be confident of a murder charge being successful as witnesses were coming out of the woodwork. Hugo was alarmed to hear that. Patrick had said nobody could have seen him, but the solicitor assured him that these were extremely unreliable witnesses, alcoholics and petty criminals, so d'Alton would reduce them to dust.

The spring turned into summer, and Liam was deep in study for his first year exams. He had not managed to get home since Christmas. Hugo suspected the dean of trying to put some distance between the young seminarian and the high profile case, but he could be wrong. Liam seemed sure it wasn't the case, but every time he asked for a weekend off there was some reason invented as to why it was impossible. They kept in touch by letter, seminarians weren't encouraged to use the telephone except in emergencies, and in a way, Hugo preferred it. They were able to be more honest in letters somehow. Patrick asked them not to leave him out, to keep him in the group and not have private communications. They were taken aback when he first said it, but when he described the sheer bloody awfulness of prison life, any distractions were welcome, and the long hours of boredom was a perfect breeding ground for paranoia and imaginings. So each letter they wrote went to the other two as well. The weekly letters kept them all connected and for Hugo it allowed him to live who he was, even just for the few minutes it took to read it. They didn't ever say anything about his sexuality in the letters for fear of their being intercepted, but just to know that Liam and Patrick knew and accepted him was enough.

Because he was the one engaging the legal team, it was through him that any progress was reported so he also wrote to Mrs Tobin who filled Helen in and, of course, Father Aquinas.

'There was a telephone call for you when you were out, sir,' Patterson informed him as he came in the door from the stables. 'A Mr Fenton, the private secretary to Mr d'Alton. He left a number for you to contact him upon your return. It is written down on the pad beside the telephone.'

'Thank you, Patterson.' Hugo was pensive. Maybe a date had been set.

'Good afternoon, Hugo FitzHenry here, Earl of Drummond,' he introduced himself. Normally, he didn't bother with his title, but it was expected when dealing with that irritating man.

'Ah your lordship, yes. Mr d'Alton asked me to contact you to make you aware that a date has been set for the trial on the twenty-fourth of November. He will arrive in Cork on the evening of the twenty-third and will be staying at the Intercontinental Hotel and taking chambers in a legal practice in Washington Street. These expenses will be billed directly to your lordship.'

Hugo glowered once more at the audacity of the man.

'Fine,' he replied through gritted teeth. He was defiantly being told rather than being asked, which irked him. He didn't care about the money; it was the offhand attitude of d'Alton that annoyed him.

'Mr d'Alton will meet with his client the evening before the trial and brief him on the proceedings for the following day, but he will not be available to anyone else prior to the event under any circumstances. Should you wish to communicate to him in any way, please do so in writing through me, and I will see that he gets it.'

'Considering it is me who is hiring d'Alton to provide the best defence money can buy for my friend, I should think he would talk to me.' Hugo couldn't help himself.

'Precisely the reason he is not in a position to, your Lordship. He will be providing expert defence; therefore, he needs to remain focused on the trial without any interruptions. Thank you for telephoning, your Lordship, if there's nothing else?'

Hugo was being dismissed. While he was uncomfortable with the sycophantic way some people behaved around him, he wasn't used to being dismissed out of hand like that.

'No, that's all,' he managed to reply.

'Very well then, goodbye.' And the line went dead.

The trial began and after several requests, Liam had managed to get a few days off to attend the court. Hugo had promoted the head stable lad to temporary manager and employed four new workers for the estate with Tom keeping a close eye. He was out of the wheelchair but needed two sticks and got tired easily. It wasn't ideal, but it was the best Hugo could organise. He needed to be in Cork.

Mrs Tobin sat tensely beside Liam. Helen's sister offered to take care of the girls during the trial. She had little ones of her own. They often visited with Helen so Connie and Anna were happy to go and play with them. Liam knew his mother was dreading having to endure the details of her dear friend's death gone over in such detail for the whole world to hear. The papers were full of nothing else, and she tried her best to protect Connie and Anna from it. Kathleen Lynch had been a quiet person, a country girl, but she met and married the charming and good-looking Joe Lynch against her parents' wishes, and they disowned her because of it. When things went wrong as they did within weeks of the wedding, she had nobody to turn to. Her family would have told her that she had made her bed and now she may lie in it. One sister, Kit, did keep in contact with Kathleen, unbeknownst to her family, but she died of cancer when Patrick was small.

People around Chapel Street were not unkind, but they gave the Lynch family a wide berth over the years because of Joe's behaviour. Mrs Tobin was her only friend. Kathleen had given her good advice around that time of the business with Seán and that hussy next door, she had told her lift her head and look everyone straight in the eye. She did nothing wrong and neither did her husband, and people behaved towards you the way you let them. It was great advice.

They discussed often what Kathleen should do, usually after one of Joe's outbursts. Even with her deeply held Catholicism, Mary Tobin firmly advocated that her friend should leave her husband, but the other woman's faith was deep, and in her mind, the rules were the rules. In later years, Joe would go missing for protracted periods, and a peace would descend on the Lynch family for a while. But, like a bad penny, he kept turning up. Mary prayed for forgiveness for the thoughts she had, wishing when they pulled a body from the river, which was not uncommon, that it would be that of Joe Lynch. It seemed to be a cruel twist in the tale, that poor Patrick would spend his life in jail for what he did.

D'Alton had flown into Cork again, to yet another flurry of excitement. He was staying in the luxurious Intercontinental Hotel on the banks of the south channel of the River Lee. Liam had never even been inside it, but he heard it was supposed to be out of this world. The barrister had accepted Hugo's apology for his anger at the bail hearing, so thankfully, was still on the case, but he was as sanctimonious and patronising as ever, according to Hugo. In his letters, Hugo regularly ranted about how much d'Alton's attitude rubbed him up the wrong way. Liam got a pang of sadness reading them, wishing he could see Patrick's face and hear him tease Hugo about how he was used to being treated like the Lord of the Manor yet he couldn't take it when someone had the audacity to challenge him. That banter went on between them all the time in the carefree days before this nightmare took over their every waking thought. Liam wondered if it would ever be the same again.

D'Alton went to see Patrick the night he flew in, and neither Liam nor Hugo knew what went on. Funnily enough though, Patrick's impression of his barrister was in total contrast to Hugo's. In his letters, Patrick always spoke of him in glowing tones, but perhaps it was because he wanted Hugo to know how grateful he was and to complain about the superior attitude of the cripplingly expensive legal services would have seemed unappreciative.

Patrick had written a brief note last night saying that he was doing all right and was nervous but hopeful, thanks to Mr d'Alton. One of the prison officers lived up the street so he had delivered the note to Liam.

The trial seemed to take ages to get going, and the courtroom was packed to capacity. The press gathered in even greater numbers than they had before, but Liam also recognised several lads they had gone to school with, neighbours and friends, in the public gallery. Sure, some of the interest was ghoulish but, mostly, people just wanted to support Patrick.

The testimonies of various down and outs and petty criminals, including the red-haired man, seemed interminable. They went on for two days, and the judge was constantly threatening to clear the court if the noise level wasn't reduced. Liam and Hugo found the whole experience frustrating. True to his word, d'Alton swept in and out of the court, communicating with nobody but his secretary Archibald Fenton. The accounts of what happened that night varied wildly, with tramp after tramp giving evidence, most if not all of which was decimated by d'Alton. Discrediting alcoholic tramps and petty criminals was beneath him, it didn't even challenge him, so he exuded an air of boredom. He could be observed examining his perfectly manicured nails or focusing on the elaborate carvings on the ceiling of the courtroom while the witnesses gave their evidence, often with colourful graphics, only to ask one or two pointed questions to totally bamboozle the tramp in question, much to the delight of the gathered crowd. If it wasn't so serious, it would be very entertaining. D'Alton was a showman all right. He was popular with the crowd and Patrick's story was everywhere. The whole city was behind him.

The last witness for the prosecution took the stand. He was dressed in a garish blue suit that was several sizes too small, stretched across the vast expanse of his back. His red hair was long and dirty-looking and his beard unkempt. His face, puffy through years of alcohol abuse, revealed some scars and when he spoke, it was obvious he was missing several teeth.

'So, Mr...' d'Alton checked his notes, 'O'Mahony.' Liam detected a smirk in the barrister's voice at the use of the title to describe the dodgy-looking man in the witness box.

'Let me be clear, you run an establishment as a licensed premise that seems to be without a name or indeed a valid public house licence on the outskirts of Cork city.' He cast a glance at the jury, making them complicit in the exposure of this man as a petty crook.

'Well, it's not exactly a pub,' the red-haired man began.

'No, indeed, though you do sell alcohol at this location, do you not?' D'Alton's blue eyes were innocent.

'Well, yeah like, but only to friends...' O'Mahony muttered.

'I'm sorry, Mr O'Mahony, you *sell* alcohol to your *friends* in a pub that's *not actually* a pub. A fact that will no doubt be of considerable interest to the Gardaí and Inland Revenue in due course. Now, let us return to the night in question. You say that you saw the defendant attack the deceased outside the premises.'

'Yeah, he bate him up and kicked him when he was down...' O'Mahony was just warming to his theme when d'Alton interrupted him again.

'And you saw this yourself?'

'Yeah, that's what I'm tellin' ya,' the man growled impatiently.

'And what did you do?' d'Alton asked calmly.

'Wha?'

D'Alton spoke slowly as if to a particularly dim child, causing a slight ripple of laughter in the court.

'Do, Mr O'Mahony, what did you *do* when you saw your friend Joe Lynch being attacked? What action did your take?'

'I done nuttin',' he protested, fear that he was to be blamed in some way creeping in.

'You done nothing.' D'Alton's plumy tones highlighted the grammatical error, again causing a chuckle. Liam could see the man on the stand growing murderous in his rage at being the butt of these jokes and naked hatred shone from his bloodshot eyes. D'Alton was totally unfazed and carried on.

'So, you want this court to believe that your dear friend and associate of many years duration was being allegedly battered to death in front of your very eyes, Mr O'Mahony, and you tell us here today that "you done nothing". Is that correct?'

'I was far away like, in the pub, well in my place, so I couldn't get out to him like,' O'Mahony was backtracking.

'But I thought this alleged incident took place immediately outside, where according to your earlier statement, you saw everything. Do we take it then, you are saying, let me be very clear so I understand you, Mr O'Mahony, that you were too far away to intercede in any way to defend Mr Lynch from his alleged attacker?'

Liam watched the man try to figure out the best answer. D'Alton was like a snake, weaving O'Mahony's own lies tighter and tighter around him. It was mesmerising.

'Dat's right, I couldn't a done nuttin cause I was inside and...'

'Come now, Mr O'Mahony, you are seriously asking this court to believe that you were near enough to see the alleged event unfold, and near enough to identify my client as the perpetrator of this alleged attack, but too far away to do anything about it?' D'Alton's voice had changed from mocking and superior to whip-like precision.

'He was outside like, and I was inside, an' I heard him, roaring like...'

'So you were not outside the pub that's not a pub at all now? Is that what you are telling the court? Because either you were there and did nothing, stood idly by while a man was beaten to death, or even was complicit in some way with the assault, or you were *not* there and therefore cannot identify my client as the perpetrator. Which is it to be, Mr O'Mahony?' D'Alton never took his eyes from O'Mahony, daring him to admit either story. Liam was fascinated, whatever O'Mahony said he was going to come out badly. Sensing he was about to be put into the picture in a damaging light, O'Mahony made a decision.

'I wasn't there,' O'Mahony muttered.

'Please repeat what you just said so the jury can hear you, Mr O'Mahony,' d'Alton asked politely.

'I wasn't there. I was inside minding my own business. They all saw me, I never left the bar...' He gestured to the collection of down and outs sitting together on a bench.

'Well, if they are your alibis, Mr O'Mahony, I'm sure you have nothing to worry about.' D'Alton smirked at the public gallery to a ripple of laughter. 'No further questions, your honour.'

To the fascination of the crowd, the barrister managed to infuse his last statement with utter contempt for the witness. The clerk indicated to the huge man that he should stand down. As he walked past d'Alton, he stopped and gave him a threatening stare, at which the barrister gave the slightest of smiles.

The crowd settled in for the juiciest part of the tale as Patrick took the stand. The excitement and anticipation at what he might say was palpable in the room. Liam's mother squeezed his hand as they tried to project their love at him across the courtroom.

The prosecution began by ham-fistedly trying to make Patrick admit that he hated his father and wanted to kill him. The young junior counsel was cocky and clearly resented the star status of d'Alton and so was showing off and posturing for the press.

Patrick seemed calm and answered truthfully but without detail. Liam thought he came across very well, humble and respectful, but spoke clearly and confidently. D'Alton must have schooled him before he took the stand. Once it was the defence's turn to cross examine, the barrister was gentle.

He asked him about his childhood, about how Joe treated the family, about his mother's murder. He spoke about Connie and Anna and the impact Joe Lynch's violence and drinking had on the family. He talked about Patrick's relationship with his mother and sisters and how he took care of the family as soon as he was able. Patrick was shown to be a wonderful young man, and he was returned to the dock.

Father Aquinas was called as a character witness and spoke in such glowing terms about a boy who despite all the odds got a scholarship to St Bart's, excelled there as a student and sportsman and had a successful career ahead of him. His employer Jim O'Neill described a hard-working, honest young man, who as far as he was concerned wouldn't hurt a fly. D.I. McMahon described the events of the night as explained to him by Patrick but went on to add that he knew Patrick well through his dealings with the family after Mrs Lynch's death and was very impressed by his integrity. He also managed to slip in that the deceased was well known to the Gardaí. The prosecution objected on the grounds that it was irrelevant, and the judge instructed that it be removed from the records, but it didn't matter, it was said.

As the detective left the stand, he passed them by and smiled and nodded briefly. He had done his best for Patrick despite being a witness for the state.

Through the witnesses, d'Alton painted a picture of a sweet boy, who had turned into an admirable young man, all against the back-drop of a violent and abusive father. He skimmed over the events of the night in question, only saying that when this boy witnessed his father laughing at the brutal way he killed his wife, he could no longer contain the anger he justifiably felt. He asked the jury, 'Would not each of us do the same?'

Patrick came out whiter than white. The prosecution were making their closing arguments; the crux of the case being that Patrick did murder Joe Lynch and that's all there was to it. The barrister for the state seemed a bit disorganised despite the swagger, clearly intimidated by the presence of d'Alton, though trying to hide it. They were clearly regretting the decision to push for a murder conviction as it became evident with each passing minute that d'Alton was wiping the floor with them.

The judge called for a half-hour recess before the closing arguments were heard. Some of the crowd gratefully filed out of the courtroom, others staying put for fear of losing their seats. Liam needed some air, and Hugo needed a cigarette so they all trooped out. A slight sleety drizzle added to the already gloomy, cold day. As Father Aquinas raised his huge black umbrella, they all huddled underneath it. It looked like it was going well for Patrick except, as Hugo pointed out most succinctly, he did actually do it.

'That was so nice of Inspector Mc Mullan, wasn't it?' Liam's mother said.

'I know,' Helen agreed. 'I bet that will really help, I hope it will, anyway.'

'D'Alton is playing a blinder, Hugo. No matter what you say about him, he's as good as they say he is. He managed to make all those drunks look ridiculous,' Liam said, batting away the cigarette smoke. 'And he made mincemeat of your man O'Mahony.'

'God, he's terrifying looking, isn't he?' asked Helen. 'No wonder poor little Anna nearly lost her life when she saw him. Mr d'Alton made him look like a right eejit though.'

'Yes, he's doing well, I'll concede that. I still think he's an idiot.'

'Well, I hope he never runs into that O'Mahony fella again. Did you see the way he looked at him, like he'd happily have throttled him there and then if he could?' Father Aquinas smiled.

'Somehow, Father, I can't see them mixing in the same social circles.' Hugo grinned and stubbed out the cigarette. 'Now, we better get back in, I suppose.'

As they made their way along with everyone else back into the courthouse, they spotted the Garda inspector just outside the door of the courtroom. Liam felt his mother grip his hand and lead him over. The others shuffled back in.

'Thank you for what you did for Patrick,' Mrs Tobin began.

'No need, I was only telling the truth.' He smiled kindly. 'I hope it all works out as well as it can,' he added.

'What do you think will happen now?' she asked. 'I've never been to a trial before, thank God.'

'Well, I suppose the prosecution is now realising that they should have gone for a manslaughter charge first day, but they obviously thought they could make a murder charge stick. Your man d'Alton is after putting paid to that plan anyhow, so if I were a betting man, which I'm not, I'd say the prosecution will have to say they'll accept the lesser charge. After that, who knows?'

'Well, thank you for everything you've done for us so far, not just now, but before, when my friend was killed, we appreciate it,' Mrs Tobin said sincerely.

'Well, Mrs Tobin,' he began.

'I've told you before, please call me Mary, please.' Liam was surprised to hear his mam say that.

The detective smiled shyly and went slightly pink. 'Well, Mary, if there's any justice, the jury will go easy on him. Now we better get back. Sure maybe I'll see ye after?'

Liam was bemused as they made their way back to the public gallery. Was he imagining it or did there seem to be a spark of some sort between his mam and the detective? He knew from Mr O'Kelly that D.I. McMullan was a widower and a thought crossed his mind that maybe it would be nice for his mam to have someone in her life. He was probably jumping the gun, it might just have been a friendly chat, but he hoped not. They'd spoken a few times in recent weeks about the custody of the girls. Apparently, he even called in for tea one day.

The entire court was hanging on d'Alton's every word as he made his closing statement to the jury. Helen on one side and his mother on the other squeezed Liam's hands so hard he feared the blood supply would be cut off. Hugo chewed the inside of his cheek as he did whenever he was nervous for as long as Liam could remember. Father Aquinas gripped his rosary beads in the pocket of his soutane, fervently praying. The old priest reminded Liam of a swan, serene and collected on the surface, but paddling like mad underneath. Apparently, he and Father Xavier had words when Xavier said Patrick should face the full rigours of the law and his name should be removed from St Bart's roll of honour in the light of his actions. Liam only heard about it from his mother, who knew the woman that cleaned the monastery and overheard the argument. He didn't know the outcome of the exchange, but he could guess, and Patrick's name stayed where it was.

D'Alton walked slowly up and down the length of the courtroom, making eye contact with every member of the jury. After what seemed an interminable wait, he spoke.

'Gentlemen of the jury, normally, I have my closing address worked out before the trial begins at all.'

Liam looked at Hugo, the plummy tones of the barrister were considerably toned down. There was even a hint of a Cork accent coming from his lips. He realised the jury were 'salt of the earth' and decided to speak in their own terms, using their vocabulary. The metamorphosis was remarkable and mesmerising to watch. Liam would swear his hair was a little less shiny, less coiffed, and he had definitely lost his imperious demeanour. All of a sudden, he was like someone you could meet in a bar, not the Glue Pot maybe, but definitely somewhere mere mortals would congregate.

'But as I stand before you today, I'm deliberating. I've never defended a client in Cork before, and I imagined it to be like Dublin, or other cities where I've conducted cases, but I was wrong. Cork is an unusual place, a city and county with a proud rebel past, a place where people don't take slights lying down. If you take on a Cork man, I now realise, you'd better be prepared for it to go all the way.'

Liam couldn't believe it, he was buttering them up, and they didn't even know it. They were nodding sagely, agreeing with every word. Some allowed themselves a self-satisfied smirk, that this Dublin jackeen came down here expecting to find eejits, but he soon changed his tune.

'What has this to do with the case, you might wonder? You are intelligent, hard-working men, and you are proud of your city as well you should be. You don't want murderers roaming around unchallenged, people taking the law into their own hands. Of course, you don't. Joe Lynch was a violent, malevolent, abusive, bully. He was also an alcoholic, that is true, but he was all of the above, with or without drink. Well, you might say, that's all well and good but that's not a reason to kill him. I mean if citizens took it upon themselves to get rid of every person they didn't like, no matter how valid the reason, then society would be in anarchy, isn't that right? The Bible tells us that we must not kill, and indeed, we shouldn't.' They nod and agree, eating out of the palm of his hand.

'But gentlemen, as both you and I know very well, that is not what happened here. This was not some vigilante heroism gone mad on the part of my client, quite the contrary. You've heard what kind of a lad Patrick is, his employer, his former teacher, a very well-respected man of the cloth, who comes from a long tradition of Christian adherence to God's law, his many friends, all know him as a kind, upstanding, decent young man. A young lad whose only capacity for causing pain to others is when he puts the sliotar over the bar from the sixty-five-yard line below in the park.' The gathered crowd chuckled and several jury members smiled. Any reference to the beloved sport of hurling, especially from a Dublin man, would be met with approval. Father Aquinas winked at Liam. D'Alton was like a magician, weaving his spell.

'Patrick Lynch is not a murderer. He's one of your own, a grand lad who had the misfortune in life to draw the short straw when it came to fathers. Joe Lynch shoved the four-year-old Patrick in windows to steal, though even at that age he begged him not to. He knew, even at that young age, the difference between right and wrong.'

How d'Alton could tell what was going on in the mind of four-year-old Patrick nobody thought to ask.

'He watched, before he was big enough to do anything about it, while Joe Lynch beat his wife when he was drunk, but also, and this is *vitally* important, gentlemen, also when he was sober. It's not enough to just blame the drink in this case. This man did nothing but irreparable harm to his family, and yet, despite all this, Patrick Lynch pulled himself up by his bootstraps and gained a scholarship to one of the most prestigious boys' secondary schools in the country. He studied, he made friends, he helped his mother and sisters, and he played hurling. He is on the face of it, a normal lad but as you now know, he is anything but. He is exceptional.

'The news that his father had murdered his mother shook young Patrick to the core. As well as unimaginable grief, the main thing he felt was guilt. Lynch senior had been missing for weeks, Patrick went off to work that day, never thinking for a moment that his father would turn up, but turn up he did, and with such violent intent that it left his wife Kathleen dead on the floor of their home, battered to death with the leg of a table in front of her two terrified little daughters.'

He paused and allowed that horrific image to solidify in the imaginations of the jurors. The muted sounds of the street outside were the only sounds that could be heard. The gathered legal people were as entranced as the jury, even the elderly judge seemed to be captivated.

'The fact that Patrick couldn't have been there to defend his family from this brutal and unprovoked attack was playing on his mind, but he focused on the task at hand, helping two little girls cope with the loss of their mother. He was resigned to the Gardaí's inability to find his father, and he tried as best he could to put it to the back of his mind. He was not a man intent on revenge, he had, along with the diligent members of a Garda Siochana, come to the conclusion that Joe Lynch had absconded to England. Patrick was working and supported by what I must say is one of the most loving and caring groups of people I have ever met. He kept going.'

Liam caught Father Aquinas glance at the compliment and smiled wryly.

'The girls were back at school, life was going on. He was doing his best. He used to like going to dances, what young lad doesn't? But that all stopped, every penny was for his sisters, and he slowly was rebuilding the family home into a place where they could feel safe.'

Liam nudged Hugo and cast a glance at the other side. The prosecution looked worried. If ever there was a David and Goliath situation, this was it. D'Alton was unstoppable.

'It took two events to drive this young man to do what he did. Firstly, Joe Lynch arrived to the little girls' school and terrified them. Patrick was trying valiantly to assure them that they were safe, and they were just starting to believe it when their father arrived outside the classroom window of the youngest little girl, only six years of age. The poor mite was petrified. The second was when Patrick tracked him down. Lynch was mid flow of a story. This story cast Lynch himself as the hero, a formidable force, who was, much to the delight of his gathered *comrades*, relating the tale of beating his wife to death, for not having his dinner ready.' D'Alton cast a disdainful glance in the direction of the witness box, and Liam was sure each juror could visualise the tramps as they lied one by one. Silence again. D'Alton stood, as if observing a moment's silence out of respect to Kathleen Lynch.

'Patrick watched this macabre pantomime progress through a broken window and when, to rapturous applause and gales of laughter, his father left the building to relieve himself, Joseph Lynch was singing, singing to himself, a man without a care in the world, in Patrick's own words. He saw in his mind's eye the haunted looks on his little sisters' terrified faces, the image of his dead mother, unrecognisable due to her injuries, lying on a slab in a hospital morgue, and the reason for all this misery and pain was laughing and singing. Well, he just snapped. He beat him and kicked him, he punched him, and yes, he choked him. But Patrick Lynch did not plan to murder his father; he did not set out with slaughter on his mind. He was just a boy, who was trying to defend his family from a man who should have been their protector but was, in fact, their tormentor.

'Joe Lynch, a man whose health was in a very poor state, due to years of alcohol abuse and living rough, did not survive the attack. Patrick did not call the emergency services because he realised there was no point. Lynch was dead. It was over, and he went in a daze of distress to his friend's house where he confessed and agreed to be taken into custody.'

The silence crackled in the dry courtroom air. The entire courtroom hung on d'Alton's words.

'Gentlemen, Patrick Lynch is in jail on remand. He has two little sisters who need him, he is not a violent man, but he was driven to extremes by the extreme nature of the abuse the Lynch family suffered at the hands of his father. Patrick's attack was almost certainly a factor in the death of Joe Lynch, but *he did not* murder him. On those grounds, gentlemen of the jury, you must acquit him.'

D'Alton addressed the judge, 'The defence rests your honour.'

Hugo and Liam watched in frustration as the clerk of the prosecution approached the clerk of the defence and handed him a note, which was quickly passed on to d'Alton. They longed to know what it contained, and d'Alton remained pokerfaced. After a moment, he inclined his head slightly in the direction of the young barrister for the state, John Delaney.

He spoke up, 'Your honour, in the light of the evidence and testimonies heard, we would be willing to accept the lesser charge of manslaughter in this case.' Liam could hear the desperation in his voice, he now realised he should never have pushed for a murder conviction; d'Alton was just too good an opponent.

The judge considered for a moment and raised his gavel but there was no need to bang it, a silence had fallen over the courthouse once more.

'I want to see both counsels in my chambers now please.' He waited for the clerk to call everyone to rise, and he slowly moved in behind, followed by Delaney and d'Alton.

'What's going to happen now? This is good, isn't it?' Helen was worried. O'Kelly was talking to Patrick from beneath the dock, and Patrick had to lean down to hear what he said.

'Yes, very. Inspector McMullan said this might happen. D'Alton wanted a manslaughter charge first day but that young prosecutor wanted to make a name for himself by beating the celebrity lawyer in court,' Liam said.

'O'Kelly said he was warned that d'Alton would wipe the floor with him, but he was too cocky. The fact that they're now saying they'll take manslaughter is good news.' Hugo prayed he was right.

Before the conversation could continue, the judge re-entered, followed by the two men. Liam wished he could be down in the dock with Patrick, he must be sick with nerves. They couldn't see his face as he had his back to the court, but Liam and Hugo knew he was doing his best to remain stoic.

Silence descended once more as the shuffling of people rising and sitting subsided.

The judge seemed to be looking at some papers on his bench, and Delaney and d'Alton sat back in their places. D'Alton looked calm and relaxed, almost smug, while the prosecution team were tense.

'Will the defendant please rise?' the judge said.

Patrick rose to his feet and faced the judge.

'Patrick Joseph Lynch, as you are aware the prosecution has now changed the charge against you to manslaughter. So, to the charge that on the eighteenth of December 1977, you did commit the crime of manslaughter of Joseph Thomas Lynch at the premises of Tinker's Cross, Cork. How do you plead?'

Hugo observed Patrick from the back and was afraid the whole courtroom could hear his heart beating.

'Guilty.'

Urgent whispers and sighs of either excitement or relief or grief filled the air.

'Very well, your plea has been noted.' The judge then turned his attention to the jury. 'Gentlemen of the jury, thank you for your time and patience. You have performed your civic duty admirably and I now exempt you from jury duty for life in recognition of your service to the state. Thank you, you are dismissed.'

The jury remained seated as did everyone else in the courtroom.

'I will now put this case forward for sentencing two weeks from today in order that a probation report can be filed. Take him down.'

Patrick was led through the door at the back of the stand and didn't even get to catch their eyes before he was led away.

Father Aquinas and Liam were chatting with Helen and a few other friends of Patrick's inside the courthouse but Hugo needed a cigarette. The case was becoming of more and more interest to the press and Hugo watched as they clamoured for a photograph of d'Alton as he emerged onto the slushy street. Most unusually for him, d'Alton was attempting to slip away unnoticed and despite the press efforts to get a statement from him, he resolutely ignored their questions. He seemed to have ditched the team of young lawyers and even the secretary who followed him everywhere. The barrister seemed to be scanning the streets for a taxi. Impulsively, Hugo went to the corner where he'd left his car, he jumped in and seconds later was at the front of the building. Leaning over at the kerb, he opened the passenger door.

'Jump in,' he called to d'Alton, who was elbowing his way through the throng.

Gratefully, the barrister sat into the Ford GT40. Hugo revved the loud growling engine, sending the pressmen with their cameras jumping back in fear of their lives. Taking advantage of the space in the crowd, he drove out into the street and turned away from the busy city traffic. Once they were several streets away, d'Alton spoke.

'Nice car,' he remarked.

'Yes, it's the one extravagance I allow myself. My father would probably have a stroke if he saw it, but I do love it. The seats are a little low to the ground. Are you comfortable?' Hugo asked as he manoeuvred around cars, pedestrians, and delivery trucks.

'Yeah fine. Thanks.'

Hugo was a bit taken aback at his casual speech and the fact that the plumy accent was by now altogether gone.

'Where shall I take you?' Hugo asked. 'You'd better lay low for an hour or so, I suppose, if you don't want to talk to the press. I would imagine they'll make for the Intercontinental; every paper has been full of it for weeks.'

'Indeed. They love a bit of salacious gossip, but we've left it as we want it. We can't do anything further until the sentencing. Can we just get out of the city for a bit? I'm tired and hungry.'

'Er...okay,' Hugo said, unsure of what he should do with him.

Hugo glanced over at him as he drove along country roads. He seemed so different to before. Not the supercilious snob he was used to, or even the practical but dismissive way he was when Hugo apologised months earlier, and certainly not the larger than life character he presented in the courtroom. It struck him how peculiar this Geoffrey d'Alton was. It was like he had different personas, and he could alternate them at will. The pompous attitude, along with the affectations of dress and gestures were gone. Patrick said that whenever he spoke to him in the prison, he was calm and practical and quite approachable. O'Kelly told Hugo that he's never seen anyone with such an encyclopaedic knowledge of the intricacies of the law as he instructed him to look for precedents that could be implemented in the defence. Then that performance today, just an ordinary man asking other ordinary men to be fair and decent and do the right thing. Despite his dislike, Hugo found himself intrigued by him.

'Could you take me somewhere to eat? I won't get to fly out until tomorrow at this stage, I suppose,' he said with what sounded like regret. 'Thankfully, we don't have to wait for a jury to deliberate.'

'How would it have gone if they'd had to decide, do you think?' Hugo asked.

'They would have been nine to three in favour of acquittal, initially, it would have taken one full day to convince juror number five, and the other two, seven and eleven, would go together so once eleven cracked seven would go, too.' There was no speculation in his voice, he was definite.

'How can you be so sure?'

D'Alton smiled at Hugo's scepticism and explained, 'When I was closing, and indeed, throughout the case, I was having some investigations done. It will be in my bill. Juror number five was married to an American, who was murdered on their honeymoon nine years ago, the killer was never found so he might want revenge on any murderer he comes across. Either way, he's not rational on the subject. Number eleven is a former brother from an order of enclosed monks in England, came home three years ago, but is fervently religious. The brothers were not fanatical enough it seems, that's why he left, to follow his own, even more exacting form of Christianity. The other man, number seven, is a homosexual who is attracted to number eleven though that is a total waste of time, but will vote with him to impress him. The nine who will vote for acquittal are from Cork city and suburbs and see Patrick as one of their own, seven of the nine are involved in a hurling club.'

Hugo was flabbergasted. D'Alton had never mentioned any such investigations going on.

'So everything you said, all the stuff about the Bible and Father Aquinas following God's law and the hurling, it was all aimed at specific people on the jury.'

'Yep.' Hugo noticed that he looked exhausted and seemed reluctant to speak. Hugo suddenly had an idea.

'Well, I can take you to Greyrock if you want some dinner and a comfortable night's sleep. Nobody will look for you there. The press know you're staying in a hotel in the city so they'll track you down if you go back there. '

'Fine. Thank you.' And with that, Geoffrey d'Alton leaned his head back and despite the speed of Hugo's driving and his deliberate manoeuvring around corners, he fell fast asleep.

Hugo didn't know why but he felt relieved that d'Alton agreed. He wanted to discuss the case with him, not just because of Patrick but because of the psychology of the whole thing. The way he played that jury today was nothing short of miraculous. He had them in the palm of his hand and yet there was something so enigmatic about him. He found himself wondering as they drove along, who was the real Geoffrey d'Alton.

They pulled up at Greyrock, and Patterson emerged onto the gravel. He tried to conceal his disdain at the light blue sports car but failed as usual.

'Welcome home, Master Hugo,' he said.

D'Alton woke as the car door was opened.

'Patterson, Mr d'Alton doesn't have a valet or any luggage so if you could show him to the Coral Suite and arrange for him to have everything he needs. And tell the cook that we'll eat in an hour.' Turning to d'Alton he said, 'I'll freshen up as well, and I'll see you in the drawing room for an aperitif as soon as you're ready. Patterson will direct you.'

It felt good to be home again. During the weeks leading up to the trial, he'd been commuting every few days between Greyrock and Cork, meeting the legal team, helping out Mrs Tobin with the girls, and keeping Liam informed.

Hugo washed and dressed for dinner. He wondered if he should go formal. Geoffrey d'Alton might like that sort of thing; it would appeal to his snobbish side. The funny thing about him was, though, that Hugo was starting to suspect that it was all an act. D'Alton wasn't what he seemed and his chameleon-like changes were intriguing. He considered black tie for a moment and instantly dismissed it. He changed into jeans and a light blue shirt and combed back his now wet, blond hair. Patrick and Liam always teased him about his hair, calling him goldilocks but Hugo didn't care. His hair was short now, even more than it had been allowed to be in school, and still as curly as it was when he was a boy if it was allowed to grow. He had bulked up from all the physical work he enjoyed on the estate. He liked to be exhausted going to bed, it stopped his mind dwelling on other things. Grinning at the mirror, he thought he looked okay.

The whiskey decanter glittered in the glow of the soft lighting and a fire crackled merrily in the grate of the drawing room. The heavy damask curtains were pulled, and Hugo settled himself beside the fire with a drink, the ticking of the grandfather clock the only other sound. He wondered how the evening was going to go, would the conversation be awkward, or would d'Alton be impressed with Greyrock. Hugo was proud of his home, not in a pretentious way he hoped, but it was part of who he was. It was however only a part of it, and if all went well with Patrick and he got a light sentence and life went back to some version of normal, maybe he would look up his uncle as Liam suggested. Since the night Patrick turned up telling him what he'd done, life had gone in a kind of blur. Incredible to think almost a full year had passed. He was so busy and preoccupied, but at least, it took his mind off the fact that he wasn't normal.

His eyes fell on the portrait of his mother and smiled. He missed her bubbly presence around the house. At least she had finally stopped telling of some wonderful girl that he should meet if only he would ever visit her in London. She had been dogged in her determination to get d'Alton, for which Hugo was now eternally grateful. His mother, while adoring on one level, was very tied up with her own life. She was relieved to relinquish the responsibility of the estate and was happy that Hugo seemed to fit the role of Lord of the Manor so well. He wondered once again if she had any inkling as to his real nature. It was hard to know. Now that this nightmare was drawing to a close, he could focus once more on his own life. Looking around Greyrock, the pain of never producing an heir to take it over was as sharp as ever. Of all the crosses he had to bear, that was undoubtedly the worst. He felt such a failure.

He wondered once again about Martha and prayed she was all right. He had heard nothing from her in over a year and while Tom said once or twice that she'd written to him, he gave no indication that he wanted to discuss it with Hugo. He was only her previous employer; he had no right to know anything. His cheeks burned with shame when he thought about their last encounter. How she thought she could fix him. Poor Martha, she couldn't understand, nobody could. Who could blame her?

In his more optimistic moments, he thought perhaps it was possible to live a little of the life he wanted to, somewhere like Paris, for a few days a couple of times a year. Or maybe it was a ridiculous and dangerous notion. The idea of ever having a relationship, or even an encounter with a man filled him with such a myriad of emotions that he couldn't even determine which took precedence, excitement certainly, terror, and if he were honest, shame. As he sat there in the peace and quiet, he remembered all the nights he cried, prayed to God, begging him to take this away. As a child even, he knew he was not as a boy should be. Those nights in school with Xavier prowling, the terror, the pain, the fear, he forced them to the back of his mind.

All around the walls of the drawing room were hunting trophies and watercolours of sporting events. He hated shooting and had no interest in cricket or rugby. He was so grateful for the father he had, who never forced these things on him, or who didn't send him off to board at school when he was five or six as so many others from their class did. He knew that Hugo was happy playing around Greyrock with Martha and the animals and that such an environment as a public school in England would have been torture. Hugo felt once again the sharp pang of loneliness for his father. He wished more than anything that he was there, that he could talk to him. He would understand, he knew he would. The best decision his parents ever made for him was sending him to St Bart's, though it must have been a worry, and surely caused a few raised eyebrows with friends. But without Liam and Patrick, life would be unbearable. He was lonely, his nature made him so, as trusting people was impossible, but to know that they both knew what he was and accepted him as such meant the world. He knew they made an unlikely bunch, him, the Lynches and the Tobins, but he had so much more in common with them than he did with any of his so-called peers.

His reverie was interrupted by the door opening. D'Alton entered wearing jeans and a white shirt that Hugo recognised as Patrick's. He must have left them here on one of his earlier visits, and d'Alton and he were similar in size. Hugo smiled his gratitude at Patterson as he backed out of the room. D'Alton's hair was wet from the shower, and he smelled of a musky scent. Hugo felt a lurch in the pit of his stomach, so intense it almost left him breathless. The piercing blue of the older man's eyes shone in his face and a smile played around his lips.

'Well, what a house, you must love it.' D'Alton's voice was different again. Familiar almost, with a hint of an accent Hugo had never heard him use before.

'Yes, yes I do,' he said, trying to recover. 'Can I get you a drink, Mr d'Alton?' He hoped his voice sounded normal.

'Just d'Alton, I just use my surname, I never liked Geoffrey. Stay where you are, I'll help myself.' D'Alton walked over to the sideboard and poured himself a whiskey and added a cube of ice from the bucket. He sat opposite Hugo on the other side of the fire.

'Cheers,' he said, raising his glass. 'And thanks for the hospitality, I've often passed here and wondered what it was like.'

'Really?' Hugo got the impression that he seldom left Dublin on the rare occasions he came back to Ireland.

'Yeah, I'm actually from Cork, so…' d'Alton grinned, enjoying the effect of this revelation on Hugo.

'Cork? I thought you were English or maybe an Anglo-Irish family in Dublin—that was perhaps how you knew my mother. And you live in France, don't you?' That was the accent. He knew he'd heard a trace of the sing-song.

D'Alton threw back his head and laughed. Hugo thought it was the most wonderful sound he'd ever heard. That lurch in his stomach again, what was happening? Sitting in the Queen Anne wingback chair, a glass of whiskey in his hand, Hugo realised that Geoffrey d'Alton was the most attractive man he'd ever seen. He was confused, he thought this man was a pompous snob with all his affectations and his rudeness, but then the way he was in the court, the way he was with Patrick, it was all so confusing and unsettling.

'No, I'm not from aristocratic pile, I'm afraid. I met your mother on a few occasions over the years. We have one or two mutual friends. She's a charming lady,' he said with a hint of a grin that suggested she was a handful. Hugo knew he was right as well, once Lily FitzHenry made her mind up, there was very little that could withstand her will.

'So I've met her a few times in London and once or twice in

France, of course. At things in Antibes, as well, she knows a lot of people your mother. I live there most of the year, just come back for cases, here, or in London really, occasionally in the United States. It's nice there...sunny.' The understatement made him grin.

'But you're from Cork?' Hugo was fascinated by him.

'Midleton, well, outside Midleton. I grew up on a small farm, tiny by comparison to this place. I loved it, there was a lake on the farm, only a little one, and I used to go down there, and really, it was the most magical place. You can't get at it by car, only on foot, and when I needed to escape, I would sit on the lake shore, fish, swim if it was warm enough. But I knew that no matter how much I loved it and my parents—they were lovely people—I couldn't stay. So, I managed to get a scholarship to a school in Dublin, worked hard, went to university, did my bar exams, devilled, and worked in London as a junior counsel, then senior counsel, before taking silk, becoming a QC,' he added by way of explanation. 'I was lucky to get recognition on some high-profile cases, and then I was in demand. So I can more or less pick and choose what cases I want now.'

Before Hugo had time to ask another question, dinner was announced.

They walked down the stairs to one of the small dining rooms, d'Alton stopping frequently to admire artwork or to ask about portraits. He seemed fascinated by Hugo's lineage and watched him intently as he spoke about his various ancestors. The fire was lit in the green dining room, the one the FitzHenrys used to use for small dinner parties when his father was alive. It could seat eight and was cosy and intimate. Candles burned on the sideboard, and the room felt like a cocoon. A lovely painting of his parents on their wedding day hung over the fireplace, and Hugo remembered just sitting on the rug in the weeks after his father's death gazing at it. As they sat down, he told d'Alton about it.

The meal was delicious and consisted mostly of produce of the estate. D'Alton ate with enthusiasm. The conversation flowed easily, and Hugo realised that this man sitting opposite him was the real d'Alton.

'You seem very different than the way you come across initially,' Hugo said, emboldened by the fine claret Patterson had dug out for the occasion.

Again the hearty laugh.

'Acting. That's the trick to success in my game. If they knew, the opposition, the press, whoever, if they had any idea how ordinary I really am, I wouldn't hold the mythological status I do, and I'd lose more cases. So, I have some personas I adopt, mostly the stuck-up barrister, who looks down his nose. While it irritates people, it also intimidates them, in the early stages anyway, and that gives me advantage. It's all an act.' D'Alton smiled as if it were the most logical thing in the world to present yourself as totally different people.

'Right, when Patrick said you were nice and approachable and all that, Liam and I were amazed. We thought you were a bit of a snob, to be honest,' Hugo admitted.

'A bit! I'm an insufferable snob, looking down my nose at everyone, but it works. Your friend Patrick is a good lad and his father was a bastard by all accounts, so the world is much better off without vermin like that. I just hope the judge sees it that way when he's handing down the sentence. He will have to serve some time either way, but I'm hopeful he'll suspend a lot of it and even what he does serve can be reduced by good behaviour. Anyway, no point in speculating, those old judges are a law unto themselves, literally, so they are unpredictable to say the least. If it is excessively harsh though, we'll appeal, anyhow.' He shrugged and rapidly changed the subject. 'You three and the old priest seem like an unlikely bunch of pals if you don't mind me saying so.'

Hugo found himself explaining about St Bart's and the friendship he had with Liam and Patrick and their families and why they meant so much to him.

'Thank you for taking the case, I know it's not your usual thing...' Hugo began.

'Well, I'll be honest, it was the fact that the client was the Earl of Drummond that drew me in, along with persuasion from your dear mama, but every so often a case comes along that I really want to win, not for me, though that's always nice, but because it's the right thing to happen. Patrick Lynch should not spend his life in jail for this, he did kill his father, but sometimes, that's forgivable.' He chuckled.

'Well, whatever your motivation, we only have a chance because of you. The way you analysed the jury, broke it down and spoke to each one of them, the way you made them feel like you were someone they could meet down in the pub...well, it was mesmerising.' Hugo felt instantly foolish for being so gushing and reddened in embarrassment. *Pull yourself together,* he berated himself, *you're like a schoolgirl with a crush.*

D'Alton sat back in the chair and gazed at Hugo saying nothing. Hugo wanted the ground to open up and swallow him. What if d'Alton suspected, he was so astute, so well able to read people it was entirely possible. Hugo's mind went into a spin, what would he say, how would he withstand cross-examination.

'I lied,' d'Alton said quietly.

'About what?' Hugo managed to croak.

'I lied when I said the reason I took the case was because you were the Earl of Drummond. I couldn't care less about that. I'm from a very ordinary background and I just happen to be good at the law, but money, social status, doesn't impress me, really. I have a lot of money, far more than I need.'

Hugo knew the conversation had taken on a whole new tone and wondered where it was going.

'How old are you, Hugo?' he asked.

'Twenty, I'll be twenty-one next month.'

D'Alton sighed deeply and ran his hand through his hair as if he was weighing something up in his mind. Putting his hands together on the table, he exhaled.

'I know I must come across as awful, Hugo, and I'm sorry if your friends think I'm rude, I will apologise to them as soon as all this is over, but as I said, it's part of the game. It's how it all works. I don't want you to think that's who I really am, though. When I said I lied, I meant your title wasn't the reason I took on the case...you were.'

Suddenly, d'Alton didn't seem as self-assured as he always came across.

'Me?' Hugo was confused.

'Yes. That day you rang O'Kelly and he told you that you'd need a miracle or me, he explained to you that I probably wouldn't take the case, didn't he?'

Hugo nodded, remembering the despair he felt.

'Yes, and my mother contacted me a few days later and said you would. I didn't care why you were on the team. I was just relieved that you said yes.'

'Well, the reason I agreed was we have a mutual connection. Your mother and I.' He smiled, that enigmatic smile again.

'Who?' Hugo asked.

'Piers FitzHenry, your uncle, I believe.'

Hugo was confused, his uncle, the one banished to France by the family because of his unnatural tendencies, knew d'Alton?

'Yes, he's my father's brother. My father kept in touch when he was alive. I never knew Mama kept in touch. I met him once or twice as a child…'

'He said he met you at Ascot and again at some family function in Derbyshire, I think he told me, but you were younger. When I refused the case initially, nothing personal, but it doesn't really work for me to be in Cork, I'm afraid of having my cover blown.' He grinned. 'But when Lily rang and explained that you were not just her son but also Piers's nephew, well, she asked me to help you if I could. So I did.'

'I don't remember him, not really. Do you know why he left?' Hugo asked cautiously.

'I do. It's one of the reasons I also live in France.' Time seemed to slow down as the weight of what d'Alton had said settled between them. Suddenly, several thoughts struck Hugo at once. The foremost being of course that d'Alton was homosexual.

'So, that's how you knew the juror was…' Hugo said in wonder.

'I suppose I'm more finely tuned to these things.' He chuckled and watched for Hugo to react to the acknowledgment.

Another thought struck Hugo.

'Are you and Piers…?' he tried to keep the dread out of his voice.

D'Alton laughed aloud. 'God no! I know that to you at forty-three I must seem ancient, but he's too old even for me! The grey hair makes me look older, I know. I went grey very young most fortuitously, it fits with the image. No, Piers is just a friend, but he is a thoroughly nice chap, and I know he'd love to meet you again. Your father told him a lot about you and he always hoped that you would make contact, but he doesn't want to initiate it for fear of how you'd react, I suppose.'

'I planned to when all this was over, maybe even visit…' Hugo said. It was a nice thought that he had an uncle who wanted to get to know him.

'Well, I know he'd love that.'

A silence descended between them as Hugo tried to process what was happening.

Despite all the thoughts and misery and wishing and praying, he'd never considered what he would do when he met another man like himself, and now, when he least expected it, he was having dinner in Greyrock with not only a homosexual man, but an incredibly attractive one who knew his uncle. There was a bizarre but wonderful symmetry to it.

'Is it, you know, in France, possible to…em…?' Hugo wanted to sound urbane and worldly, but he knew he sounded like a little boy.

'Well, homosexuality is illegal, no two ways about that, but the French have a different attitude towards sex in general and tend to turn a blind eye to all misdemeanours in that regard so long as you don't flaunt it. It's quite acceptable, for example for men, and for women too in some cases, to have affairs. Everybody knows it, but it's never admitted. It's kind of the same with us, there are certain places we go, bars and clubs, where so long as you are discreet, you can meet people and take it from there.'

'I'm...' Hugo said. Though he knew d'Alton probably guessed that he wanted to say the words but failed.

'I know.' D'Alton smiled.

'But I've never, I wanted to…well, I didn't know what I wanted, actually. Mostly for me not to be this way, I suppose.' Hugo smiled sadly.

'We've all been there, Hugo, believe me. Why do you think I worked so hard for as long as I can remember? I didn't know how I was going to do it, but I knew I had to get away. There was no way I could get married and take over the farm and have a load of kids as would have been expected of me, so I just studied day and night, literally for years, to find a way out. And I did, get out, I mean. It's harder on you, though, the responsibility of this place, the legacy…'

To his horror, Hugo felt tears sting the back of his eyes. Patrick and Liam had been kind and Martha was too, in her own way, but nobody ever understood before, really knew what it was like to feel so outside, so different.

'I can't imagine it being…I…when I was at school…there was a priest…he used to come into the room…' Hugo allowed the suppressed feelings of shame, despair, and horror to bubble to the surface. The words flowed from him like a torrent, the pain, the terror, the disgust. Words he had never told another soul were tumbling over themselves as he unburdened himself of the sickening weight he'd carried for years.

'I don't know why he picked me, he must have known…' Hugo finished, trying to catch his breath.

D'Alton put his hands on Hugo's shoulders, his piercing eyes boring into Hugo's own.

'Listen to me, Hugo. That was not your fault, that man was, is, a criminal, a paedophile. He would have done that irrespective of what sexual orientation you were. He is the one in the wrong, not you. You were a child; you should have been protected not preyed upon. It was not your fault, do you hear me, none of that was your fault.' He drew Hugo to his chest and held him tightly. Hugo felt drained but relieved.

'Maybe you're right, but either way, I'm such a failure. If I were an ordinary person, this would be hard to bear, but for me, I will be the last of the FitzHenry line, and I can't bear it. We've been here in this house for centuries, literally for hundreds of years a FitzHenry has been the Earl of Drummond. It doesn't mean much anymore, to anyone outside. I mean Ireland is a republic, for goodness sake. From their perspective, it's a title awarded by a foreign king and all that, and I have no desire to lord it over anyone, but to let the title die with me, to sell this house, I just can't bear the thought. I walk down the halls and feel my ancestors' eyes on me, the disgust, the disappointment...'

Quickly, he wiped his eyes with the back of his hand.

He cried and cried, and the other man just rubbed his back and soothed him, kissing his head and allowing him to sob.

'It's all right, Hugo, it's all right. You are not alone. I promise you, you'll never feel this alone again for the rest of your life. The estate is a huge responsibility, and I understand your attachment to it and the weight of history on your shoulders, but you can't change who you are. We've all been where you are now, I see so much of myself in you. I remember the pain, the sheer bloody terror, the shame and guilt, the self-loathing, but they're wrong. The church, the state, the courts, they're all wrong. We're not unnatural, we're not disgraceful, we are not the things they say we are. We are people, men and women, who are just…I don't know, wired differently or something. Not wrong, just different.' D'Alton wiped Hugo's tears with the pads of his thumbs and hugged him tightly. Hugo wanted to stay in the safety of that hug forever, to never have to leave this room, to never have to return to a world where he was a freak of nature, an aberration, a failure.

A log sputtered in the fire, and the sound drew him back to the present. Patterson could walk in at any time, and Hugo couldn't begin to imagine his reaction to the master of the house sobbing in the arms of a house guest.

Reading his mind d'Alton said,

'Hugo, I'm much older and much more experienced than you in most walks of life, but I haven't forgotten what it feels like to be so alone, so conflicted. Okay, I didn't have a big estate and a title into the bargain, that's an added strain no doubt, but I'm glad we had this time together, and I meant what I said, life can be good, fun even sometimes, when you're like us, but you must be careful—very, very, careful. Go and visit your uncle, maybe even look me up when you come over, we could go out to dinner. I could introduce you to some young chaps I know.' He winked and smiled, and Hugo's heart skipped a beat. Disentangling himself from the hug, he sighed deeply.

'Now, we need to be back in Cork in the morning, so I suggest we get some sleep. My flight is booked for nine thirty. Your valet very kindly allowed me to use the telephone so I've told Archie where I am, he worries. We'll need to be on the road by seven, so up at six. And I need to put my mask back on.' He smiled again. 'Goodnight, Hugo.' He kissed his head once more and left the room.

Hugo fought the overwhelming urge to drag him back, to kiss him, to never let him go again. But he realised he would only embarrass himself. D'Alton was certainly nothing like the man Hugo and the others imagined him to be, he was the complete opposite. He was kind and funny and gentle and very ordinary, really. The whole thing was an act, but nobody could ever know that. He wasn't going to be interested in an inexperienced kid. All the electricity he felt when d'Alton touched him was one-sided. D'Alton was a kind man, who made Hugo feel normal for the first time in his life. If this was going to be the future, falling for every man he met, then he had a ridiculous life ahead of him. He chided himself once more, trying to force himself to think clearly. That night, he lay awake, knowing d'Alton was sleeping down the hall and wishing more than anything that he was lying beside him.

The following morning, they left before breakfast in order to get back to Cork.

'How are you?' d'Alton asked in the car as they drove down the avenue.

'Fine thanks.' Hugo was business-like, friendly but not needy. Inside he was crushed that d'Alton was leaving again.

D'Alton nodded. 'Did you sleep?' he asked.

'Yes, thanks,' Hugo lied. He supposed the last thing d'Alton wanted was a kid mooning over him, so he started telling him about the horses and the breeding programme they were running.

They stopped at a roadside café and got a quick breakfast. The conversation was sparse, both men were lost in their thoughts. The easiness and trust of the night before had evaporated in the cold early morning. It was as if d'Alton had put back on his armour, and Hugo couldn't reach him. All night, he thought about the confidences they shared after the revelation that he was homosexual. The fact that d'Alton was from Cork was the most surprising, he seemed so sophisticated and worldly, yet when he spoke of his childhood home last night something changed in him. He looked younger, more vulnerable, somehow. He had clearly loved his family and his home, but he was exiled because of who he was, self-imposed exile, admittedly, but exile nonetheless. He told Hugo about his sister Jennifer and her three children who lived in London with her English husband. He visited them often, and he could tell they were close.

For Hugo, it was a torturous drive. As well as being worried about the outcome for Patrick, he felt guilty about how much he longed to ask d'Alton if they could see each other sometime, but he hadn't the courage. Clearly, he wasn't interested, why would he be? The thought that d'Alton would be gone from his life forever filled him with despair. He had said last night that maybe they could meet in France, have dinner, but that was probably just something he said to make him feel better.

'Hugo, could you take the next left turn please?' D'Alton's voice broke through the silence as they were approaching the city from the east. His voice startled Hugo as he snapped out of his thoughts.

'Okay, of course, is there something you want to see?' Hugo asked.

'Sort of, my parents' house where I grew up is down here. They are both dead now, as I said, but the place was sold a few years ago since neither Jennifer nor I wanted it. I don't know who lives there now. My memories of this place are mixed, not because of my parents, they were lovely people, they made so many sacrifices for me, but I never fitted in.'

Hugo drove on in silence.

'Just right here at this small junction.'

Hugo found himself driving down a narrow road with grass growing up the middle.

'You can pull in here at the wide bit; we need to walk from here.'

Hugo sat in the car, wondering where d'Alton was going and wondering if he should go with him when there was a sharp rap on the glass.

'Well, are you coming?'

Hugo unbuckled and followed d'Alton into a wooded area. It was freezing cold, and they could see their breath on the November air. The frost glistened white all around but once they were under the canopy of evergreen trees, not a sound could be heard. They walked on for ten minutes, getting deeper and deeper into the woods. Hugo followed d'Alton's footsteps, just a few paces behind. The only sound was of their labouring breath as the ground rose steeply. The gnarled roots made it difficult underfoot, and Hugo wished he was wearing more suitable shoes than his polished leather brogues. As they reached what looked like the brow of a hill, the ground fell away sharply and they clambered down. Hugo lost his footing, and d'Alton put out his hand to steady him. The moment their hands touched, Hugo felt a crackle of electricity.

Where were they going? The Scotch pine stretched upwards to the gunmetal grey sky. Even though it must have been around eight in the morning, it was still only barely light.

As they made their way down the incline, Hugo spotted a small lake below. Reeds choked the circumference and a small timber shed, which had a little jetty attached, stood silently to the right of the path. D'Alton walked on, the path only wide enough for one, and Hugo followed.

As soon as they reached the door of the shed, d'Alton took a bunch of keys from his pocket and locating a small one, opened the new-looking padlock. He pushed the door open, and it creaked on its hinges.

'I've had renovators and builders working on this place for a while, it drove them crazy to bring everything in on foot, but I insisted.' This was the only explanation d'Alton gave.

Inside, Hugo was amazed to discover not a shed but a little house. There was a tiny but perfectly functional kitchen, a large double bed with a beautiful, colourful patchwork quilt, and an open fire with a large comfortable-looking couch. At the back were double glass doors leading out onto a little deck that had an uninterrupted view of the lake and the woods. It was beautiful.

'Is this yours?' Hugo asked.

'Yes, I bought it as soon as we sold the home. I used to come here as a boy, it was just an old shed then, and it was my sanctuary. I had a small boat, and I used to go fishing, read, dream, cry, everything, here in this shed, or out on the lake. My parents owned it as part of their land, but nobody ever used it so when we sold up, I insisted on keeping this part. I had it done up, and I get a local man to keep an eye on it for me. I come down here every few months, usually after a big case. Nobody knows where I am, and I stay a few days to recharge. Read, sleep, walk, that sort of thing. When I'm working, I kind of block everything else out and focus one hundred percent on the case, which can be exhausting. I love my place in France, but it's a very social house, lots of people dropping in for drinks and so on. I enjoy it, but this is my bolthole when I want to check out of the world now and again. I've never brought another living soul here before.' As he spoke, he looked directly at Hugo.

'It's wonderful, lovely, so cosy, well, it would be with the fire going I imagine. You're so lucky to have this; nobody could even find it.' Hugo wanted to say how flattered he was that he was the only person d'Alton had ever brought to this place, but he couldn't find the words.

'Everybody needs someplace, even if it's a hut in the woods, someplace where they can go, just to be alone with their thoughts.'

'I know,' Hugo replied wistfully. 'I own a huge estate but even then, I don't know, I don't get much time or space. There was a tree house, Martha and I—we were best friends as children—used to play there.'

'Is she still around?'

Hugo found himself telling d'Alton the whole story of the last time he's seen her.

'Well, I think it's what most men like us have tried, just to see if we could. I did something similar years ago when I was in college, I didn't get quite as far as you because I think the girl realised I wasn't...I don't know...anyway, I knew then that women were never going to interest me in that way.'

Hugo smiled ruefully. 'She was being kind, thought she could fix me, though up to then she had no idea, which surprised me. I suppose I think I might as well have it written on my forehead, but afterwards she was nice, supportive, well as much as she could be…' He shivered. The shed was cold but not damp.

D'Alton stood looking out of the windows at the lake.

'Thank you for bringing me here.' Hugo's voice sounded strange to his ears.

'You could use it if you wanted…' d'Alton began.

'I wouldn't come here without you, it wouldn't feel right.'

The silence hung between them. Hugo didn't dare to divert his gaze from the vista outside and d'Alton's back as he stood still. The older man's voice eventually broke the stillness.

'Would you like to come here with me sometime? When this is all over and you've had time to think about things.' D'Alton still had his back to the room, and Hugo felt the tension and weight in the air between them.

'I'd love to.'

He moved towards d'Alton and didn't allow himself to think about what he was doing, if he did, he would surely stop. Hugo stood behind him and put his arms around him, resting his face against d'Alton's back. Several moments passed and then he turned around to face him.

Hugo looked straight into his face and their eyes locked until d'Alton leaned forward and kissed him.

Time passed as they stood there kissing. Hugo wanted the moment to never end. For the first time in his life, he felt alive inside, real, like a normal person.

'I'm too old for you. You know that, don't you?' D'Alton smiled.

'No, you're not. You're everything I've ever wanted. Nothing about this is right in the eyes of the whole world so an age difference is the least of our problems.' Hugo grinned. All traces of insecurity gone. This wasn't just a fling or a schoolboy crush, he knew it. D'Alton brought him to his special place; the only person he'd ever brought there, this was real. They stood in each other's arms, just enjoying the moment.

'D'Alton?' Hugo suddenly felt reckless, unafraid.

'Yes, Hugo?'

'Is it this simple? I'm new to this so...'

'Well, in matters of the heart, I've found things can be as simple or as complicated as you want them to be. There are a myriad of reasons as you say why we shouldn't be together, but you impress me so much. From the time I first met you, and that unlikely bunch you are friends with...' Hugo delighted at the sound of his warm chuckle and looked into his eyes once more. He knew d'Alton liked them, and it was true they were an odd mixture. 'I knew then that there was something unique about you. You don't care for class or title or position in life, you choose your friends based on their attributes, you're fiercely loyal and generous and kind and, of course, you are rather good-looking, as well...'

D'Alton's smile melted his heart.

'I realise you don't know me, not really. I wear a mask most of the time as you've seen. But I've shown you more of the real d'Alton than I've ever shown anyone. I trust you, Hugo, and in my experience of humanity, that is something to be doled out very cautiously. Maybe we'll get on each other's nerves, maybe you'll discover the whole gay world, and I'll be just your first crush, I don't know, but I do know that I don't want to walk out onto that aeroplane and never see you again.'

'You know I have to stay here, manage Greyrock...' Hugo desperately wanted a future with this man, but it was vital he understood the ties that bound him.

'Of course you do. But Hugo, we can see each other often. Aeroplanes are wonderful things, you know.'

'Really? Can we do that? I'm terrified and excited and worried all at the same time.'

'I know you are because I am too. Now, let's get this case over, we'll wait until the sentencing. Technically, I don't need to be here. O'Kelly or a local barrister could handle it, but I'd like to be. I need to go and focus on this other case, but I'll be back in two weeks, and we can talk some more then. The case is in Paris, but I'll be back at my house for a day or two at the weekend so I'll telephone you then.'

Two weeks sounded like eternity, but the spell was broken, they had to go back. Hugo felt guilty at how much he wanted to stay, but d'Alton was right, it was too complicated until they knew what was happening with Patrick. They stepped outside and locked the padlock and when he did, d'Alton took another small key off the ring, identical to the one for the padlock.

'That's for you,' d'Alton said, and kissed Hugo quickly on the lips.

Hugo had been given so many gifts in his life, ponies, holidays abroad, a huge estate, but no gift he'd ever received ever meant as much to him.

'Thank you, d'Alton.'

CHAPTER 24

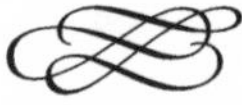

Liam heard voices downstairs as he was packing his bag to go back to Maynooth and wondered who was calling so early. He'd spent a few days at home with Mam and the girls after the trial, and Hugo went back to Greyrock. He was anxious to get back there as things were piling up after his weeks of absence due to the trial. He popped in after dropping d'Alton to the plane the day after the trial and had been in great form. D'Alton had spent the night at Greyrock to avoid the press after his amazing performance at the trial, and Hugo was really optimistic about Patrick's hopes of a light sentence.

Mam tried to get him to stay, but he insisted he had to get to the estate. She was living in terror that he was going to kill himself in that fancy blue sports car. Liam smiled at the memory of his mother's face when she saw it, revving loudly on the street outside, and Hugo grinning with the top down. It wasn't in his nature to be flashy, but this car was his pride and joy. Liam was glad something was giving his friend happiness as he often seemed like he had the weight of the world on his shoulders these days. They'd have been lost without him, and of course, his money, in Patrick's case. They had got the best in the business in d'Alton, even if he was a bit of a snob, you'd have to admire him.

Patrick really liked him though and trusted him, which was the main thing. Liam still was trying to take in how Patrick was able to kill his own father. He understood why he did it, God knows Joe Lynch had it coming, but to actually extinguish the life of another, whatever the motivation, was something Liam couldn't comprehend. Still, he prayed that the judge would see that Patrick wasn't a danger, a killer on the loose, he was a desperate man led to desperate measures. Life could be peaceful for his friend, for the first time ever, when he got out. Liam had battled for so many nights with his conscience. To kill was to break one of God's commandments; there were no provisos in it. 'Thou shalt not kill'—end of story. But should you pay forever for something that wasn't cold blooded, or if the victim wasn't innocent himself? Eventually, Liam came to the conclusion that only God could judge Patrick, not him, or the courts or anyone else. He believed that Patrick should be freed and allowed to take care of his sisters as his mother would have wanted.

Things were good between Patrick and Helen. She was such a nice girl, and Connie and Anna loved her. They would make a happy family given half a chance. That flashy one he used to knock around with had never made an appearance after the funeral, but Helen stuck by him, even though they didn't have any kind of understanding. Nonetheless, she visited him regularly and wrote every day. To the best of his knowledge, the subject of romance had not been broached. Patrick explained that until he had something to offer, there was no point.

He was in generally good spirits, Liam and Father Aquinas visited every chance they could, and d'Alton really did seem to have given him hope.

'Liam,' his mother called up the stairs. 'Father Aquinas is here to see you.'

'I'll be down in two minutes.'

He rose and dressed, he was probably supposed to dress in his clerical garb, but he felt uncomfortable in it. He hated the reverence his old neighbours displayed towards him now, like he was somewhere above them when he was just the same Liam Tobin they'd known all their lives.

He looked out the window at the golden fish on top of St Teresa's and made a silent prayer, 'Please Lord, let your will be done but if your will could be to let Patrick away with a light sentence, that would be really great.' He rolled his eyes and sighed in exasperation. What sort of a priest prays that a murderer gets off with taking a life? He despaired of himself, wishing for the millionth time that he could be more holy. He thought of his fellow seminarians, with their earnest faces and serious demeanours and the way they seemed rapt in prayer. There seemed to be serenity to them, like they were on the way to being saints already while he was very much a mere mortal.

He, on the other hand, condoned Hugo's homosexuality, wanted Patrick to get away with murder, wasn't full of divine thoughts, and his prayers lacked the piety and devotion of his fellow students. He desperately wanted to be a priest, he loved God and believed him to be a kind and loving force in the lives of all those who followed him. That thought kept him going through his many moments of doubt. God wouldn't have given him a vocation surely if he didn't intend him to use it.

He could hear his mother clucking around like a hen and though it was driving Liam mad, he was trying not to let it show because it was just her way of coping with everything. It was the same when Daddy died, he remembered, making tea, fussing over food, cleaning the house, all the things that seemed so irrelevant at the time. She'd had so much to deal with, that business with that woman next door, Daddy leaving, and then his death. She and Mrs Lynch were there for each other through thick and thin, and he knew his mother felt the death of her friend keenly.

She was all of a dither today though, and Liam knew why. She confided to him last night that D.I. McMullan had called to see how things were after the trial, but it had led to him asking her to go out for afternoon tea to the Imperial Hotel in town with him someday next week. Liam was so touched when she raised the matter, clearly embarrassed, but it was to ask his blessing.

'I think it would be a great idea, Mam. Sure he's a lovely man, and he's on his own as well, why shouldn't you have another chance at happiness?'

His mother cried and told him that there was never going to be a replacement for Seán, she wanted Liam to know that, that he was the great love of her life, despite everything.

'I know that, Mam, of course, I know that, and Daddy knew it too. He's up in heaven looking down and wishing you well, he wouldn't want you to be on your own forever, and with Con and the girls away...'

She nodded, grateful for his approval. She missed the girls, and she hoped that when Con got married, maybe they would get closer if God blessed them with children. Hilda's mother had passed away last year so maybe they'd have need of a grandmother. She confided to Liam that she prayed about it. Liam reminded himself to have a word with Con and ask him to include their mother a bit more. Con was grand, he didn't ever mean any harm, but he could be thoughtless. The girls were a dead loss he feared. Kate was firmly planted in England and not showing any signs of wanting to come home even for a visit, and the twins, well, maybe it was better that they stayed in Dublin out of the way based on the get up of them the last time they came home. Maybe he could write to Kate, ask her to invite Mam and Connie and Anna over for a visit.

'Well, it's only a cup of tea. Nothing more. And sure we'll see...' She seemed unsure.

'Do you like him, Mam?' he asked gently.

'He's very nice, very gallant, if that word is still used these days. He's a gentleman, just like your dad was, God rest his soul. And he makes me laugh, it wasn't until that happened that I realised how rarely I laugh these days. No doubt, people will talk, but sure people will always talk...'

Liam was transported back in time to when he was a small boy, looking through the crack in the door at his Mammy and Daddy laughing long after he was supposed to be asleep, and Daddy hushing her because she'd be laughing so hard at something he'd said. He wanted that for her again, she deserved it.

The only other bright spot in her life was him and his vocation to the priesthood. He wondered how she would feel if he told her he was filled with doubt about his suitability. He wished he was sure, sure that he wouldn't make a total mess of it even if he did manage to pass through the seven years and get ordained.

He finished dressing quickly. It was freezing upstairs, he could see his breath on the air. The girls were fast asleep; he'd seen them sprawled on his and Con's old bed when he'd gone outside to the toilet earlier. He'd hopped from foot to foot. He had forgotten how difficult an outside toilet was in the winter. He was getting used to the comparative comfort of the seminary.

Father Aquinas was at the bottom of the stairs.

'I thought I could walk you to the train, Liam, before you have to get back to the seminary, maybe stop for a cup of tea somewhere if we've time.'

Liam looked at the old priest and wondered, not for the hundredth time, how he was ever afraid of him. He'd shown such kindness to Liam over the years and, indeed, to Patrick and Hugo as well, standing up for them to other priests, who may not have seen the same potential in the three unlikely friends. Patrick used to call to the monastery often in recent times. In his letters, he would tell Liam and Hugo about how everything was up there, and he spoke with such gratitude for the support the priest gave him, especially when his mother died. If the worst happened, and Patrick did get a long sentence, Father Aquinas would visit him, Liam knew that for sure. In lots of ways, it made him being away in Maynooth a bit easier, knowing he was taking care of things here.

'Good idea, Father, that's a long journey he has this afternoon. The fresh air will do him good, but be sure and wear your warm coat and don't forget your hat, sure you won't, Liam?'

Pulling on his coat and a hat and smiling at his mother fussing over him, Liam and the priest made their way out onto the street.

He kissed her on the cheek. She was always sad when he went back.

'Bye, Mam, sure I'll be home for Christmas so it won't be long at all.'

'I know love, God bless. I put a few scones and a fruit cake in your bag.' She hugged him tightly and let him go.

Father Aquinas and Liam fell into step as they walked down the hill towards the city.

'A lot happens under the Goldie Fish, doesn't it, Liam? It looks like any other street in any other town, but an awful lot happens here.'

'It certainly does, Father, of late, especially. How do you think it's going to go with the sentencing?' he asked, knowing the priest had no more insight than he did.

'Well, if he doesn't get a light sentence, it won't be for the want of trying on that Mr d'Alton's part that's for sure. He was wonderful the other day, wasn't he?'

'Yes, amazing. He came across so differently than the way he is, much more approachable.'

'Ah, Liam, there's more to our Mr d'Alton than meets the eye. What would you say if I told you he's from Cork?' Father Aquinas's eyes twinkled with merriment.

'No! He can't be, with his big plummy accent and the get up of him, go way outta that,' Liam laughed.

'Well, accent and all, he is! He's from down Midleton direction. But he got a scholarship to Clongowes Wood. Very bright by all accounts. He studied law and then went off to England, where he picked up the accent, no doubt, but yes, he's a scholarship lad the same as you and Patrick.'

'How did you find that out?'

'Sure, Liam, I'm a priest and sure don't you know priests know everything?' the old priest replied with a wink.

'Well, I'd better hurry up and develop this great bank of knowledge so. At this rate, I think I'll be the thickest priest in Ireland.'

'You'll do fine, so you will. Anyway, the thickest priest in Ireland is a much contended title, you've brains to burn boy, always had. Are you finding the studying hard going?'

Liam debated expressing his worries to Father Aquinas. He'd worked so hard to get him into the position where he could even apply for the priesthood, admitting any doubts felt like letting him down.

'No, not the studying, that part's grand. I like it, actually, but I just wonder if I'm cut out for it…' The words flowed from him like a torrent, all the fears and misgivings he had until eventually he stopped talking, there was nothing left to say.

The silence was easy, and Liam knew Father Aquinas wasn't a man to rush into pronouncements. He was more cautious than that.

'I'm sorry I shouldn't be dumping all this on you after you've been so good to us, and today of all days, when Patrick is all we should be thinking about.'

'Liam, we've talked about the Patrick situation a thousand times. It's in the hands of God now, or at least in the hands of the judge, who is hopefully being directed by God. So we might as well talk about you. Firstly, I am not going to dismiss your concerns, the old 'yerra you'll be grand' kind of attitude meant lots of men and women wound up in the religious life when they shouldn't have and are now in positions where they can vent their frustrations on those in their care, so it's important you are making the right choices. Secondly, no matter what you choose, I am proud of you. You had a tough time, not as bad as poor Patrick, but tough all the same. Losing your father under those circumstances and the effect it had on your family, well that wasn't easy, but you got your head down and did your best, and I admire that in you. Because, Liam, that's what anything is about, a good priest, a good doctor, a good parent, a good teacher, it's not about getting it right all the time or knowing a hundred percent that you are making the right choices, it's about doing the best that you can. We're human, flawed, we make mistakes, we get it wrong a lot of the time, but once you can look yourself in the face and say, I'm trying my best, then what more can God ask of us? You say you're thinking about hurling and cake and your mother when you should be thinking about theology or philosophy, but that just makes you normal. Now, tell me this, and I want a straight answer, do you think about girls at all?'

Liam was stunned; he didn't know what to say.

'It's not a trick question, Liam. I'm not trying to catch you out, I just want to know if you can do what is the hardest part of being a priest for a lot of men, giving up female companionship, falling in love, sex, family, and all the rest of it.'

Liam didn't know what to say. His gut instinct was to deny he ever thought about girls, to deny he ever harboured an impure thought, but that wouldn't be true.

'I think I can do it. I'm not saying the thought of girls has never entered my head. Of course it has, and I see Patrick going out with this one and that one, before, I mean, and I'd wonder what it would be like, but I love God and if he wants me to be celibate, I will be. Maybe when he gives you a vocation, he takes away the desire a bit, so you can cope with it. That's not my biggest problem. Being a terrible priest, that's my problem.'

Father Aquinas burst out laughing.

'Liam Tobin, you never lost it! You'll be a grand priest and do you know why?'

Liam shook his head.

'Because you are kind. You see people in trouble, people who might need help, and you do your best. You understand people, Liam. I know some of the other fellas might seem fierce holy altogether, but a lot of them are raised as priests since they were infants, like little hot house flowers they were, the rough and tumble of the real world never touched them. They were never in a house where the man is drinking and battering his family, or a house where a young woman, who had her own problems, fixated on a married man and ruined his family. They don't know what it's like to have a life foisted upon them, the pressure to be something you're not and feeling the weight of everyone that went before you on your shoulders day after day. They wouldn't know what to say to a woman or man who might be worried what the neighbours would say if they tried to find a bit of happiness with someone late in their lives. They never knew a day's poverty nor had to search their conscience when what they knew to be right wasn't what the church taught. Who are they fit to minister to? Only their own kind, who don't need it, anyway. You, on the other hand, have lived, here, under the Goldie Fish where all human life is found, with all its frailties and rough edges. That's why you'll make a great priest because you'll understand. Sometimes you just need to listen. You don't need to have all the answers but just be there for someone, and you can do that, better than most.'

Liam tried to digest what he said, especially the part about his conscience and the church teachings. Father Aquinas didn't miss a trick that was for sure. Everybody had their challenges, their own set of worries, and he noticed everything. He was probably referring to Patrick and his condoning of the breaking of one of God's commandments, but he wondered if the priest had any inkling about Hugo.

'Thanks, Father. I do often find myself at loggerheads with the church's teachings, especially of late, I mean how can I follow the vow of obedience if I'm totally opposed to the church's rule on something?' Liam asked.

'Well, I don't know the answer to that one, and I don't think a priest exists that hasn't had to battle with that at some point. Not anyone that takes his vocation seriously, anyway. I've had moments myself, times when what the church taught and what I believed to be right were totally opposed. I'll give you an example, I saw mothers there when I was in the school having baby after baby, year in year out and no money to provide for them, and yet the church says to interfere in the procreation process is a sin. I can't stand over the church's teaching that a man and woman who are married should abstain from normal marital relations if they don't want to risk a pregnancy when science has developed a way for them to do that. I've probably shocked you now, but I just want you to know that we all face dilemmas at some time.' Liam felt the weight of his impasse lift a little. Just knowing that Father Aquinas felt it too helped enormously. He was a great priest, kind, compassionate, and dealt in the real world.

'We are human beings as well as priests. We're not exempt from moral dilemmas, far from it. I remember one particular occasion, one night a few years back, when I gave a bottle of whiskey to a violent drunk to make him forget an incident. Was that a sin? Technically, it probably was, but having him remember and take his revenge on two innocent young lads was, in my eyes, much worse.' Liam smiled. It was the first time Father Aquinas ever referred to that night in all these years.

'I don't know what the answer is, except to say this. I ask myself, what would Jesus do? If he was here right this minute and you could ask him about somebody who was not living in a way that the church deemed to be right, and you could ask him to decide, what would he say? Generally, I think he would say as he did in Corinthians, "And now these three remain, faith, hope, and love. But the greatest of these is love." I think if there is love, and the motivation is love and not hate, or bitterness or revenge, then how can love be wrong?'

The two men shared a glance that said a thousand words. Father Aquinas knew about Hugo, Liam didn't know how he knew, but he knew he did, and he was giving his absolution in as far as he could. Liam looked forward to relaying the details of the conversation to Hugo sometime in the future. Hopefully, Patrick will be there too. Liam imagined the three of them some evening in Greyrock, sitting around the fire analysing the whole lot. He wished for both of his friends long life and happiness but given the life paths they were on, it wasn't looking likely.

CHAPTER 25

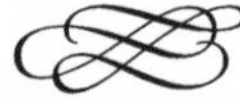

The week after the end of the trial passed in a blur for Hugo. As he sat one morning in his study, he despaired of the amount of work to be done. It was bitterly cold, so all the animals were inside and that made the workload double. Feed, staff, water, vet visits, all were needed, and someone had to run the entire operation. His absence from the estate meant that paperwork had piled up and while Tom was doing his best, Hugo could see he was not back to full working capacity. He doubted that the old manager ever would be, but he would never dare raise that topic with him.

Tom Courtney was a taciturn man at the best of times and made no secret of the fact that he thought the generation of today compared most unfavourably with those that went before. To be fair, Hugo knew Tom's feelings included him in that, but his disdain was not reserved particularly for the young earl. He felt that way about all young people.

Hugo wished he was more approachable but even his father had treated Tom with kid gloves. He would have loved to enquire about Martha to find out where she was, maybe even write, though what he would say he had no idea. Perhaps, he often told himself it was better to stay away. She knew perfectly well where he was. If she wanted to hear from him, she could easily make contact. He felt awful about that day in the tree house, how horrible it must have been for her to endure his rejection afterwards and then the disgust when she realised that he really was the abomination he told her he was. His cheeks burned with shame at the memory of that day.

Since the conversation with d'Alton and the visit to his little house by the lake, Hugo felt a lot better, less of an outcast, less alone, but now that d'Alton was gone back to France, that glow of acceptance was fading fast. He was home in Greyrock, and he had to keep telling himself that it was going to be all right. It was all very well to have conversations with exotic men who lived in France in the dead of night over bottles of wine, to think it was all normal. That *he* was normal, but the harsh reality was very different. He wished he had someone to talk to, Liam was gone back to the seminary, so that was out, and Patrick was still languishing in jail. He would have loved to phone d'Alton, but he was only gone a few days, and he said he'd call. He didn't want to seem like a lovesick teenager, so he'd just have to wait. Hugo tried not to worry. D'Alton explained that when he was in a case, he was all consumed by it, blocked out everything else, so he said he'd call when it was over. Also, he didn't trust phones in hotels or public places. His cases were often high profile with potentially disastrous consequences for some very influential people, who would love nothing better than to expose the famous Geoffrey d'Alton as a homosexual, so discretion had to be paramount. He said he'd call when he got back to his house in Antibes, and Hugo just had to hold on to that.

The days seemed long though, waiting for d'Alton, waiting for a sentence for Patrick, wondering what had become of Martha, and all the time the work in Greyrock piled up. It was probably just as well he couldn't talk to Liam or Patrick.

Anyway, while Hugo was incredibly touched that Liam had chosen friendship over his deeply held faith on the subject of homosexuality, he still hated the idea of forcing his friend to deal with the reality of

Hugo's attraction to men. The thought of Liam struggling to accept him in an actual relationship rather than a notional one made him cringe. Patrick, too, was accepting and non-judgemental in theory but if anything came to pass between him and d'Alton, Hugo knew he would dread telling them.

As he sifted through the endless bills, receipts, requests from tenants, vet reports, Department of Agriculture directives, invitations to events in the area, he felt guilty. His father would have never allowed things to become so chaotic, but he had so much on his mind lately, the needs of the vast estate were pushed aside. He swore that by the end of today, no matter how long it took he would get to the end of his overflowing in-tray. As he started, the phone rang.

'Hello, Greyrock, how can I help you?' he said absently. He heard peculiar clunking noises and realised the caller was ringing from a payphone.

'Oh hello...hello, is that you, Hugo?'

'Mrs Tobin? Yes...yes, it's me. Is everything all right?' Hugo was worried. He knew Liam's mother hated using phones so something must be wrong.

'Oh yes, pet, everything is fine, but I got a letter this morning, and I just don't know what to do about it. From the bank on the South Mall. The letter says that...' Hugo heard the rattle of paper.

'I set up a standing order, Mrs Tobin,' Hugo interrupted her. 'I didn't ask you because I knew you'd say no, but please take it. Every month some money will be lodged in there for the girls and for you. The bank will send you out a book so you can just go in and withdraw whatever you need. I don't have personal experience, but I hear children are expensive, so I wanted at least to alleviate any worries you have in that area. We can revisit it as soon as we know what's happening with Patrick but, in the meantime, please, will you just use it?'

'But, Hugo, you can't do that. I mean, it's a ridiculous amount of money, you need your money for that big place of yours and...well, whatever else you need it for...' She was flustered.

'Mrs Tobin, I have more than enough money, let me assure you. Please let me do this, it remains between you and me. I owe you for a lot of dinners.' He smiled.

'Hugo FitzHenry, you do not indeed owe us anything, you're like a son to me and having you in our house, well, you're just one of the family, fancy and all as you are.' He could visualise her standing in the draughty telephone box on Patrick Street and felt a wave of love for her.

He would never have children of his own, any nieces or nephews, but he had the Tobins and the Lynches and he cherished them.

'Thanks, Mrs Tobin, that means a lot. Now, not another word about the money, all right?'

She sighed. 'All right, Hugo, just until we know what's happening. I'll get them something nice from Santa Claus and maybe coats and shoes and that sort of thing so, if you're sure.'

'I am,' he said as the phone began to beep.

'I'll go so, I'm about to get cut...'

Hugo grinned as he returned to his paperwork. Maybe Mrs Tobin and Liam would bring the girls to Greyrock for Christmas. Patrick's sentencing would be decided and at least the endless waiting would be over. Maybe even Father Aquinas could visit, and Santa could come for the girls down the big chimney for the first time since Hugo was a boy. The thought of filling the house with his dear friends gave him a warm glow. After the chaos of the trial and his misery at his situation, things were looking a little brighter.

He worked all morning. Patterson brought him sandwiches and tea and insisted on opening the windows when he entered as he claimed he couldn't see Hugo through the cigarette smoke.

'Patterson! It's freezing, close the bloody window,' Hugo exclaimed as a pile of papers fluttered off the desk in the stiff breeze.

Patterson closed it though he exuded disapproval through every pore as Hugo retrieved the pile.

'Thank you, Patterson,' Hugo said with a smile. 'I'll cut back, I promise.'

'You're welcome, Master Hugo,' he replied and left the room, mildly appeased.

Hugo spotted an envelope with familiar writing addressed to him that had been buried under stacks of bills. It had been posted two months before. He slit the envelope with a beautiful, pink mother-of-pearl letter opener. He dreaded to think of Patrick's reaction if he saw that, but it had been at Greyrock forever.

Inside was a letter, but there was also something else.

Hugo stared, stunned. With shaking hands, he unfolded the letter.

Dear Hugo,

Right, I've started this letter around a hundred times. The waste paper bin beside me is overflowing. I just can't find the right words. So I'm just going to spit it out as your friend Patrick might say.

I'm sorry I left so abruptly, I had to. I couldn't explain to you, well, because I knew how you would react, and I didn't want that. I didn't know what I wanted, to be honest, but I definitely didn't want you doing the 'right thing' as I knew you would.

I wish I could see your face as you read this, to judge how you're taking the news, but I can't. The thing is, Hugo, I discovered I was pregnant a few weeks after that day in the tree house. I know you might think I'm a wanton hussy based on the way I seduced you, but I swear to you what happened wasn't planned on my part, it just happened. You, my best friend, were so sad, and I just wanted to make you feel better, I suppose.

God, this must sound like total gibberish. Anyway, I'm going to keep going. I didn't say anything because I didn't want you to think I'd tried to trick you, to get Greyrock or something. There was only one other before you, and I told you about that. Well, anyway, I knew you'd suggest we get married but that would make nobody happy in the end, would it? Least of all our son, so I decided it was best to go. My father knows, but I made him swear never to mention it to you or anyone else, so I'm sure he's not breathed a word. I told him that I knew you'd marry me if I told you and that I didn't want to marry you nor you me. He was not pleased as you can imagine, but I told him I was going to stay with Mammy's sister, my Auntie Betty in Birmingham. So that's what I did. The baby was born last May, and he's a lovely little fellow. I wanted to call him after you but yours is such an easily identifiable name, I decided against it. His name is William, after your father, and he looks just like you, blond curls and blue eyes, and he makes us all laugh with his chuckle.

I'm sorry that I didn't tell you sooner, but I hope you understand. I've met someone over here, a really nice man, and we're going to get married. He knows the whole story. I would never betray your confidence, Hugo, but if we are to be married and he is to be in William's life, it is only right he is in possession of all the facts. Terence, my intended, is a lot like Dad, actually, quiet and trustworthy. He won't ever say it to anyone, I give you my word.

So, my dear Hugo, there you have it. I've wrangled with this for months, often deciding to leave well enough alone, but I know how much having a child to pass Greyrock on to means to you, and I figured William might be your only chance, so that's why I'm writing. If you choose to ignore this letter, I understand, and there will be no bad feeling from my side. I don't want anything from you but if you want to be in your son's life, in some capacity, as he grows up, Terence and I would be happy to accommodate that.

I enclose a photo of William taken last week and my return address. Take your time, Hugo, there is no pressure. William will grow up happy and healthy in a loving family whatever you decide.

All my love always,
Martha and William

HUGO PICKED up the two-inch square photograph and stared at it. A smiling baby beamed back at him. Martha was right, he thought, William looked just like him as a baby.

'Hello, William,' he said, his voice croaking with emotion as tears ran down his cheeks.

He sat there, just staring at this baby boy's picture. How could this be happening? He was unsure about religion at the best of times and even questioned the existence of God on occasion, but he was overwhelmed with a feeling of gratitude. Gratitude to whatever force was at work to have allowed him to become a father, to have a son, not just for himself, but for Greyrock. Martha was a wonderful friend, and he believed her completely when she explained her reasons for staying silent until now. He wasn't angry that she didn't tell him once she found out she was pregnant. Poor Martha, what an incredibly difficult situation to find oneself in. Tom must have been livid; it certainly explains his reticence on the subject since she left. She was right. If he'd known, he would have offered to marry her and that would have been disastrous for both of them.

Hugo kept looking at the smiling baby and felt instant love. He couldn't wait to meet him, his son. He repeated the words over and over to himself, 'My son, William.'

Martha didn't send a telephone number, just an address, so he promptly wrote her back.

My dear Martha,

I'm sitting here in the study trying to take in this wonderful news. I'm sorry it's taken me so long to reply, but I only discovered your letter this morning. So much has been happening here, too much to go into now, but I've not been here in Greyrock much of late, and I let the paperwork and correspondence slide, I'm afraid.

Martha, can it be true? I am a father and that beautiful little boy is my son? I can hardly believe it. Perhaps, I'd have more doubts if he wasn't the image of me as a baby. Remember the photograph in the oval frame on the sideboard in the downstairs drawing room? It could be William. I'm so touched you called our son after my father, he would have been as well, he always loved you Martha, as I do.

I can't tell you how much it means to me. You could have said nothing, you could have just lived your life, got married and been happy, and I would have known nothing of my child but your generosity and selflessness means more to me than words can ever say.

I want to see him, to hold him, to show him Greyrock, to teach him how to ride a pony, but Martha, I'll do whatever you want. I'm just eternally in your debt for what you've done. You make the decisions, you are his mother.

But, just say the word, and I'm on the next plane.

I can't believe this is happening, it's amazing.

I want to shout it from the rooftop.

All my love,

Hugo

CHAPTER 26

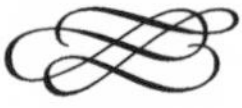

Patrick looked across the battered table at Helen.

'I do, of course, I like you, you've been amazing...' he was struggling to explain.

'Well, it's just I know the type you go for, you know, the very glamorous girls, and I'm not that and so I just want to know if I'm wasting my time?' The whole speech came out in a rush as if she'd practiced and practiced it and if she didn't blurt it out now, she never would. Her cheeks were pink with embarrassment.

Patrick leaned over and held her hand. Though strictly speaking there should be no touching, the warder on that day was half blind.

'I have nothing to offer you, Helen, not a single thing. I'm going to be sent to prison for years and even when I do get out, sure what will I have to offer someone like you? No job, no prospects, and a criminal record following me around forever. How could I make any plans, you've been so good to me and to the girls, I'll never be able to repay you. I just can't ask you for anything more than friendship. You should find someone else,' he finished miserably.

'But you thick eejit, can't you see? I don't want anyone else, I just want you.' Tears of frustration shone in her eyes.

'I can't ask you...the sentencing is tomorrow, it could be years and years...' he tried again.

'I'm not asking you to ask me anything, I'm telling you that I want to be your girlfriend and someday maybe more than that. That's what I want and if I have to wait for years, then so be it. Mr d'Alton is hopeful, and so am I, that it won't be for too many years, but however long it takes, I'll wait. I just don't want to wait for a fella who doesn't want me. I just wanted to know where I stand.'

In the year since his arrest, Patrick had really got to know her and he'd never seen her so emotional. She was tough and determined and full of craic despite her demure exterior. He hated girls that turned on the waterworks every five minutes, but Helen wasn't like that.

'I don't know, Helen. I'm mad about you, of course I am, you're lovely and funny and kind but I...'

'Stop right there, Patrick Lynch.' She put up her hand to stop him talking.

'I love you. Do you love me?'

Suddenly, Patrick realised that she was serious. She loved him, and she wanted to wait for him. It seemed such a huge sacrifice, but it was what she wanted. She seemed adamant.

'I do. I really do. And on top of it, Connie and Anna, and Liam and Hugo, and Mrs Tobin, and even Father Aquinas, all love you too. I don't know who sent you to me, my mam maybe, but Helen Dunne, if you'll wait for me, I swear to you the minute I get out of this place, we'll get married if that's what you want.'

'It is, more than anything.' And she allowed the tears to flow unchecked down her face as they held hands tightly.

'But there is one condition,' he said gravely.

'What?'

'If I get more than ten years, I'm letting you go. I don't want to hear from you, no letters, no visits. If I'm going to have my youth taken from me, I couldn't bear to have yours taken as well. You have to give me your word that you'll agree before I propose. Do you promise?'

Helen knew he was serious, and she had to agree.

'I promise,' she said, though she knew in her heart she would always wait for him.

Patrick pulled a thread from his rough prison issue shirt and clumsily tied it in a loop. The warden was deep in conversation with a colleague and had his back turned, so Patrick got off his seat and went down on one knee beside Helen.

'Helen Dunne, I've no idea why you want to marry me but if you do, I'm asking you formally. Will you do me the great honour of becoming my wife?'

Tears shone in her eyes as he put the loop of thread on her ring finger.

'I'd love to.'

By now, the warder had turned around and was observing the scene.

'We just got engaged,' she told him as if he couldn't see for himself.

He grinned, the sight of the two young people clearly in love, bringing a bit of joy into the grey visiting room. 'Right, well good luck to ye, I suppose. At least he won't be annoying you by leaving the seat of the Jacks up, not for a while.'

Though the humour was dark, for some reason Patrick and Helen found it hilarious, and they laughed till they could hardly breathe.

They sat in the same coffee shop across the street from the courthouse the following morning, this time with d'Alton and Mr O'Kelly, all trying to keep the conversation going but failing miserably. Liam thought d'Alton was different, he seemed nicer but still quite standoffish. Perhaps he was worried about the outcome, as well.

They were gathered on the steps outside awaiting the opening of the court and for the circus to begin again. Geoffrey d'Alton's most notorious cases emblazoned the front pages complete with several photos of the man himself.

'This seems to be more about you than Patrick, Mr d'Alton,' Father Aquinas said with a smile.

'Well, Father, the media do love a David and Goliath story and since I often defend the David rather than the Goliath, I suppose I have gained some notoriety. Though not always, of course, sometimes the giant can be the injured party also.'

He was smooth, Liam gave him that. Intelligence gleamed in his eyes, but he was unreadable. Liam wondered if being good-looking, and d'Alton certainly was a handsome man, helped in court. He suspected it did. Even though women couldn't serve on a jury, men too were drawn to good looks and tended to trust the word of beauty over ugliness. If d'Alton had reinvented himself, and it seemed that it was the case, he's done a comprehensive job on it. Liam definitely got the impression that mentioning that they knew of his humble origins wouldn't be welcome. Even he couldn't have failed to be impressed by Greyrock, and there was the distinct feeling that fine dining in mansions was much more d'Alton's style than reminiscing about the good old days when he was poor.

He glanced at Hugo, who was gazing at d'Alton. He looked entranced by him, hanging on his every word. That was a turn up for the books, Liam noted. Last time he checked, Hugo couldn't stand the man. He'd had to go back to Greyrock immediately after the trial so he didn't get a chance to talk to Hugo properly since then. He wondered if d'Alton was married. There was no mention of a wife or family and given the vast amount of coverage he received, if he had one, surely it would have been written about. There was something about Hugo that morning, something different, it was hard to put his finger on it. It was probably nervousness and anxiety over the sentencing.

The courthouse opened, and they trooped across the road. Once again, the cameras and the journalists surged and demanded a statement from d'Alton. This time he obliged and all traces of the nicer version of him disappeared. Back was the plummy accent and his condescending air as he addressed the gathered hacks.

'Please stand aside and allow us access immediately.'

Amazingly they did, his tone brooked no argument.

Liam, Hugo, Father Aquinas, Helen, Mrs Tobin, and Mr O'Kelly followed in his wake once more to a hail of camera flashes. Several of them called Hugo by name, by his title, this really was story gold, but he ignored them.

They were called into court where the public gallery was already full. The judge was announced and took the bench. This time, Patrick turned around to see who was there and managed a watery smile. Each one of them was sending him strength and love, and Liam hoped he could feel it.

D'Alton sat at the defence table with Mr O'Kelly behind him. The prosecution barrister, Delaney, sat on the other side, looking nervous.

There was the usual shuffling before the judge addressed the clerk of the court and several legal people approached the bench. There seemed to be endless coming and going.

'Can he not just get on with it? I'm going to be sick, I can't wait…' The normally cool Helen was very stressed.

Liam leaned over and patted her arm. 'I know, Helen, it's torture, but you've been so tough for so long, just hold on…'

'I can't bear to think of him down there on his own, not knowing...' Her normally stoic countenance dissolved into tears. Mrs Tobin held her hand and comforted her. Father Aquinas sat like a statue, gazing straight ahead, his face unreadable. Liam knew he was deep in prayer.

Twenty minutes passed and there was an endless stream of legal people in and out but nobody else left the courtroom. Other cases were being tried in other courts but for everyone in court number one, the fate of Patrick Lynch was all they could think of.

The judge cleared his throat and silence descended.

'Will the defendant please rise?'

Patrick stood up, and they could see him in profile. Liam thought he looked much younger than his twenty-one years, more vulnerable.

'Has the probation report been compiled?'

'Yes, your honour,' said the clerk, handing him a document.

'Can I get the probation officer,' he checked the name on the report, 'Oscar Fennessy on the stand please?'

A tall thin man approached the witness box. Patrick said he was a nice man, he trained the under-twelve hurling team in St Finbarr's so they had a lot to talk about. He was confident that Mr Fennessy would give a good account of him.

'What are the findings of your report, Mr Fennessy?'

'I found the defendant Patrick Lynch to be a young man of good and honourable character. He behaves well in prison, does all that is asked of him and is polite and courteous to all those with whom he has dealings. He was, in my opinion, driven to commit this act by extreme circumstances, and it is very much out of his character to behave in such a manner. It is my considered opinion that he is extremely unlikely to reoffend. In addition, as the court is aware, there are two young girls, his sisters, currently in the care of a neighbour, who have lost both their parents. His presence in their lives would be to their betterment, in my opinion.'

'Has he shown remorse for his actions?'

This was a question they were dreading. Patrick wasn't sorry, and he said he would not get on the stand and say that he was. D'Alton advised him to do so, but he refused. Liam tried to convince him to lie under oath as well—yet another action which led him to question his suitability for the religious life—but he thought Patrick was mad to jeopardise his future over just words. Nobody could get through to him.

Two days before the sentencing, Liam had begged his friend to say he deeply regretted killing his father, even using the emotional blackmail of Connie and Anna and how he would be depriving them of him in their lives over just words.

'You don't have to mean it, Patrick, for God's sake, just say it,' Liam pleaded.

'Lie under oath? Is that what you're telling me to do, Father Tobin?' Patrick snapped.

'No, well yes, but for the greater good,' Liam was adamant.

'No, Liam, I've done wrong things in my life but killing him wasn't one of them, and I won't say it was. I'd do it again given the chance.'

Liam left exasperated with his friend.

'Yes, I believe the defendant is truly sorry for what happened.'

Hugo and Liam exchanged glances and then gazed at Patrick, half-expecting him to jump up and shout he wasn't sorry, but thankfully he remained silent.

'Very well. Thank you, Mr Fennessy. I would also like to hear from Detective Inspector McMullan, who led the investigation into this case.'

Liam caught his mother's eye.

'Is the defendant known to you, Inspector?'

'Yes, your honour, but only since the day of his mother's murder. Up to that point, Patrick Lynch was not known to the Gardaí.'

'And what opinion have you formed of him based on your acquaintance?'

'Your honour, I have found Patrick Lynch to be an exemplary young man. He is hard-working, honest, and has acted as the protector of his family since he was old enough to do so. I have had occasion several times to engage with his father, the late Joe Lynch, and he was of a criminal mindset. He was a violent alcoholic who tormented his family. Patrick is nothing like him. He is abstemious in his ways, he has a wonderful network of support around him, and he is, in my opinion, of impeccable character. I would also like to echo Mr Fennessy's comments, Patrick Lynch has two young sisters who are currently being cared for, most ably, by a family friend, but they miss him. They have had a lot of trauma in their lives and the absence of their brother is exacerbating that situation.'

Liam saw his mother lock eyes with the detective's across the courtroom for just a second. There was understanding there; he hoped things worked out for them.

'Thank you, Inspector.' The judge seemed to be considering for a moment what he was going to say next.

He turned his attention to Patrick and looked at him for what seemed like several minutes but was probably thirty seconds. Helen's fingernails dug into Liam once more. The tension in the courtroom was palpable.

'Patrick Lynch, I'm going to ask you a question, and I want you to remember that you are still under oath, do you understand?'

'I do, your honour,' Patrick answered clearly. His voice betrayed none of the anxiety that his friends knew he was feeling.

'How do you feel about your father now?'

Liam begged the Lord that Patrick wouldn't tell the truth. He tried to telepathically connect to his friend, 'Just say you're sorry.'

'I hate him, your honour. He gave my family a terrible life, my mother especially, and I'm glad he's dead.'

The courtroom filled with a kind of silent apprehension. Liam realised he was holding his breath and quietly exhaled with a sinking heart. Patrick surely had done terrible damage to his prospects by admitting that.

'Is that all you have to say?' the judge asked.

'No, your honour, it's not. I wish he hadn't killed my mother, I wish my sisters and I still had her in our lives, but we haven't. I did beat him up and he died as a result, but I didn't set out to kill him. I'm glad he's dead, but I'm sorry it was I who did it.'

Hugo whispered to Liam, 'That's as close as he's going to get to an apology.' And Liam nodded.

D'Alton gave Patrick an almost imperceptible nod, and Hugo realised that just like everything else, the barrister had orchestrated the last few minutes. He had written that speech for Patrick. He knew he wouldn't apologise, but he got him within a reasonable approximation of it.

The resonant tones of the judge filled the silent but packed courtroom.

'There is no excuse for what you did. You should have left matters in the hands of the Gardaí. Instead, you chose to take the law into your hands. It is unacceptable from any citizen to exact retribution or punishment from those with whom they have a grievance, legitimate or not. The structures of the law exist for that purpose, and therefore, people who deem themselves above the law must be punished. You took a life. Everyone in the courtroom heard all the reasons why and many sympathise, but the fact remains that you took the life of another. I am therefore sentencing you to six years in prison, with four suspended. Take him down.'

He banged his gavel and rose to leave. The gathered crowd rose as they tried to process what they just heard.

'Six with four suspended...' Helen began.

'He's served almost one already. That means he'll be out in a year,' Father Aquinas said with a broad grin.

'Less probably, he'll get something off for good behaviour,' d'Alton added, having left his seat to join them.

Hugo fought the urge to hug him. Instead, he stood beside him and briefly squeezed his hand. D'Alton squeezed back, their hands hidden from view by his gown.

Liam and Father Aquinas exchanged a silent prayer of thanks to what they both were sure was the intervention of the Almighty, and Helen and Mrs Tobin wept tears of joy.

'We're getting married!' Helen announced through her tears, having promised Patrick she would say nothing until the hearing. She wouldn't have to renege on her promise to forget about him. He'd be out and home and able to start their lives together.

'He proposed yesterday, but he said we could only go through with it if he got fewer than ten years.' The small group were overjoyed, both at the sentence and Helen's announcement.

'Welcome to the gang, Helen,' Liam said. 'I hope you realise we are a package offer. Not only do you get Ireland's most loved jailbird, but you get me and Hugo too!'

'And Connie and Anna, and Mrs Tobin, and Father Aquinas,' Hugo added with a grin.

D.I. McMullan made his way across the courtroom to join them. 'This is good. Honestly, this is the best we could have hoped for.'

Liam saw his mam redden slightly when the detective protected her from being bumped as the crowds surged to get out. Liam recognised an elderly couple in the throng beside him as Mr and Mrs Murray from the huckster shop up the lane from Chapel Street. Mrs

Murray was always nice to them as kids on the odd occasion when they got the money for an ice cream or a few sweets.

'Hello, Mrs Murray, Mr Murray,' Liam addressed them.

'Ah, Liam, how are you, pet,' she replied. Her husband nodded and smiled. He was always a man of few words but everyone on Chapel Street liked them.

'Not too bad, Mrs Murray. The lawyers say it was the best we could have hoped for. Thanks for coming, I know Patrick appreciates it.'

'He's a grand boy, always was. And that Joe Lynch was a trial and a torment to that family and no mistake. We said a prayer the judge would go easy on him, didn't we, Pat?' she said, nodding at her husband.

'Indeed, we did. Every candle in the church has been lit for Patrick, you tell him that. Father Mac can't say all the Masses that people have petitioned for him. Make sure he knows that, Liam. His neighbours were all praying for him.'

It was the longest sentence Liam had ever heard Mr Murray say in his whole life.

'I certainly will, Mr Murray. He'll be heartened, I'm sure, to know that.'

'He's lucky to have you and Hugo. I know we should call him some fancy name now, I suppose, but I still remember him with his blond curls, buying up every sweet and cake in the shop.' Mrs Murray smiled.

'Oh, whatever you do, call him Hugo. He'd hate it if you changed now. We are so lucky, but then he's like family to us.'

'He is, I suppose, by now. Mrs Lynch, God rest her, loved to see him coming and ye young lads above in St Bart's. Anyway, God bless you, Liam, and sure someday soon we'll be calling you Father Tobin.' Mrs Murray smiled.

'Mrs Murray, you've called me Liam my whole life. Please don't ever call me anything else,' he said with a sigh.

'Maybe, Father Liam so,' she said with a wink and patted his hand.

They shuffled on out the door.

Eventually, the crowd thinned and the small group stood together.

D'Alton was placing his papers into an expensive leather briefcase, engraved with his initials in gold on the top.

Hugo and Liam stood and were each waiting for the other to speak. Liam cast a sidelong glance at his friend and was surprised to see a peculiar look on his face. It was as if Hugo didn't know what to say.

'Thank you, Mr d'Alton, for all you did...' Liam began.

D'Alton looked up from his papers and smiled.

'Well, as I said to you before the trial, this is as good an outcome as we could have expected. A sensible judge who did the right thing, it's an eventuality rarer than you'd imagine.' He grinned wryly. 'I think the judge is quite convinced of the inherent goodness in your friend, but justice must be done, and more importantly, justice must be *seen* to have been done. The fact that he has already served some time in prison means he should be out with good behaviour within six months, I would imagine.'

'Six months? Really? That's incredible. Can we take you to lunch? To say thank you,' Hugo asked, praying his voice sounded normal. He was filled with a sudden terror that even after everything that had happened between them, d'Alton was about to walk out of his life forever. He felt in his pocket. All day, he'd been turning the key d'Alton had given him round and round in his pocket. Suddenly, it didn't feel like enough.

Liam noticed the way Hugo was acting and couldn't figure it out. Normally, he was confident and when it came to the barrister, he was business-like and almost curt, barely hiding his dislike for the man.

D'Alton smiled at them, and for the first time, it seemed genuine.

'I would love to, I really would, but I'm needed in London this evening. I was due to appear at the Old Bailey and luckily the case was adjourned, which allowed me to come here, but I do need to get there as soon as possible. I will telephone you in the coming days to answer any questions you might have and to discuss anything you are unsure about. I've come to have quite a personal interest in this case, and I'd like to see your friend freed as soon as we can. In the meantime, you will be able to visit him, keep his spirits up, and tell him I said that it went very well indeed. Now, gentlemen, I believe my car is waiting to take me to the airport and so I'll take my leave. I will speak to you soon,' he said again, looking directly into Hugo's eyes. And then he was gone.

Father Aquinas left to say Mass, and Mam and Helen made for Chapel Street. Helen had promised the girls she'd take them for a puck around with their hurleys. She was determined to make great hurlers of them, and they wanted to show Patrick how good they had become in his absence. They practiced every moment they could, and Mrs Tobin sighed in mock despair at her gable end being used as a target once again. In reality, Liam knew she loved to hear the constant thudding of the leather ball against the wall, being 'pucked' as it was known, with great strength. It reminded her of the days when Liam and Con were doing the same thing.

Eventually, having shaken hands with countless neighbours and friends, old schoolmates and total strangers, Liam and Hugo stood alone in the courtroom.

'Would they let us see Patrick, do you think?' Liam asked. Hugo was lost in thought.

'What? Sorry, I wasn't listening, what did you say?' Hugo turned back to him.

'I said do you think they'd let us in to see Patrick this afternoon.'

'I don't know, we can try I suppose...'

'Hugo? Are you all right? You seem a bit...distracted or something.' Liam was worried.

'Me? No, no, I'm fine, really. I...I'm just relieved this whole thing is over, you know. Patrick soon to be a free man and the girls back with him and everything as it should be, you know?'

Liam nodded understandingly, but he knew with certainty that for the first time ever, Hugo was lying to him.

CHAPTER 27

Patrick was no longer a remand prisoner having been sentenced so when Liam and Hugo requested a visit they were surprised to be given permission. Mr O'Kelly had explained to them outside the courthouse that even with a remand prisoner, visitors can't just turn up whenever it suited them, all the more so with a convicted felon. But Patrick's case had caught the imagination of the whole city and the governor had once played hurling for Glen Rovers, Patrick's team, so he was being particularly lenient. Liam didn't care why they were allowed in, but he was glad they were. He had to go back to the seminary in the morning, and he wanted to talk to his friend before he left.

'So, d'Alton reckons this is the best possible outcome...' Liam was saying.

'Yeah, that's what he told me would happen. He came to see me last night and spent ages coaching me on what to say. I'm so grateful to him, honest to God, I am, like, without him, I'd be looking at life in jail for murder. He's one in a million, you know, you'd think a fella like him would be all stuck up and full of himself, but he's so normal, like one of us, y'know?' Patrick looked exhausted.

'You look like you haven't slept for days,' Liam said.

'A combination of worry about the trial and some eejit roaring his head off all night in the next cell. I think they sedated him in the finish, probably for his own good, because if the other fellas got hold of him in the morning he'd be a dead man,' Patrick said with a huge yawn. 'What I wouldn't give for a night in my own bed.' Changing the subject, he asked, 'Was Helen gone straight way after? Was she all right?'

'She was grand, she said to tell you she was thinking of you and that Connie and Anna are getting to be brilliant little camogie players. They're driving Mam half-cracked pucking the ball against the wall all day and night, too, if they were allowed.' Liam grinned. 'Oh, and she mentioned that ye were engaged...' he added with a chuckle.

'Did she?' His face lit up. All night he was hoping that his sentence would be light, not just for himself, but for Helen and the girls as well. She mustn't have changed her mind then, he thought gleefully.

'Yeah, I can't wait. She's great, isn't she?'

'She's wonderful and far too good for you!' Liam joked. 'But we told her she was getting the three of us for the price of one, she seemed relieved.'

'I hope the girls are not too much of a bother for your mam, she's been so good...'

'Don't be mad, she loves having them, and she secretly loves the sound of the sliotar on the gable. I was telling Hugo earlier, it brings her back to the time when we were small before everything went wrong. Helen said she's got the afternoon off on Friday so she'll be in to see you then. She's a great girl, Patrick, she really is...'

'I know, she's lovely. I'm mad about her, to be honest. I can't imagine anyone sticking by a fella like me, but now it looks like I might have a bit of a life, y'know? I used to think what was the point? Like, even if I did get out in a few years and she waited for me, sure what prospects have I then with a criminal record? She deserves better, I thought the right thing to do was end it before we even began, and let her meet someone who has a brighter future...but now, things look so much better. Mr O'Neill came to see me a few days ago and told me there would always be a job for me in his office so at least we won't starve when I get out, and I'm going to do up the house properly and make it really nice for Helen and the girls, and we can live in peace for once, with no fear that he's coming back.'

'I'm so glad you said you had remorse, but how come you decided to, at least partially, admit you were sorry? You were adamant you wouldn't when I spoke to you last week,' Liam asked.

'I know, sorry about that, Liam. I shouldn't have been so snappy with you. Mr d'Alton talked sense to me. He explained that the judge wanted to give me a really light sentence, it's what the public wanted too but by me refusing to say I was sorry, he'd have to take it into consideration when he was sentencing me. He convinced me into it if I'm honest, asking me did I want to miss the girls' communion or your ordination, Liam. That my stance would be cold comfort day after day in this place. He's persuasive, I can tell ye that.'

'He's a bit of a mystery that Mr d'Alton, all right. Still, I'm glad he was on our side. I bet that young Delany lad is licking his wounds somewhere today. Isn't that right, Hugo?' said Liam, kicking Hugo under the table. He'd not said a word since they got in and had been behaving like a sick calf all day.

'Ow! Yes, absolutely, I totally agree,' Hugo responded, rubbing his ankle and wincing in pain.

'With what?' Liam asked him.

'What?'

'What do you totally agree with?' Liam winked surreptitiously at Patrick, involving him in the joke.

'You, what you said,' Hugo said defensively.

Patrick smirked. 'Okay, out with it, what has you on another planet today?'

'Nothing, I'm fine.' Hugo sighed in exasperation.

'Hugo, we know you, and we know something happened so you better tell us or we'll be imagining all sorts...and that's worse.' Patrick nudged Liam. 'Isn't that right now, Father Tobin?'

'Oh undoubtedly, Mr Lynch,' Liam went on. 'On top of that, it's the height of bad manners to keep secrets from your best friends.'

Hugo sat back in the hard tubular steel chair and looked keenly at both of them.

'I don't even know where to start,' he said quietly.

Liam and Patrick exchanged a glance, whatever it was, it was serious.

'The beginning is usually a good place.' Patrick smiled.

'Right, well...' Hugo took a deep breath. 'You remember Martha? That I grew up with?'

'Yeah, what about her?' Liam was confused.

Hugo told them about the day in the tree house and the letter and photograph arriving.

They were stunned into silence. Patrick being first to recover said, 'Well, Hugo, em...this is good, isn't it? Like, you hated the fact that you wouldn't have a family of your own because...well because of everything, so now you have a son and the title and all that stuff is safe, so it's good, isn't it?'

Hugo nodded. 'Yes, it's great, and Martha said she and her husband would be happy for me to be involved in William's life and everything. I wrote, and she replied immediately, I'm going over to see him next week. I just can't believe it. I mean what are the chances...'

Liam asked the question that was on his and probably Patrick's mind.

'And did the...experience with Martha, you know...change your mind?' He prayed Hugo was going to say it did because his friend's life would be so much easier.

'No, quite the opposite, actually. It was awful. And there's something else I need to tell you both. I've met someone.'

'I knew it!' Patrick exclaimed. 'Well? Who?' he whispered.

'Don't go mad now, and it's very early days,' he registered their shocked faces. 'But we talked a lot about everything, and we both, well we like each other, and we're going to try to see each other again and see what happens...' Hugo's face was lit up, and Liam suddenly knew what he was going to say.

'It's d'Alton,' he added barely audibly.

Liam and Patrick were stunned. All joking gone as the seriousness of what Hugo was telling them sank in.

'Well, Hugo boy,' said Patrick. 'He's sound out! I don't know what ye were going on about him being all stuck up and all that, he was always great to me, talked to me in a way I understand and all that. I wouldn't have had him down as being...that way...but you couldn't have picked anyone better. Hey,' a thought suddenly struck Patrick, 'does he know about the baby, about William and everything?'

'He does. He's going to come with me. Not to see him the first time, obviously, but to England, just for moral support, I suppose. He's really happy for me. He knew how much not having someone to pass it all onto was destroying me. I don't want to burden the little chap if he doesn't want it, then that's sad but his choice, but I'd like him to have the opportunity at least.' Hugo sounded relieved to have told them.

Liam struggled to find the words. He could never tell Hugo, or even Patrick, of the internal conflict raging within him. There was so much to process, extramarital relations resulting in a child out of wedlock, knowing his friend was a homosexual was one thing, but congratulating him on actually pursuing that life, condoning the actual act, it was all flying in the face of everything he was being taught by the church that he loved. He knew that the next thing he said would never be forgotten by either of them, so he chose his words as carefully as he could.

'He's a great man and a decent human being and you are too, you deserve to be happy, and I hope that you will be.'

'As I said, I don't know yet, but it turns out he knows my uncle in France, just as acquaintances, really. Piers—that's my father's brother over there—asked him to take this case and to help me out if he could. Apparently, my uncle wanted to be in touch with me for years, but it's been so long and since my father died, he didn't know what kind of a reception he'd get. I'm going to visit him for a few weeks when all this is over. Maybe go to see d'Alton as well...'

Hugo looked to Liam, just like the unsure-of-himself little lad they met that first morning in St Bart's, trying desperately to look calm but in turmoil inside. All the teachings of the church seemed irrelevant in an instant. Hugo was his friend, he was a good, kind, generous man, and he clearly loved another man of equal quality. What could possibly be wrong with that? They weren't hurting anyone, they were bringing joy and relief to so many people. Surely they deserved a little happiness for themselves. The biggest source of distress to Hugo was the lack of an heir and now that was solved, as well. None of this was orthodox and was breaking every rule, but Liam thought back to that day all those years ago when they were out on the horses on his and Patrick's first visit to Greyrock, and how lost and alone his friend seemed then. He wished him all the happiness and luck in the world. He recalled the chat he's had with Father Aquinas, the reference to Corinthians, saying that love is the most important thing of all and all his doubts melted away.

'Maybe Patrick and I will come to visit too for a day or two sometime if it wouldn't cramp your style?' Liam asked.

'Oh yeah, a Catholic trainee priest and an ex-con will do wonders for your image, Hugo. We'd blend right in.' Patrick smiled ruefully.

'You will, d'Alton will see to that.' Liam smiled at the pride in his friend's voice. 'And we'll definitely go to France, I'd love that.'

EPILOGUE

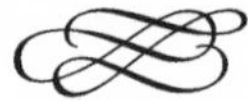

Seven months later

'Well, are we ready?' Helen fixed the ribbon on Anna's hat and checked Connie's patent leather shoes for shine. She knelt down in front of them. 'You girls look so beautiful. I know for a fact that your mammy is looking down at you from heaven, and she is so proud of you both. She's showing you off to all her friends up there, saying, "Look at my Connie and my Anna, aren't they the most gorgeous girls in the whole of Cork?"'

'Or the whole of Ireland,' Anna added as she always did.

'The most lovely in the whole entire world,' said Patrick, giving them a squeeze.

'Here, let me do that.' Helen smiled, brushing Patrick's hands away as he was fumbling with his tie.

'I'll soon be going back to a collar and tie every day. I can't believe that by Monday I'll be back in O'Neills. It's going to be great; I hated that scratchy prison material. Mam always washed my clothes, and they were always lovely and soft and smelled nice, too. I've very sensitive skin. I hope you know, the future Mrs Lynch, so you better figure out how to keep all my shirts nice and soft.' He laughed, dodging a swipe from the damp tea towel Helen was using on a stain on her skirt.

'We're modern women, Patrick, isn't that right, girls? He'll be doing our laundry while we're out training to win all Ireland medals for camogie. We're too busy for cooking and cleaning and all that,' Helen said, mock stern, and the girls giggled again. They loved the banter Patrick and Helen shared.

'But you make lovely things to eat, Helen, nearly as nice as Mrs Tobin, doesn't she, Patrick?' Connie insisted.

'Praise indeed, Miss Connie.' Helen smiled affectionately.

'She certainly does. Helen is the best cook, the best girlfriend, and the best hurler in the whole of Cork, and we are very, very lucky to have her.' He put his arms around her waist and drew her in for a kiss.

He'd been out of prison a week and everything seemed new and shiny to him. The old shabby streets of his childhood now looked warm and welcoming, his neighbours were all happy to see him back among them. Connie and Anna couldn't bear for him to be out of their sight even for a moment in case he left again, but he and Helen reassured them that he wasn't going anywhere. They were getting married in September and spending their honeymoon in Greyrock, complete with all the servants. Hugo was going to France so they'd have the place to themselves. It was all arranged, and they couldn't wait.

'We'd better go,' said Helen, getting up on her tip-toes and kissing him on the nose, 'before these two little women decide they want to go hurling in their best frocks.'

Connie and Anna giggled. They loved Helen so much, it was clear to everyone who saw them together. She had worked hard with the help of the neighbours to get the house painted and looking welcoming before Patrick came home. He couldn't believe his eyes when he was released. He came into a bright, clean, little home with a stew bubbling on the stove and the firewood crackling. The weather was chilly even though it was summer, but he was secretly delighted. He could sit on the sofa cuddling Helen on summer evenings when the girls were gone to bed upstairs, though she always left before eleven. Times were moving forward under the Goldie Fish but not so fast that a single man and woman could spend the night together without tongues wagging. He wished she could stay but, at least, they didn't have long to wait.

'So Hugo, what does one do at an Irish-Catholic ceremony? While it was the religion of choice of my parents, I must confess to having quite forgotten it all. Yet another cause of my eternal damnation, no doubt. Flagellate oneself in guilt, confess all? Denounce that upstart Luther for scuttling the whole applecart back in sixteen whatever?' Piers asked with a mischievous wink over delicious kippers and poached eggs in the dining room.

'Leave him alone, Piers,' d'Alton demanded as he filled his plate from the bain marie placed on the sideboard so the guests could help themselves. Hugo was busy pouring tea and serving toast and grinning. Tom was back on his feet and crankier than ever, but it meant that Hugo got to take off to France once a month for a few days. It was the perfect combination. He loved Greyrock and was always happy to get home, but he also looked forward to his visits to Piers and d'Alton.

'Yes, leave me alone! I'm not exactly the most devout or anything, but it means a lot to my friends so no smart remarks please, Uncle.' Hugo knew Piers was only teasing him. They'd got in touch after the trial and, within five minutes of the first telephone conversation, it felt like they'd been close for years.

Piers and d'Alton arrived from France yesterday and had spent the day out on horseback as Hugo showed them all over the estate. Hugo had taken Piers to the family plot where for the first time he saw his brother's grave. Piers loved Hugo's father and regretted not returning for his funeral, but he hated the prospect of returning to Ireland. He had been threatened with exposure and arrest when he was discovered with a young man in his late teens and only escaped because he was the earl's brother, on the promise that he would go and never return. He'd only come now under the considerable joint persuasive powers of d'Alton and Hugo. They left the graveyard and went for a walk, allowing Piers some time alone to say goodbye properly.

They wandered down to the seashore and found themselves on the same little beach where Hugo had confided in Liam all those years ago. As Hugo recounted the story, reliving the dread and despair of those years, d'Alton sat on a rock, listening intently. They were so happy and relaxed in each other's company, they saw as much as possible of each other. Hugo had been to France four times and had been amazed and delighted at the life he found there. D'Alton took him to clubs filled with people like them and where Hugo felt inconspicuous. It was wonderful. Of course, caution was paramount and d'Alton was ultra vigilant, but Hugo didn't doubt even for a moment how he felt. They loved each other, and Hugo knew he could face anything once d'Alton was by his side.

The visit to Birmingham was better than he could ever have imagined. D'Alton went with him, and they met Martha and Terence and, of course, little William. Martha was right, Terence was exactly like Tom, though friendlier, and Martha whispered to Hugo that Terence's brother was also 'one of your lot' and they were best of friends, so there was nothing to fear.

William sat on his father's knee and smiled and drooled at everyone. Photos were taken and d'Alton and Terence took William for a walk while Hugo and Martha talked.

'Thanks, Martha. I can't believe I have a son, he's so beautiful and smiley and everything. It's just amazing.' Hugo thought his heart would burst with joy.

'He's a little dote, all right. So, what are we going to do?' Martha was ever practical.

'Well, I'll go with whatever you want. I'd like to support him financially if you and Terence would allow me, and be in his life, visit him, and someday if you could bear it, have him come to Greyrock.'

'Do you want him to know who his father is?' Martha fixed Hugo with a clear eye.

'Absolutely, if you are happy to have him know, though the hardship if there is any, will be on you, the gossip, and all of that back at home.'

'That doesn't bother me. I can't imagine living there again, but I want William to know who he is, who his father is, and where he came from.' Martha was confident. She seemed different to the way she was in Greyrock. The move had been good for her.

Hugo held his childhood friend's hand, and they chatted about the future of the next Earl of Drummond in the evening sunlight in the back garden of a terraced house in Birmingham.

Liam and Patrick had never met Piers, but Hugo knew they would love him. He was hilarious and outrageous and made no apologies for his homosexuality, but in public he was every inch the respectable older gentleman. Hugo knew they would welcome him into the family. He was excited to bring all his people together. Of course, they all knew d'Alton and while Liam and Patrick knew the nature of the relationship, the others didn't. D'Alton half-hinted that he had a lady friend in England, and people seemed to accept it. He said he enjoyed coming to Greyrock for the hunting and fishing. Since it was so far from their experience, they accepted that as well. Piers told people that his better half passed away, which was true, neglecting to mention that they weren't married and that she was a he.

'Oh, how I yearn for the days of the carriage, all that leg room,' Piers moaned as he folded himself into the back seat of Hugo's car.

'Yes, but you'd have had to have left yesterday.' Hugo smiled. 'This is so much quicker.'

'I am an elderly man, Hugo, be gentle and please slow down,' Piers howled theatrically at his nephew.

D'Alton winked at him over the roof as they settled into the front seats.

Hugo drove slower than usual though still fast by anyone's standards, and as they passed the turn-off for d'Alton's little house on the lake shore, d'Alton leaned over and placed his hand on Hugo's. They'd gone there overnight for the first time a few weeks earlier, and it was the most wonderful night of Hugo's life.

Liam shaved carefully with the water basin he'd brought up from the kitchen; he didn't want any nicks on his face today. He fixed the Roman collar and made sure that the buttons of his soutane were done up correctly. He brushed his hair back and looked in the small mirror on the wall of the bedroom he'd slept in his whole life. Con was gone already and he had to admit it had felt nice to have him in the other bed last night. He even threatened to throw a hob-nailed boot at Liam for old time's sake. Hilda reprimanded him saying he'd go straight to hell for injuring a man of the cloth, causing laughter from everyone as they drank endless cups of tea and devoured the huge amount of baking Mammy had done in preparation for their arrival. Hilda was good for Con and brought out the best in him. The girls were arguing over access to the newly installed bathroom, and Liam hoped they wouldn't look too much like showgirls when they were finished. They seemed to be carrying lots of bags of war paint and he'd caught a glimpse of some very garish outfits hanging on the wardrobe door yesterday. Still, it was great to have them home and seemingly at peace with each other. He knew they found the sight of him in clerical garb hilarious, but he was happy to take the slagging. It was better than the reverential looks he got from the neighbours.

He went over to his small dressing table and took out the book he kept at the back of the top drawer. It was an old cowboy novel about Indians and the Wild West, one Daddy used to read to him when he was a small boy. In it was the only photograph he had of his father, in the background at a wedding. The photo was blurred and out of focus and time had faded it further, but Liam still recognised his father smiling in the back row.

'We'll never ever forget you, Daddy, and I pray you are happy and at peace now. Today is going to be a lovely day but you know you're in the heart and thoughts of every one of us. Look down on us and help for everything to go smoothly, will you? ' Liam said to him. He spoke to his father regularly and felt his reassuring presence often.

He walked across the street and up the hill to St Teresa's, stopping to admire the Goldie Fish that was glistening in the bright July sunshine. Father Aquinas once said that all human life was here, under the Goldie Fish, and how right he was. Liam had originally hoped to go on the missions when he was ordained, but he was changing his mind. What he'd really love was a parish, just like this one, where he understood the people and might be able, even in a small way, to help them with all the trials life would throw at them.

Donal McMullan was standing outside, looking slightly nervous, and was only paying half attention to his brother Brendan, who as best man, was trying to keep him calm.

'Ah Liam, don't you look every inch the priest now in your soutane. Your Mam will be so proud of you.' Donal said sincerely, shaking Liam's hand.

'You scrub up well yourself, Donal,' Liam said with a smile. 'I think Mam is on her way, the girls are bringing her over so you better go in, in case she sees you.'

'Right-o, Liam, she'll murder me if I see her first, let's go, Brendan.'

Liam could see the church was full, and he was pleased for Mam and Donal. She had been worried at the start that people wouldn't approve of their relationship. Even though Seán was dead for many years as was Donal's first wife, there was still stigma to a second marriage. Not that widows shouldn't remarry, but courting again at their age was a little unseemly. But as Father Aquinas often observed, the people that lived beneath the Goldie Fish might not be the most cosmopolitan in the world, but they looked after their own, and there were many in that church who remembered big Seán Tobin and wished his wife all the happiness in the world.

Liam was giving the bride away and then the Mass was to be concelebrated with Father Mac and Father Aquinas with him on the altar. He had resisted, saying he was happy to be in the congregation, but when Father Aquinas said his mother would be so happy to have him up there with the priests, he felt he had to do it. One of the aspects of the priesthood that didn't sit right with him, maybe it never would, was how respectful people were, even people who'd known him his whole life. Suddenly, they spoke in hushed tones to him and seemed excessively devout. He'd love just once for one of his former school friends to tell him a dirty joke or have a neighbour tease him about Maynooth losing the inter-college hurling final, but it seemed priests, even student ones, were above all that. He thanked God once again for Patrick and Hugo, they never treated him differently.

He and Helen were getting married in a few weeks' time. Patrick wanted to be back at work first so that he'd have a few bob to make it a really nice day for her. Hugo didn't offer to pay, though both Liam and Patrick knew that he would be happy to. Hugo understood that Patrick needed to restore his pride after his ordeal, and he wanted to restore his life by himself. They made such a happy little family, Patrick, Helen, and the girls. The months in prison went quickly, and it was lovely to see Connie and Anna smile again.

Hugo too, seemed so much happier. The life he had with d'Alton was difficult, and it must be a terrible strain to have to hide, but they travelled to meet each other often. Hugo was bringing both d'Alton and his uncle Piers to the wedding today so everyone was looking forward to meeting him. Little William was visiting Greyrock with Martha and Terence soon, and they were all being invited down to meet him. Mam had been a bit shocked when he told her about the baby, but she soon recovered. Hugo FitzHenry could do no wrong in her eyes.

Con dashed across the road along with another few stragglers, late as usual. He'd joined a few of the neighbours in the Glue Pot for a quick one before the Mass. If Hilda smelled the beer on his breath, she'd kill him so he was sucking mints furiously. The two brothers shared a conspiratorial smile as he slipped into the church.

At last, the door of their little house opened and Mam came out. She was looking lovely in a lilac dress and jacket. The girls had been fussing over her since dawn and though she claimed they were driving her cracked, Liam knew she was thrilled they were there. The twins had calmed down a bit, though they did still look a little on the racy side, and Kate was in really good form. She confided that she was seeing a man in England, a divorced man at that, and was worried how everyone at home would take to it. Liam reassured her that in the light of the madness that went on regularly around there, it would be a five-day wonder. He urged her to bring him home for a visit, and anyway, what business was it of anyone's what went on in his past? He counselled her to bring him home and say nothing about any former wives to the neighbours.

'You're going to get into trouble as a priest if you're going to be going around telling good Catholic girls to hook up with English divorcees, Liam Tobin!' She smiled as they enjoyed tea and buns in Thompson's Bakery the day he picked her up from the boat.

'Oh Kate, you don't know the half of it.' He grinned.

The girls handed Mam over to Liam and slipped into the church. Mam didn't want any bridesmaids or anything like that. In fact, the wedding had become much bigger than she imagined at first, and she was conscious of not showing off.

'So, are you right?' Liam smiled down at her, offering her his arm.

'I am, pet, as I'll ever be.' She paused and looked up. 'Is he looking down on us, do you think?' Her eyes momentarily sparkled with tears.

'He is, Mam, and he's wishing you all the love and luck in the world. You deserve it.'

The End

UNTITLED

Thank you for reading my story. I really hope you enjoyed it. If you did, I would be so grateful if you would consider reviewing it for me. Feel free to follow me on Facebook at Jeangraingerauthor or check out my blog on www.jeangrainger.com.

Read on to preview another Jean Grainger novel.

SHADOW OF A CENTURY

Scarlett set the alarm on her new cream Mini Cooper. It emitted a satisfying beep as she crossed the underground parking lot of the *Examiner* Building. She felt a surge of pure joy. For the first time in her whole life, everything was perfect. She looked great, an expensive new wardrobe saw to that, and she knew that she was unrecognisable from the insecure girl she had once been. The elevator doors opened and she stepped in. The young cub reporter from the sports desk nodded, and then stared at the floor. She smiled to herself. She didn't intend to be intimidating but she was now senior staff so the kid probably didn't know what to say to her.

As the elevator ascended to the fourteenth floor and the editorial suite, she had to remind herself once more that this was really was happening. Her years slaving for Artie on the *Yonkers Express* were behind her and here she was, a senior political correspondent for the *Examiner*, one of the biggest nationals in the country.

She glanced at her iPhone. It was odd that Charlie hadn't texted; he usually did, to check that she had gotten up. He was always gone by 5 a.m. on the nights he could stay, but last night he couldn't make it. She understood. In his position, his time was rarely his own. She smiled as she thought of the private messages he was sending her on

Facebook last night while he was supposed to be deep in discussion with the representative of a powerful lobby group for tax reform on a video conference call. Ron Waters was a crashing bore according to Charlie, and a Republican through and through, so he was never going to vote for Charlie or his party anyway, but he had to be seen to show willingness. He promised he was trying to get her some face time with the guy, though, for another high profile *Examiner* piece.

The elevator door opened and the bright, modern, busy Newsroom buzzed in front of her. Hundreds of screens flashed images, and lots of reporters, IT people and administration staff seemed to teem constantly from all directions. She breathed deeply, almost inhaling the atmosphere and didn't miss Artie and his chain-smoking ways one little bit. She made her way with enthusiasm to the office of Carol Steinberg, the editor in chief.

Scarlett could hardly believe she was heading into her eighth month of working here, the time had flown by and her star was definitely on the rise. The piece she had done on the extremist Islamic mullah on the Lower East Side was garnering a lot of attention. Her pieces on Charlie were also getting her a lot of column inches, much to the chagrin of many of the other journalists in the city. Carol's text saying 'Get here ASAP' had come through when she was driving into the office anyway. She was looking forward to the meeting. The urgency of the text suggested some exciting development. Scarlett knew that Carol had a reputation as ball-breaker, that she intimidated almost all of the staff, but Scarlett admired her. She had to be tough to get where she was and one day Scarlett intended to hold a similar position.

Was she imagining it or did the noise in the office, usually so deafening, suddenly drop to a murmur? The political team were standing together at their corner by the bank of flat screen plasma TVs. She wasn't imagining it; they had all stopped talking and were staring at her. They must be really ticked off about the mullah story, she thought.

She pushed open the opaque glass door of Carol's office and entered the sumptuous surroundings. The TV beside her desk was live paused, and Scarlett instantly recognised Charlie's handsome features, stilled in mid-sentence.

'I'm assuming you've seen this?' Carol's voice was quiet but lacked her usual warmth.

Scarlett was nonplussed, 'No, is this from today? I haven't seen…'

Carol interrupted her by pressing play on the remote. Charlie was unshaven and tired looking. He looked as if he'd slept in his shirt. His familiar voice filled the office.

'Words can't express my regret. I have offended my party, the good people of this city who elected me, and most painfully of all, I have let my family down. I feel deep shame and embarrassment at my reckless and unprofessional behavior, and though I don't deserve any special favours, I would ask you, ladies and gentlemen of the press, to restrict your interest to me and to leave my family out of this. They are innocents in this whole thing and are suffering enough at this time. Thank you.'

Charlie turned away and went back into the offices behind him in a hail of questions and flashing cameras.

'I don't understand.' Scarlett's voice cracked. 'What happened?'

Carol gazed at her with thinly veiled fury.

'Last night Charlie Morgan was in a video conference meeting with Ron Waters, the Republican senator. Morgan was sending him some data to support a point he was making, but he inadvertently sent him a message of an explicit sexual nature, clearly intended for someone else. The message also mentioned *this* newspaper by name. To add insult to injury, the message went on to outline how boring and stupid Morgan thought Waters was. Waters immediately reacted and exposed Morgan, who has, about an hour ago, admitted that he is having an affair with a journalist, the person for whom the message was intended. In addition, he has told the world who that journalist is.'

Scarlett felt nauseous. Blood thundered in her ears. This wasn't happening, it couldn't be. Charlie would never do anything like that to her. He couldn't, he loved her.

'I took a chance on you, Scarlett. You are only twenty-six, very young to hold the position you did.' Scarlett heard her use of the past tense and every fibre of her being prayed that this wasn't happening.

Carol went on, her voice icy, 'I appointed you over others who have more experience, and who felt they deserved it more than you. I thought you had something, that's why I convinced the board to take you on. I'm at a loss for words. How could you throw everything away, everything you've worked for, and more to the point, how could you have dragged us into this mess with you? We pride ourselves on the highest standards of journalistic integrity here at the *Examiner*. You have let us down, very badly. To have an affair with a politician for someone in your position is to relinquish all moral and professional authority.'

Carol's tone conveyed nothing but disgust. 'Your in-depth interviews with him that we printed have made us look as foolish and corrupt as you are. But to be involved with a married politician, especially one whose unique selling point is his position as a family man, something you wrote about with such empathy... words escape me, Scarlett. I'm so disappointed in you. I thought you were so much better than this. Get your things now, rather than coming back for them, and try to get away without the gathering press outside seeing you leave, though they are already circling the wagons.'

She paused, and then added coldly, 'And Scarlett, if you give any interviews about this I'll drag you through every court in the country. Do I make myself clear?'

Carol got up and without a backward glance left the room.

'There she is! Scarlett! Scarlett, over here! Just turn around! C'mon Scarlett ...'

Scarlett emerged from the car and pushed her way up the steps to the front door of her brownstone, blinded by the incessant flashing of cameras as she pushed through the heaving mass of bodies. Every hack in New York was out in force, circling like vultures. News anchors smugly did their pieces on camera down the street. The fact that the target was one of their own had obviously made it even more tantalising for them. Many of them resented her growing profile, and felt she was too young and had come out of nowhere, so they were thrilled to see her crumble. No such thing as loyalty in this business, she thought, while trying to keep her face immobile.

She fumbled for her keys in the bottom of her new Prada handbag as the reporters jostled and pushed to get closer to her. Her red hair was escaping from the chignon she had hastily tied in the car, and she could feel the make-up slide from her face as she began to sweat. Despite her best efforts to look calm and collected, she was cracking. She couldn't find the damn key, and her hands began to shake badly as she gritted her teeth, determined not to cry, refusing to show any weakness. They'd love that. Not that anything could make this situation any worse, but to have her tear stained face splashed all over every tabloid and gossip show in town would be the final straw.

'Come on Scarlett, just one shot. At least this way you get to look good!' There was a collective cackle.

Would she have been any different if it was one of them? If she was to be honest, probably not, except that salacious sex scandals were not really her thing. Mercifully, she finally found the key, and despite her shaking hands, managed on the third attempt to get it into the lock. She quickly slipped inside and slammed the heavy door shut, leaning her back against it, adjusting her eyes to the relative gloom of the hallway. Relief flooded through her. Everything was as she'd left it this morning. The highly polished mahogany staircase gleamed, its snow white carpet runner fluffily breaking the austerity of the architecture. The house smelled exactly as it had done, of lilies and cleanliness, an oasis of serenity.

She went into the kitchen at the end of the hallway and immediately shut the blinds. Alone, in her new beautiful home, she disintegrated into wracking sobs. The strength that held her together for the past two hours suddenly drained out of her. The paintings, mirrors and everything else she had gathered so lovingly over the years were invisible to her now. That was it, it was all over. Her life was over. This just couldn't be happening. That press conference playing over and over in her head.

How could Charlie have hung her out to dry like that?

Dreading what she was about to see, she typed 'Charlie Morgan confesses all' into YouTube. She watched in horror as he explained that he was a weak, foolish man who loved his family, and he deeply regretted his inappropriate liaison with the political correspondent Scarlett O'Hara.

Facebook, Twitter and bloggers were already on the puns. Torturing herself, she scrolled through, "Charlie's Scarlett Woman," "Morgan really has Gone with the Wind," "Frankly my dear." It went on and on and on.

Scarlett hated her name. She used to dread meeting new people and enduring their shocked expressions, the attempts to hide a smirk, or the all too common 'did you know there was a movie...?' When she met Charlie, he told her he wanted to be her Rhett Butler. She felt a sharp stab of pain at the memory. Normally anyone who would have said such a thing would have felt the sharp end of her tongue, but he was different. Even though he constantly joked and teased her about it, she forgave him. She forgave him everything, and then he betrayed her.

CHAPTER 2

Scarlett sat on her Roche-Dobois oatmeal sofa that had cost almost a month's salary. She fought back the panic at the thought of her mortgage and credit card bills now that she was unemployed. She could hear the raucous laughter of the journalists outside the door. She longed for someone to help her, somewhere to go, but she realised that in recent years she had had no time to keep up friendships. She avoided her mother, and she had no other family. Charlie took up any spare time she had, waiting for him to call, or grasping precious moments with him. Without him and her job she had nothing, absolutely nothing. A feeling of hopelessness, something she had not felt for so long, came creeping back.

She was drawn back to another time, another sofa, in a dingy run-down apartment in Yonkers. The familiar feelings of terror threatened to choke her as she remembered sitting on her mother's lap, in the calm after the cops had picked her father up yet again. She could only have been four or five, trying with her little hands to stem the blood from a cut on her mother's face or holding frozen peas to a swelling injury. She would say prayers to the many Catholic saints represented on the damp walls of the room, that her mother wouldn't die. Lorena took her faith seriously, and the only thing that equalled her faith was her love of movies. She would tell Scarlett how she was named after the most beautiful woman in the world, and then, when she knew it was safe, her mother would draw out her old cookie tin from under the table and show her the pictures from her old movie magazines. To Scarlett, the names of Vivien Leigh, Fred Astaire and James Dean were as real as her mother and father. It was one of the many things about his wife that drove Dan O'Hara mad, and when he was mad he was terrifying.

She remembered the titters from the other children and the outrage from Sister Teresita in St. Peter and Paul's Elementary when she announced that she was not, as was Catholic tradition, named after a saint, but instead after the most beautiful woman in the world.

As she became a teenager, though, she learned to hate her name. The childhood innocence was laughed out of existence by bullies and teachers who jeered and mocked. She tried several times to shorten it and did everything she could to get a nickname, but nothing would stick. She was born Scarlett O'Hara and Scarlett O'Hara she was going to stay. She was teased mercilessly.

Dan O'Hara, Scarlett's father, was regularly to be seen staggering drunk around the streets of Yonkers, bellowing abuse at passers-by and scaring kids. He was from County Mayo in Ireland and had come over to the United States as a young man full of dreams and ambition. Life was going well for a time, and he met and married Lorena, a fragile hot house flower from Georgia, whose southern charm beguiled the young Irishman. But things soon turned sour. Dan was a charmer, good looking and smart, but work-shy. He always wanted to make a fast buck but never did any actual work. He had a friend who worked in construction who offered him job after job, but Dan would scoff, claiming that manual labour was for 'fellas too thick to do anything else.' He always had a scheme going, some kind of a scam to get rich quick. He convinced several people to invest in his so-called business opportunities, and to a man they lost their shirts on them. Eventually, he was untouchable and started drinking. He was unwelcome in the more respectable establishments, so he hung out in grotty, smelly bars, and over time, he was even barred from them.

The blame for his failure was never his own. No, it was Lorena and Scarlett's fault. They were holding him back, he used to snarl. If he didn't have them hanging on to him, he'd be making a fortune out west. His disappointment with life was expressed by using his beautiful young wife as a punch-bag. Scarlett had hated him.

When Lorena opened the door to the police, the winter Scarlett was fifteen, they told her Dan had walked in front of a truck. She tried her best to compose her face into that of a grief-stricken widow. Scarlett remembered Sergeant Kane, who'd been coming to arrest Dan for all sorts of offences over the years, not the least battering his family, sending the other officer to wait in the car. He sat down in the tiny living room and said, 'That's it Lorena. You and Scarlett are safe now. It's over.'

Lorena looked as if a huge weight had been removed from her, though she was in a daze of disbelief. Scarlett remembered Sergeant Kane explaining how her father had been killed instantly; he would have known no pain. Witnesses said he seemed to be very unsteady on his feet as the truck approached.

'What kind of truck was it?' she asked, only mildly curious.

The sergeant tried his best to remain composed, professional, but he'd known this misfortunate family a long time. Though he normally hated bringing news of this nature, in this case it was a blessing. Fighting a smile, he said, 'A Guinness truck.'

Scarlett's abiding memory of her father's untimely death was of her mother and Sergeant Kane weeping with uncontrolled gales of laughter.

Life got much easier after that, in lots of ways. Lorena, who was becoming even more zealous about her Catholic faith as the years progressed, gave the teenage Scarlett enough freedom to do as she wished. Lorena had been raised Baptist, but Catholicism appealed to her dramatic nature, so she had converted when she married Dan. She loved all the pomp and ceremony, and every spare wall of her house was adorned with icons and statues and holy pictures. She had a particular love of the more gruesome ones. In the hallway there was one of St. Stephen being stoned to death that really used to freak

Scarlett out. The house was a source of cringing embarrassment, but since she wasn't that close to anyone anyway, she didn't have to endure kids from school seeing the macabre décor of her home.

School was fine. She loved English and had a great teacher who inspired her to think for herself. He often lent her books or printed out articles for her to read about world events. She wished she had blonde hair and tanned skin. Failing that, she would have really liked to look like Gloria Estefan, but her Irish heritage gave her flame red hair, alabaster skin and emerald green eyes. Boys tended to steer clear, their parents warning them off because of Dan, so she kept herself to herself. One guy had asked her to the prom, but she declined. He was good looking and seemed nice, but there was no way she was having him come to the house. Scarlett remembered her mother's disappointment when she said she wouldn't be going. Lorena had bought her a dress, but Scarlett couldn't face going, nor could she explain to her mother why, so she sat in her room and read instead. She loved travel books, especially the books by the *BBC World News* Editor, John Simpson. He wrote with empathy and intelligence about places Scarlett could only dream of, Afghanistan, Iraq, Russia. She devoured his books and dreamed of one day visiting those places.

In her final year at school, she signed up for a trip with her political science class to hear a Bostonian congressman who was touring high schools in the tougher areas of New York. He was a noted self-server, and it looked good for the electorate that he cared about those less well off. He was part of a National Education Taskforce that was allegedly asking the students what they thought should be done to improve educational standards in disadvantaged school districts. He was a pompous ass, as she recalled, and patronised and flirted with the girls in her class. He tried to flatter her during the coffee break, asking her questions while all the time ogling her breasts. He repulsed her. At the end, the girls were given an opportunity to ask him any questions. The teacher, Miss Fletcher, was obviously a fan of the congressman and giggled and fawned whenever he addressed her. She'd prepared a long list of sycophantic questions and distributed them among the students, giving him ample opportunity to explain just how wonderful he was and how marvellous it was that he would ask their lowly opinions.

For no reason other than to knock him off his stupid perch, Scarlett raised her hand to ask a question. It was not the one on the card distributed by Miss Fletcher.

'Where do you stand on the subject of Gay rights?'

It was 2007 and the St Patrick's Day parade in the city was drawing the usual controversy by continuing to ban the Gay, Lesbian, Bisexual and Transgender groups from marching. She had read about it in the paper that morning over breakfast. Miss Fletcher went pink and stammered, 'I…I'm sorry Congressman Bailey. That was not an authorised question…' she glared with unconcealed horror at Scarlett.

The congressman gave a slimy grin and said, 'That's quite alright Deanna... I mean Miss Fletcher.' The teacher had blushed and giggled again. 'I'm sure this little lady didn't mean any offence.'

He turned towards Scarlett. 'Now then my dear, a nicely brought up girl such as yourself need not concern herself with such things. I'm sure that nobody at St. Peter and Paul's wants its young ladies discussing a matter that is, after all, a mortal sin. The church is very clear on its position on that subject, and as a devout Catholic I would vote with my conscience.' His smug self-satisfied smile made Scarlett want to punch him in his stupid fat face.

That was the day the Scarlett decided she would be a journalist.

CHAPTER 3

She walked into her beautifully decorated bedroom. The kingsize bed dominated the sunny space, and dust mites danced in the shaft of sunlight that streamed through the glass doors that led to a small balcony. She caught a glimpse of her reflection in the full length mirror that formed the doors to her walk in closet. She looked awful, pale and dishevelled, eyes red from crying. Though the room overlooked the little communal garden at the back, she quickly closed the blinds in case one of the hacks managed to get in and perch himself in a tree, waiting for the perfect shot with his long range lens. She sat on her bed, and held a pillow up to her face. It smelled of him, of his faintly spicy cologne. How often had she gone to sleep in his arms, only to wake alone. Always the same story. She was transported back to the early days of their relationship, before she became used to his early morning disappearances.

Scarlett recalled vividly how the alarm of his cell phone cut through the darkness. She stirred, wrapping her legs around him, willing the piercing ringtone to stop, her face buried in the back of his neck, her arm around his chest.

Charlie groaned and gently removed her arm. 'I have to go.' He kissed her palm as he tucked her arm under the sheet.

'But it's only...' Scarlett picked up her phone, '2 a.m... for God's sake.'

Charlie ran his hand through his tousled brown curls. 'I know but I said I'd take C.J. to school. First day and all that. I can't just rock up at 7 a.m. You know that.'

'What will you say?' her voice was steady, betraying none of what she felt.

'Oh, a meeting ran on, something like that. Don't worry about it. I'll try to call later.' He padded into the shower, washing all traces of her and her house from his skin. He asked her not to wear perfume in case Julia smelled it on his clothes, even the shower gel she bought was fragrance free.

Feigning sleep, she heard him slip out. He'd walk the two blocks to the subway and take a cab from there. Despite his passionate nature, Charlie Morgan was very careful. She tortured herself imagining him slipping into bed with Julia, she all concerned that he worked so hard. Then she'd wake in the morning, looking fresh as a daisy and prepare their two adorable children for school. She was beautiful in a really natural way, no botox or plastic surgery. Her hair was naturally blonde and her skin tanned to a golden brown since she played often on the beach with the kids. She was on several worthy committees and was always in the papers. The perfect politician's wife.

Scarlett lay down on the bed and pulled the cover over herself, glad of the warmth. Though filled with self-loathing, she tried think. It wasn't all her fault. She had never intended for things to turn out like this. She was doing a profile piece on him in the run up to the election and had met him and Julia at home. Carol was amazed and delighted she had managed to secure a feature piece on him. He was notoriously private about his family, and Scarlett knew it was a really good mark for her, especially since she had only been with the *Examiner* a few short months. He repeatedly explained to the media that his children and his wife did not run for election, and so he wanted them to have as normal a life as possible. This 'family comes first' attitude had won him lots of votes in a world where most politicians used their kids to further their own campaigns.

During the interview, the Morgan children, then aged five and seven, played angelically with educational and sustainable wooden toys while munching happily on carrot sticks and hummus. Julia sat on their large comfortable sofa beside her husband. If you had to draw the perfect American family, the Morgans were as close as you could get. The perception was that Charlie Morgan was a powerful man, unafraid to do what was right, but despite that, an all-round good guy. Scarlett was terrified but managed to hide her nerves as she asked intelligent and pertinent questions. Artie had set the interview up for her, but made her promise to take the credit. Her old editor was more like a father figure to her, and though he made out like he was insulted that she had left him and got the job at the *Examiner*, she knew that really he was proud of her. He knew Charlie Morgan's father from years ago, so pulled in a favour.

The interview was wide ranging, sounding Charlie Morgan out on issues from abortion to gun control, and he presented a compassionate yet realistic case for everything. Broadminded, liberal, he appeared to have his feet very firmly planted in the realpolitik of twenty first century America.

So impressed was she with him, that she wrote an uncharacteristically flattering piece on him, admitting that she had been looking for flaws but there just didn't seem to be any cracks in the image he presented to the world. All really was as it seemed. Of solid New England stock, he had graduated from Harvard and chose to leave the family business to his brothers and entered politics. Julia was his childhood sweetheart and they seemed happy. As he sat in the sunny living room of his Montauk home, he looked handsome and relaxed. Not slimy or aggressive or sexist or any of the other traits she'd come to associate with politicians. His brown, slightly curly hair was well cut to look casual, and the light blue linen shirt and Levi 501s fitted him perfectly. His skin was tanned dark brown from a summer sail-boarding with his children.

It was at moments like this that it struck her how far she'd come from the cowering kid of a crazy alcoholic Irishman and poor old Lorena. She had kept her promise to herself and studied hard for her last year at school and graduated, then went to the local community college to study journalism. There was no way Lorena could have afforded to send her to one of the big colleges.

She did well and managed to get a job on a local Yonkers newspaper, writing about local charities and reporting on town council meetings. Artie Schwitz, the editor, was a small old Jew who liked the spark he saw in Scarlett. He remembered Dan from his days drinking and roaring around the streets and decided to give his daughter a chance. She was tenacious and dogged in her pursuit of stories, often scooping the bigger publications, and it was through her persistence she managed to increase the circulation of the *Yonkers Express* to record numbers. The interview she had done with the mullah from a radical Islamist mosque on the Lower East Side, who had refused all interviews before, plucked her from obscurity. In a letter that she was sure was correct, written in his native tongue, she'd told the old man from Iraq how she had gone to night school to learn Arabic. He agreed to talk to her and explained the despair and fear in Moslems in New York in the wake of 9/11. It was an unimaginable scoop for their small paper and led to a huge surge in circulation.

Her coverage of 9/11 continued to be very well received, and when she wrote a feature on the reaction of the Islamic community of the city to the terrorist attacks one year on, with the blessing of the mullah, she won the prestigious Carter award for journalism, the youngest ever recipient. She knew she was on the rise, and when she saw Carol Steinberg at a press event, she approached her and asked her for a job. Carol had smiled politely and suggested that she email her resume to the *Examiner* office. Two weeks later she had an interview. Life since then was a whirlwind. She bought a small house, a car and a whole new wardrobe on the strength of her new salary and the money she had saved over the years working for Artie. She was on top of the world.

Charlie made no reference to the fact that his father had asked him to do the interview as a favour to Artie, and she was grateful to him for that. In the months that followed, they would meet at events and they were always friendly. Then one night in Atlantic City, after a

Democrat campaign meeting, they found themselves staying at the same hotel. He invited her for a nightcap in the small residents' bar, and not realising his staff had gone for the night, she agreed.

They talked and laughed until the early hours, and she found herself telling him about her father. Not used to drinking, she poured her heart out, about the violence and fear that overshadowed her childhood. Her anger at her mother for not leaving, for not keeping them safe from him, and her anger at Lorena for giving her such a stupid name, it all came out. Charlie said he loved that she was called Scarlett O'Hara and that she was every bit as hot as Vivien Leigh.

He listened without judging and congratulated her sincerely on how far she'd come. Undoubtedly the whiskey played a part, for she had never told anyone about her past, but Charlie was easy to talk to. She felt she could trust him. They met a few more times after that night, both knowing an affair was inevitable. And so it began, she was his mistress, the other woman. She looked at herself in the mirror some mornings and said that to herself, but those sordid, dirty little words just couldn't be applied to what she and Charlie had. With him, it was honest, it was love.

She tried to block out Julia and his children, the eldest now about to start middle school. If the relationship was good, he wouldn't be seeing Scarlett. That's what she told herself. He never gave her any of the standard lines, that his wife didn't understand him, that he was only staying for the sake of the kids, that they'd be together properly when the kids left school. He simply never discussed it. His life with Julia was one thing, his life with Scarlett something else completely and never the twain shall meet.

She pretended that it suited her, that she was so taken up with her career that a full-time relationship would be just too restrictive. But as the months went on, she knew she was lying, to him and to herself. She never raised the subject with him, probably, she told herself, because she wasn't at all sure of what his reaction would be. He told her all the time that he loved her, that she was not like anyone he'd ever met, that she was gorgeous, but still she was not convinced. If he had to choose, would she be the one? He used to joke that she was his

Vivien Leigh and always signed his texts 'Rhett' or just 'R'. She always thought it was cute, though she wished he could have chosen something other than her ridiculous name to make jokes about. In the cold reality of what had happened, she realised that he wrote R in case anyone found the texts. Charlie was protecting himself.

And now, the worst possible thing had happened. She'd destroyed everything she'd worked so hard to build.

Available at most online retailers

ACKNOWLEDGMENTS

This is a book about friendship. It's about the closeness you can have with people to whom there is no blood connection but yet are central to your happiness. The family you choose for yourself. I have been extraordinarily fortunate in my life to have known deep and lasting friendships and, for all of them, I am eternally grateful. If I had one wish for my children it wouldn't be fortune or career success, though of course that would be nice, it would be that they would be surrounded by people who make them feel good about themselves, who don't judge, who support them in the good times and the bad, who can make them laugh.

This book holds a special place in my heart, and of all of the books I've written, these are the characters that are hardest to leave. I wanted to write a book about friendship because I have personal experience of such loyalty and love as exists between Liam, Hugo, and Patrick. I hope my friends can see our relationships reflected in theirs.

I would especially like to thank those friends who help me to get my books to print. In particular, my editor Helen Falconer, and my proof-reader Vivian Fitzgerald Smith for their wonderful insights. Once again, I could have achieved none of this without my dream team of first readers, those I trust with my new born bookbaby to be kind but honest. The wonderfully witty and charming Jim Cooney, Joseph Birchall, the co-founder of the Irish Indie Publishing Experience Support Group, my mother Hilda, who, while she is never anything but utterly biased in favour of her firstborn, is a source of tremendous support. Tim O'Riordan, himself a wonderful songwriter, who kept my story in the strangest of places and whose opinion I value hugely, and finally my best friend, the gorgeously funny and kind Beth-Anne O'Dwyer, who I can talk to forever, who makes me laugh so much, and who I know has my back, always.

Thank you to all my friends, how grateful I am to have you. Some scattered all over the world and some within the throw of a stone. I love you all and cherish your presence in my life, be it once a day or once a year. You know who you are.

To my gang, Rob, Colleteo, Lia, Jack, Ellen, Barbara, Pete, Ruby, Renee, D-daw, Daniel, Tadhg, Millie, Ais, Simon, Johnny, Hil, Conor, Sórcha, Eadaoin, and Siobhán. Ye know what ye mean to me.

And finally, I have to thank once again my husband Diarmuid, who always cheers the victories and gives me courage in the darker days. Thank you for everything, mo rún, mo chroí, mo stór.

Made in the USA
Middletown, DE
21 December 2020

29055395R00210